ALICE'S TRADING POST

ALICE'S TRADING POST

A NOVEL OF THE WEST

KERRY DEAN FELDMAN

FIVE STAR
A part of Gale, a Cengage Company

LIBRARY OF CONGRESS CATALOGING-IN-PUBLICATION DATA

Names: Feldman, Kerry Dean, 1940– author.
Title: Alice's Trading Post : a novel of the west / Kerry Dean Feldman.
Description: First edition. | Waterville, Maine : Five Star, 2022.
Identifiers: LCCN 2021011878 | ISBN 9781432879419 (hardcover)
Subjects: LCSH: Lakota Indians—Fiction. | Racially mixed women—Fiction. | GSAFD: Western stories.
Classification: LCC PS3606.E3866 A78 2022 | DDC 813/.6—dc23
LC record available at https://lccn.loc.gov/2021011878

First Edition. First Printing: January 2022
Find us on Facebook—https://www.facebook.com/FiveStarCengage
Visit our website—http://www.gale.cengage.com/fivestar
Contact Five Star Publishing at FiveStar@cengage.com

Printed in Mexico
Print Number: 01   Print Year: 2022

To my father, William F. Feldman, who passed on his love
for the land where I grew up.
And, Native American daughters, mothers, and
grandmothers, whose courage inspires me.

ACKNOWLEDGMENTS

I am deeply grateful to the Native American and Alaska Native women who shared their life stories with me.

Don Stull of the University of Kansas read most of these pages, offered crucial suggestions and moral support to see it through. His vast knowledge of Native American cultures and histories alerted me to better ways of presenting aspects of Alice's life and times.

Ms. Toni Lopopolo, my fiction writing mentor in California who read most of these pages, suggested and made edits, challenged me, had me read different kinds of fiction, taught me how to put a scene on paper with vividness. She was executive editor at St. Martin's Press before offering her extraordinary writing workshops. We corresponded via email and I completed a few weeks on *ooVoo* with two of her other writing students near the East Coast, who also offered helpful suggestions for many chapters.

Phyllis Ann Fast (who earned her PhD in anthropology from Harvard), my friend, colleague, and former student, encouraged me to write this novel from a Native American woman's perspective. She provided insights into how, for example, the twentieth-century male fascination with female breasts was not as pronounced in the nineteenth century. Phyllis was of Koyukon Athabascan descent on her mother's side, and the great-niece of Walter Harper, the first man to reach the top of Denali (Mount McKinley). The Harper Building on the campus of the University of Alaska Fairbanks is named after her aunt, who was the first Alaska Native woman to graduate from the university.

G. Richard Scott, currently at the University of Nevada, Reno, read the first draft of my effort to write a novel about this era when he was at the University of Alaska, Fairbanks. His positive comments gave me confidence to write the current novel as I have.

Two of my former students, Christine Brummer and Jyl Wheaton, provided valuable insights. Christine read the entire novel, writing a critique that helped my perspective on Alice Callahan/Army Girl/Sweet Medicine Woman as a girl learning how to be a woman. Jyl, of Kootenai Indian descent on her mother's side, from Idaho, taught me about some of the complexities of being of mixed descent and a young woman, sharing with me (in her later MA thesis in anthropology at Oregon State University) how her mother was indecently treated in the 50s as an elementary student who did not speak much English. Jonathan Bower, an Anchorage writer and musician, gave helpful comments on an earlier draft.

My wife, Tami Phelps, walked the Bighorn Battlefield with me one summer, made a black and white photograph of death markers of two Cheyenne warriors just over the hill from the famous Custer hill. She hand-painted the photograph, and it now is part of the permanent collection of the Anchorage Museum of History and Art. Tami offered critical insights into nuances of a woman's life. Tami's family is from Hot Springs, South Dakota, where many years ago we went to visit her family, and her brother who lived nearby in Buffalo Gap. Her family took me on a marvelous tour of the Black Hills. Those experiences provided the background I needed of the area, the Black Hills, Buffalo Gap, and its history, plus more than four hundred historical sources.

Kathryn Marie "Peaches" Hauk-Feldman, my mother, taught me to read, write, and argue about current events. She was raised like a boy to be the main hand on her father's farm and ranch, which helped me understand the rugged qualities of many Native American women, while still being quite feminine and good mothers. When we moved to the small town of Terry (pop. 500) from dryland farming across the Yellowstone River, an older neighbor boy threatened to beat me up if my dog strayed into his yard. She told me never to fear a bully, bought boxing gloves that day, and taught me how to defend myself with my fists. I was five. I never feared anyone physically from that day on. She gave me a love of Montana and the west, its wildness, and an awareness that women had to do the same things better than a man to be accepted as an equal. She published two novels about her life as a homesteader's daughter in Prairie County, Montana: *Mathilda* and *The Spring Tender*.

My father, William "Bill" Feldman was nicknamed *Wegie* when he was six because patrons at Young's Café in Terry, Montana, where he cleaned tables in 1916, thought he was a Norwegian. (He couldn't speak English. His dad spoke German.) He exemplified for me much of the western manhood of his era, 1910 to late twentieth century; a man of few words, his word was his bond, a simple faith, rarely swore, accepted no handouts, never shed tears, superb athlete, could ride a horse all day and dance all night. He knew how to grow wheat, corn, dig irrigation canals, feared no one, worked sunup to sundown, taught me sports. He could build a house, mine for silver, catch trout with a piece of corn. He said an early draft of this story was "the best story about the west" he ever read, "but, it's not a western." I agreed. Our downstairs library, which mom insisted we have, housed his collection of Louis L'Amour and Zane Grey westerns, which were all he read except the *World Books A–Z* (a couple times). He helped me avoid historical errors in the novel, such as the number of buffalo in the U.S. before the 1880s, now estimated at sixty million (I thought there were ten million).

Amos Feldman, my paternal grandfather, died in Terry, Montana, when I was five. I asked to be raised up by my dad, to kiss his cold lips in his casket. He was a railroad man from West Salem, Illinois, whose sons often spoke German until they were in school (as least that's true of my father). Grampa Amos told me stories about riding with Buffalo Bill Cody, hunting buffalo. I believed him until a few decades later when I looked at Bill Cody's years. Those stories brought to life the land around me, making that era seem close to me.

Mike and Kate Hauk, my maternal grandparents, originally from Perham, Minnesota, homesteaded in Prairie County, Montana, before they turned twenty years of age. They were one of the homesteaders who didn't give up. Grampa Mike was county commissioner for twenty years, served two terms in the Montana House of Representative, and one term in the Montana Senate. They taught me to love hard work, music, family time, late night pinochle card games, the smell of wheat and horse sweat. I used all those sense experiences in fleshing out the life of Alice Callahan.

JoAllyn Archambault, the director of the American Indian Program at the Smithsonian Institution, alerted me to the enduring importance today of the Lakóta custom of *giveaways* to honor moments in a child's life. In her lecture at a meeting of the Society for Applied Anthropology, at a session honoring my mentors, Robert A. and Beverly H. Hackenberg of the University of Colorado, Boulder, she noted that although men often take charge of distributing the gifts, it's women who prepare the food and do most of the preparation work. I invited her to give that lecture. She comes from a distinguished Lakóta family and holds a PhD in anthropology from the University of California, Berkeley.

Crow athletes whom I competed against in high school sports for four years, especially legendary Larry Pretty Weasel, were boys who revealed themselves as young men like myself, wanting to do their best. I have always, since those days, thought of Indians/Native Americans and First Nations people as like me, not as exotic Others.

My sisters, Koleen, Mary, and JoAnn, helped my writing over the years by offering insights about a woman's life and thinking that never occurred to me. My brothers, Peter and Michael, gave me support and great encouragement.

Sister Mary Ruth was the first educator in my life who noticed my fiction writing talent, sending me out of her junior year English Composition class to write short stories for two teen publications. Both were accepted and published.

Brie Caron Anderson-Feldman is my amazing daughter who has supported me on all my endeavors. Watching her become a woman helped me see life from the viewpoint of young Army Girl.

Every writer should be as fortunate as I to work with two outstanding editors assigned by my publisher. The distinguished

Acknowledgments

Canadian author and editor Gordon K. Aalborg provided the first edit of the manuscript, saved me from numerous peccadillos, and wrote kind praise for Alice's story. The distinguished editor Marcia LaBrenz copyedited the novel, digging deep into its entrails to raise important questions about word usage and all that a good historical novel requires.

And lastly, I thank and acknowledge the authors and storytellers—Native American and others, men and women—whose writings guided me in the historical and cultural aspects of Alice's story.

PROLOGUE

Alice's Trading Post burned to the ground on Beaver Creek outside Buffalo Gap, in 1995. A metal box under the charred pine floor contained a woman's moccasins resting on recordings made by our dear friend, Homer *Half Big* Phipps, ninety-five years of age. Mr. Phipps was a Native American volunteer veteran in World War I at age seventeen and was our dear irascible friend. He made notes and recorded stories of his grandmother, whom we knew as *Miss Alice,* who gave us gingersnaps when visiting her Post. He passed away in the fire. He wanted the stories of her life added to those told, he said, *"by soldiers, miners, historians, and the endless trail of suck-ups coming to these parts."*

Our society transcribed her stories and his notes as he wished, and put them in a sequential order, honoring his wishes.

Buffalo Gap Historical Society

Buffalo Gap, South Dakota

2019

*Please note: In our report, č sounds like *ch,* š like *sh,* η like *ng,* ž like *j.*

★ ★ ★ ★ ★

PART I
WILLAMETTE VALLEY

★ ★ ★ ★ ★

CHAPTER ONE
COLUMBIA RIVER,
OREGON TERRITORY: 1874

Hold it right there, bear . . .

The bear caught wind of my first woman moon. Before I could shoot he lifted his curious eyes away from the white oak acorns he'd knocked from low limbs. Going on thirteen snows, I never thought my life would change like it did when I became a woman. He came at me with grizzly claws, teeth, and a roar. My woman blood wanted to crawl back inside me but I tried to stay calm, took aim at the bear's nose, the only place to bring him down with one shot except a shell in his eye. Shells bounce off a bear head like pine cones.

My carbine jammed, I grabbed the barrel, waved the metal like a club, yelled how Chub taught me, "Hey, wahoo, GIT!" The bear hesitated, gave thought to what I said. The thought held little interest; he got his anger on, roared at me again.

I dropped the carbine, grabbed my knife with both hands on the handle, blade up, ready for whatever the bear had a mind for. Maybe stick him in the belly, slice up, find his heart. I was bundled in furs that day so I hoped his teeth would not get too deep. I backed away, stumbled due to my fright, fell to the Willamette earth, summer pine smell clinging to soil. The first part the bear got was my head in a wolverine cap—my favorite—so I hoped he wouldn't chew holes in it. I took a breath, opened my eyes, looked around a bear mouth. Bear's breath, when inside the mouth, smells worse than entrails of an outhouse hole. Bear tongue washed my face.

My head bones cracked—*I'll never see blue sky again, never taste Ma's camas cakes* . . .

A rifle shot. Me and the bear hit the ground.

Chub pulled the bear jaws, freed my head. I let loose of my fear, peed my buckskin, warm water I hadn't felt on my body since I turned five, peed myself during a night dream.

"Grease your bloody Springfield 'fore you do bear," Chub said, like he shot a squirrel. "Told you before, Army Girl, now you know why. Listen up next time."

He shot that bear in the eye. I never saw a bear shot that perfect in my whole life. Words of thanks never found air because Chub, my stepfather, walked away. He hollered back, "Don't lay there, Girl. Get your knife, skin him out. I got traps to check. Your ma will have dinner."

I tried to get calm, stop shaking, took off my boots and buckskin, stumbled to the river to soak pee off me and my clothes. I sat in cold water, took a deep breath, and flopped back on the sedge grass, arms wide, looked at blue sky, happy to see sky and taste Ma's cakes when I got back to our cabin.

I greased my Springfield good after that, kept the copper cartridges clean, too.

After Ma birthed me, she wifed Mr. Angus Tunbridge, a white trapper from the Grandmother's Land. Folks called him Chub. He gave a Winchester lever rifle, two pinto horses, and a pile of winter furs to Ma's family in the Willamette Valley to have her for his wife. Mr. Tunbridge came full in the belly but good looking when he shaved his face. He didn't get whiskeyed up like my real father, Ma told me, and stood a head taller, too. I never met my real father. I took Ma's word for that. Folks we come across thought I was Chub's daughter.

My life was hard from snow to snow, but I loved my life in the valley—the greened hemlock, cottonwood, fir so tall they almost touched clouds. I pulled chinook from the river in baskets Ma made from grass and roots. Helped her pound berries, watched her make flour she baked into cakes. I never had pets, Ma kept two spotted frogs and a pair of turtles she got from a pond, the frogs so small they fit on my palm. The turtle laid four eggs, size of peas, that hatched. I took more interest in turtle babies after starting to become a woman. Interested in baby deer, too, squeezed out from a mama deer in the woods, and ground nest meadowlarks that hatched, fed by their folks till they could fly. Someday I'd have to leave my nest but I figured the time for that was far away.

My stepfather raised me like a boy, taught me to hunt, feel at home in woods, talk sign with Indians we came across. He showed me how to blow through tree bark to make rabbit sounds for my snare, walk barefoot in snow to get my feet tough, jump naked in river ice holes, wrap warm in hide with the hair turned inside. I knew the difference between wolf and cougar tracks, to shut my eyes when I trapped in moonlight—my eyes got no glow. In a knife fight, how to hold the blade up, kick an enemy in the belly, find his throat with my knife if he didn't drop his.

Ma cut my hair short like a boy in our log cabin, that way she didn't have to worry none about washing and fixing curls. Long hair might get caught on brush when I hunted. I learned to shoot beaver eye at fifty paces, keep the shot away from the hide. Get a hide soft by chewing the skin, tan scraped out deer hide with my pee. Had me a good time.

Indian and white blood in me made my skin look like a fair-skinned doe's, winters. Summers, I got skin dark as wet cedar. After my womanhood began, my bosoms stuck out under my deerskin tunic. Hid them best I could, embarrassed me to look like that.

Ma wouldn't teach me her tongue, only white man talk, that way I understood the ways we had to live, not get killed because of what kind of blood flowed in my body or how I talked. She kept me out of Mission school after what a man there did to her privates when she was a girl.

One thing Chub warned me, "Stay clear from J Boys, Army Girl. Can't trust a J Boy." That began my interest in J Boys. Later I discovered Chub was right, but I still liked J Boys.

At barn dances, I felt shy, never danced, but had an eye for a certain boy, my body changing and that changed my thinking. He had an eye for me, too—Jeremy Hackney. Chub said he was a J Boy I should stay clear of. Youngest boy of widowed Mr. Jedediah Hackney, who had five boys, all with a J name like their pa. Mr. Hackney cheated Chub on fur trades.

Chub took us in his horse-drawn wagon to settlers' barn dances, of men with Indian wives like Ma. They danced happy all night—waltzes, quadrille, and long line contras. You listened to what the dance leader said about how to do a contra, dance with everyone in the line before a dance ended. At a dance the summer I turned woman, I got my punch from a bowl same time as Jeremy Hackney got his. He wore baggy knee knicker-bockers, long socks, boots, him thinking he looked sharp as the black and white woodpecker with red feathers on his chest that thrilled girl woodpeckers outside our cabin. A lock of brown hair curled sweet from under Jeremy Hackney's wool cap.

He showed me a smile. I looked down, wanted to run, but stay, too. He looked at my little bosoms, too long for a quick punch bowl look at a girl. I stuck out my bosoms—first time I knew what they might be for besides nursing a baby. The J Boy spilled punch on his knickerbockers.

"You talk?" I said, watched him wipe punch off his pants.

"Course I talk," Jeremy said, looked in my eyes.

"Can I ask you something?"

"What?"

"I never asked this before."

"I'm Jeremy Hackney, what's your name?"

"I don't like my name."

"What should I call you, then? *Girl?*" He laughed like a crazy bird.

"That would be good," I said, looked him sharp in the eye to stop laughing if he wanted to keep talking.

"Want to talk outside, Girl?"

I forgot what I was going to ask. We slipped outside, went past wagon teams tied to trees. He held my hand.

"Don't fall," he said, giving a reason why he held my hand. I didn't think that's why he held my hand.

Fall air, clean, no clouds, more stars that night than ever.

"How old are you, Jeremy Hackney?"

"Goin' on fifteen."

"I'm goin' on fourteen, myself."

I needed the extra digit added to my age, didn't want to look like a kid to him, pretending to be my protector. When we were in the barn, I saw his eyes, sawdust color, same as my favorite horse. I loved the horse, couldn't tell that to Jeremy Hackney, though, about why I liked his eye color.

"What you want to do when you grow up, Girl?" Jeremy says.

We stopped under the biggest fir tree in the clearing around the barn. I wanted to kiss him on the mouth. Jeremy asking me dumb questions about what I want to do when I grow up. He should be thinking—what does this girl want *now*?

I never, ever, kissed a boy. Never, ever thought about doing that till I got on my moon. I'm thinking—maybe some changes might be all right.

"Never thought much about when I grow up."

I look at his lips, gentle sawdust eyes, back to his lips, try not to sigh. *Be a man, J Boy* . . .

Jeremy takes a deep breath, "Well, you have to think about that, Girl. Someday . . ."

Jeremy Hackney acted like a man, how I wanted him to act, put his arms around me like he done it before with girls. I moved into his arms, wished for the first time in my life I wore a madder dress, or calico skirt, even a blouse.

His lips mushed mine, I stepped back. He knew he put his lips too hard on me. I grabbed my skinning knife from my sheath, pressed it to his neck, his eyes got big, not moving with the blade at his throat. I take his head in my free hand, "Like this, J Boy." I show Jeremy how a girl, heading to woman, wants a kiss from a boy. Like a butterfly touching a daisy.

Kissing ended. I almost forgot to open my eyes. I was in love, first time.

Jeremy looked at me. "Girl, I got it. I never done this before. Would you move your blade away from my neck? I'd kiss you how you want it."

I put my skinning knife away, pulled him to me. We kissed and kissed—how he wanted the kissing, till we heard violins play a waltz. I never wanted kissing him to end.

Chub began his looking at me when I dressed in our cabin. He snuck up on me, too, bathing in rivers.

"What you bloody looking at?" I said, first time I caught him at the Willamette River where I bathed. I trusted Chub like Ma said. I liked him, he taught me how to swim in rivers, made me a rope swing over the Willamette, never yelled at me except when I hunted wrong. I could not figure why he stared at me naked.

"I'm not looking at you," Chub said. "Am making sure you're safe when you bathe."

I knew he lied. I asked Ma, "Why does Mr. Tunbridge look at me when I bathe in the river, get dressed?"

Ma looked at my little bosoms, my face.

"He's not looking at you, daughter. Not much to look at. Stop such foolish talk."

Ma feared to admit what Chub had going. She had over thirty snows, her lovely plum skin looking like a prune needing water compared to her younger self, though still the most beautiful woman in the valley, Indian or white. Maybe she worked too hard roasting roots over smoke, tanning hides for my clothes.

I heard them talk by the river, Ma telling Chub he made me nervous looking at me when I dressed or bathed.

"I don't *look* at her," he said.

"Whatever you do with your eyes, Chub, *stop it*," Ma told him, and she meant it.

Chub stopped his looking, least for a while. He headed with Ma and me back to his homeland, the Grandmother's Land, what they call Canada. Indian wars would give him less trouble there, he said, get more for his furs.

I took a last look at our cabin by the river, tried not to cry, but tears flowed, leaving my home, Jeremy Hackney. I dried my wet face, got ready to become a woman in the Grandmother's Land, meet another boy.

I didn't know this was the beginning of my troubles, the hard journey of my life, why I thought of myself as Troubles Girl.

CHAPTER TWO
FORT BENTON
MONTANA TERRITORY: 1874

Chub's loaded wagon bumped us along the Mullan Road, leaving Oregon Territory. We came to the little town called Fort Benton that sprouted around an old army fort, alongside a river called Big Muddy—sorry sight of a river, compared to the Willamette or Columbia. What came strange to my eye—Big Muddy flowed to where the sun came up, not like the Columbia. Seeing that river gave me pause in how I thought about this earth. Not only was I changing in mysterious ways, but this earth held mysteries, too.

We came in on the mudded Front Street, willow and cottonwood leaves headed to gold. Our wagon poked along behind buggies and jerk-line mule teams hauling freight for mercantiles and whatever gold hunters had a need for. I could hardly sit still seeing the people all dressed up, strutting on boardwalks.

Chub had our bear hides, beaver, some fox pelts. He was looking to trade for a new Henry rifle, beaver traps, and a packhorse. Maybe a whiskey jug.

My bosoms now growing like Ma's only mine looked like chokecherries, not melons like hers. Maybe I'd meet a Fort Benton boy, Indian or white no matter, who wanted to talk to a girl heading to woman. Hold my hand like Jeremy Hackney.

Chub dickered with an old Scot name of Mr. McFadden at his trading post on the outskirts of the town. The old trader robbed Indians who came to trade with offers of whiskey, Chub told us. Chub had no mind for whiskey except a jug that might last him through a winter. Ma never drank whiskey and told me not to drink, I never did.

"One horse and a Hudson blanket," the old thief said. "Folks wear silk top hats these days, not beaver. A beaver only get ya three silver dollars. Check around, man, if ya don't believe what I say."

"Two horses, three Hudsons, and a Henry, with shells for a season. And a jug, not watered," Chub said.

They agreed to dicker more next day. Meantime, we heard stories about the old trader.

Mr. McFadden had seventy snows in him. A chief to Piegan Blackfoot and other Indians around Fort Benton for his younger days at the Fort Union trading post in the Dakotas, for the Sioux scalps he took. He spoke Crow, they said, better 'n a Crow. Had one of the biggest hungers in a man, too—took a hundred Crow and Blackfeet wives, down to one Crow wife when Ma, me, and Chub came to his post.

"He has no body in battle," Indians said about Mr. McFadden. "Big medicine. Bullets, arrows, go right through him."

McFadden went hand to hand with Blackfeet when younger. Two Blackfeet scalps hung over the stove in his trading post. I saw Indian scalps hid in homes of Chub's friends. Those scalps of Mr. McFadden got my attention. Beneath the old man's skin hid a killer with considerable know-how when he cut Indian scalps. Did that include my scalp? At that time, it was not clear to me I was Indian. Chub viewed me as a white girl because my father was white.

Next day, Chub saw Mr. McFadden look my way when I wide-eyed dresses, boots, hats, coats, blankets, carbines, candy sticks, and saddles he kept for trade with whites. I never saw so much stuff; wished I had one of his Winchester lever carbines. A carbine Winchester came shorter than a rifle, easier for me to aim, load shells quick if I missed on a deer or elk.

Chub said, "Friend him, girl, give him a smile. You got a smile, a pretty one. Don't look peculiar around folks I got to trade with."

I smiled at the old man best I could in my buckskin tunic, loused-up skin pants, leather boots Ma sewed, and the wolverine cap from the critter I trapped, cut, stitched together myself. Bear teeth holes were now in that cap, but Ma sewed them up. The bushy tail of a wolverine hung down my back. I came short for my age, not pretty Ma told me; my looks and regalia must have been a sight to behold. All I saw was snot wantin' to drop from the old Scot's nose. Mr. McFadden had gray bushes above his eyes, like a wolf.

I got excited, eyes about come out my head, seeing Mr. McFadden's pet baby beaver.

His young Crow wife had milk in her bosoms because she nursed her baby. She squeezed her mother milk to a saucer for the beaver. *Dee*lighted me to know a woman could feed a beaver from her own body. I petted the beaver, held the sweet little critter in my arms. Had me an interest coming in kids. The baby beaver cried like a human baby; the Crow woman's baby cried. Their songs, a *doo*ette to my ear.

Ma told the old thief she'd like a porcupine necklace, a calico dress for her and one for me. Ma liked to dress up for parties, rub berry juice on her cheeks, look at herself in a mirror.

I never wore a dress, calico or not, but figured her words made good trade talk.

The old man grabbed two dresses, smiled my way, I smiled back. I thought the gifts were part of the trade. He gave me gingersnaps, too.

I heard talk about me staying with Mr. McFadden. I could not believe my ears. Mr. McFadden offered three packhorses, four Hudson blankets, a Henry, and cartridges for a season, for me and Chub's pelts. He said he never gave that much before for a wife and pelts. The Crow girl put too much time on her baby; Mr. McFadden wanted another wife.

"Ya won't have to cook for me," he said to Ma. Crow mothers cooked for their daughter's husband and he had a Crow wife.

I looked at my ma, cried. More sadness and tears than I ever knew. "I don't want to wife this old man. I don't know how to wife nobody," I told her.

"You're not pretty, daughter," Ma said. "We come far from our people. You give us not much to offer in trade, and we got to take the offer while we can."

I pulled away when Ma tried to hug me.

"No, don't leave me here," I said, all tears and sadness. "Don't leave me, Ma. Take me with you."

"A chief here," Ma said. "He'll pass on soon. See how bent he walks, an old spruce ready to rot. All this will be yours, my daughter. Treat him good and when we come back, we can live with you."

I thought my ma loved me more than life, but maybe she feared Chub would take me for his woman, throw her out. Or maybe she feared he'd put his hands on me?

I ran to woods the night before she left, cried more tears than I knew could come in me. I went back when I heard a wolf howl close by, and two drunk Indians peed under the willow where I shed those tears. If I had a gun, there'd have been a quiet wolf.

Next day I watched Ma leave, thought I saw a tear in her eye when she climbed in the wagon.

"Ma," I screamed. "Ma, don't leave me!"

Folks on the boardwalks turned to see why I hollered. I slipped in the mud; my legs flew high and I fell on my back. I rolled over, facedown, spread my arms on the earth, let tears run. I looked up; Ma never looked back.

I had me an old Scot to live with as his woman, a man who cut Indian scalps that hung over his stove. Had me some white blood, time to learn to live white, I reckoned, keep my scalp. Wait for Ma to come back for me.

To understand my life, I'll tell about Ma and my real father. If family peculiarities could be thought of as quills, I got porcupined when I came into this world.

CHAPTER THREE
MY MA, MOLLY

"When a white man wants you, daughter, he looks at you like a beaver skin. A woman's got to know how to work with that."

First words from Ma for my womanhood when she thought I had enough snows to understand. Going on ten snows, I had no idea what she wanted me to know.

I was skinning out a beaver I shot near a stream that ran to the Willamette River. The beaver would not come out of his lodge. I had to spend a whole day smoking him. That day the idea came to me. I thought over her stories about how I should use my future womanhood. Here's what I came to: beautiful women like my ma might not have much sense.

A man give me the eye, like he looked at a beaver skin, would find my knife at his throat.

Since I didn't come a beauty like Ma, I wouldn't have to worry none about such things.

Ma, called Molly by whites, came with a bit of the feral. I had me a ma on the untamed side. No matter to me because I loved her more than anything in my world, and I learned from her what I needed to know to survive the times we lived.

I didn't know that, then.

Ma came all Indian.

I came half 'n' half.

The soldier first laid eyes on Molly when he watered his horse at the army fort in the Lower Willamette Valley. Even the horse

29

thought what happened a curious sight. On that spring morn she came to the fort wearing her prettiest doeskin dress, and a camas blue blanket around her shoulders. The week prior she'd noticed the soldier looking at her.

That morning she walked tall and proud alongside her uncle, a chief of local Friendlies. Molly felt the soldier's eyes on her but stared straight ahead like a proper Indian girl. Her uncle came to the fort to give the remind to the army that provisions promised his people never arrived and miners in the area ignored more treaties than the settlers.

That valley had good land for planting after settlers wiped out the green fir, hazels that turned gold before snows fell, even oak groves. They burned off the camas, bear grass, the tarweed, too.

The soldier, who never saw beauty in any woman like flowed in Molly, Indian or white, a lovely willow swaying in a breeze. He got tangled in his horse harness, took a dive headfirst in the water trough. His horse jumped, gave the soldier a stare, horse eyes big as an owl's at the sight. The horse opened wide his mouth, gave what Molly told me looked like a horse laugh. Her uncle offered a hand to Stump, what Indians called the soldier for how short he stood, his uniform dripping water. He lifted himself out of the trough with her uncle's help. Horseflies and mosquitoes flitted around his face. He stood wet, head to foot, water washing his dusted boots.

Molly pulled up her blanket to cover her laugh.

"I tripped," Stump said. He stuck the wet hat on his head, tried to look like a soldier.

This troughing unfolded in Oregon Territory, 1856, in the White Man Winter Count. Give or take a digit.

Stump lifted his officer cap to Molly, tried to look the gentleman, even if a soaked wet gentleman, with red and gold hair, the ends curled sweet like gooseberry petals when not wet.

"How might you be this fine day, Miss Molly?"

Proper Indian girls didn't talk to strangers, specially blue-coats leaking water. Molly looked to her uncle, waited for a sign what she should do. Her uncle gave thought to the situation, squinted at Stump, made sure he saw a soldier, not a spirit having fun. Her uncle looked to the sky, maybe to ancestors for guidance, a few clouds rolling there. The chief gave a little nod to Molly that could have looked like he twitched a no-see-um from his nose.

Molly smiled at the soldier, a warm Indian girl smile, the soldier not even tall as her in his boots. Molly watched trough water run off his sideburns. She looked at the ground, the proper way for an Indian girl to look if a man gave her the eye. But this was Molly, not just any Indian girl. Ma followed rules up to a point, the point being if the rules held something she wanted.

Molly loosed her blanket, looked the soldier in the eye, looked away, shy.

Stump took the opportunity to survey Molly's figure with the Ireland eyes the white man God gave him, from her beaded moccasins up her eighteen snows legs under her dress, to the braided belt that held her waist, to her bosoms swelled with womanhood.

He stared on her bosoms too long for a man's quick peek if he wanted his look kept to himself.

Molly sucked in morning air, pushed out her bosoms, showed the soldier her lovely fawns.

"Good today, sir. Thanks for asking."

The soldier looked up to her face, forgot he even asked a question. Molly closed the blanket, turned to leave with her uncle, removed the blanket from her shoulders to let the soldier gander at her backside, how she swayed like a willow in her maiden slow walk. Stump stepped back to take in what she

31

showed him.

He troughed himself again, this time arse first.

Like I said, Ma came with good looks. Her cheeks were smooth and full as wild plums, her teeth white as the inside of a clamshell, with a figure that let you know the difference between the man and the woman.

Maybe Ma wanted to help her people. But, thinking back on the story, knowing Molly and how she thought, I reckon she wanted what twenty-five dollars a month officer pay might get her in calico dresses, pretty hats, fine leather shoes with heels.

"That soldier," Molly said to her uncle, feeling Stump's eyes on her *be*hind, swaying like a soft bush in a breeze, "give me to him. Your problems with these soldiers will go away."

Her uncle looked at Molly, kept his thoughts to himself. Next week Molly moved to Stump's officer's quarters. She lived with Stump in the finest wood-framed fort house, faced to parade grounds, a deck above the porch to review troops. The house had lace-curtained windows, a brick fireplace, and more rooms than Molly knew how to fill.

Stump bought her dresses shipped from Philadelphia around the tip of South America.

And her people got the provisions, which was her people's way for a man to show his respect for a woman who married him—gave gifts to her family. She thought she was now married, showed him every day and night all she'd learned about being a wife from her mother.

CHAPTER FOUR
MY PA, LIEUTENANT STUMP

"I'm not your husband, sweetheart," Stump said. "I can't marry you, though I want to. I truly do."

After getting in her soldier husband's robes for four snows, Molly told folks she was Stump's wife,

"Why aren't you my husband?" Molly said, swatting a rug of bugs and ash.

"My church won't allow me to marry a heathen, and my folks would not understand me marrying a squaw."

She told him not to call her a squaw, had no idea what the word meant, threw him the rug to finish cleaning it himself.

"I don't think of you like that, honey, that's just how white folks talk. I'm not your husband till we make promises in a church," he said, and that was that, he thought.

Stump's folks sailed across the Great Water, became farmers in the Midwest. When he met Molly, he had only twenty-five snows. He graduated near the middle of his class, out of an army learning school called West Point, so he got sent to Texas. Chasing Comanche and getting fried in Texas hell, not to his liking. Army chiefs sent him north to Oregon Territory to keep peace among reservation Indians, white settlers, and gold miners who went broke in California.

Stump came north with an even shorter lieutenant Molly's friends called Weasel. That lovely valley filled up fast with white men like Stump and Weasel, two steps ahead of flunk in what

33

they tried till then. The white man plan seemed to Molly's people to turn that sweet valley into a dump for white folks who had not done well elsewhere.

Stump and Weasel called Indians, all the warring tribes there, red nigras. Molly never saw a nigra so that word didn't bother her none.

Because of Molly, Stump stopped that kind of talk. Her uncle also gave Molly's cousin, his own beautiful daughter same age as Molly, to be in the robes with Lieutenant Weasel, who graduated from West Point one step under Stump.

To her people, Molly and Stump were married. Molly thought herself Stump's wife, like her Aunty Nell and the settler, Mr. Waller.

Molly got all riled up, more than once about him not thinking she was his wife. "Why we need a church to be married?"

"Sweetheart, calm yourself, please. A church is where the white man God lives, our Great Spirit."

"I know about churches. Folks at Mission school up north called me a savage and heathen, gave me the white man name, Molly. I got tired of weeding their pea and potato gardens. I bit a Mission man's ear who put his hands under my dress, on my privates. I ran away, came home, never went back to a church."

"I never knew that, about your life, sweetheart," Stump told her. "Can we talk about this later?"

Indians starved those days on the north Pacific coast—Klickitat (like my ma), Coquille, Chinook, Klamath, Modoc, and Rogue River Indians. The government took what was their land and meat, and the supplies they promised the Indians rare showed up, and then not on time. Stump and Weasel knew what hungry Indians could do if they got an anger on, what they could do to settlers who invaded their land.

Yakama scalped three prospectors because the treaty with a long-winded governor to allow the prospectors would not go in effect for four more years. Potentates in Washington City sent an Indian agent to talk to the Yakama about the murdered gold hunters. They slit the agent's throat, took his hair. Killed his horse, too, because they hated all the lying. Cascades done in some white men and women and children. Stump and Weasel rounded up the Cascades after that killing.

The Cascades stared at their feet, looked guilty, stood in a line while the soldiers inspected their muskets. Stump and Weasel nosed each musket barrel, handed over nine of those Cascades to the judge for hanging.

"How you know those Cascades killed anybody?" Molly said, riding in a horse-drawn wagon north to the hanging. "Maybe those Cascades only hunted deer before you checked their muskets."

"Justice must be served, honey," Stump said. "Cascades might scalp your people again, when your people wander into their land. I look the other way on that and you know why, sweetheart." Stump nuzzled her neck.

"Because I clean you up when you come home whiskeyed up? Warm you in the robes?"

"Never heard you talk like that before, honey."

"Squaw girl. Good in the robes. What your soldiers say about me," she said, angry.

"I'll tell those soldiers to stop that talk or send them back to Texas. Thinking on that hellhole should keep their tongues in the right place."

"There's more to me than what they say."

He got curious. "What might that be?"

"I would show you, if you marry me in your church," Molly said. "If I become your wife, in how your people see me."

At the hanging, Molly turned her head when they hung the first Indian. "Take me out of here, NOW," she begged Stump. "I can't bear to watch. Their families are here." Stump watched the next man get the noose around his neck. The man's relatives and friends watched, crying, in the Indian crowd that was forced to watch. Stump cared about Molly so he put his arm around her and led her away. That day Molly learned they could hang her just because she was Indian. When I heard that story, I wondered if soldiers hung half Indians like me, and which half they'd hang.

Molly got all dressed up, a warm clear day, going on a mission. Stump would marry her in his church, or he'd be out of luck for what she had in mind that day. She tapped Stump's arm to stop the horses, reached behind the buckboard for a tanned deer hide she brought.

"Bring this, sweetheart," she said, smiled sweet, nodded to grass near the woods. "I want to show you how I, as your wife—if I had me a husband—would spend afternoons with you, if you found a church that married heathens. Or, I'll find another man who marries me to get what I will give you today."

She jumped off the wagon, held a parasol to keep the sun off her fancy dress, swayed toward the Garry oaks and bigleaf maple grove. Stump quick put on his officer hat, grabbed the deer hide, ran to catch up with her.

She studied the grove, closed the parasol, said sweet, "Here. I like the grass right here."

Tall grass near the alders made way for the hide Stump plopped down.

When he moved for her too fast, she said, "No, sweetheart, not in your uniform, with those dirty boots."

Stump yanked off one boot, then the other, near tore off his uniform, piled everything one on top of the other like squirrel stacked provisions. He stood quiet in his long johns, hands hiding his privates, officer hat on his head, waited for what she told him to do. Molly pulled up her fancy dress, lifted the dress over her head, tossed the cloth like a thought she didn't need. That was my ma, unlike most shy Indian girls, and when she set out to do something, nothing stopped her. The tossed dress scared swallows roosted in oaks, so many they gave a greened feather cloud to the sky. Bird omens, she thought; meaning she should maybe fear Stump and the army.

"When I'm married," she said, "fine lady picnics like this coming for the man who marries me, in a church."

"You being a mite unfair here, honey?" Stump said.

In their home at the fort, she performed her wife duties at night, but never like this. She could see he liked what he saw waited for him. She smiled, lifted her petticoat.

"No need for this, what you think, sweetheart?" She pulled the cloth over her head, lay the petticoat gentle on the grass. Stump sat down in his long johns, grabbed a blade of grass to chew, nervous.

"And you like this, sweetheart, my plum pack?" she said. She meant the corset under the petticoat that held what she called her plums.

"Golly, sweetheart," Stump said, looked around, feared someone watched. "I never saw one of those garments except in a magazine. Where'd you get it?" He tossed away the chewed grass, furrowed his brow to hear the answer to his curious question.

"My cousin used her schooling to add this to an order you sent for presents for me."

She undid corset hooks, tossed the pack. The corset landed spread open like a done-in swan. "How does this *squaw* look now? Like a lady? A wife? Good. Now, about finding us a preacher."

"Oh. Yes, sweetheart, like a goddess in bloom. I hear a preacher comes around before winter. I could . . ."

"You look into a preacher, Stump, if you want more fancy

lady picnics."

Even if she could not save the Cascades, Molly said the picnic got her the wedded promise. Stump gave his word, the promise of an officer and gentleman of the U.S. Army of the West.

Before the preacher came, Stump received new orders, packed his trunk in the bedroom of their home at Fort Hoskins.

"War?" Molly said, tears flowing. "More hostiles to put on reservations?"

"No, Molly, honey," he said. "War might come between white men. Some folks keep nigras for slaves, use them like animals. Get free work done."

"You on the side of the nigras?"

"Of course. The Great Spirit don't approve of work done for free."

"I'm proud of my husband," Molly told him, "helping nigra people."

"I'm not your husband, Molly. Remember, no church wedding? Sweetheart, maybe you could visit me in Washington City? They assigned me to train militia and recruits to protect the city, though if war comes, should not last long. Lots of churches and preachers in Washington City. I sure want more picnics with you, sweetheart."

Molly hesitated none, "Oh, I will come. Be your wife, have fancy picnics, wherever you ask."

Molly wasted no time, began packing her bags that night. A few days later, Stump headed east. Not long after, Lieutenant Weasel and the soldiers went east to fight the war. The army shuttered the fort, sold the land to settlers.

Molly had no word from Stump. She'd come to love him, feared he got shot or forgot about her. She took her plum pack to the pit she dug for roasting camas bulbs in front of her folks' place, lit the fire, tossed the useless corset to the fire. A soldier galloped fast down the road, waving wild. She gave a sweep of her hand to the soldier, grabbed the corset from the fire, wiped dust and sweat onto her dress, went to meet the soldier.

"A parcel for you, Molly. And a letter. I am to read you the letter."

Molly invited the soldier to sit in front of her folks' home. Had Stump got killed? She took a deep breath. "Read the letter, soldier. I'm ready for what you read."

The soldier read her the letter.

Dear Molly,

I am sorry I could not write sooner. More to be done than we thought to defend the city. I will have a leave. I want you to come visit, if you still have feelings for me. Come with volunteers we bring to the fight. I sure have feelings for you, sweetheart. I would ask the question proper if you come. Might help me, too, to move up ranks if I have a wife and family. I include a parcel for you that has money for your trip, for dresses, too. Bring a chaperone of your choosing. Maybe ask your aunty, who lives with the widowed settler, Mr. Waller. If you can come, want to be my wife, put your X on the paper this soldier carries that will be returned to me. I will meet you at the B&O train station in Washington City.

Your loving soldier.

Molly, hands shaking, wrote a big X on the paper. The soldier tipped his hat, stuck the paper in a leather pouch, gave her his congratulations, galloped off. Molly saw in her mind the family she would have with Stump—babies she carried in her body, nursed with her own milk, kids' hands held by their ma and pa. A lovely girl for a daughter, whose hair she combed. A handsome boy for a son, though not short like Stump. Being a wife and ma was all she ever wanted. She would come back now and again to visit her family but wouldn't have to cook camas under sod in a pit. She'd be a fancy officer wife.

She jumped bareback on her horse, rode fast as she could to her uncle's home to tell her cousin the news. Excitement ran through her legs like she never felt before, her legs tight around the horse.

"Oooooo," she squealed, hollered through the alders, waved her arms at anyone she came across.

Her uncle stood quiet on the porch of his home, dressed in overalls, boots, and a straw hat with a hole cut for the feather he wore. He watched the girls talk. Molly's cousin was happy for Molly, but sad she didn't get a letter from Lieutenant Weasel. Molly's uncle knew he might not see his niece again but was pleased to see Molly happy and off his hands for a husband.

"Finish weeding the garden," he told his daughter. "Maybe a letter from your soldier will come later. Ask Molly for supper."

Her uncle eyed the shack, figured what he'd do with the gifts to come from the army—a new front door, roof that didn't leak. The army must understand his people's way for getting a niece moved off his hands in marriage even if the army didn't know much about honoring treaties.

CHAPTER FIVE
BLOWIN' UP WILLARD

"Will have me a box of dynamite, daughter, a whole box. Stole from these miners around here, how I get the box, blow up that Willard. I will roast duck on the remains with my feet up, like a lady. Will need your help to get the duck, daughter."

Molly told this story for my womanhood while I licked liver grease off my fingers from a porcupine she cooked, eleven snows now in me. I snared the porcupine so she would have quills to sew on her doeskin dress. The liver looked on the pink side, but I said nothing. Molly wasn't good at cooking liver or anything else, except camas cakes, but least I didn't have to cook. Didn't have to do the sewed quills, neither.

We sat on a log, alongside a campfire on the banks of the Columbia.

I thought Ma talked about some man that done her wrong, name of Willard. But why did she need more than one dynamite stick to send Willard to his *re*ward? Since Molly got done what she set her mind to, I put my mind to how many duck I'd need for the party.

Quite a trek to Washington City for Molly and her Aunty Nell, with soldier escorts and Union army recruits. Her aunty, a woman on the large side due to the settler farm food she ate, brought a skin bag of bear grass she cut while picking huckleberries in the hills, and split willow roots. She bided her time on the trip making a grass basket for a wedding gift for her niece.

41

Mr. Waller loved Molly's aunty, treated her good. Molly hoped Stump would give her a husband like Mr. Waller.

Their travels began on a wagon behind a team of army horses, loaded with their trunks and bags, creaking over mountains on the new built army Mullan Road to Fort Benton on the Big Muddy River, Montana Territory. A noisy steamboat gave them the first ride folks took from Fort Benton to the Mississippi. After they docked on the Mississippi, they rode a wagon pulled by army horses to a train heading east.

They found themselves on a B&O that gave off steam and noise at a station north of the capital. They never felt such heat and wet air like at that train station overflowing with dressed-up folks, waiting for families and friends.

"How do I look?" Molly said to her aunty, primping in their compartment. "Like a lady?"

She grabbed a towel, wiped sweat from her hands and neck. Her Aunty Nell laughed, checked out her own bonnet in the mirror. "I have to wear a bonnet? Don't like bonnets," Molly said. "Bonnets hide my hair and I can't see around me."

"I looked at picture magazines of Mr. Waller. Ladies wear bonnets these days, niece," her aunty said.

Molly opened her trunk and took out a bonnet that matched her dress, added a shawl. They wore silk dresses to their necks, bustles on their *be*hinds, corsets under the dress. They wrapped their hair in buns at back, under the bonnets. The only part of Molly and her aunty that looked Indian was their face, color of their skin.

They looked at each other, held hands. Molly's feet stomped, itching to go.

"Ready," Molly said.

Their trunks were delivered to the station where Stump stood in his uniform, pressed and clean, officer hat in hand. A porter came to help Molly and her aunt to the station. He grabbed their smaller bags, took them to Stump.

"These your fine-looking squaws, Officer?"

Blood crawled up Stump's neck to his face. He pumped a fist in the porter's face, "Where's your manners? These women are not squaws."

"No, sir," the porter said, backed up. "Didn't mean no disrespect."

"Get your nigra arse outa here," Stump yelled.

Molly learned that day what army folks meant when they called her people red nigras.

Passengers from the train give her curious looks. "What you staring at?" Molly said, took a step at the closest woman, lifted her dress for the skinning knife hid in her garter. The lady almost fell on the track in her run to get away. The sight gave Aunty Nell a chuckle. Folks moved to the far wall of the station when the Indian woman got a hug from the smart dressed officer, pistol at the waist.

Stump took them in a carriage to the Willard Hotel, center of a town bigger than those women ever laid eyes on. Bigger than hotels in Oregon City on the upper Willamette where Molly went with Stump for army business and parties. She'd learned to dance the quadrille in calico dresses and moccasins like other Indian women who wifed soldiers and settlers.

Carriages coming and going in Washington City, horse drops decorated the dirt streets. Molly and her aunty never saw a building like the Willard, windowed all around.

"Climbed so high, had to lean back, see where the windows ended," Ma told me, her hand high above her head. "Somewhere near clouds."

Stump took Molly and her aunty to the counter at the Willard Hotel. The desk clerk, in a black suit too big, looked at Molly and her aunt, excused himself.

He got the manager.

"Officer?" the manager said, as his paw fiddled the gold chain and watch in his vest. He eyed the women, "What can I do for you?"

"Reserved a room for my lady, Miss Molly. Another for her aunt. I'm paying. Rooms ready?"

The manager drummed fingers on the counter, took a breath, let the air out slow.

"Of course, Officer." To the desk clerk he said, "Sign them in."

"*Squaws?*" the clerk said.

"This soldier fights for our union. Whatever he needs for his relaxation, see he gets."

In her room, Stump gave Molly a bigger hug than at the station.

"Missed you, honey," Stump said.

"Missed you, too, sweetheart. I want you to know, I don't like when they call me squaw. I have no idea what that word means. And I didn't come to relax, I came to marry."

"I don't like that talk, neither," he said. "Pay no attention to what folks say. You look real good, sweetheart. Prettiest gal in Washington City. Tomorrow night, me and some of the boys got up a party. Forget this war for a night. I will find us a church, after."

Next day Stump picked up Molly in a carriage, took her to see the sights and shop for a fancy dress. Molly never saw such a city. Top part of the Capitol building not yet stuck on, soldiers coming and going, forts and cannons on hills, canals with water that gave off smells, streets with flies and garbage not picked up. Stump told her the war was not going easy like the army hoped. They might have to burn out the enemy, burn crops, homes, put to the sword to whatever lingered, to end the war.

"What we learned at West Point, sweetheart," Stump said, slapped the horses along. "Take the war to the enemy's homeland. Always attack, like Napoleon said, *toujours l'audace.* What I do, Molly, honey. What I'm paid to do, always be *auda-cious.*"

Molly never heard of Napoleon, but the man must know something if the army followed what he said. She put his words to mind. The most audacious thing about Stump, Molly said, was how he looked. Stump stood short with long arms and a pinhead under his officer's cap. But he had a smile and feelings for her that won her heart. Molly had feelings for him, too, missed him terrible, worried each day he would get shot.

Stump took Ma and her aunty to the party next night got up by army officers and militia leaders that guarded the city—a dance party at the Willard ballroom, gas-lit brass chandeliers polished and shining bright. A band played music Molly never heard before. Ladies were draped in silk from across the Great Water in all colors—blue, pink, yellow, even green, decorated with lace trim, what they called rosettes, gloves up the arms to the elbow. They waved hand fans to keep their painted faces cooled.

Molly learned to dance in Oregon City like other Indian girls married to settlers and to soldiers, but they danced to fiddles, a squeeze box, and upright piano. She could waltz dance, too, hold up the bottom of a dress so she wouldn't step on the hem. She learned to sway like a lovely daisy in a summer breeze. But this dance at the Willard looked different to Molly, and the music sounded like nothing she ever heard. A dressed-up man waved a skinny stick in front of the band.

More officers and militia men were in that ballroom than Molly thought in the world—soldiers in clean blue uniforms, bow tie at the neck, white gloves. The party dress Stump bought showed off Molly's beauty and plums. Officers with more stars and gold shook hands with Stump, gawked at Molly, how tall and proud she stood, so lovely, with the bustle showing off her maiden *be*hind and her plums. She hid a laugh at her aunt, who looked even bigger in a dress with the bustle.

The wives of the officers took notice of the attention given to Molly's beauty. "Get a smell of her skin? Indian smell, near nigra," she heard one say.

"Smell worse than nigra to me," the other lady said. "A nigra smell come in from the wild."

Molly and her aunty slipped to the ladies' room, powdered their noses, looked in the mirror. Her aunty sprayed herself and Molly with a sweet smell bottle from her party purse.

"Put more here." Molly pointed to her bosoms. "I'll stuff those fine-lady noses between my plums if I hear another word about Indian smells."

"Don't get riled, niece," her aunty said. "We got women like them back home. Remember, Molly, you're a chief's niece, not just any girl."

Aunty Nell took her seat along the wall in the ballroom, angered, fanned herself calm. Molly bit her lip, waited nervous outside the ballroom for the go-in entrance walk with Stump. She had to dance good like the wife of an officer who hoped to move up ranks—her part of the wife deal.

46

CHAPTER SIX
DANCING THE GERMAN

What happened seemed a funny sight to Molly.

Two lines formed at the door to the ballroom, gents' line of roosters on one side, hen line next to roosters on the other. A hen's left wing wore a long glove, touched the man's wing high on his right, the other wing of the rooster held behind his back. Roosters bowed, hens curtsied and did a hen strut to the ballroom, ready it seemed to Molly to lay eggs. Both the roosters and hens did bird walks and strolled around in circles like they could not find the nest.

Molly took a breath, touched Stump's hand with hers, began her long leg sashay into the Willard ballroom.

The problem came in her hip sway, too much for a grand walk, but that was how Molly walked, on the untamed side no matter the occasion. And her long leg steps got looks from the ladies who did little bird steps. The bustle on her *be*hind moved the way the leader of the band waved his stick. Other ladies hid faces behind fans to cover a laugh at her savage walk. But a officer with more stripes than others clapped at the sight of Molly. All the officers had to join in what their chief did, clapped, too.

More woman talk reached Molly after her grand walk.

"See nits in her hair? I saw white specks. Lice. Indians eat dog. Wigwam dog have lice."

"I won't have her over to my house, or the squaw man who brought her. Hard to get rid of lice in a child's hair."

Molly tried to pay no mind to the talk but the lice talk

angered her. Her family kept her hair clean growing up, never had lice. Aunty Nell shook her head, *No, niece, let it go.* Molly paid no heed, walked behind the lady doing the lice talk where women talked, stuck her heel on the hem of the lady's dress. When the lady headed to the champagne table, the dress tore from around her bosoms; she screamed, ran out of the ballroom.

Molly asked Stump to kindly get her a glass filled from the bowl.

Molly sipped her champagne, heard an officer with chin skin hung down his neck say to another, "What's a red nigra girl doing here?"

"Squaw man brought her. Him in from the west. She's a good-looking redskin, you got to admit, for a whore," said the other officer.

The skinning knife Molly had in her garter itched to get grabbed, stuck in that soldier.

Then came the most peculiar kind of sashay of the night, what they called the cotillion. Some called that dance the German. Two ladies held a rope, men walked or jumped across the rope. Ladies lifted the rope gentle to tangle the feller, give everyone a laugh. To Molly, the German seemed the most lunatic way to dance she ever saw.

"I'll have a try with that rope," Molly told Stump, her second glass of champagne bubbling her head. She eyed the officer who did the whore talk.

When that feller stepped over the rope, Molly gave a *YIP,* yanked the rope, caught him square on his manhood sack. He gave a holler, grabbed himself between his legs, fell to the floor, did a vomit of what he ate that night.

Aunty Nell hid her laugh with the fan.

"You did that on purpose," the wife said to Molly, wiped her husband's mouth.

"Mercy, me. So sorry, I truly am," Molly said. She got herself more bubbly.

Stump heard the talk about Molly. The remarks about her being a squaw with lice nits embarrassed him, made it unlikely he'd get more stripes, move up ranks.

Next day, Stump talked with Molly in her room at the Willard. "I've been thinking, sweetheart," he said.

"Me, too," she said, so happy. "What church will we . . . ?"

Stump waved his hand, "Now might not be the best time to marry."

Molly sat down on a stuffed chair like her legs got roped, said to him, "What are you saying?"

Stump squirmed, tried to smile, "Honey, I could get killed in this war, leave you a widow before we settle down. That's not what I want for you."

Molly could not believe her ears. "No, you fear you won't move up ranks, marrying a squaw, that's what you fear. Don't lie to me. Why don't you tell those ladies to eat horse shite from the streets of their fine city. I thought you loved me."

"I do love you, Molly. That's why . . ."

"You lie!" Molly hollered, so loud Aunty Nell heard them in the next room. Molly had words for him no lady spoke, unless he broke her heart, made her look a fool to her people.

"You lice licking dog, Stump. You . . ."

Stump got tears—that stopped Molly's angered words. He cared about her.

"What you say is true, Molly," he said. "I want to move up ranks and I love you, never met a girl so pretty and so good to me. But my folks and these army women—let's wait till after the war, honey?"

"How can you do this to me, sweetheart?" Molly said at the B&O station, tears flowing.

"Not the right time," Stump said, wanting her gone, no more

squaw talk to embarrass him, keep him from moving up ranks.

"When, then?"

"After this war we can settle down?"

"You lie to me, Stump? Like you did to bring me here?"

Broke Molly's heart when he sent her packing, no church wedding. Aunty Nell held Molly on the trip home, like a baby doing her tears. Her aunty's half-done wedding basket got tossed to the stinking Potomac River.

But Molly was with child when she headed home. That child was the lightning spark on this earth that became me. The beginning of me looking to find where I fit on this earth, the beginning of my journey. The only words I got from my father— *Twojur Lahdass*, Always Be Audacious.

My father never came back to the Willamette after the war, never knew he had an Indian daughter. Ma swore many snows later, waving her skinning knife, "If Stump got out of that war alive, and I ever come across him, I will separate your pa from his manhood."

Ma unkindly named me Army Girl.

She married Angus Tunbridge, his Indian style wife.

And, going on fourteen snows, I got traded to Mr. McFadden to be his woman.

CHAPTER SEVEN
MR. MCFADDEN
FORT BENTON

"Ya don't know how to move, ya peedy lass," Mr. McFadden yelled after I slept with him in his robes. Called me skinny—peedy. I'd cut his old throat 'cept I might get hung like Molly saw white men do to the Cascades and I'd never see my ma when she came back to get me.

His old face, craggy as a mountain beneath his white hair, threw those words at me because I didn't know how to move my skinny body to please him. He whacked my fanny.

"Ya got what we ain't tried," he said. "Maybe a fresh squaw prefers her duties like four-legged shaggies perform theirs. Buffalo style."

He rolled me over, lifted my *be*hind, tried to shove himself in me there. Made me bleed. This old man crazy? I knew he would laugh if I cried. I didn't want to give him a laugh. I looked for a knife to open his throat. I'll get you, will bloody get you, make you pay, I was thinking. Had to be careful so I didn't end up hung by the neck, what Molly saw happen to the Cascades.

When I did no better for him in his robes, Mr. McFadden said, "We will marry, lassie. You will be my wifie. Maybe the Lord will bring me in holy matrimony what ain't coming my way."

He threw out the Crow woman, my only friend, whose tongue I learned. He never asked me if I wanted to marry him. He gave me a fine yellow blouse for a top, a brown cotton skirt he shipped up the Big Muddy, a white lace veil for our wedding

51

day, and found us a preacher.

For the wedding, he put on a long black coat, a black tie that needed pressing, a shirt made of white silk, and black suspenders he got from a undertaker who got taken under himself. The black trousers hung loose on his sparrow legs. He found two sober steamboat captains to witness this wedding, and Miss Brenda, for what he called my bridesmaid. Miss Brenda ran the finest bordello in Fort Benton.

The preacher at that chapel, where we stood all dressed up, learned I was a heathen.

"Mr. McFadden, you cain't ask our Lord to bless a marriage if both partners ain't baptized. Even a Scot, livin a heathen life, must know that."

Mr. McFadden narrowed his eyes, slapped his knee.

"How might we correct that little matter, Preach?"

We walked over what hog, ox, and horse drop on streets—me in the wedding blouse, veil, and skirt.

I got baptized in Big Muddy water. What the water poured over me was supposed to do, I couldn't wonder. I took me a bath the night prior.

"We marry tomorrow," I said to Mr. McFadden. "The water poured on me looked dirty, smelled of upriver pee. I need me another bath."

We married next day.

Mr. McFadden gave me more news to get me wifie.

"I got you a calico dress. And a fresh scraped doeskin dress I traded for. See if they fit. Ya got to look proper for my wifie. I ain't some hand to mouth trapper."

"I don't like dresses."

"No matter what ya like, you're my wifie."

"Ma never said I got to wear dresses."

"What else Ma say? That she cared about ya?"

He knew where to stick the knife in how I felt. I took off my skin shirt and pants in his log cabin next to the trading post. His bedroom smelled of old man, everywhere the stink of tobacco, old man sweat, wood smoke from the fireplace, garbage not thrown, waiting for me to toss. He smoked his briar pipe, watched me undress, his bushy eyebrows near grown together, his eyes the strange color like the sky.

"Come here," he said.

"I haven't got this dress on."

"No need. I want ya skuddy."

Nights, when I crawled skuddy in his bed without the lantern lit, I put on a nightshirt he gave me, before he did old man things on me. Never touched me with the lantern lit when I was skuddy.

"Come here," he said.

I didn't want the strap, or slap of his hand, so I went. He sat on a wood chair, needled cushion bottom and back. He laid his pipe on the bear rug, ran his rough hands over me, over my bare shoulders, down my chokecherry bosoms, squeezed my bosoms like sourdough biscuits.

"Can I put on my clothes?"

He gave the matter some thought, waved his paw to the fireplace behind me where wood popped in flames.

"Fetch me my pipes, behind the woodpile. Gonna have us a party. I feel lonesome this night, miss my home."

I got the bag of pipes he kept on the floor next to the fire. He liked to keep his pipes and skins warm when headed to winter though he never played those pipes around me. Wood pipes stuck out the bag made of dog hide, stitched tight, a white man contraption I paid no mind to.

On my return with his pipes, he threw off his slippers and trousers, pulled his shirt over his head, got himself a green leaf color wool skirt from his dresser, but didn't give me the skirt. The coot put the skirt on himself; his sparrow legs showed under the wool. He pulled on his white silk shirt.

What craziness Mr. McFadden had a mind for that night got my chilled skin to crawl.

The dog hide bag fit under his arm. He took in his mouth one of the pipes stuck in the bag. The noise made when he blew in the pipe knocked me back; my hands hid my naked privates. The noise from the bag sounded like hounds begging for dinner before they croaked from starvation.

"Ya dance, wifie. I play us the tune."

His eyes came to life, fire glow reflected in his eyes that before looked empty.

"Dance?"

"Course ya can dance," he said. "Any savage knows dance. Crow dance after they take scalps, like devils."

"I ain't Crow."

"No matter. The Lord gave woman the dance. Ya got the parts of woman so ya must have the dance that go with the parts."

"I'm cold. Don't have my clothes on."

"I'll start with 'My Home in the Hill.' "

He blew to make music, marched in his skirt around the room, moved his head to show me how to dance. I watched, bobbed my head, moved my shoulders up, down, the hound noises finding my bones. Heels of my feet moved up, down; my hips saw what my feet did, came alive. A leg lifted, then the other. I laughed, having me a good time. I got in behind the old coot while he blew on his pipe, noise coming from his dog hide bag. Me, naked as a bird behind a old feller in a skirt.

Outside, Fort Benton hounds took up the tune.

Then, something happened. Dog bag music struck a part of me I felt deep in my bones. My feet flapped faster; my head did a bob like the weather iron in a wind on top of the trading post. First time in my life I enjoyed dancing. Mr. McFadden blew and played music faster when he saw me kicking my feet like he taught.

Every time I heard chicken squawks after that, I got the remind of dog bag music.

Making music tuckered Mr. McFadden so much he fell asleep in his rocker, after he downed scotch malt, had a cry about his dead folks. I got some rest that night, no old husband to bother me in the robes. His set of pipes became my friend in my time of need.

Next night, Mr. McFadden sat me front of the fire to tell me stories, get me on the civilized side, he said. I put on his new doeskin dress, my old moccasins, and red shawl around my shoulders. Woman clothes gave me a strange feeling—soft, like the insides of a cattail. Mr. McFadden, in his rocker by the fire, held a picture on his lap of his family. Him, his old folks, a brother and sister in the picture where he got birthed across the Great Water. All dead, 'cept him.

"To get ya civilized, wifie, ya got to know stories. Will take more than white woman's clothes to make ya civilized."

"That so?"

"Am gonna tell a civilized story by an English bard, taught by my auld pap, who taught me at his parish school to read, know the Holy Book, do my numerals. That awfy bastirt, rest his soul, taught me well. This story is about a fellow name of Hamlet. Well, Hamlet was the son of a big chief in Denmark. After Hamlet finds his father dead in the garden, his father comes back as a ghost. The ghost of his dear auld pap, the King, comes to the son, tells Hamlet he got done in by his brother, the laddie's uncle . . ."

"Wait, husband. I don't follow the story."

"Haven't even got the story going. Dead King's ghost comes to his son."

"Ghost? I never heard about ghosts."

55

"You a savage and not know ghosts? Every savage knows ghosts. What their whole way of thinking comes from."

"Savage?"

"Wifie, trust your husband. The savage flows in ya, in your blood."

I told him—tell your story.

"A ghost is the spirit of the dead man after the man meets his Maker, jumps this mortal coil. Dies," he said.

"Hold on, husband. A man dead be a dead man. Same for the bear or wolverine and the beaver. Nothing left, what once walked the land, alive."

"And I got ya baptized? Shame on me. If ya don't know ghosts, can't stop the heathen flow."

"A skinned-out wolverine ghost ever steal something from your porch?"

"Ya don't get the point."

"You ever bed the ghost of a dead woman you been with in the robes?"

"Ya don't bed ghosts. Lord, save us. This is gonna be hard."

"Tell your story, husband."

He settled down, took a swallow of Scotch mash, leaned back in his rocker, told me more about Hamlet—get me civilized.

"The uncle that killed Hamlet's father marries Hamlet's ma."

"That's what civilized folks do? Marry the wifie of the man ya done in?" I said.

"Damnit, lassie. NO."

"My ma's trapper comes back, kills you, he's got to marry me? Take care of me because he done you in?"

"Lord save us, No. Will take me longer than when it came to me. When I first laid eyes on ya, seemed the bonnie lass. Wanted ya for reasons only the Almighty knows," he said. "Here's the problem, using stories of the English. English people, who tell that story, are the crock of shite from the hound. *Ith mo chac*, I

56

say to any English."

"*Ith* . . . What you say?"

"*Ith mo chac*—eat my shite. Least ya know *shite*, right?"

I practiced his words till I got his words right, learned his civilized talk about shite. Mr. McFadden said the problem to civilize me was he used a tale told by shite-eating English. Next night he would try again, with a tale from his tribe, a Scot story about some feller name of Ivanhoe. If Scot tales were as good as their dog bag music, a longer night would come than before.

Next night, I listened best I could—no ghosts in the Ivanhoe story. Mr. McFadden got blootered from his scotch mash. A chief of two tribes in Mr. McFadden's land headed home from a war. Those two tribes of the chief could not get along. Ivanhoe fought a one on one, with somebody, not sure who. Why, I don't know that, neither. Ivanhoe had his eyes on a lovely woman he should not want, Rowena.

Dumbest story I ever heard. I fell asleep on the bear rug.

Mr. McFadden gave up on stories to civilize me.

Every day, I'd run to the Fort Benton levee whenever I heard them shoot the cannon that greeted steamboats with whiskey, passengers, and supplies that traveled up the Big Muddy from St. Louis. See if Ma came back for me, know if I saw a tear in her eye when she left me. Ma never stepped off a boat. With the Crow girl gone, I had to heat the old man's skillet, cook his grub. I didn't like to cook about as much as get in his robes. But I could not please him in the robes.

By the lantern in his bedroom, he said, "I'm sending ya to Miss Brenda's for learning how to please a man who paid a heap. Pack up. Come back when ya learn how."

"How to please you in the robes?"

"Lemme be clear, ya peedy lass. How to proper shag a man who paid a heap for ya."

I felt alone in this world though people moved round me—

Indians in buckskin with feathers in the hair, white trappers, gamblers, miners and mercantiles, wives, kids, steamboat woodhawks my age. But none of them cared about me.

My predicament fell clear to my mind.

I had Indian and white blood, not sure which was me or how to live like the one or the other. Being white and Indian is not something in the skin. It flows in the mind, how to reckon what comes your way when you could go one way or the other. I knew I came a girl to this world but till then it made no difference, 'cept I squatted to pee. Each new moon, I got the remind I was a girl.

Mr. McFadden shamed me when he sent me to Miss Brenda's bordello. But, to keep my scalp, I'd learn to shag like a wifie.

CHAPTER EIGHT
MISS BRENDA'S BORDELLO

Miss Brenda came up on a steamboat with her fat basset hound, Pancake, to make her fortune, retire, she said, go back home. Some of Miss Brenda's women came up the Big Muddy, but mostly she kept Indian girls at her bordello who got traded by their fathers for whiskey. There weren't many women in Fort Benton to give a bordello time to trappers and steamboat captains; or to the young wood-hawks who kept the steamers fired up with cut logs; or to the keno gamblers who looked to enjoy what gamble money could buy. Made no sense to me, paying for what should come from a giving heart, one to the other. White men figure dollars give the road to whatever they have a hanker for.

I had no idea how to be a woman with Ma not around. I had to learn what I could from Miss Brenda, stay alive till Ma came back for me.

Miss Brenda's hair had new ribbons every day, wild rose paint on her cheeks. She wore silk dresses with humps on her *be*hind that made her arse look like a well-fed bay horse when she walked on the Front Street boardwalk. Sheriff Healy called her a whore, but tipped his hat to her. She paid top dollar for the moonshine he left in back of her bordello. He sold whiskey to Indians in the Grandmother's Land at Fort Whoop-Up before mounted police sent him packing. That made him what they wanted for a sheriff in Fort Benton. Miss Brenda ran a good business is how the sheriff looked at it.

My first night, she bathed me in a brass tub, washed my hair in hot water heated on the stove, gave me a clean nightie to wear in the bunk room with Indian girls, older than me.

"See you in the morning, dearie," she said.

I didn't speak the tongue of the Indian girls, so we didn't talk in the bunk room. And maybe I didn't look Indian enough to them. I cried myself to sleep.

After breakfast in the kitchen next morning, Miss Brenda had me to her room.

"Put this dress on, dearie. After I brush your hair, fix you up, you'll come with me to church. Got to let town men know we have a new girl."

I put on the white cotton dress, sashed at the waist. "You've been with a man before or I wouldn't let you work here," she said, looked me over like she studied a mare for sale. "But you don't know how to please a man, what Mr. McFadden told me. Like anything worth doing, it takes practice. You're with experts here, dearie."

She laughed.

I sat on a cushioned chair in her room while she brushed my hair with a silver-handled brush. My hair now hung long down my back. "Mr. McFadden paid me good, so I'll let you keep most of what you earn. A woman's got to look after herself if she ever wants to get ahead in this world, husband or no husband. Men die, dearie. Can't take care of us when they're buried in Boot Hill."

The brush flowed through my clean, good-smell hair like a hand through water, got my whole self, soft. She could tell I liked how it felt, said I could have the brush when I left. I brushed my own hair, looked at myself in her mirror, turned my head to see my hair shining like Miss Brenda's, though mine was the color of coal, not honey like hers.

I looked at myself, wished my face weren't round like a silver dollar but heart shaped like hers.

"You know about money?" Miss Brenda said, while I brushed my hair.

"Some."

"Not many ways a woman can earn money, that's why women marry, dearie. Not me. A woman where I come from, St. Louis, might earn only five dollars a week working at a store, a little more selling what she sews. But here," she took my arm, looked me in the eye, "for a ten-dollar night, my girls keep six. Easy for them to make twenty-five dollars a week. A hundred a month. Buy property or cows, someday own a ranch, or give money to their families. I might buy me a husband when I get back to St. Louis. A rich woman can buy any husband she wants."

I gave attention to her words, Miss Brenda teaching me how to live a white girl life.

She took a small brush, put red paint on my lips—some got in my mouth. Tasted awful. I spit it out.

She laughed. "Here, you try. Use my mirror." I could not find my lips with the brush even looking in the mirror. She took the brush, told me, "Put your lips together, like this. I am going to make you look like a beautiful actress. And, dearie, we are the best actresses in the world."

I did what she showed me. After painting my lips, she told me to rub them together. I stared at myself in Miss Brenda's big mirror, could not believe my eyes. First time I saw me looking like my ma, though not as pretty. Scared me to see how I looked—becoming a woman.

"Dearie, when men look you up and down like last night in the parlor, don't shake a fist in a man's face when he does that. *Shy* makes a man want you more, pay good money to have you."

"I don't want a man wanting me."

She told me someday I might want a man looking my way.

"I'll never want that," I said. "Not if I got me a gun. Or my skinning knife handy."

"Shush," she said. "I won't make you do anything. You decide when you're ready."

Some nights when Miss Brenda fixed my hair, I gave a rub to her hound. That dog liked to sleep on my bed in the bunk room. His ears hung under his chin, his belly about touched the ground, with a spotted coat like a pinto horse. Nights, when tears came to me in the bunk room, Pancake licked my cheeks.

The hound's want to put his tongue on my sadness stole my heart.

I learned from other girls, through peepholes, how to please a customer, bathe him in a brass tub of hot water, crawl naked in the robes with him, make sounds, howl like a she-wolf. Make a man feel important like a chief even if he smelled or was drunk. Show him how to put on a French skin so us girls didn't get diseased. How to do what Miss Brenda called popping a man's cork.

I said I'd try popping a cork with the cute wood-hawk, not much older 'n me.

I never asked his name.

Miss Brenda let me use her room. I got him on top me, him more nervous than me. When I had him in me, far as he could get, held him there, like when I had to pee, but had to hold, then let loose. Held him, let loose.

I sent that boy to the moon, best I could tell from how his face got red, eyes bugged out, and he fell on me like he died, moaning, "*Gawd. O, Gawd.*" Peculiar time, seemed to me, to pray.

He begged for another trip to the moon. "Do me again. I paid a week's wages for you."

I told him to go home, I wanted to take Pancake for a walk by the Big Muddy.

"Listen to me, you whore!" he yelled, made a fist above my face. "Do me again or I'll . . ."

I grabbed my skinning knife from beside the bed, put it to his throat. "You'll do what? You want to keep your tongue, or do I cut it off, stuff it down your throat, call mama to come get her little boy?" I cut a nick in his throat, put my finger to the blood, let him see me lick my finger, know he had a savage girl he tried to scare.

He stuck his legs in his trousers, ran home.

Not many men wanted me because I was skinny. Made me right pleased I came skinny, though I had nice curving legs, muscled like my ma's. Pancake was always at my feet waiting for handouts.

Miss Brenda put me at the Quarter Hole to eat grits by the bucket, get fat, take care of business. There were holes in the wall big enough for a man too busy, or no money for the whole woman, to stick his organ through, have his organ worked on till he felt done.

I laughed and cried, told her I could not do that. No. Mr. McFadden said Indians were savages, that savage blood flowed through me, told white man stories to get me civilized. Seemed to me the Quarter Hole went along with other white man civilized ways. One day, a customer shoved his organ through the hole with four small bells stitched under the skin on four sides, what the man told folks he learned from a Borneo *Sul*tan, to *de*light ladies there who wanted more from their men than the Great Mystery gave them.

What to do? Lick the smelled-up ugly thing? Rub the turnip head? Bang the stalk, make the bells tinkle? I tried all I knew on that mystery, not sure what might send him away, done in. Miss Brenda's basset waddled to the room, like he owned it, ready for his hardtack and gravy lunch. Never saw a critter with such begging eyes like that dog. He stole my heart, his tongue hung out his mouth like he didn't know where to put a tongue big as his head.

I gave a little whistle. "Come here, Pancake."

That dog came when I whistled because I slipped him bear grease. I loved bear grease, reminded me of when I hunted, roamed free, ate roast elk leg dipped in bear grease for supper. A dog will eat whatever don't smell skunk, even eat his own shite if he forgot he made that particular drop.

Pancake waddled his fat self to the organ with the bells stitched in. I let him see me rub bear grease over the top, down the sides, hear bells jingle to my touch. Pancake licks his lips, gets the go ahead from me. His tongue washed the feller's organ like he found the best bear grease he ever got to lick.

Contented sounds of the customer from the other side of the Quarter Hole wall. Pancake eyed me, begged for more of what made him the happiest dog in the territory. That sweet hound got all he wanted. Indian girls covered their mouth, their laughs would not upset the customer. For the first time at the bordello, Indian girls liked me. I was now Indian in their eyes, made a fool of a white man.

Later, the customer asked Miss Brenda if the woman of his organ's *de*light might be had for a night.

"Who did so well for our Borneo Sul*tan?*" she said, proud of some girl's talent at the Quarter Hole.

The other girls looked to me because Pancake been my idea.

"Lou Ellen, ma'am," I said.

She threw her hands in the air like she heard the tallest tale she ever heard but sent a runner to find Lou Ellen for a big dollar night. Lou Ellen was born a man across the Great Water where the sun rose, and flowered into what folks said was the most beautiful woman in Fort Benton. Maybe Lou Ellen had him the name, Loo Lin, before he became a woman in Fort Benton. We wondered how the tinkle feller and Loo Lin spent their night but heard no complaints.

Loo Lin sucked on a pipe at night after work with his friends, asked me if I wanted to join him. I looked in once, said no. Peculiar smell to what they puffed on, their eyes wet and colored like a roan horse, before they passed out.

I never thought what we did at Miss Brenda's was what preachers called a sin. I thought it was not respecting of us girls.

Mr. McFadden was right pleased when he got me back after I learned how to shag. My body held memories of dirty men, drunks, some that throwed up, their ugly words about me in my ear, and in my heart flowed shame. My hate for Mr. McFadden dug deep in my bones for what he did to me.

CHAPTER NINE
SIOUX DEVILS

One cloudy morn, different Indians stood in front of the counter at Mr. McFadden's trading post.

"Sioux," Mr. McFadden told me behind the counter, disgust from his throat at the thought. "Sioux devils. Do business out their fanny flaps."

One of them Sioux devils had the name Lone Wolf. He piled buffalo hides on the trading post floor to trade for carbines. Indians weren't to get guns and shells, but Mr. McFadden had no worry about goverment rules. The carbines came by fire-wagon up the Big Muddy from Fort Lincoln in the Dakotas, for the Govner of the Territory Army in case Territory Indians tied their ponies' tails for war.

"Just business," Mr. McFadden said, eyed the buffalo hides piled carbine-high on his floor, stuck a bookmark in his *Ivan-hoe*, walked out from behind the counter. "I'll be a mite richer off these Sioux devils. Shut your mouth, lassie, don't let 'em know I'm going to cheat their stupid arses."

Why'd he talk like that to me?

A handsome face on Lone Wolf, smooth as a river stone. He snuck glances my way like he saw a lovely flower. When Mr. McFadden looked the other way, he smiled at me. I wore the calico dress Mr. McFadden gave me, a pink bow in my hair, how Miss Brenda taught.

On Mr. McFadden's counter, I opened a book writ by a feller Mr. McFadden called Custer, with his picture in the book. Mr.

McFadden said Custer took lessons in stuffing animals because he loved to stuff critters as much as shoot Indians. I looked at Custer's face in the book, a ugly river-otter face. but I had my mind on the handsome Indian Mr. McFadden dickered with.

I never been with an Indian, looked down when Lone Wolf gave me the eye. They couldn't be worse than a white man, not as awful as Mr. McFadden. Sure enough, what Miss Brenda and my ma said held true. Lone Wolf could not take his eyes off me when I looked down, shy of his eyeing me. I looked right at him, what my ma taught in her stories when I skinned the beaver, up in his eyes, him standing more 'n a head taller than me.

This could be my way out of this crazy place, I was thinking, not listen to no more *Ivanhoe,* dance skuddy to dog hide noise coming from a wind bag. Become wife of a good hunter, what with all those hides he and his three friends brought for trade. Get back to roaming free, look for my ma, try living an Indian life.

What living Indian meant was not clear to me, though. Not at all.

Mr. McFadden had his keno card game that night and getting blootered with his friends.

I snuck to meet Lone Wolf by the Big Muddy where I got baptized in the blood of the feller from a tribe that wandered in a desert beyond the Great Water. I looked around, made sure we didn't get spotted by some nosy kid, who'd tell Mr. McFadden where I was, get a gingersnap *reward,* hang Lone Wolf and get me whipped.

I didn't know Lone Wolf's tongue; he moved his hands slow, in sign, gave me a porcupine quill necklace. He was on the shy side now that we sat alone. He played his flute for me, a real gentleman. Flute music didn't do much for me but he liked to blow in the wood. He was older 'n me, some, in buckskin that had seen better days. In his eye came a J Boy look, the kind that warms a girl's heart, like an invite to a party that's just for the girl. Chub said to watch out for J Boys, but in my mind if I could hunt bear, no reason to be scared of a J Boy Indian.

He signed I could run off with him if I wanted because Sioux had no mind to trade more with McFadden. Never knew an invite like that from a handsome man, spoke with just his hands, could curl my toes in moccasins like it did. I took a deep breath, held it, let the air out slow, got calm. An owl hooted above us. I looked up, saw stars beyond tree branches, a black sky filled with more candles than I ever saw before. I thought on what my real father said to Ma for how to win a battle—Always Be *Audacious*. Lone Wolf had his eyes lowered while I thought on his kind offer. I looked at the owl, at the sky that gave a dark blanket over the Big Muddy.

A call came to me from the owl, a bird omen? It was all I had to go on for my life: *Go, Army Girl, and don't ever look back.*

I looked Lone Wolf in the eye, signed fast as two hands could move, *I want to go with you.*

He said a word in his tongue I didn't know, Wašté. *Washtay,* how the word sounded. I opened my arms to him, thought that was what he had in mind, some sweet time, maybe I'd pop his cork.

"Hókahé," Lone Wolf whispered when we started up; another word I didn't know.

I thought the word meant "I love you," in his tongue.

"Hókahé, sweetheart," I said, touched his face tender, a face I might come to love, if'n I got to know him and he was like he seemed that night.

He squinted at me like he saw the prettiest girl he ever laid eyes on. He sat up, signed what I will never forget. "We lay together later. When you know me better, sweet woman."

He gave me a smile that want to break my heart. Not like

them fellers that came to Miss Brenda's.

I smiled to him, signed, "Later."

I wanted to hug him for what he did for me—risk his life. I gave him a peck on his cheek, a taste of what was to come his way later. He touched his cheek where my lips been, like no woman ever done that to him before.

Next day I grabbed my doeskin clothes, moccasins, skinning knife, beaver boots, and necklace from Mr. McFadden—all I had in the world. When I went to get the silver handle brush Miss Brenda gifted me, I saw Mr. McFadden at the Quarter Hole in line behind young wood-hawks. He liked bordello girls that way when he had business. I went to the room on the other side where all them fellers poked their organs through. The Piegan girl at Mr. McFadden's hole moved aside. I picked up Miss Brenda's shears on my way.

I saw his organ, opened the shears. The old man's organ waited for the Great Mystery to wake up what he shoved through. That organ hurt me, hurt my pride. He shoved that ugly manhood in me where only a devil might go, made me bleed. I owed his manhood nothing.

Like Stump said to Ma when those Cascades got hung—justice being served. This time, a savage half 'n half girl's justice.

The girl at the Quarter Hole ran away, her eyes big as the moon. I put my hate for the man in my hands, gave a squeeze. The tip of his ugliness flew, blood flew, and I flew out of there to meet my new husband, ride to my life with the Sioux.

Lone Wolf stole four horses of Mr. McFadden's, scored big coup with them horses, and stealing a wife from a white man scored big coup, too. I didn't know any of that Sioux coup stuff then. We rode hard to get out that town before the drunk sheriff came after us.

★ ★ ★ ★ ★

Part II
My Sioux Life

★ ★ ★ ★ ★

CHAPTER TEN
JOURNEY TO LONE WOLF'S VILLAGE

The arrow dug deep in my horse's head.

The horse squealed something awful, stumbled. I leaped off before he hit the ground. Lone Wolf's scouts, who rode ahead, galloped back to help us fight. A flock of arrows flew from bushes, I kept my head down, hid behind my horse. Lone Wolf galloped to get to me. He yelled, but I had no idea what he said in his tongue. I grabbed my skinning knife. More arrows thumped my dead horse.

We'd wandered into a raid, boys trying to steal our horses. They ran away when they saw they had a fight with warriors not feared of dying. One of our scouts rode down a boy, brought him to us.

Lone Wolf studied the arrows in my horse, the feathers on the arrow. "Psalōka," he said, disgust in his voice. I didn't know the word. He took his knife, walked to the boy, about my age. Our scouts made the boy kneel. I got nervous—he going to cut the boy's throat?

The boy looked at his captors. "*Bishkawíke!*" the boy yelled in his tongue, not feared of what came his way. I was impressed.

Surprised me because I understood what the boy said. I heard talk from him like I learned from the Crow wife of Mr. McFadden. We had ourselves a Crow boy. I laughed at what he said to the men.

Lone Wolf glared my way, put two fingers to his forehead, signed—*You know the boy's tongue?*

I put two fingers to my head, signed, "This boy said he didn't know you were Sioux or he'd not try to steal your horses." I lied about what the boy said to save his brave but foolish life.

"Who does he think he attacked?" Lone Wolf wanted to know, suspicious of my translating.

I asked the boy what other varmints he raided for horses. The boy studied me, more curious about me than I ever saw in a face. "Isaashpuushé!" he said, spat on the ground.

I signed to Lone Wolf, "Cheyenne."

The men sat in a circle on the ground to decide what to do with the boy—kill him, let him go, or take him with us for a son. I went to the boy, on his knees in the hot sun. He spoke to me but I didn't like what he said.

"Why call me a name like that?" I asked him. "I saved your life, little boy. I never told the men what you said. You can now stay alive—for your mother."

"You didn't tell what I called them—*bitch dogs*?" he said.

"No, I never told them. Or you'd be dead."

"I am not afraid to die."

"Tell that to your mother."

The men ended their council. They stood around the boy, Lone Wolf motioned for me to come to the circle, signed, "Pass water on this pup. We count coup on him, return to his people a coward who did not die brave."

I signed I could not do that.

"You want us to turn our backs when you pass water on him?" Lone Wolf said.

"That's the only way this boy lives?"

"Yes. Or we cut his legs, he can't walk, leave him for hawks."

I put two fingers to my head—Yes, I'd pee on the boy. Lone Wolf motioned for the warriors to look away. I went to the boy, loosed my belt, took down my buckskin trousers. "Maybe you talk nice next time to a girl who saves your life?"

I peed on his feet. He grit his teeth, stared me in the eye. I kept peeing. When I got done, I pulled up my trousers. He said words to me I will not repeat. The men laughed, let him go.

I wanted time to thank the horse for giving his life for me. I knelt, touched his head gentle, took the blanket from his back. Lone Wolf gave me another horse of Mr. McFadden's.

Tears crawled down my face at what happened that day, though I never let the men see me cry.

That's how my Sioux life began.

I spotted Lone Wolf's village in the distance, on flat prairie alongside what he signed was Elk River—slow moving, wide, not deep. We'd come a new moon's ride from Fort Benton. Far off I saw hills and mountains, pine trees in those mountains like in the Willamette Valley. Got me heavy of heart thinking of the pine and hemlock where I hunted. I had me a rope swing on a dead ponderosa tree in the Willamette Valley. Would take a run on a log, hold the rope, swing out naked and chirping like a bird over a river, let loose, have me a swim.

Here's my problem, I figured. Till I got on my first moon, I had a good life. I lived like a boy, trapped streams, hunted bear and fox, bathed in rivers, ate what Ma cooked. Womanhood brought me only trouble in my life. After I became a woman, men wanted to put themselves in me. I had to figure how to stay alive till Ma found me.

I'd been thinking about meeting his family, wondering if they'd like me. I smelled bad, slept under stars, rode for miles under hot sun and rain. I wasn't pretty, Ma said, and now I looked like I'd come from a pig wallow. I asked Lone Wolf to stand guard while I bathed in the Elk River; white folks call it the Yellowstone.

I took off my buckskin, walked into the water. Cold like the Big Muddy, but clean and clear. I sat down, lay back, floated on water under a sky that never came to an end. After a while, I sat on the bank under a willow tree to dry off. I combed my hair with Miss Brenda's silver handle brush, put on my moccasins, took my doeskin dress from my bag, got dressed up best I could. Lone Wolf nodded he liked how I looked. I took a breath, got ready to meet his family.

Out from Lone Wolf's tipi, in the last circle of their camp, walked two women, each standing with folded firm arms on each side of the tipi, studying me as if I was an apparition. There was an older one and the most beautiful woman I ever laid eyes on except for my ma. One would become my protector, the other would want me dead. My dear husband forgot to tell—he already had a wife.

Lone Wolf, a Oglála Sioux, had a beautiful Húŋkpapa Sioux wife—Medicine Feet Woman. When his wife saw me, she stared angry at Lone Wolf, screamed, ran into their tipi. His mother looked to the sky, prayed for what her son would need from a higher power in bringing me home. Sioux men could have more than one wife, I learned, often sisters, but were supposed to talk it over with the first wife.

Not the life I hoped for with Lone Wolf.

His wife put out the word that the crazy woman, me—the witkówiŋ Lone Wolf brought home—should sleep with her eyes open. What his people called a witkówiŋ was a woman who gave herself to a man without him giving horses to her family to show his respect.

His wife had ten snows more than me, stood a head taller, knew how to fix her hair pretty, had great beauty, and cooked good.

Not my talents.

I slept with my skinning knife under my wolf hide pillow. I feared her. Next day, I took a walk under cottonwoods, thought about my predicament.

I wanted a family, somewhere to fit in this world, Indian or white. I wanted that more than anything. My first go at family with Ma and Mr. Tunbridge, part Indian and white man way, had a good feel till my stepfather wanted me for his woman. Next try, the white man way with Mr. McFadden, got me bordello time. Now, third try, livin' Indian, got me a co-wife who wanted me dead. I had to figure how to co-wife with a woman who wanted to slit my throat.

When everyone in Lone Wolf's family knew Medicine Feet Woman and me had no chance to co-wife any better than angered badgers in a parfleche bag, Long Wolf's mother, Eagle Nose Woman, gave a plan to her son.

"Your new wife needs her own tipi, my son," Eagle Nose signed, mending her son's winter mittens.

His mother had gray hair, wore a clean doeskin dress with dyed porcupine quills sewed around the neck. She eyed me, probably wondered why I wanted her son. She never scolded him about nothing, best I could tell. Few slaps behind the ears when he grew up might have done some good but Sioux didn't raise kids that way.

Lone Wolf had near twenty-nine snows. He sighed when he learned what his mother wanted. I wondered what seemed impossible difficult for a man to get me my own tipi—hunt buffalo, stitch their hides together, stick the hides on pine poles. Move in.

Men listened to their mothers around a camp. Lone Wolf's mother had a Húŋkpapa husband, dead from a fight with blue-coat soldiers. She liked me because I worked hard. The village gave her respect—she never got in the robes with a man before she married, her husband gave many horses to have her for his wife, and she honored his memory by not taking another husband.

"You will live next to my mother's tipi," Lone Wolf signed.

"You do not know how to cook but you surely know how to make a tipi?"

"How would I know how to make a tipi, my husband? Like how would I know you had a wife, unless you told me?"

"I'm sorry I forgot to tell you about that."

"Anything else you forgot to tell me?"

"No." He looked embarrassed. "My mother will teach you how to make a tipi." I wondered what else he forgot to tell me.

His mother began her teaching. A husband got the lodgepoles and buffalo hides, near fourteen. The wife worked many moons, depending on help, to get hides ready, fix hides to poles. Had to be a dew liner, too, made of skins, head high on the inside of the tipi, keep cold air trapped out in winter and cooler, summers. Some tipis got dyed on the outside if a man liked the color of his horse or some other color. If the marriage ended, the wife kept her tipi. His mother showed me drawings on tipis of a husband's deeds in battle, or him swiping horses. Women's deeds, making a tipi or quilling a baby's cradle, got painted inside the Great Lodge of the camp.

No one tried to make a tipi alone. Friends gave a hand, and family, but I had no friends, no family except Lone Wolf, his blind uncle, a co-wife who wanted me dead, her sweet little daughter, and my husband's mother, who doted on her only child like he still nursed on her bosoms.

My husband worked many days getting lodgepoles for my tipi. I had pride to see him going to mountain woods a half-day's ride away, return near sundown, dragging pine poles behind packhorses.

Summer sun warmed prairie grass, buffalo herds not far away. With all those buffalo hides he brought to Mr. McFadden's for trade, I figured Lone Wolf would soon get all we needed. He hunted before the rest of the camp woke, snuck back at night. He'd see buffalo but hit nary a one with his bow or carbine.

He confessed the problem—something else he forgot to tell me. "I cannot shoot a bow or máza wakháη good, my wife. All I hit is dirt or dust. You will not tell?"

"I will not tell," I assured him. I pondered what he told me, walked across the clearing in front of our tipi, held up three fingers. "How many fingers, my husband?" I signed.

He squinted, motioned for me to come closer. Folks watched, eager for gossip around a camp. Not much privacy in a camp. "Núnpa?" he said. He signed, "Two?"

"I three fingered you, my husband," I signed and told him. I was learning his tongue as fast as I could. "You can't see good. Why you shoot nothing even if you stand next to the animal."

Lone Wolf needed eyeglasses, what Mr. McFadden wore on his nose when he read a book. Maybe why Lone Wolf's father got killed, why Lone Wolf showed no hunting skill as a boy, figured himself a failure. His father and uncle covered for him, best they could, but with his father dead and his uncle blind, his limits as a hunter stood out. His band gave him those buffalo hides to trade at Fort Benton.

I had me for a husband the worst hunter to ever call himself Sioux.

"My husband, get your máza wakháη. You and me are going to hunt buffalo." I couldn't cook, sew, quill, or bead, but I could shoot a beaver eye at fifty paces, my talent, and moving fine in the robes if my husband ever decided I knew him well enough for that. We'd have a wonderful family life if Medicine Feet Woman cooked, got over her jealousy, and I had my own home.

I was falling in love with this handsome man, first time in my life I felt like that. If he needed help to hunt buffalo, I'd give a hand.

CHAPTER ELEVEN
LONE WOLF'S BUFFALO HUNT

I put on my buckskin tunic and trousers, leather boots, braided my hair in two long braids with a cloth bow at the end. We rode out on Mr. McFadden's horses before the sun rose, Lone Wolf in the lead. We took four more for packhorses. I never hunted buffalo, but I had nary a hand or arm tremble, taught to hunt by Chub. I'd work on living a proper woman life after the hunt. I didn't like the beading part of a woman's life. The men joked, whatever didn't move in camp got beaded by a woman.

Aŋpétuwi, what Lone Wolf called the sun, gave a straight up shine when we found fresh buffalo chips. Buffalo might walk in a line like ants, he said, follow ruts from doing the same trails.

Over a ridge we spotted the herd, bulls with pté and calves while they enjoyed lunch. We tied our horses to sagebrush, crawled to the top of the ridge for a look. I wanted wind coming at me, the buffalo between me and the wind, to hide our smell.

"Crawl through the grass, other side of those buffalo," I signed to Lone Wolf. "Chase them my way."

"My wife shoots a máza wakháŋ?"

He cocked his head, looked at me, his curious chickadee look that I'd come to love. He filled my heart when he chickadeed me; I wanted to pop his cork.

"Go, my husband. I could knock horns off a bull from here."

Lone Wolf crawled through the grass. I hoped he would not crawl into rattlers. Rattlers fouled up Lone Wolf's try at water

80

boy and horse guard on his first pony raid. He lost the horses when a rattler came after him and the men nearly got done in by Shoshone. The men laughed, told him to live a wíŋkte life, with women, if snake scared him.

I spotted Lone Wolf running at the buffalo from the other side, waving the robe. The buffalo stirred up dust, headed my way, but to an angle that gave me a shot behind the head, like Lone Wolf said to shoot buffalo.

I hid behind sage, had target practice, if the truth be told. The buffalo had no idea where the shooting came from. I finished off what we needed.

A scared pté and her calf ran in my direction. No time to reload, not a rock or tree to hide behind. I jumped up, waved my carbine, tried to scare the buffalo to take another path. What I didn't know—buffalo need glasses. I probably looked to that pté like a buffalo, maybe her leader. They ran wild my way.

"No! Hey! Git! Wahoooo," I hollered, fear crawled up my neck. I turned and ran, her hoof stomps beat loud in my ears. Never knew I could run so fast, my braids banged against my head. What else I didn't know, buffalo can near outrun a horse. I tripped, fell hard, rolled over and over, but held onto my carbine. I screamed loud for Lone Wolf to help me. The buffalo heard my peculiar sound, slowed her run. I watched her, she watched me while she ran at me. She sniffed, got my smell, stopped her run, breathing hard, ready for a fight to protect her calf.

I jumped up, grabbed my carbine by the barrel, heated though it was, charged her, waved the carbine like a club, yelled, "Wahooo. Heyyyy. Heyyy!"

The buffalo lowered her head, short tail swinging behind her, slobber in her nose. *Uhohh.* Her calf wandered near her, waited for his ma to let him know what to do. If she ran me over, stomped me, my life would end.

Twenty paces from her, I stopped, dropped the carbine. We stared, one at the other, the buffalo and me. I hoped she didn't think me a wolf. She gave a look like I was not worth her time, ran away, her calf following. I sat down, let out a breath, waited for my dear husband.

Lone Wolf jumped across prairie like a grasshopper. If you want honor as a *wičaša*, a Sioux man, you don't grasshopper hop because you brought down some buffalo. You hop at a dance or making fun of enemy in battle.

Lone Wolf, though, had the spirit of a boy. That's why he stole my heart.

"Put me down," I signed, when he swooped me up in his arms. He put me down. We had buffalo to skin before hawks and coyotes figure they got a free meal.

We worked on those buffalo the rest of the day. I felt proud what we did that day.

Lone Wolf signed while we cut meat, "My wife won't tell?"

"My husband shot many buffalo today, is what I will tell." Sioux didn't mind if women hunted, if they wanted to, and knew how. But I feared the reputation I came with, not being a proper woman, had no need for more wood tossed to that fire.

Lone Wolf gave thanks to his Great Mystery, and the buffalo for giving themselves to us. He sprinkled tobacco from his neck pouch over the head and back of the buffalo. Why'd he think they gave themselves if he had to scare them my way and they almost ran me over? The trapper taught me the fight came between me and a critter. Don't rile a bear from the front. Don't hunt moose in the rut or I'd find antlers up my arse. Chub never told me to make thanks to what I hunted. Made me feel good to think buffalo offered themselves.

Lone Wolf took a bite of buffalo heart, offered some to me. I declined.

We took four of the hides to camp, and all the meat our

packhorses could carry. The men wanted to know what medicine came to Lone Wolf to get more buffalo than any man that summer.

"Sweet medicine," he signed. "Came to me in a dream." The village sent a party to get the rest. Lone Wolf gave meat away. Seemed a peculiar thing to do, give away what we hunted, but I said nothing. He got much honor from the people for his giveaway.

"Sweet Medicine Woman," my husband said, his face in my neck. I heard the new name he gave me, *Pežúta Skúyawin*, the new name for his people to call me. *Payjootah Skooyawin*, how the words sounded. In his tongue, *win* means woman; *Pežúta* means medicine; *Skúya* means sweet.

Warmed my heart, him talking like that. I wanted to pop his cork. How could I let him know—it was time for me to be his wife in the robes?

I got wore out scraping meat stuck to the hides, pounding out muscle, beating in buffalo brain fat and berries his ma picked, making the hides soft with a sweet smell. My ma tanned hides, I knew some of what to do. But now I am the woman, making my own home.

I stretched hides after a soak in the creek, smoked them to keep bugs away, did all that because I wanted his mother to admire me, and I needed the hides for my tipi. My arms became strong, muscle showed like I never saw muscle in a woman's arm. Women who looked at me like a no-account wiktówiη, who spread her legs for any man, invited me to gossip around fires, sit with them when they sewed or quilled. The women knew they shouldn't gossip about their men, but they sure did. Some women knew sign and helped me learn their tongue.

Finally, I had my own tipi.

I held my head high when women came to see my new home.

Beautiful, how poles peeked from the top. I could move smoke flaps when I had a fire lit inside. Lone Wolf's hunt got painted on the outside by his mother, him shooting the buffalo. My home smelled like fresh leather, a place where I'd be safe. I put sweet smell pine cones around the edges, buffalo robes around the center fire ring.

Lone Wolf came to my tipi that night, dressed in clean buckskin. He smiled, gave me his chickadee look. I ran to him, put my arms around him. He turned his cheek for my lips, removed his eagle feather.

We got undressed, lay on my buffalo robes, no fire lit so we put no shadows on the walls, our private time. My first night in the robes with Lone Wolf as his wife. I hoped I would please him.

He moved slow, made sure I was ready. Softest hands on a man I ever knew. He got me ready. I felt cannons go off inside me when he put himself in me. Colors of the rainbow shot through me, up my head, and all I saw were colors. I had no idea being with a man might do this. Orange color first, blazed like leaves in the fall. I tried not to make sounds but I could not stop the joy in me I never knew before. Then came blood red color, sun yellow, white lightning flashes—the color I liked best.

When white color came, I left this earth. I hollered so loud I probably woke the Sioux dead. I had such a good time, forgot about popping his cork, but he got all he wanted. I woke him up later, while he snored, let him know I wanted him again. This time, I let go being a lady, showed him all I learned at Miss Brenda's, but with love in my heart. I learned what being in the robes with a loving man might offer.

That night I became a woman. I wanted my husband in the robes forever.

What to do about my co-wife? Medicine Feet Woman wanted her knife across my throat. I couldn't blame her—I took her husband. Had to figure how to co-wife and not get my throat cut.

CHAPTER TWELVE
SETTLING MATTERS WITH MY CO-WIFE

Winter came to our village; snows deep, the river iced over. I wrapped in a buffalo hide, took a walk in the woods, my breath froze on my nose. What to do about my co-wife? I couldn't sleep, feared she'd sneak in my tipi, cut my throat. She put a knife hole in my favorite wolverine cap when I wasn't around, let me know what she'd do to me if I hung around.

I had to figure a way we could co-wife or tell Lone Wolf he had to choose one of us. I got me a plan. Might not be the proper Sioux way for women to settle a difference but would be mine.

While we gathered firewood outside camp, I watched Medicine Feet Woman put wood in her young daughter's arms to take to camp. She wiped snow from her eyelashes, looked angry at me, gathered more wood. Other ladies left with their arms loaded with wood. Medicine Feet Woman and me were alone in the woods. I faced off with her, pulled a knife from my belt, tossed the knife at her feet. She knew what I meant.

"Do what you want, wife. I have no fear of you," I signed.

She scared me, but this was not the time to let her know. She was a grown woman, a head taller than me, raised tough like Sioux women. I pulled my skinning knife from under my skirt, ready to use what Chub taught me about fighting with knives. Medicine Feet Woman dropped her firewood, grabbed the knife, came at me.

"You're not Lakóta!" she yelled in my face. "You spread your

86

legs for any man, like your mother!"

I could not allow that kind of talk, not about Ma. "Don't talk like that about my mother, ya peedy old mare."

"What you call me? Take that back, whore girl."

"All right, I take that back, old dog hide bag."

Medicine Feet Woman came for me, knife in hand. I dodged, kicked her belly like Chub taught. Medicine Feet fell facedown in the snow. I grabbed her hair, long and silky; I forgot for a moment what we fought about. I yanked her head, held my skinning knife to her throat.

"You're a dead woman if you don't open your heart to me," I yelled. Medicine Feet Woman went still, my knife at her neck. I let her go, didn't want to hurt her, wanted her to accept me, let me belong to their family, fit in someplace on this earth. Medicine Feet Woman did something Sioux women should not do except when mourning the dead. She shed tears, held her hurt belly, cried without making sounds.

Near broke my heart. I liked Medicine Feet Woman, wished I had all the woman in me she had in her. I'd studied how she fixed her hair, sat like a proper woman around a fire. I wanted to be like her, become a proper woman folks respected.

"You steal our husband's heart," Medicine Feet Woman said through tears that ran down her froze cheeks. "You can tell the women you beat me up but don't tell I cried."

I helped her to her feet.

"I won't tell."

Medicine Feet stopped her tears. The problem, she said, was not only her jealousy. Women in camp joked her because Lone Wolf brought a witkówiη home, me.

I put an arm around her, best I could, given how tall the woman stood.

"I fight them if they talk like that," I said.

She smiled, warm sunshine on me that froze day, said, "I will try to like you, co-wife, and not feel jealous."

"I didn't know Lone Wolf had a wife," I told her, "I would not have rode off with him."

"I believe you," she said. "Our husband should have asked me. If he took my sister, that would be all right. But, you . . ."

"I'm sorry he didn't ask. I have a favor to ask—would you teach me to live like a proper woman?"

Medicine Feet Woman smiled, held my hand gentle, put two fingers to her head. She understood, would teach me. She wanted to know how I got what Sioux called me, *Akičitawiŋ*— Soldier Woman—before our husband gave me my new name. I told her about Stump in the Willamette Valley, how my mother abandoned me at the trading post to the old Scot.

"I am sorry about your life," she said. "But if Long Knife soldiers fight how you fight, we would sing few songs of victory."

We smiled at each other, like sisters. "I will not tell you have a Long Knife father," Medicine Feet Woman said. "Our *tiwáhe* will be your mother."

Their family would be my mother is what she said. Felt good to hear those words. She looked shy, said, "And would you teach me how to please our husband better in the robes?" She looked away; I heard her giggle. I got to laughing myself.

"If you want," I said. "Not hard to learn. Will teach you what I know."

"Pilámayaye, co-wife." She thanked me.

She got me laughing again, thinking on what we were going to teach, one to the other. We hugged, fell to the ground, laughing, arms around each another in the snow. Lone Wolf found us that way, nodded approval of his wives, now friends. She spoke low in my ear, "No need to tell our husband about the fight. We only tell a husband what he needs to know."

We never told him about the knife fight.

I wanted a family, now I had a family. Hard to have a family without my ma. If I had a daughter, I'd never do what Molly did, give me away. Nothing worse, in the white or Indian world. I wondered why she did that to me.

Later, while we mashed dried chokecherries and wild plums, dripped elk fat to make pemmican, Medicine Feet told me how Lone Wolf courted her.

"My brothers put a chastity belt on me when they saw I might become a crazy woman for a sweet-talking man with few horses like Lone Wolf. My brothers said they would kill Lone Wolf if they caught him trying to cut off that belt."

"Chastity belt?"

"You never heard of a maiden belt?"

After Mr. McFadden, bordello work at Miss Brenda's, I had no idea what she talked about. A girl learns chastity from her mother. Ma was what Medicine Feet's people called a crazy woman, a witkówiŋ when she lived as a wife with Stump. Some men might like to get in the robes with a witkówiŋ, not give horses to her family to show his respect but tried never to marry a witkówiŋ. Their folks worked on that learning of their sons. But Lone Wolf showed kindness by taking me with him, didn't want to make me a witkówiŋ. I had no family for him to give horses to show his respect. He waited for sweetheart time till after I had my own tipi.

Medicine Feet Woman pushed hair out of her pretty eyes, left red berry juice on her cheeks while we talked about how she became the wife of Lone Wolf.

"To court me, men lined up in front of my family's lodge, waited their turn to stand under their buffalo robe to talk with me, to have privacy from families.

"When I came out of my seclusion lodge, my family gave a feast to let everyone know I was ready for marriage. I sat in the Maiden Circle, no one challenged my family's word, a man never had me.

"Lone Wolf played a lovely flute, sweet-talked me like no other man. My heart burned for him. One night, he took my hand, led me to the woods. He cut off my chastity belt, risked his life to have me. I gave him all my maiden that night. Ready to die if my brothers found us."

Hearing her story, I had something I wanted to tell her.

"I am sorry what I called you."

"You mean, 'old mare'?"

She pointed to her face, how beautiful she looked, laughed till I feared she'd cry.

I looked down, ashamed of my words, hugged her.

Medicine Feet Woman said, "Lone Wolf sent six horses to my family after our night in the woods, nearly all he owned. My brothers could use those horses to get wives for themselves. They stopped thinking him a worthless wičaša. Lone Wolf will not do that in battle but will risk his scalp for a woman who makes his heart sing."

"How old were you when you ran off with Lone Wolf?"

"Sixteen snows. Lone Wolf, twenty-one."

I felt no jealousy about their love story. I had a weakness for love stories. Lone Wolf risked his neck to get me, too.

I ran in my tipi, dug in my special bag, ran back to her. "For you," I told her.

I gave her my silver handle brush. Medicine Feet Woman's eyes got big, took the brush, ran it through her hair. "Wašiču hairbrush?" she said.

My curious look at hearing a word new to me, sounding like *washeechoo,* brought her mouth to my ear. She whispered, "They are people like your father."

I put two fingers to my head, understood. I put the peculiar word to mind that her people had for white men—something about "fat" in the word.

Wished I had a ma like her. My time came to teach her. She wanted to know how to please our husband in the robes. No one near us while we pounded pemmican outside my tipi, I told her what I learned at Miss Brenda's bordello.

"We start with what's called popping a cork. You know the wašíču jug with the firewater they trade for furs?"

She put two fingers to her head, had seen those crazy-water jugs around camp. She leaned close, I could talk quiet, her lips together, ready to learn words a woman needs to know.

"What keeps the firewater from spilling they call a cork." I had to use the wašiču tongue for the word. I didn't know her word for cork.

"Corkg?" she said, making the sounds as best she could, like I tried to make her peoples' sounds.

She tried to get her mouth, best she could, around a new word in the wašiču tongue. I put two fingers to my head that she got the word right. I took a strip of dried buffalo meat hanging over our fire, put the meat on a deer hide on the grass, pounded the strip with a hammer stone.

"To get a man's love to flow hot for you, you got to pop his cork."

"Oh," she said, looked down, shy of what we talked about. Eyeing me, curious, she said, "Well, go on."

"When you have the man in you, far as he can get, you have something you can do."

"Pop his corkg when I have him in me?"

"When he's in you. You, under him, works best."

"Hard to pop a man's corkg if I am on top?"

"A lot harder. Under him works best. You find muscle in you, right where you got him in you. Like trying not to pee when you need to pee. You know?"

"Yes. Yes." She got excited. "I know how to hold when full up on a long ride."

"You got to practice holding. Give a try now, you can practice anytime, no one knows."

Medicine Feet Woman gave me a doubting look but held herself still.

"I think I hold now."

"Let loose. Hold again," I said.

Girls walked by to get firewood, gave us a greeting. We waved. Medicine Feet kept practicing, waited till the girls reached the woods, threw back her head, laughed till tears came, wiped berry juice from her cheeks. We held hands and laughed.

"That will pop a man's *corkg*? Let him drink a woman's firewater?" she said, doubting what I told her.

"Send the cork to the moon, sister, the man, too, best I can tell." I looked down, shy of what I confessed about my talents in the robes. "Sister, I have something else to tell you, help you look forward to having our husband in your robes."

"For me?" She looked down, shy.

"You can't tell nobody. Our secret. Sometimes, think about another handsome man who catches your eye, when you're in the robes with our husband."

"WHAT?"

"Trust me, sister. What I learned at Miss Brenda's."

She eyed me, grabbed a piece of pemmican, chewed slow, thought on what I told her. Put two fingers to her head, understood.

"*Pilámayaye*, sister," she said, thanked me for giving her my secrets.

"*Tókhi wániphika ní*," I said, wished her luck with our husband.

Lone Wolf forgot to tell me one other thing when he asked me to run off with him. Bluecoats wanted to stick his people on reservations, end their free roaming life. He tried to calm my fear that this was not a time for us to bring a new spark of lightning to the world.

I was thinking on having a baby, Lone Wolf's child. I had a fire in my lodge when he tried to calm my fear. He sat against the bone backrest, faced the tipi flap, puffed on his pipe. We watched Medicine Feet Woman cook outside in a metal pot from Gift House Indians who lived around army forts that handed out rations. I never saw a woman more happy to cook for a man after she learned how to pop his cork, him not eager to leave her tipi for mine.

"These rivers and valleys are old friends to us. Long Knives hunt for us like blind wolves. Nothing to fear, my wife," Lone Wolf said.

He spoke like he knew what he talked about.

But our band's war leader, Crazy Horse, had scouts, war councils, spies in the hills, runners going to other bands, and plans for how to slip a camp if bluecoats came for us.

I knew bluecoats had spies, too, because those spies roamed all over, especially among fur traders. Mr. McFadden spied for the army. I saw him send reports to a soldier name of Beecher who would send the reports to an army general named *Sher i dan,* a name I'd come to hate.

They say a woman who was a relative of Mr. Beecher's wrote a famous book.

I had much to learn about my dear Lone Wolf.

I loved him with all my heart, though he was not a good hunter, and he had no vision power to see the future. Even in the spirit world, only thing that happened when he went Crying for a Vision in a mountain, didn't eat for days, he passed out.

Least he spent more nights with Medicine Feet, gave me some rest.

CHAPTER THIRTEEN
MY HONEY TONGUE HUSBAND

"I want the Old Leaders to invite me to join the Akičíta," Lone Wolf said, his voice deep, wild bee honey to my ear. We lay together in my tipi. I liked him letting me know what he wanted for himself and our family. He wanted to walk proud among the men, but a man had to show bravery in battle, count coup by stealing horses from enemy, if he wanted to get the invite to join the Akičíta—those asked to guard the camp and protect us in war. Lone Wolf got third coup four times touching dead Pawnee. At least those coup allowed him to look for a wife. But he never counted first coup, never touched an enemy in a battle with his hand or coup stick. This flowed from his poor eyesight; he couldn't see if a warrior was Pawnee or one of his own. The only horses he stole belonged to an old white man.

I looked like a woman now, fuller hips and bosoms. I had Lone Wolf's child inside me, though I did not yet tell my husband, waited to see if the baby would stay in me. "How might you get the Old Ones to invite you to join the Akičíta, my husband?"

I pulled the buffalo robe up to my chin.

"Swipe Crow horses," Lone Wolf said, not happy about sneaking in a Crow village to steal horses.

A man needed friends to go on a raid, but no one wanted to raid with my dear Lone Wolf. They poked fun at Lone Wolf on his first raid as a water boy when the rattler scared him. They joked him to get a wíŋkte calling. W*ingtay*, how they said the word, the *n* sound not clear, in the middle. Lone Wolf had no wíŋkte heart. A man became a spirit man, dressed like a woman, if his dream calling flowed down that path. Lone Wolf had a wíŋkte friend named Friend of Otter. He was sweet on Lone Wolf, though my husband had no attraction towards him. He was my husband's only close friend.

I thought on what my husband wanted. It came to me what could be done, though I feared my love for my husband would take me into the peculiar world of men.

"Maybe you get Friend of Otter for a water boy and pony guard for a pony raid? This woman would help her husband swipe Crow horses."

Surprised me—Lone Wolf said he would give thought to my offer. No man with any sense would take such a plan, but Lone Wolf believed in my medicine, even when I told him I had no medicine, just luck and skill with a carbine.

I almost fell over—next day, Friend of Otter joined our raid plan.

"You need Crow clothes," Friend of Otter said, sitting in my tipi, giving a sweet look at Lone Wolf. Friend of Otter went on a pony raid before he learned in a dream he had a wíŋkte calling. He found more interest in the handsome Crow warriors than their horses, which gave him pause on his way to becoming a warrior.

"Here," Friend of Otter said, opened his parfleche bag, pulled out Crow buckskin. He spent time with Crow warriors when they made a truce between neighboring villages and he kept their spare clothes as souvenirs.

"My favorite," he said, held up a deerskin shirt, dyed quills sewn round the neck. "I do not want in any shooting or scalping."

Lone Wolf squinted at Friend of Otter, tried to figure if Friend of Otter had enough bravery to hold our ponies when we snuck in a Crow camp.

"You won't have to shoot or scalp nothing," he told Friend of Otter. "I was water boy and pony guard when I was a boy. Just keep our fast horses watered and hold them till we get back."

I cut my hair short in front, the way I looked roaming forests with Ma and Chub. I fixed my hair in a ball in front, showed my husband and Friend of Otter how to fix theirs the Crow way. Crow men cared a lot about their hair. I saw some that had hair that flowed down their backs, all the way to their moccasins.

"If Crow speak to us, let me talk. I speak some Crow. You say nothing," I told them.

A few days later, Lone Wolf, Friend of Otter and me rode out early, before others in camp woke. We brought dried buffalo *pápa*—pemmican—in our parfleche bags, and three faster ponies for our getaway. I wore leather leggings, eagle feather in my hair, buckskin shirt to cover my full bosoms. I looked like a man. My belly with the baby, not yet showing.

We rode across lovely prairie. I hummed while we rode slow, tried to calm my fear.

"You got the Crow clothes?" I said to Friend of Otter.

Friend of Otter touched two fingers to his head, serious, no smile. To tell the truth, I found him a strange man, a man who dressed like a woman, yet stood bigger than most men.

He really liked my husband. I feared he might have jealousy of me, not certain if he'd look out for me if we got in a fight.

At night, when we bedded down, coyotes yipped, howled, serenading grass and sky. I loved how they sang, one to the other. I wondered what they sang about.

"You want more children?" I said to Lone Wolf, resting under a buffalo robe in a dry creek bed. After the raid, I would tell him we had a child on the way, make him proud.

"I want a son. I love my daughter, but I want a son. Show him how to hunt."

I didn't point out his limits as a hunter. Friend of Otter looked lonely by himself.

"Sleep near us, kolā," I said. "Stay warm." I called Friend of Otter *kolā*, my close friend, what men called each other. Friend of Otter and I dressed like men on this raid; why not use man talk? Friend of Otter moved his robes near us. We were like family.

Noon the third day, we came to a ridge, below were more 'n a hundred lodges. Crow rode in from other villages for what seemed a celebration, pony drags pulled behind horses. We studied the village to see where they had guards, my heart drumming in my chest. Swiping Crow horses no longer seemed easy. Lone Wolf rubbed his chin, more nervous than I ever saw.

"Crow dance like rabbits in a moon," he said. "We ride in at night, like we come to dance."

Friend of Otter looked calm. He had no fear of a man's life, but it didn't make sense to him. No small man, taller than Lone Wolf by near a head, two heads taller than me, with a chest broad as the Elk River. He had arms and legs like cottonwoods, could end a Crow life with one of his huge hands.

Lone Wolf and Friend of Otter got their medicine bundles, rubbed stuff up their horses' noses, on manes and tails, to make their horses fast. They sniffed medicine themselves, for protection, offered me some, but I declined. I found it a curious sight, being a heathen to any religion.

The sun slipped below the edge of Makhá, what my husband's people called Earth. Crow fires lit the village below like fireflies in a meadow. We mounted up, rode slow down the ridge. At the entrance to the village, we slid off our horses, tied them to alders, walked past two old men sitting on logs, talking.

The old men looked our way, studied us. My knees did a

wobble. The old men reached for their knives, I got ready to run. They laughed, showed knives to each other. We had not even got in the village and I wanted to run. Lone Wolf fingered the medicine bundle around his neck.

We made our way through the village, looked for horses staked outside tipis—these would be the Crows' fastest, with a feather braided in the tail, good medicine for a fight.

We headed in the direction of the dancing and whooping, spotted a pinto staked outside a tipi, a fire lit inside. Lone Wolf said those tipis would have a woman at home, her husband at the dance, an easier horse to swipe. But at the sound of our walking, a man ran out of the tipi to see who eyed his prize horse.

"My wife is sick," he said. "Leave my horse alone, thieving dogs." I said I hoped his wife felt better, that we were headed to the dance. We decided to split up, draw less attention, meet at the dancing.

A Crow girl, maybe sixteen snows in her, smiled flirtatious when I quick-stepped past her tipi. I probably made a better-looking man than woman; didn't please me none. I lowered my eyes, strode long-legged best I could past the girl, looked out the corner of my eye for a good horse. I saw two fine geldings. Geldings could outlast a mare, even a stallion. I met Lone Wolf at the dancing and drumming where Crow whooped and hollered.

"I saw three horses no one watched," Lone Wolf said.

"I saw two," I said, teeth banging together like they did on the first bear hunt on my own.

"May the Great Spirit protect you, my wife," Lone Wolf said, eyebrows twitched, scared as me.

"Oooo, you, too, my husband."

We walked separate back through the camp. I snuck to a gelding, cut his rope, ambled like I owned him. A hound yapped at my feet, made old folks outside tipis look my way. I grabbed a stick, whacked him. The dog squealed, ran off, old folks laughed. The flirtatious girl slipped beside me, asked if I needed help to water my horse.

"Am a married man, cousin," I said, in a low voice. "My wife would cut your nose if we head in the direction you want."

She flipped her head, took her pretty self away.

I got back to Lone Wolf, him tying the rope of a pinto to an alder. I wanted to ride out of there, NOW, fast as we could get.

"*Wašté*. Two more," he said.

"You *witkó*?" Was my husband crazy?

"Two horses are not enough, my wife. We need two more, Sweet Woman." His hound eyes begged.

"No, my husband! They might have a trap set. These are CROW."

"Please, my wife. When they dance, Crow eyes are no better than baby birds out of the shell."

"No, my husband."

"One more, for each of us?" He looked at me sweet, with his begging eyes, mouth open, head perched sideways, his chickadee look that stole my heart.

"All right. One more for each of us," I said, a decision I would regret.

Back we went into their village. A boy my age practiced a dance outside his folks' tipi, a magpie feather in his hair, knife in hand. He practice-danced a story from his life. I could not believe my eyes, the boy whose feet I peed on.

He spotted me, stared, his eyes got wide. He put a hand on his knife.

CHAPTER FOURTEEN
A PECULIAR CROW FAMILY

"I like the story you dance, cousin," I said to the boy, waved friendly, hoped he wouldn't recognize me dressed in man clothes.

He came to me, no smile, suspicious. "I know you, cousin?"

"I'm from the Kicked in the Bellies. Never met you, but I like the story you tell."

He eyed me up and down, patted his knife blade, narrowed his eyes, looked closer, smiled at my praise. "Not much I did. Raided enemy for horses, peed on a Sioux scout I ran down, got away with his horse."

"Good for you, cousin. You are very brave." I moved on fast.

The Crow girl followed me, the girl who noticed me earlier. I told her to leave me alone, but an older man joined us.

"My sister says she likes you, cousin," he said, something in his voice more than a friendly greet.

"Just going to the dancing," I said, tried to ease away.

"Come to our lodge, got something to show you," he said, "unless Little Man thinks he is too good to talk to our family."

I smelled his breath. Firewater filled his belly, looking for any disrespect I showed to cut me, protect his sister's honor. They got on either side, each took an arm. Off we went to their lodge in the last circle of the camp. I've never been so scared in my life, walking to their tipi, except when the bear mouth had my head.

I perked up when I spotted a sorrel gelding with a feather in his tail staked outside their lodge. I began to figure how I might get his horse.

The girl's handsome brother was Fox Tooth, his pretty younger sister was Yellow Cloud.

A kettle hung in the tipi above a fire, their family at the dancing except an old aunt singing Crow Praise Songs for a dead husband. A baby slept in a crib hung from a pole. Yellow Cloud birthed a baby without a husband, and Fox Tooth was on the prowl for a husband for his sister, to take her off his hands. Bonds between a Crow brother and sister could be stronger than bonds between a Crow woman and her husband. When she married, her brother got the horses given for her.

"You eat with us, cousin, and drink with me," Fox Tooth said, pulled his knife, waved the blade in front of my eyes. Blood on that blade. A J Boy, for sure, I was thinking.

Fox Tooth sat me next to his sister near the fire. He got a whiskey jug, handed the jug to me. I found myself with what seemed the only drunk Crow in the camp.

"I have a sick stomach tonight, cousin," I said, rubbed my belly, carrying Lone Wolf's child.

Yellow Cloud put her hand on my belly, rubbed gentle. She said her rabbit soup would make me feel better. Sioux didn't allow women to eat rabbit soup when with child, but I couldn't tell her. Fox Tooth stared, his eyes narrowed in the firelight, waited for any disrespect I showed his sister to let out his craziness. His hand rubbed the knife in his sheath.

"My sister is a very good cook," Fox Tooth said. He motioned with his chin for his sister to get her buffalo horn spoon. "You offend our family if you do not eat her soup. Best soup in camp, cousin."

I pretended to sip from the jug, corked it, laid the jug on the robes. His sister scooped soup in her buffalo horn, handed the horn to me, blinked her gorgeous eyes. Her lovely eyes were probably how she got with child and no husband to show for it.

Fox Tooth laughed, uncorked the jug, chugged firewater, leaned back, closed his eyes. He corked it, fell back, no longer of this world. His aunt sang her mournful song.

Yellow Cloud smiled sweet to me, pushed the buffalo horn to my mouth, slipped closer.

"Yellow Cloud treats a warrior good," she said. "Cooks, cleans, sews; would have her husband's horse ready for battle. You want Yellow Cloud for a wife?"

I gave thought to her question.

"I have a wife, Yellow Cloud," I said. "Meanest woman this side of the moon. She would kill you if I brought you home. She's fatter 'n your mother and rips the head off dogs that steal her meat."

That didn't stop her.

"I like you," she said. "My brother will kill you when he wakes if you do not take me for your wife. He killed the man who gave me a child and ran off. My brother cut out his heart, ate it. Fox Tooth did that for my honor. Yellow Cloud does not drink firewater. You throw away your fat wife. No woman is good as Yellow Cloud at making a man's heart sing."

She stood, lifted her doeskin dress, showed me her legs—long and lovely like my ma's.

"You like me?" she said. "You have a name?" She had a soft voice that would make any man's heart flutter.

Her brother snorted, looked ready to wake. I rubbed my chin, tried to figure how to get out of their lodge, and swipe his horse.

"My name is Thunder Walks, of the Kicked in the Bellies."

The girl's aunt sobbed, crawled out of the lodge, "Have to relieve myself," she said.

"Strong legs you have," I said to Yellow Cloud, pretended to sip soup. "Thunder Walks likes strong legs on a woman."

She jumped me. I dropped the horn, her hand moved gentle between my legs. A surprised look in her eyes. "Where's everything?" she said, her eyes wide as an owl's.

Somebody had not taught this girl how to be proper, but, to tell the truth, I liked her spirit. And her brother was the most handsome Crow I ever saw. A peculiar situation—a lovely girl's hand between my legs, and me thinking what a handsome brother she had. If I made a mistake in how I handled her offer, he would cut my heart and eat it.

"Everything crawls inside me when a girl jumps me, and her brother, who ate her last man's heart, sleeps nearby," I said, which was the truth, or would have been, if I was a man.

"My brother will sleep all night. Thunder Walks want to go to the woods? Yellow Cloud make lightning with Thunder Walks. You will thunder like never before, never see lightning like Yellow Cloud lights up in you. You throw away your fat wife. Yellow Cloud will get fat for you."

"I never thought about that," I said. "You light me up in the woods, get fat later? Tell you what, we go for a ride. I take your brother's horse. You get dressed up, take your time. Bring a buffalo robe, meet me at the alders. We will spend the night together, and tomorrow we come back; you'll be my wife. I throw my wife in the river."

Yellow Cloud grabbed a robe, held the robe modestly in front of her.

"How many horses you give to my family to have me for your wife?"

The girl, all business now, was getting horses for her brother.

"Four."

Yellow Cloud's eyes didn't move, stared at me like I didn't understand what she offered.

"Five," I said. I only knew one more Crow number.

She looked up at the stars through the tipi top, bored, shook her head.

"Ten."

That got her interest, her eyes moved quick, left, right, thinking on my offer. I was out of numbers.

"My whole herd for Yellow Cloud," I told her.

"Éeh!" she said, jumped with joy. "Yes. Your whole herd for me, to show how you respect me. You take my brother's horse, then people do not know I ride off with a man. I will be faithful to you, and you will get a baby, my son. We will sing your praises when you are rubbed out in battle."

I thought over what she said, told her, "No man can do better than that offer. I will take your brother's horse, like you said, meet you outside camp." I felt awful for what I did to the girl, but my dear husband needed the sorrel more 'n her brother did.

I slipped out of their lodge, untied the rope to the horse, walked calm as I could to the alders. Lone Wolf waited, his scared eyes twitching.

"What kept you, my wife?"

"Eating and making relations. No time to explain, my husband. Let's go."

We mounted up, held ropes to our four stole horses' ropes, trotted toward the ridge. I hoped Friend of Otter waited for us, like he said he would.

A Crow hunting party rode by, eyed us. Lone Wolf said *Hau*.

I expected arrows in my back after he opened his mouth. We rode faster. Yellow Cloud would discover me gone, with her brother's horse, let out her tremolo, the high-pitched cry of a woman's sadness that could wake the dead.

Friend of Otter waited on his horse, holding our fast horses' ropes. The high sound of Yellow Cloud's tremolo filled the night.

"What happened?" Friend of Otter said, fear slid up his face.

"Crow coming after us," Lone Wolf said.

We jumped off our slow horses, jumped on our fast ones.

"Ride, cousin!" Lone Wolf said.

"No need to tell me, cousin," Friend of Otter said.

We kicked our horses. A bullet whizzed by my head, then another. The Crow had carbines, and stirred up dirt behind us in the moonlight, screaming death chants. They hoped to scare us to drop the ropes to their horses. They'd haul us back to roast if they caught us, and Fox Tooth ate my heart.

"Ride!" Lone Wolf hollered.

I never kicked a horse harder, never hoped more that we'd not run into gopher holes. I prayed for the first time. Friend of Otter tumbleweeded past me. The man could ride. But we had to hold ropes of the horses we stole and our slow ones. Crow scored ground on us. I was not of a mind to be caught by Crow as a horse thief.

"Keep riding, husband," I yelled to Lone Wolf, his legs flaying his horse.

I reined mine, gave the rope on a Crow horse to Friend of Otter, pulled out my carbine, took aim. First shot missed. I slid off, sat down to rest my arms on my knees and shoot. If I missed, they would be upon me. I saw me tied to a stake, a painted Crow deviling in my face while he lit brush at my feet for a Sioux roast.

The lead Crow fell back off his horse, then another. They slowed, checked on their wounded companions. Four horses and a witkówiŋ's honor was not worth taking lead. They followed slow, out of carbine range, yelled taunts, feared we had an ambush waiting. If they followed, we would let their horses loose, save our scalps.

Fox Tooth shouted, *"I'll eat your heart next time we meet, cousinnnn!"*

Not bad, for a Crow. I had words for him, *"Ith mo chac, cous-innnn!"*

Lone Wolf whooped in the night, a horse thief of Crow, his heart flew high. Mine, too. We slipped in the Psáloka camp, cut their best horses, escaped with our scalps. Friend of Otter sighed, happy to be done with our foolishness, and to get out of men's clothes, put on his doeskin dress.

Lone Wolf and me got back to our own clothes, rode slow the rest of the night.

Lone Wolf and Friend of Otter prayed thanks to their spirit helpers.

Before we came to our village, Friend of Otter and me separated from Lone Wolf, snuck to our lodges. My husband rode in next day, leading four Crow horses behind him, sitting high, free hand on his waist. He squinted to see who came to watch. The village cheered at the horses he stole.

The men bragged about victories and counting coup. They ought to, I reckoned—counting coup could get you killed. I'd cook, live a proper woman life taught by Medicine Feet Woman.

My dear husband got an invite to join the Akichíta. Filled him with pride. "Now I will count first coup in battle," Lone Wolf told our family around a fire.

His mother sad-eyed those words, tried to smile. Her son had courage but that could get you a dead son.

Our *tiwáhe* rose in honor when Lone Wolf brought those horses to our village. My child would come from a honored family, and I proved useful to my husband. I held my head up high when I walked out of my own home; I was wife of a warrior.

CHAPTER FIFTEEN
BECOMING A MOTHER

I learned to quill, decorate a baby basket, do what women competed for honor in doing, but I never won awards for how I quilled or beaded. Those were Medicine Feet's talents. How a woman put beads straight on a hide was a mystery to my mind.

My belly grew big and round like a beaver lodge.

I gathered wood with Medicine Feet Woman when water gushed down my thighs. I dropped the wood, took Medicine Feet's arm, did a fat goose waddle to my tipi. She told our husband to stay at his mother's tipi while we got ready. She left me, went to her tipi to feed her daughter. I lay alone on buffalo robes in my tipi, night came. My husband removed the skin tarp that kept out rain, let me see sky. Full moonlight peeked through the hole above me where poles came together. My hands on my belly felt the baby kick. A wild woodpecker in my belly—kicked harder, then no kicks. I slapped my belly, did this baby want to play? A boy, a girl?

Scratches on my tipi. Medicine Feet came in, smiling happy, with a deer hide and skin cloths in her arms. I removed my clothes, stood on the deer hide she put on the ground, took hold of the pole Medicine Feet Woman put up in my tipi. She wrapped a rawhide rope around my belly, above the baby, pulled it tight to pull the baby lower. She did her pulling, moved the baby lower.

A long time later, I squatted. Medicine Feet Woman showed me how, rubbed my back, wiped sweat from my face with a wet cloth. I knew how muscle cramps felt in a leg if I hunted all day alongside the Columbia and forgot to drink water.

I wanted to die, to holler for my ma when the birth pains came. My body cramped, starting in my back down low, came around front. Go and leave, go and leave. When the pain left, I hoped this birthing would come to the end. Then pain came again, I bit my lip to not scream.

Later, moon glow was gone from my tipi, and—all sweated up—I pushed out a baby. Medicine Feet Woman caught my baby, a boy. He cried his lungs out—had me a baby who let me know what he had in mind. I took him, hugged his oily little body, a surprised look in his eyes at coming new to this world.

He stopped his holler when his mouth found my bosoms. He sucked like he wanted to pull my insides inside him. I was feeding a baby from my body—hard to believe. Medicine Feet helped me to my robes, lay me down, washed blood off my baby.

"I sleep here tonight," she said. "Clean you up after your baby goes to sleep. I will put in the ground what we bury after a woman gives birth." She put more wood on coals in my firepit. I lay on my robes, thought about my ma, if this was how she birthed me, wished she could see her grandson.

Next day, Medicine Feet gave me a cradleboard she made, beads and shells sewed in the hide. So pretty, tears came to my eyes. A strap on the cradleboard would let me put the strap around my head, carry my baby on my back, free to pick berries or fight enemy with my hands.

Women came with gifts—blankets for my baby, soft diapers made from deerskin, food; I wouldn't have to cook for a while. Friend of Otter sang wíŋkte prayers over my baby, gave him his secret name. He tied eagle feathers to my baby's cradleboard— medicine to keep him safe.

"Wašté," Friend of Otter said to me. He said I did good in

how I birthed my son.

We named our son Flying Eagle in honor of Lone Wolf's dead grandfather.

I had my own child to care for; my heart wanted to burst with joy and love and pride. Lone Wolf walked proud around camp. I felt happy beyond words to tell—wife to a man who cared for me, a mother to a child, and I had a loving family. Our son would bring honor to our family. I had a purpose on this earth—keep my baby alive and happy.

Soon after, our family moved with all the lodges for better buffalo hunting, to a gathering of more Sioux and Cheyenne than I imagined could come together in this world. I looked forward to making new friends, meeting women from other bands, show our son the beautiful world waiting for him.

Chapter Sixteen
ROSEBUD CREEK BATTLE

Scouts galloped into our camp at Rosebud Creek, stirred up like I never saw men get the excite. Bluecoats, led by a man they called General Three-Star, were coming for us, with Crow scouts in the lead, going to stick us on reservations, have us live a penned-up cow life. The soldiers, scouts said, looked like a herd of blue buffalo swarming up the grassy slopes.

What the scouts said scared me, I ran with my baby to my tipi. Why'd they attack us?

Lone Wolf tore open my tipi flap, eyes afire, rushed to the leather bag behind his bone backrest. I wondered what he kept in that bag. Shakes came to my legs when I saw the excitement in Lone Wolf's eyes.

"I will join the fight, my wife," my husband said. "We will attack Long Knives before they get to our women and children and old ones." He grabbed clothes from the bag that I never saw him wear before. I tried to hold my words.

I gave up on holding words.

"Did you talk this over with your mother?"

"Yes."

"And . . . ?"

"She does not want me to go. But if I must fight, I should fight brave but not foolish. My father fought foolish his last fight. I gave her my word."

He stuck his legs in a pair of sky color leggings, beads down the sides. War clothes—that's what he took from that bag.

110

"My father's," he said. "Made for him by my mother. He gave them to me to make him proud in battle." He pulled a pair of moccasins from the bag, beaded blue and white like the leggings. Looked like he dressed up for a party. He put on flannel breechclout better than I ever saw him wear, wrapped the red flannel over the old loincloth he wore. He put the flannel under a belt around his middle, the flannel flowed to his feet. He never gave me or Flying Eagle a look. I felt tears want to flow, looked at our son in my arms, then at his father. The world of men made a bond between a boy and his father that I understood that day.

Our son watched his father dress for war.

But why he got all fancied up was a mystery to my mind.

"Those pouches, my wife."

He motioned to leather pouches hung on a pole. I never paid mind to those pouches. He let me look in a pouch—tail of a wolf, an eagle feather—his war medicine for a fight. He shirted his chest and arms, slung a rawhide rope around his head and under one arm. Put his medicine pouches on the rope, but still didn't come to the end of getting dressed up. He took a black blanket from his bag, belted the blanket around his middle— looked like the skirt Mr. McFadden wore when he blowing music from a dog hide bag. The belt holding the blanket had shells for his carbine.

"Why you get all dressed up for a fight, my husband?"

It made no sense.

"I will not look like a poor man if Crow lift my scalp. I want that man to know he killed a warrior."

I was sorry I asked. Lone Wolf touched our son's cheek. I lay our son on a robe, gave my husband the hug of my life.

"Come back to us, my husband, walking on two feet, not carried in a blanket, missing your scalp. You want me to fix your hair, then enemy who scalp you get pretty hair?"

Lone Wolf gave his chickadee look to my peculiar question, laughed, knew I joked him. We heard a scratch on my tipi. An Akičíta friend of his, Rises at Dawn, rushed in, a bonnet of eagle feathers in his hands. Rises at Dawn had himself a nickname around camp, Rooster.

"I have a hurt leg, cannot fight. You want to wear my uncle's war bonnet?" Rooster said.

They fit the bonnet on my husband. I have to say, Lone Wolf looked real good with all the feathers down his back. They got my paint cups, ones his mother and me used to paint his buffalo hunt story on my tipi. Rooster put paint on my husband's face, how Lone Wolf told him. "More black around my eyes," Lone Wolf said. Rooster took the brush, painted more wolf eyes on my husband. My dear husband would scare me if I saw him in a fight. Lone Wolf grabbed his carbine, coup stick, war club, scalping knife, looked my way. Out they went to the fight.

"Hókahé!" they yelled,

Other warriors joined them, yelling, "Hókahé."

They ran for their horses staked outside camp.

I thought Hókahé meant "I love you" when Lone Wolf said those words to me alongside the Big Muddy. Now I learned what the words meant—"Let's go. Charge!"

I never prayed much, but whispered a prayer for my husband, "Wákaŋtáŋka be with you, protect you, my husband."

For two nights our family ate meals in Eagle Nose Woman's tipi, said nothing, one to the other, about our fears. Late the second afternoon, men returned on foot, some riding tired horses. A few chanted victory songs, others quiet, mourned friends who were killed or shot up. No sight of our husband.

I put my arm around an old woman crying for her son wrapped in a blanket red with his blood. Tremolo cries of women flowed through camp. Medicine Feet comforted an old father kneeling beside a son's bundled body, a boy he'd never again hear laugh. No sight of Lone Wolf.

Our family gathered in his mother's tipi. We tried to eat, but Medicine Feet's daughter wouldn't eat; she sat quiet, feared her father would not return. Near sundown, folks ran to our lodge. They saw Lone Wolf riding slow on his horse. We ran to him, dirt covered the paint on his face, smeared from sweat, the feather bonnet hung like a plucked goose on his horse's neck. Lone Wolf slid off, said nothing, quiet from what he saw at the fight. His mother gave him a hug.

"Good to see you, my son. We have something for you to eat."

He took the bonnet from the horse. "We fought all day, my mother. Long Knives will leave us alone now," Lone Wolf said. "We had a good fight, beat them good."

He counted second coup on a dead bluecoat, said he'd like to count coup on a live one. Big difference, husband, I wanted to say, held my words. We didn't see Lone Wolf again that night.

He went alone to the woods to pray his thanks for living through the fight.

Next day, we loaded pony drags to go with Cheyenne and other Sioux to better hunting grounds. I put Flying Eagle in his cradleboard, looped the strap around my forehead, the cradle hanging down my back for the walk behind Lone Wolf. He rode his war horse, our other horses pulled pony drags. Medicine Feet Woman held her daughter's hand, Painted Calf Girl, who was old enough to walk on her own—happy her father came back alive from a fight. She hugged him tight after the battle, tears of thanks in her young eyes.

Warriors guarded us on our journey, ready to protect us if bluecoats attacked. Word had gone out to Gift House Indians to join us, hunt buffalo, do a Sun Dance, live free of bluecoats who wanted to turn us into cows, live fenced up. Many warriors and families snuck away from fort Gift Houses, joined us. Food might be scarce, a lot of ammunition shot up, but we had repeating rifles, bows, clubs, knives, tomahawks, and a fighting spirit like I never saw before.

Medicine Feet Woman whacked a mosquito sucking blood from her neck, said, angry, "Wašíču!"

"Why do wašíču not leave us alone?" I said, not understanding why the white man, wašiču, wanted all the land.

"Wašíču do not understand us," she said. "They will never understand us."

She looked at me, the recall in her eyes how I came half like those who would never understand their way. She offered me wasná she made, to make up for her unfriendly thought.

"Milk for your baby will dry up if you do not eat."

I had a dry mouth, tongue swollen, back ached. I said nothing, chewed her pemmican. The sun felt hotter than a sweat lodge. We found a berry patch for something wet for our throats. We lived like sisters, Medicine Feet Woman and me.

Cheyenne friends who traveled with us told Lone Wolf they heard a man on the Big Muddy River offered a *re*ward to anyone who killed me, brought him the necklace he gave me. Bring him my head if they wanted no doubt they got the right woman. I didn't worry about the old Scot—he was far away. What Indian would hunt for my head, for an old Scot *re*ward?

We came to the beautiful valley where flowed *Peži Slá Wakpá*— Greasy Grass River, what Crow called the Little Bighorn.

CHAPTER SEVENTEEN
GREASY GRASS CAMP
1876

Grassed hills, gold colored from the hot sun, sloped down to that lovely curving river. Water flowed under a beaver lodge at the south end, as far as I could see. Sagebrush and yellow flowers peeked from grass on our walk to our Oglála circles, and wild turnips everywhere. Cottonwoods and low bushes greened the riverbank. Lodges perched on the setting-sun side of the river that snaked through the land, with smoke climbing from their tops.

I took in a breath, proud, seeing all the people. My people.

All the free Sioux in the world camped alongside the river, their lodges staked in circles. It looked like a town, peaceful, with boys fishing, old folks sitting on logs swapping yarns. Horse herds roamed prairie grass on the ridge above the river. The seven circles of the Sioux gathered to make winter hunting plans. Cheyenne and Arapaho friends joined us, too.

When we came to the Oglála circle, our band's war chief, Crazy Horse, smoked a pipe with his friend, Touches the Clouds, a Minneconjou chief. I lowered my eyes when we walked past them, I was a nobody. They said Touches the Clouds stood twenty hands tall, a seven-foot chief who towered over Crazy Horse. The main chief of the Minneconjou, Lone Horn, died the winter before. Now his four sons lead their bands—Big Foot, Roman Nose, Frog, and the man Crazy Horse smoked with while us women set up tipis.

The most handsome Húŋkpapa man I ever laid eyes on

115

joined their pipe smoking. "That man?" I said to Medicine Feet.

"Two Horns," she said, pounded a stake to keep her tipi stuck to the ground if strong winds blew. "He mourns for his wife and children. They died of white man's sickness. He is Húŋkpapa Lakóta, like me. He lives with Sitting Bull's people. You ready to set up your lodge?"

Two Horns looked my way; I lowered my eyes. I had a husband, no longer a girl who might want a handsome man's eyes look her way. I set up my tipi with help from Friend of Otter. Medicine Feet made supper for our family and Friend of Otter. My reputation as cook earned me cleanup.

Our band's circle claimed the middle of the tribes camped for a few miles along the river. At the south end was a Húŋkpapa friend I got to know at Rosebud Creek, Moving Robe Woman. After supper I took Flying Eagle in his cradleboard, went to chew pemmican with Moving Robe and her brother. The whole camp readied for a dance that night, a drum beating, stomping dance. We'd mourned our dead for four moons. Time now to celebrate living, even when chased by bluecoats across our land like buffalo, but ready to fight.

On that night came sweetheart dances for young folks to look for each other, find a wife or husband. Sioux knew when to live quiet on earth and when to twirl like a twister, stomp like the male prairie chicken trying to get the hen to notice. Howl like a wolf who had no sweetheart time in a hundred moons. They sang they had no fear of bluecoats, sang for boys dead before they got to do a Sun Dance. For wives who didn't get to see age carved in a husband's face.

The dancing that night was the most fun I had with the Oglála. Lone Wolf taught me how to stomp, though women were not allowed to dance around a fire with the men. Drums beat to the heartbeat of earth, fires lit big that night. Young men, women, showed each other what they had; the men, hand-some, dancing, singing.

I held up Flying Eagle to let him see the life waiting for him, Indian life. People enjoying each other, the mystery of Sioux, what I tried to figure myself. Living a Sioux life flowed from something in the heart was all I could figure. Whatever Sioux flowed from, I wanted to live Sioux as long as this earth grew grass, and I was on this earth.

A Cheyenne name of Old Hand eyed me at the dance. I looked away.

It was my night with Lone Wolf, if he stopped stomping. Medicine Feet Woman knew what I wanted, said she'd care for Flying Eagle.

Lone Wolf howled all night, danced till flames died down. No matter to me, I had pride in my husband, wanted him happy now that he had warrior friends.

I had not been in the robes with Lone Wolf because I felt tired days, gave comfort to my baby, nights. I wanted time alone with my dear husband, been rubbing Lone Wolf with a sweetheart touch.

I nursed my baby in my tipi, sang him the song I made up after my ma abandoned me.

In your heart I go, mother.

In your heart I go.

A sparrow in her mother's wings.

As you go in my heart, mother.

I sang quiet, tried not to shed tears but tears came. I wished my mother never left me.

"Co-wife," Medicine Feet called from outside my lodge, "too noisy for your baby to sleep. Your Húŋkpapa friend, Moving Robe Woman, sent word you can go to their circle. It will be quiet in her lodge. Our husband will not come home till after the dancing."

I wiped tears, thanked her, got ready to leave. I bundled my baby, put him in the cradleboard, slung the strap over my forehead, took the long walk to the Húŋkpapa circle at the south end of lodges. Their circle stood close to where the swish of the river met Box Elder Creek. Four creeks ran to Peži Slá Wakpá, two on our side. Crickets made loud love songs. I walked more than a mile to her camp.

I felt safe. The Húŋkpapa paid no mind to any fear because Sitting Bull, their leader, visioned at a Sun Dance that blue-coats attacked but we wiped out every soldier. We had guards around our camp if the bluecoats didn't learn a lesson at Rosebud Creek.

Moving Robe, a little over twenty snows in age, shared a laugh with her younger brother when I entered their lodge. This brother and sister were good friends. Sioux ladies, like Moving Robe, took pride in brothers. A few moons before, her brother did a Sun Dance, fulfilled a promise made to Wakáŋtáŋka, his chest showed the wounds.

Moving Robe Woman put her cheek to Flying Eagle's face. Her husband died in a fight with bluecoats before he made babies with her. Now, every wičaša wanted her for a wife. She had great beauty, could ride like the wind, hunt with a carbine. She loved the man killed, though, still grieved him, three winters later, her legs slashed in mourning. Her younger brother took that lonely place in her heart. She offered me a robe near the fire.

I lay down with my baby, let him nurse, talked with Moving Robe, her brother, and their mother.

I fell asleep.

I heard magpies caw next morning when I woke in their lodge. No one in their lodge except me and Flying Eagle. He smelled like a buffalo wallow, cried his hunger, screamed his little head off. He had the hearty lungs of his father. Men outside swapped war stories, old men whose stories were not about bluecoats, but Pawnee and Crow they fought. I never understood why men talked about counting coup, slitting a throat, or ending a life with an arrow or musket.

"That when you lost your thumb?" an old man said to his friend.

"Cut off, in a fight with Pawnee. See?"

"Yes. See here?" the other feller said, showed something on his body. "Musket ball."

His friend said, "Have to go to the woods. If you wait, will tell you about the first Pawnee I ran down. He was brave, I let him live."

"I will go with you," his friend said. "Am watered up much as this river."

I went outside, saw those men do their old man walk to the woods, wearing red breechclouts, eagle feather in the hair, backbones more clear to the eye than what muscle gave them when they counted coup. They stood in the woods, backs to the camp, hand on a hip how men do when they water down bush, share war stories.

I went to the river to bathe Flying Eagle, feed him my overflowing milk. Meadowlarks singing—I sighted some on low bush—my favorite bird, with a gold belly, black sash round the neck. Meadowlark sing the same song over and over. I had no idea how birds learned to sing like that—brought joy to my heart. Medicine Feet Woman said their song meant good things would come.

I washed Flying Eagle in the river. He hollered his head off; I stuck him on my bosoms.

"You scare the fish," a boy yelled. Two boys fished for trout; I gave a stare. Young people should not talk like that to a mother and her child, bothering their fishing. They laughed, waved, moved down the river below the beaver lodge. In the distance where the sun came up, a huge dust cloud floating our way.

"Ahhh, buffalo," I thought. I finished bathing my baby, walked back to our circle. Lone Wolf slept next to a log. I put a tatáŋka robe over him to keep off the flies and mosquitoes. His eyes rolled, watching a dream. I got a clean blanket in my tipi for Flying Eagle, happiness in him now, chirping like a magpie.

"I love you, my son," I said. "Your father and I will have pride in our son when he becomes a warrior."

Lone Wolf appeared at the entrance of my tipi, said he'd check on our horses. I felt angered he didn't ask if I had a good night like he had. I put two fingers to my head, understood what he said, but didn't care what he did. He snuck up behind me, put his arms around me, pulled me gentle to himself. Felt good, his arms around me.

"Maybe, after I water the horses, sweet wife?"

He melted my anger when he talked like that. I gave him a smile.

I wouldn't see him for a while, I headed to Moving Robe's lodge where I could get lunch from her mother. I cradled Flying Eagle in my arms, not in his cradleboard. I wanted to feel my baby close to my heart. I walked past Crazy Horse and the Hokši Hakakta, Last Child Society, the last-born men from families. Eagle Elk, another member I knew, stood with them. I didn't know others. Lone Wolf got birthed a first born, he could not join the Hokši. No one messed with them. They knew no fear in battle, the wildest of the wild, bravest of the brave. They looked after each other in battle, like a wolf pack. Crazy Horse looked at me, the only time till then that his eyes met mine. I looked down, a nobody.

"I will throw away my life in the next one," a young Hokši said—a pledge before a battle.

The war talk filled me with fear, sent a tremble down my

body, but no wašíču with any sense would attack this many warriors.

Moving Robe Woman met me with her ash stick, on her way to dig thíŋpsiŋla—prairie turnip. More prairie turnips with the purple flower than I ever saw on the walk to our camp.

"Eat, then join us," she said, her voice, happy, how girls talk when friendship flows. I loved prairie turnip—pound the root to make delicious soup—said I would. I didn't tell her I'd dig turnip after my sweet time with Lone Wolf.

"Lovely here," Moving Robe said, her arms open to take in the lovely day.

Unusual calm that day.

The sun beat down past straight overhead when I finished eating in Moving Robe's lodge, thinking about Lone Wolf, the feeling he would give me. Maybe we would go to the woods. I liked it with him in woods, leaves and sky above his head, how we first came together at the Big Muddy, me looking at stars, him saying hókahé. Got me a laugh, thinking on what I thought that word meant, that he loved me. The word would always mean both to me: I love you, Charge.

Warriors rode wild through camp, shouted Long Knives came for us. My heart jumped to my throat. The dust cloud where the sun rose was not a buffalo herd. A cloud of death headed our way.

"Nataŋ uskay! Nataŋ uskay!" women yelled. "They attack!"

I wasn't raised Sioux, didn't know how to steel my heart for war, face death with a yell. I cradled my baby in my arms, ran fast as I could toward our Oglála circle a mile away. I had to stop because warriors ran to their horses every which way around me, waved war clubs. Naked men ran past me with scalping knives in hand, trying to find a horse to ride.

"To the woods!" the men yelled to us women, kids, and old

people—pointed north.

Battle cries rose from our men. Boys younger than me wild-eyed the ridges around us, fear fighting with what gives the excite to boys—count coup, make a run at enemy, touch enemy, not get themselves killed. Dance about their bravery after the fight, impress a girl.

Touch enemy? Count coup? No, I thought—end their lives if they come to harm families, without a warning, attacking people who thought they lived in peace. Moving Robe Woman ran back with the women who dug wild turnip. I could tell, Moving Robe prepared her heart for war. She caught me on my run to my lodge.

"Too far to the woods. Stay with us, we will protect your baby." Moving Robe grabbed me, pulled me toward her lodge, showed no fear. "They will be dead wašíču," Moving Robe said, a confidence in her voice I didn't have.

Long Knives whooped and rode at us from the south, blowing bugles, flags waving, shooting shells into our camp. The bullets tore through tipis, hit women and men trying to get to the fight.

A leader of the Húŋkpapa gave orders for warriors to mount up. Men grabbed any scared horse at hand. The air filled with angered, buzzing bees, bluecoat shells ripping through tipis. A Húŋkpapa gramma fell facedown, blood flowed on her doeskin dress from the bullet in her back.

I got fear, more than I ever knew fear.

I'd knocked over a hornet's nest when I trapped with Chub and had to hide under a blanket while hornets raged around me. That day I saw our hornets swarm bluecoats, to avenge deaths in our camp from that first attack.

Moving Robe's father ran to her, yelled through the screams that a soldier's bullet took her brother's life outside camp. Moving Robe screamed her sadness, fell to her knees. She got up, wiped her tears, no fear in her eyes, went with her father to get a horse to avenge her brother. I ran with my baby to hide on the ground in Moving Robe's lodge.

I felt a tug in my arms while I ran, where I cradled Flying Eagle. A soldier bullet tore through my baby's eye, nicked my arm on the way out. Flying Eagle's other eye rolled, tried to look at me one last time. His eye stared blank, empty of life.

"Eeeeeeeahhhhh," I screamed, not believing what happened.

A Húŋkpapa warrior charged by, near knocked me over.

"Never been a better day to die!" he yelled.

"No," I said. "Nooooo. Not my baby!"

"Hókahé!" warriors shouted, charged across the river to stop the bluecoats south of camp.

I lay on the ground, covered my baby with my body, no more bullets ripped his skin. I tasted my baby's blood splashed on my lips.

CHAPTER EIGHTEEN
GREASY GRASS FIGHT

My heart filled with sadness, more than I knew could come to me. I held my dead baby, ran to Moving Robe's lodge, lay him on robes by the fire. I looked at my hand next to my baby's face, his skin darker than mine. I felt shame for the white man blood in my body. Then I understood—I wasn't a half white woman, I was an Indian woman looking at her dead Indian son.

A strange time to think about the white man blood my father gave me.

I kissed my baby's cheeks, wiped blood from his face, told him I loved him. More shells ripped through the tipi, searched for my head like angry bees. Screams outside became a wild howl at what bluecoats did that day to people living in peace. I lay over my baby's body; no more shells could hit him.

Hate came to my heart when I looked at the hole in my baby's face where once he had an eye. I looked at smoke from the fire in the lodge, drifting up. I no longer felt I was a part of this earth; I drifted in air like the smoke. Then it came to me, I understood what Sioux meant—*a good day to die,* a good day to take revenge for deaths of those we loved.

I knew what I would do. "I will kill a soldier for you," I swore to Flying Eagle. "I will kill my father if he attacks us this day." I let smoke from the fire carry my words to the Great Spirit.

Let them kill me, too—if they could get me.

Outside the lodge, Moving Robe's father brought her a horse and her brother's fighting stick.

"Revenge!" Moving Robe yelled to me. "His horse," she pointed with her chin to her brother's horse. "His máza wakháŋ, in our lodge."

Moving Robe rode across the river to the fight. Other women rode, too, and women went on foot to stop the bluecoats coming from south of us. Moving Robe looked like a wild bird in flight. A warrior yelled, "A woman fights with us, no man should hide behind her skirt."

A Cheyenne girl, Buffalo Calf Girl, rode past me to the fight, waved a six-shooter she knew how to use. Lone Wolf told me she rescued her brother at the Rosebud fight.

Moving Robe Woman jumped off her horse, held the revolver of a wounded enemy who lay on the grass, a black man wearing buckskin. I never saw a black man before that day. Moving Robe yelled at this man, aimed the man's revolver at his head, jerked the trigger. Nothing happened. The man waved hands in front of his face, gesturing to her not to shoot him. She aimed his revolver at his face, fired the gun, and he fell back. Moving Robe Woman jumped on her horse, took after bluecoats who ran to woods.

I ran back into her family's lodge, got her brother's carbine, loaded up, put his pouch of shells around my neck, ran to her brother's horse, jumped on, my buckskin dress above my knees. Flying Eagle's blood colored my face, revenge for him was in my heart.

"Hókahé!" I screamed. I rode across the river on a war horse that didn't spook at gunfire, whoops, or smoke. The horse knew more about warring than me.

Bluecoats ran to the woods alongside the river, warriors after them, setting fire to brush. Soldiers went fear crazy, charged up a ridge across the river. Warriors rode alongside soldiers who tried to cross the river on foot, whacked soldiers' heads with war clubs.

Bluecoats wading across the river gave me targets. I reined my horse, saw a soldier look for other soldiers on horseback to drag him out of the water. I took aim, squeezed the trigger how Chub taught, heard nothing due to my hate. The bluecoat fell back, floated away quiet as a stick of wood. That calmed my anger—I ended the life of a mother's son.

More to Sioux revenge than shooting soldiers. Sioux made revenge personal—warriors and women hacked off fingers and arms of dead soldiers. Hard to watch at first, then the hacking mattered none to me, thinking on my baby.

Bluecoats, less those killed in the first attack, dug in like prairie dogs high on the ridge south.

A mighty cry came from our camp through smoke, battle cries, and gunfire. Soldiers attacked the other side of our camp. I wondered why a few bluecoats were fool enough to attack many Indians from the south of our camp. Now I knew why—to get our eyes off their main attack.

Warriors screamed their anger, galloped near to death whatever horse they rode, to stop those that came at our middle—to kill our kids, women, and old folks. I kicked my horse, got in behind the warriors for the ride back to our camp. I saw soldiers charge on horses down a ravine—with shouts and yells and bugle sounds to scare us. Army flags flew above soldiers, as if flags and shouts could scare those protecting children. Cheyenne rode across the river at the bluecoats, and their women charged with clubs on foot, waded across. That stopped the bluecoat charge at our middle.

Sioux warriors attacked from where the sun set, others charged soldiers from the north. Our men now fought like blue-coats—killing, not counting coup for bravery by touching enemy.

Men in buckskin were with the bluecoats—cow boys, maybe—who herded cows on foot, is all I knew about them.

They must have joined up with bluecoats to have fun hunting Indians.

The day became roasting hot from grass fires we set, gunpowder, and dust-crazed horses stirred. For a few miles the battle moved across the hills, then Crazy Horse galloped to the battle. We cheered, got brave seeing him whip his horse, sitting straight up, daring soldiers to shoot him. We didn't know how many soldiers they had hiding, to destroy us.

He gave me courage, too, the sight of a man who feared nothing. My baby dead, I didn't care if I lived any longer on this earth, but I'd take more of them with me. I kicked my horse, hair blowing in the wind, legs tight around the horse. Boys my age, who made a fight to the death promise, ran up a hill at soldiers who jumped off a horse to aim a colt or carbine. The young ones didn't run straight at them. The war games they played came in handy—dodged left, right, dived to grass, taunted soldiers. They hid behind sage and brush, came up next to a soldier who got a stone club buried in his head, or a knife in his throat. A couple of our young boys got bullets in their brave faces.

Bluecoats made a line alongside the ridge, ready to fight us to the death.

I reined my horse. What to do? Sioux might have a battle plan, which side to go after, then a warrior fought like his own army, alongside others he knew and trusted.

Crazy Horse charged his horse at the middle of the bluecoat line. They say he had no body in battle, that bullets went right through him. No bullets hit him, hundreds fired. I never knew riding horse bareback, mocking death, could flow like a story danced to the heartbeat of the earth. His charge cut the bluecoat line in half.

A death storm gathered around those soldiers.

The smell of blood, and fires set to grass, sickened me. The terror in eyes of bluecoats got to me. I threw up my guts. I hoped Medicine Feet Woman was safe with her daughter and Lone Wolf's folks. I hoped my husband, if he came to the battle, fought brave but not foolish. Hoped he fought brave for his sake, not foolish for mine. He would not sing a victory song no matter what happened that day—soldiers killed his son.

Bluecoats along the hill shot their horse to have something to hide behind. I figured the fight must be near over if soldiers shot their horses. A warrior rode past me, yelled, "Little glory in killing such cowards."

Out from the smoke and dust, a bluecoat ran towards me, hands high above his head, fear in the man's eyes. No hat on him, short hair to not get scalped, eyes big with fright, tears flowing down his face. I raised my carbine, aimed at his chest.

The soldier fell on a knee, held out his revolver, "I give up. Don't shoot me, I beg you."

He looked Lone Wolf's age. We stared through the smoke, the one looking at the other. How could I shoot a man with his hands above his head? I thought on my dead baby, lifted my carbine, took aim. The soldier changed his mind or his surrender was a trick. He aimed his revolver at me, cocked it. My horse jumped at the same time the soldier shot and I fired my carbine. His bullet hit my horse in the head, knocked us both to the ground. I leaped free of the horse before he hit ground, lost my carbine. I could see blood where my shell found the soldier's arm holding his gun. The gun fell to the grass; he pulled a knife with his good hand, came for me.

I waited till he got close, threw dirt in his eyes, dived as far from the soldier as I could. He stumbled over my dead horse, fell hard. I tore off my dress—now I could fight him. I grabbed the skinning knife from my garter, held the blade up like Chub taught, faced off with him. He was bigger than me, but he only had one good arm. I looked around the smoky air, where I could run if I had to. Other hand fights with soldiers going on around me.

Smoke moved away, he saw a girl, near naked, blood on her scared face. I saw a white man like those on the boardwalks of Fort Benton. The soldier, wild-eyed, screamed, charged, blade high above his head. I leaped, kicked his chest before he could stab me, knocked him down. I didn't run at him after he got up. I walked slow, never took my eyes from his. When I got close, I screamed, *"Hókahé!"* and ran at him with a roar.

He turned coward, ran; I tackled him, climbed up his sobbing body. He put his good hand in front of his face, begged, "I give up! Don't kill me!"

"For my baby, soldier." My blade dug deep in his eye; blood flew from the hole I put there. He looked at me with his other eye, went still. I pulled my knife from his face.

I found my dress, put it on. Threw up my guts at what I'd done.

CHAPTER NINETEEN
TREE GRAVES

Warriors walked up hills past dead or wounded soldiers, made sure no bluecoats lived. I wandered up a hill, looked for my husband, but there was no sight of Lone Wolf. I saw a dead soldier in the grass, dressed in buckskin. He looked like the Custer I saw in Mr. McFadden's book—the same otter face. A woman yanked off his boots. Another woman ran up, looked at him. The sight angered her—she raised an arm above her head, screamed, "For all my relations!" She lifted her dress, sat on his face, shoving her anger and sorrow in that face. She gave him the treatment Sioux give those who do the worst crimes a man can do; smothered him with her bare arse.

I found an army horse, mounted up, rode down to the river, looking for Lone Wolf. The black man Moving Robe Woman shot didn't fare good. They staked his manhood sack to prairie, stomach sliced open, his own blood filled his tin cup. The cup rested on his naked belly like a grave marker.

Women waded across the river, singing the tremolo of grief. Some looked for husbands, some sang sweetheart songs, looking for a warrior they hoped survived, or a man who courted them. Women stripped dead soldiers, took anything useful. If you find use for all of a buffalo except the snort from the nose, not much was left on a bluecoat body. Cutting their bodies meant they'd have little power to harm us in the spirit world.

Dead men smell different than animals, sickened me.

I hoped my husband was safe. I looked up the hill, sighted a man his size stumbling down the battlefield. He walked slow, past dead soldiers, Indian bodies, his hands holding his bloody face. I jumped off my horse, ran to him. My dear husband, his jaw near shot off, half his face left on him.

I put him on my back, carried him to my lodge.

My husband lay in my tipi, tried to speak, looked at me as if to say, "I am sorry I brought you to our life." He closed his eyes. Medicine Feet, her daughter, Lone Wolf's Ma, saw Lone Wolf, let out a wail. His daughter looked at her father, ran sobbing from my tipi. We knew he would not live. I cried with all the pain I ever knew, fell across Lone Wolf's body. My baby and husband were dead.

The next day, warriors kept up the attack on bluecoats high on the south ridge, but scouts said more bluecoats headed our way. Camps moved out, left behind for the soldiers to burn what we could not pack quick. Some went north with Sitting Bull to the Grandmother's Land, others said they would return to reservations. We still didn't know why they attacked us.

I bundled little Flying Eagle, never thought I'd have to wrap a dead baby on his cradleboard in a buffalo hide, a baby that came from my body. My feet didn't seem to touch ground when we walked him to a cottonwood near the river, to give my son a view of me from the sky, after eagles got to him.

Our family wrapped Lone Wolf in a buffalo robe, dressed in the war clothes he didn't get to wear that day. We took his body on a pony drag, scaffolded him in the same cottonwood as his son. We sat quiet under the tree, me and Medicine Feet Woman. Lone Wolf's mother wailed her sorrow. Medicine Feet put a knife to her leg, slashed it, let blood run. She gave me her knife, pulled up my dress, pointed to my leg. I slashed my leg, blood flowed to a pool in my moccasins.

While we crammed our tipis and all we had on pony drags, Moving Robe Woman rode to our lodge, wanted me to run with her Húŋkpapa people to the Grandmother's Land. She had her brother's body bundled behind her on her horse. "Come with us," she said. "They will revenge this day, hunt us down like dogs. They have no honor."

"These are my people," I told her, looked at what was left of my family.

Moving Robe Woman grabbed my hand, held back tears. She understood, rode north with her Húŋkpapa people.

Medicine Feet Woman dressed us in widow clothes, cut our hair short while we went into mourning. We must mourn for a year.

I felt no purpose on earth. My son and husband were gone from this world.

I knew now. I was Indian. I'd die Indian.

CHAPTER TWENTY
WOLF MOUNTAIN
WINTER, 1876

"Thank you, daughters," Black Shawl said, resting on robes in her tipi.

Me and Medicine Feet Woman took turns wiping fever sweat from her face. We got asked to join with Crazy Horse's family, help care for his wife, Black Shawl Woman. She had a white man sickness in her chest. Crazy Horse met with other chiefs, planned hunts if people would eat through the winter after the Little Bighorn battle. Helping Black Shawl took my mind off my sadness. Medicine Feet told me I had to let go of my sadness, but I could not let go. My heart was dead without Lone Wolf and Flying Eagle. No one mentioned the names of the dead. Crazy Horse lost his little girl to white man sickness, he understood my sadness, that I needed to think about helping others if I was not to end my own life. Some women killed themselves, not able to live with the deaths from that battle.

We hid out in freezing mountains that winter. Some families went back to reservations, no food in the snowed woods. Wolf Mountain was more froze than I knew this earth grew cold. I thought about soldiers, hugging their forts, writing letters home, warm, getting drunk. We knew they'd come for us after the snows, to kill all of us. We'd whipped their army.

Black Shawl couldn't walk, breathing came difficult, sweat ran off her body at night. Crazy Horse watched me wipe his wife's brow with melted snow while a medicine man chanted, smoked her with sage. Whatever bad spirit had her would not leave.

Next night in their lodge, Crazy Horse spoke to me.

"You are not Oglála but are a kind and brave woman. Thank you for caring for my wife."

I looked down, embarrassed at his words. I heated more water in a kettle to make venison soup for Black Shawl. "I do nothing that Black Shawl would not do for me. Wašíču come sneaky," I said, changing what we talked about. "Like alder leaves, they clear off winter, then in the spring, more come than before. They are not going away. They never left my mother's people."

He nodded, knowing what I said was true. "There is no peace with wašíču. Only death or surrender," he said, more to himself than to me. Then he said, to himself, "How will the stories go, if I surrender?"

He meant when folks gathered kids to tell stories about ancestors. The only scar on his face was a little one near his mouth, from a fight he had over a woman he loved, before he married Black Shawl. Not a big man, he had about thirty snows. His serious eyes let me know I should think about what my life on this earth might mean. He never took scalps, they said, and his father lived a Holy Man life. His eyes looked beyond what stood around him. Where he looked, I didn't know, being young in years and not given to ponder a world beyond what came to my eye.

"Your father, your mother?" he said, aware of me staring at him. He studied my eyes, wašíču nose.

"I have an Indian mother from a Gift House where the sun sets. She gave me a bluecoat father—I never met him."

I asked if he had anger at me having a bluecoat father.

"No. Bluecoats leave children with our women. Not the child's fault. I heard you raided Psáloka horses with your husband." He laughed at the peculiarities life offers.

How'd he know I did that?

"My husband did the plan, taught me how to raid for horses," I said, looked down. He stopped his laugh, reached to his hair, untied the eagle feather he wore, gave the feather to me with both his hands.

"A coup feather, Brave Woman. I give this feather a blessing. You earned a feather on that raid. And your husband, who also fought brave at the Greasy Grass fight."

Ohítikawiŋ, Brave Woman, what he called me. I felt proud and embarrassed at his words. Considering the horse raid on Crow got me a pledge to have my heart eaten by Fox Tooth, maybe I earned the feather. Tears came to my not pretty eyes, thinking on my dear husband, how much a feather from Tašúŋke Witkó would mean to him. I looked up, said, "Wakáŋtáŋka níči uŋ ye," prayed that the Great Spirit would go with him, guide him, this wild horse man. We all prayed for him, a great wičaša, who led us in victory or defeat.

My words embarrassed him; he said no more, walked away.

Next night Crazy Horse had a friend to his lodge, the handsome Húŋkpapa man, Two Horns. Crazy Horse wanted his idea on how to care for Black Shawl. Two Horns's wife and kids died of white man disease. I gave all my attention to the sick woman, tried to. We never looked at each other, me and Two Horns. He had fewer snows in him than Crazy Horse had; folks said they raided horses together when younger.

Crazy Horse chanted low, his eyes closed. His father lived a Spirit Man life, his son knew about spirits. Surprised me when I got in his world of spirits. In the flicker of the lodge fire, I saw Flying Eagle's face, smiling. I got scared when I saw the face of Custer, who Sioux called Pehíŋ Haŋska—Long Hair. Long Hair turned his head to the side, pointed to his head like that was where he wanted me to shoot him, "L'dy, the damn guns don't

135

work." Made no sense, I got out of the spirit world.

Next day, Medicine Feet and me gathered firewood.

"He likes you," Medicine Feet Woman said, frost on her eyelashes. Even near starved, froze up, she had great beauty. Medicine Feet meant Two Horns liked me. My heart felt too dead to care about some man having his eye on me. Medicine Feet dreamed and gave her pretty woman dream to me.

"I'm not pretty, sister," I told her.

"Our husband thought you very pretty."

"The man who could not see well?" I laughed.

"Hush. Last night I heard Two Horns chant with Crazy Horse."

I gave her the ignore, piled wood on her arms. She said, "I saw him take your hand. A warrior never touches a woman's hand unless he has feelings for her."

"Witkó talk," I said, angered. Pretty women have no sense, see love everywhere. "Two Horns lives lonely, his wife and children are dead. He's sad because he knows soldiers will come for us after this winter. He fears our life will end. Take care of your life, sister. I'll take care of mine. Skies frowned when I was born. I have not mourned our husband the proper time."

She stopped gathering wood, stepped back to look at me. "Who would blame you if you opened your heart a little early? We might not live to see another snow."

"I am not pretty," I said, what Ma told me about my looks. "Two Horns wants me as a friend, not as a woman."

She looked at me, said, "Your mother lied, Little Sister. You are not ugly."

I lost patience. "I did not say my mother told me I came *ugly*. She said I was *not pretty*. Can your pretty woman head not understand the difference?"

Medicine Feet Woman would not stop her talk.

"You have beautiful eyes. Big, round, bright. Your eyes glow the way coals flame when a fire seems out. Do not scoff at my words, open your ears. You have a long neck—like a doe's leaning for river water. Strong legs, too, and skin smooth as a flute. Not too fat. Your arms are long, and strong. Your hair, if you would comb it, shines bright as a crow's wing after rain. You could use the brush you gave me."

"Stop! I have a head like a turnip," I said, close to a laugh. Medicine Feet could tell I came close to a laugh.

"And a fine nose," Medicine Feet said, giggled, covered her mouth. She loved me. We felt as family though our husband got killed.

"What about my nose?"

"Wašíču nose."

"Stop!" I said. "Here we are, at the end of our life and you talk about a nose."

Medicine Feet Woman would not stop. "And your lips are like full cherries."

I tried to hit Medicine Feet's laughing head with a stick. She ducked, I slipped, we fell on each other in the snow, how our dear husband found us after our fight, our breath froze to our cheeks. "He has a dead wife and children. Do not say such things while he thinks of them. Two Horns feels sad, needs friends, that is all he needs," I said.

"Two Horns is a man," Medicine Feet Woman said, pulled me close. "A man needs a woman. Sister, I need a man, myself."

That night, I washed my squirrel's nest hair in our tipi, asked Medicine Feet to braid it, tell stories about how she grew up, I would not give thought to what I'd do. She was like a mother to me. Friend of Otter gave a hand to braid my hair, took in her stories. Without a word, Friend of Otter left our tipi. He had a sensitive heart; we didn't wonder what stormed in him.

I put on my finest doeskin dress that night, brushed the dress clean. A woman's heart runs like a stream, flows wherever comes a beckon, between rocks that would stop the flow. Not always clear why a woman's heart meanders. A woman's heart goes where hearts go, after love and warmth. Not even a woman can stop the meander once the flow gets going.

I was supposed to mourn a year before even thinking about taking up with a man. I mourned six new moons, half the proper time, but that didn't seem too bad to me. I was a spark that flew to this earth after lightning hit, kept the smolder going, stayed alive for reasons only sparks know. I was supposed to keep burning on this earth, so I did.

Friend of Otter coughed, came back in the lodge. He waited for us to look his way, how we looked when he tried a new earring style, or a new style on his hair. He had prettier hair than most women.

"You could look," he said, in an angered voice, but he sounded different. Not Friend of Otter's voice, not at all.

He shaved his head, clean as a rock in a flowing stream, except for a sprout in the center of his head. He greased up the sprout with buffalo fat. He wore a man's breechclout, leather leggings, tunic of one of our dead warriors—a dear friend of his. Red and black paint on his face—for war. His chest, too. He had one huge chest. Friend of Otter found the man in himself.

"I will throw away my life in the next battle!" he said. He carried his buckskin dress with all the quilling, dropped his dress in the fire.

"Don't burn your clothes," I said. "Sit, talk with us."

"I am not Friend of Otter. My name is Mató Witkó." He named himself Crazy Bear. He growled like warriors do to stir up courage before hand-to-hand fights. He took a knife from his belt, cut a gash in his chest, then another, ran a leather strip through the cuts. Not a whimper from his lips while he pulled himself by the leather, blood flowing down his body. He did his own Sun Dance. He put his little finger on a stone by the fire, and, with one whomp of his mighty arm, he whacked off a top joint.

"Crazy Bear!" we yelled.

We ran to him, put our arms around him to give him comfort, blood from his finger dripping in the fire. Must be hard to be a man if you have to slash your chest, I was thinking, cut off a fingertip to prove your manhood.

We took him to the lodge of an old medicine man, Medicine Duck, to tend his wounds. We took him back to his lodge, put him to rest under robes.

Later that night in Black Shawl's lodge, Crazy Horse, Two Horns, and me, kept watch at Black Shawl's side. I wore my lovely doeskin dress, hair in braids that Medicine Feet fixed, blue cloth bows on the ends. Black Shawl lay on robes. Crazy Horse took my hand, put my hand in Two Horns's hand while they chanted. Surprised me, but I said nothing, Two Horns said nothing. Our hands didn't move from holding each other's, gentle.

Black Shawl looked at her husband, at me, at Two Horns; she eyed my pretty dress, my fixed hair. Smiled. I saw a spark in her eye.

Two Horns looked my way, "I go to my lodge."

He let go of my hand. Two Horns left the tipi. Men say things clear when they war or hunt. "Attack here." "I counted four coup." "I saw elk." But to a woman they might not speak clear in words of the heart. Somehow a woman is supposed to know what a man wants when he says, "I go to my lodge," after he held your hand, prayed in the spirit world, looked at you.

What was I supposed to do?

CHAPTER TWENTY-ONE
COULD I EVER LOVE AGAIN?

I got up in Black Shawl's lodge, knew what I'd do. Before I left, Black Shawl pointed with two fingers to her blanket.

"For me, grandmother?"

"Yes. Cold night. Stay warm, daughter, however you can. Thank you for caring for me."

I wrapped her blanket around my head and shoulders, walked to the cold, starry night.

Horses were staked outside tipis, warm fires glowed inside. No one was out that night except me and guards outside camp. My leather boots, frilled at top with wolverine tail, crunched fresh snow—the only sounds. The moon shined full above, gold in color. My heart stomped in my chest quick, I had to stop, take a breath, let air out slow, watch fog from my mouth fade to the night. Shivers ran through me.

I feared loving a man again.

Another husband for bluecoats to kill.

Two Horns had a fire lit in his tipi. On his knees, he fanned the flame, wearing a skin tunic, elk hide pants, moccasins. He spread a buffalo robe, made room for me to sit. Too much smoke in the dark for me to see his face. He sat quiet, cross-legged, back straight. I sat next to him, legs under me like a proper woman though it was not proper to be with him, without chaperones. We both knew that. I loosed my boots, took them off. If he needed a sign about how I felt about him, I hoped I let him know. Medicine Feet Woman taught me if a woman takes off her boots when alone with a man, he knows she'll take off anything.

We sat together in silence. I wondered if I had not understood what he wanted. Finally, he spoke, "Sweet Medicine Woman shows kindness to brother Crazy Horse's sick wife." He called me by the name all now knew me, the name my husband gave me. "While others sleep, Sweet Medicine Woman cares for Black Shawl."

"Not much I do for her," I said, quietly. Fire warmth on my face moved down my body at his words.

"Like the sun warms the earth, Sweet Medicine Woman brings warmth to all around her."

"To—'all'?"

Two Horns was quick as a cougar in how he moved, but slow when giving thought, looked away. He said, "Yes. All. And Two Horns feels warmed when this woman is near."

I told him I knew Two Horns had a dead heart, that I was glad I warmed his heart.

We sat on robes, watched the fire, without speaking. I wanted him to hold me.

"I have no horses to give to this woman's family," he said.

Not what I wanted to hear. "Horses? This man thinks this woman comes to his lodge, at night, without chaperones, because she has interest in his *horses*?" I was ready to give up Sioux men and their concern about horses and counting coup. I'd never been asked proper to wife a man, if that's what he had in mind. I thought the time came for a man to treat me proper.

"I didn't mean you want horses. I meant your family."

I told him I had no family, only those who took me in, here. "Stop the horse talk if you want me to stay."

"Oh. *Ohhh*. Yes. Let no more talk of horses slip from these lips. Two Horns forgot how to talk to a woman."

I told him Two Horns had not much time to remember how. He looked at me, a hurt look on his face, "Have I not said this woman warms my heart?"

"You said this woman warms the hearts of *all*. Are *all* worried about giving horses for me to warm their hearts?"

"This woman speaks how a Pawnee arrow flies, straight and hard between this man's eyes."

"Will this man tell this woman, plain, what he wants? Will his heart speak and not for *all*? Will he . . . ?"

Two Horns took me in his arms. I wanted to melt right there, held his face in my hands, my hands shaking more than I wanted, looked in his eyes.

"I go to the Grandmother's Land," he said.

"Why do you say that to this woman?"

"When I go to the Grandmother's Land . . ."

"Yes?"

"I want you to . . ."

"To . . . ?"

". . . be this man's wife."

My heart beat faster than drums at a dance. Tears slid from my eyes, I wiped them. "This woman has not mourned a year."

"This man has mourned, more than a year. They, our relations, would understand."

"And you, do you understand?" I had to know. Did he respect me?

"If stars fell in this lodge, my heart could not be happier, with you, here. Nothing else to understand," he said. I tried not to let him see how his words melted me.

I looked in his eyes, let my words flow, and tears of joy. "This woman will be proud to become Two Horns's wife. This night. But she can only join him later. She has her family to help, here."

I hoped Lone Wolf smiled at my decision. Life as we knew it

had come to the edge. The order in the Sioux world got ripped apart, and with that went rules between man and woman. What order in the world can a few make when those, more in number than leaves in a forest, think your order means porcupine squat?

I opened my heart to Two Horns, wherever he touched me came alive.

His hands did gentle touches under my dress however he wanted. He lifted my dress over my head. Pine sap popped in the low fire, gave pine perfume to our air. Sorrow that flowed through me, like bitter water, moved aside. His man smells made me come alive. I let go of worry about living proper, heard the fire crackle, felt fear leave me to ever love a man again, have a child with him. Felt strange to touch, nuzzle a man's body that wasn't Lone Wolf's. A man's body on Two Horns, and man's heart in him, not a boy's like Lone Wolf's. He played no flute, no need. I never knew a man big as Two Horns could touch gentle. I helped him take off his tunic. He lay beside me, removed the rest of what he wore. He slipped off what I wore under my dress, nuzzled me everywhere he wanted, like I gave him a field of beautiful flowers on his robes.

He picked me up like a leaf, carried me to the other side of his lodge, lay me on soft robes, pine cones scattered around the robes. I liked how he'd put those pine cones there for me, sweet smells joined fire warmth. Sadness that owned me gave way, how clouds open after a rain; rainbow colors I forgot about peeked in, moved through me to my toes. Summer lightning flashes came, lighting my body and heart. I felt love run through me like I never thought I ever feel again.

Later, we rested.

"This woman can come to you only later," I said, touched his cheeks. "My family needs me now. I must help them through the winter. This woman will come to Two Horns later, as his wife, as long as the sun shines on her."

Who knows what days we have on this earth, but considering how we spent the night, our bodies saying things our lips didn't know how to say, the words had truth.

Two Horns pulled a robe over us, held me close. We slept till sunrise. Our bodies found each other when we woke, slower, even better than before. Seemed to me, Two Horns gave the most lovely proposal and wedding night a woman could want.

Next day, Medicine Feet Woman had her *I told you* look. Opened her eyes wide, moved her eyebrows slow, up and down, asking if all went good. I flicked my eyebrows; she took hold of my hand, gave a gentle squeeze.

"See what I meant?" she said.

"Yes, sister. Thank you."

"Two Horns ask you anything, last night?"

"Yes."

"And . . . ?"

"I said *Yes.*"

"Wašté. We must not talk about our husband or your baby again. Let our sadness go."

I patted her hand, touched two fingers to my head. I'd try.

"Sister, after I mourn, will you help me to find a man?" she said.

Surprised me, she was always very proper. "Yes. Any man in mind?"

"Not yet. What's he like, Two Horns?" She moved her face close, studied my eyes.

I looked down, shy of her question. "Very tender," I told her. "All night."

"All night. How long, really?" She moved closer, her eyes intent on my answer. I knew she wanted to ask if I popped his cork but was glad she didn't ask. That was private.

"How long does the moon take to go down and the sun to rise?" I said.

Medicine Feet Woman gave a sigh, wanting a night like that. I watched Two Horns ride out with the Húŋkpapa. He gave me a loving look, put his hand on his heart, kicked his horse to move north.

"Go with him, sister," Medicine Feet said.

"I have family and friends to care for," I told her. "I owe the people who took me in, gave me a place on this earth. I always pay debts. Then I will go to Two Horns."

Chapter Twenty-Two
TONGUE RIVER RAID

Old Moccasins didn't want to bring a woman on his cow raid in the froze mountains that winter, even a woman dressed like a man. Friend of Otter had me shoot a branch from under a longtail magpie at some distance. My shell never touched the bird.

"One of my two gifts from the Great Mystery, grandfather," I told Old Moccasins.

"Sweet Medicine Woman will come," Old Moccasins said to the men who volunteered for the raid. "Anyone shoot a máza wakháŋ good as her?" No one said a word.

Old Moccasins held the pipe on our cow-stealing raid. He had bowlegs, tent-flap lids covered his eyes, but in his head flowed audacious ideas, like my pa told Molly was Napoleon's way to win battles.

"Is the woman on her moon?" Little Coyote whispered his question, but loud enough for all to hear. He feared woman mystery power might bring bad medicine to the raid. Old Moccasins looked my way, took off his fur hat, scratched his head, too embarrassed to ask the question. They had to know or I would not go.

"I am not on my moon," I said to Little Coyote, angered at such foolishness, their need to pry my life, what with the little privacy a woman had in camp. My words calmed the men.

The bluecoat chief that Sioux called Bearcoat built barracks below Wolf Mountain, at the mouth of the Tongue River where it met Elk River. They'd hang around that winter, make us pay for their defeat at the Little Bighorn fight in the summer.

Bluecoats had not been good at hunting us winters, Medicine Feet Woman said, but Long Hair's death gave them a mind to change that. The worst winter in those mountains Medicine Feet Woman could remember, snow very deep, our horses couldn't get through, stopped us from hunting. We fed bark to horses, ate the horse.

Crazy Horse sent five chiefs to talk peace with Bearcoat below where we hid. We might come in, surrender, if terms held what chiefs wanted. A runner came back saying our chiefs, under a peace flag, were shot dead by Crow army scouts camped near the barracks. Crazy Horse got more angered than I ever saw a man get an anger on—ordered a fight and a raid on bluecoat cows.

Our raiding party rode slow to sun-blessed hills high above their barracks. "Guide our path in stealing spotted buffalo, Grandfathers." Friend of Otter, still a man, prayed while we rode through.

"Surprise coming if you think you get buffalo meat," I said, riding next to him.

"They walk on four legs like buffalo, just scrawny and lazy, with short hair."

I paid no mind to what he thought we raided. But the men had questions before they risked their necks. We stopped for a talk, heavy snow falling, each flake fell like a big goose feather.

"Cousins, can we count coup for stealing spotted buffalo?" Little Coyote asked the question, fingered the medicine bundle hanging around his neck.

"Not a useful question," I said to Old Moccasins. I had no interest in counting coup, I wanted meat for our kids' bellies.

"The young woman comes with us to use her gift against Long Knives, not to tell Old Moccasins what to think," he said, more shaming of me in his voice than I thought I deserved.

Friend of Otter gave me a look—I should shut my mouth, know a woman's place among warriors.

They stood in a circle, horses tied to bush, talked about Little Coyote's question. Friend of Otter snuck close; his words came only to me. "Do not be peculiar around the men. Talk like a normal woman. You embarrass me."

"Look who talks about being normal," I said, angered at his words. My words backed him away. I felt sorry I said them, made fun of when he dressed like a woman.

The men huddled closer, talked about their predicament.

They are big four-legged we go after. Coup should be counted.

But not wild four-legged, cousin. Do we count coup for stealing dogs and pets?

But, cousin, some of those animals have horns. Takes more bravery to steal a spotted buffalo with horns than a dog.

On and on they fanny-flapped. Elk Shoulder, one of the scouts who went ahead for a look, said, "I smelled those animals, cousins. Not like buffalo. Spotted buffalo stink."

I wanted to tell him penned-up cows leave stink in heaps.

"If we eat spotted buffalo," Elk Shoulder said, "we might stink like spotted buffalo."

Old Moccasins asked if anyone had a good smell of a white man—a live one. No one smelled a live white man. Friend of Otter told them I spent time among white men, maybe I'd know if the stink of cows became part of them who ate cow. Warriors liked the smell of bear fat on their face, old elk shank hung to dry, dog boiled in a kettle, loused-up tipis after a winter. Stink depends on how you grow up with it. All eyes turned to me.

"Too young to remember white man smells who ate spotted buffalo," I said. Ma said Stump stank, but from his "constitutional"—a puke after he got drunked up.

Burnt Finger said years ago he put an arrow in a stray settler cow along the trail that went west through our land, and his family ate the cow, near Fort Laramie. All eyes turned to Burnt Finger, a man with a huge face, missing half a nose.

"And, cousin, what? What?" Friend of Otter said, impatient, not used to the warrior way to get agreement on a raid, everyone speaking his mind. "You smell like spotted buffalo after you ate it?"

Burnt Finger paused, thought on the question. He said, "You know how buffalo liver smells, if you keep it too long, and if your wife boils the liver?"

They gave thought to a unpleasant memory.

Burnt Finger said, "Spotted buffalo tastes horrible, cousins, like that liver, but I didn't stink after I ate spotted buffalo." His words calmed them.

Old Moccasins gave thought to the predicament—no coup for stealing miserable cows.

Soldier guards and Crow scouts camped near the penned-up cows, as many our scouts said as moons in a year. Old Moccasins thought we needed a trick, to draw their attention elsewhere when we swiped them.

"Grandfather, may I speak?" I said.

Old Moccasins nodded I could speak, since I asked proper. Guards meant they expected us to go after their cows—any trick we tried would get more guards, and we'd lose men in a fight. I had another plan to go with his decoy idea.

Old Moccasins thought over my plan, looked at the men while he spoke to me, "Come back safe, daughter. We will eat wašíču meat tonight."

Friend of Otter helped me off my horse near the bottom of the hill, said, "You do not have to be this brave to avenge your family. Be careful, kolā." I looked in his worried eyes, wanted to hug him for his concern. He gave me the love he had for my husband. I handed him my fur mittens, carbine, shells, and buffalo robe. He led my horse away.

I took a breath, ducked under snowed pine boughs, snuck down toward the soldier camp.

Snow fell so thick I could not see their camp clear but heard cows bawling. I made no sound, sneaking on fresh powder. I heard Crow scouts talking, spotted them standing around a fire to keep warm. I fell to the snow, didn't move. Logs on the fire popped sap in the air. I crawled to bushes behind their tipis, spidered fast around their tipis, laid flat, didn't move. I could see soldiers ahead, warming around a fire. No sight of barracks or cattle, but the cows must be near—I smelled them. I pulled out my skinning knife, did a cut on my neck. I needed blood, spread blood around my mouth and neck, rubbed snow on the neck cut, stopped the bleeding.

A soldier spotted me, grabbed his rifle. "Hostile!" he yelled.

He raised his rifle, aimed at me. I closed my eyes, wondered what dying would feel like.

CHAPTER TWENTY-THREE

MY SOLDIER PA?

"Mercy! Mercy, me," I hollered, fainted. I heard no rifle shot, only boots crunching on snow. I lay dead rat still, an eye open, saw boots run up. A soldier knelt, moved my wolverine cap to look at my face.

"A girl," the one kneeling over me said, "Speaks white, though she looks redskin."

They carried me to their barracks. I moaned in a *dee*lirium when they laid me on a table near a hot stove. "Pa, oooo, pa, save me from them savages," I talked, crazy.

"Colonel, what you make of her?" a soldier said.

I opened my eyes. Above me stood a soldier puffing a pipe, hands in suspenders. Must be the one Sioux call Bearcoat.

"Beats me, soldier. She wander in?" Bearcoat said.

"Then fainted, sir."

Bearcoat leaned down, his beard scratched my face. "Miss," he said, "your name?"

The first army officer I ever came across. Strange time to think about my pa but any officer could be him. How would I recognize him? I tried to recall what Ma told me about how Pa looked.

"Where'd you come from? Who's your father?" he said, a concern for me in his voice.

I sat up slow, "Water, please." I held my bloodied face, removed my cap. They gave me a water canteen, crowded around, gawked like they never saw a young woman before.

"Thank gawd you found me," I said. "Redskins attacked Pa's cabin over yonder, killed him, took me prizner. We done some trapping, pa and me. My Piegan ma died a couple snows ago. I thought you soldiers ran them hostiles to reservations."

"They damn well will be on reservations before I'm done here," Bearcoat said, breaking in to my story. "Sorry, miss, about your father. How'd you find us?"

"I snuck off when them savages sent me to get firewood. I followed the river, saw your smoke, but your redskins scared me, sir. Uh, *Rowena* is my name. Rowena McFadden, from up Fort Benton way."

Bearcoat stood up, looked at his soldiers. "I heard of McFadden. Sends reports to us now and again, when he's not selling guns to Indians." He looked at me, "You McFadden's daughter?"

I had to think quick. "He's my . . . uncle, sir—Pa's brother. Oooo, the horrible treatment I got from them savages." I pretended tears, did a fair job on the tears.

They went quiet, knew what I meant about what them savages did to a girl.

"Which direction you come from, Miss Rowena?" Bearcoat motioned with his pipe for a soldier to get me something to eat.

I pointed opposite where they kept the cows, "Maybe two miles as the crow flies, sir."

"Sioux? Cheyenne?"

"Some wore soldier jackets. One had a little flag."

"Those bastards. They wiped out Custer's Seventh."

"If you give me beans and hardtack, dry clothes, I will lead you to them bastirts. Revenge my pa and for what they did to me, one after the other." I looked him in the eye.

He directed they get me soldier clothes that might fit. I rolled off the table, sat on a bench, scooped warm beans with a spoon like I had not eat in days, which was the only truth I brought to their little fort. I wolfed down the hardtack, gave a bordello smile to soldiers gawking at me. After I ate, I ran a hand through my hair, stuck out my chest to get a stretch in front of their warm stove, show my feminine charms, limited though they were. They brought the soldier trousers, shirt, and jacket, I stood up, pulled my leather tunic over my head, dropped the tunic to the floor.

"No time for modesty, sir," I said, let the soldiers look at my naked charms, limited though they were. Embarrassed me to stand naked as a sparrow from neck to belly, but figured I had to, for my people. I took my time getting arms in the dirty shirtsleeves. A soldier let out a whistle. Another whispered, "Look at those sweet squaw apples, Sarg."

"I am, Freddie," said Sarg.

I turned around so's all could get a gander at my apples, cloud their minds. Put a woman's apples on a dead wolverine, white men whistle in their pants at them apples, best I could tell.

"Trousers, sir, if you please," I said to Bearcoat.

He gave me the shortest trousers they could find, yellow stripes up the sides. He told his men and the Crow to turn their backs. I appreciated his concern for my modesty, offed my skin leggings, dropped them to the floor. A soldier sighed, thinking of home, wishing he could see a woman's legs, what he left behind.

"I need a hand to help me in these trousers, if you please."

Every soldier jumped to lend a hand, except Bearcoat. I admired him for that. Too much an officer and a gentleman to put his hand on a girl's bare skin. If he's my pa, didn't want him touching my body. I rested a hand on the shoulder of a soldier while slipping my leg in the trousers. Although Ma said I came not pretty, the Great Spirit gave me legs curved nice, like fiddles, down to my ankles. To the soldiers, my brown legs gave a path up to a woman's sweetness they had in mind.

"Thank you, sir," I said to the soldier, using his shoulder to keep me upright. Another soldier volunteered his shoulder while I put my other leg in the trousers.

"Mighty kind of you, sir."

He put his hand on my bare leg, helped me. I got in those pants just fine, pulled up my fur boots, pulled my hat tight around my head. In the army uniform, I looked like the name Ma gave me when I was born—Army Girl. Ready to hunt down savages.

"Let's ride," I said to Bearcoat.

We rode through deep snow in the direction of my cabin, me in the lead, next to Bearcoat. Crow scouts rode up wild behind us, screaming—they'd spotted enemy near the barracks—Old Moccasin's decoy. The bugler gave the turnaround, off they galloped, back how we came. Bearcoat looked my way, angry. If his revolver wasn't holstered, I suspect he'd have put a hole in me.

"You! I'll deal with you later!" He kicked his horse, rode through knee-high drifts to save his cows. I dawdled near the rear of the wild charge, slipped to trees when they paid me no mind, snuck back to our camp. Wish I could have been there, see his face when Bearcoat learned his cows got stole by Indians. I kept the uniform, horse, and saddle the army kindly lent me.

The soldiers got back most of the cows, but not all. We had quite a feast that night, our first meat in many moons. Some kids threw up, not used to cow meat, but our bellies got full. And I'd done what would give my pa pride—been *au*dacious, like Napoleon said to win a war. I gave the uniform to boys for playing bluecoat soldiers in their games.

Bearcoat attacked us worse than before in those mountains, angered about Indians swiping his cows. Crazy Horse had us women, children, and old folks move away while he arranged his warriors and Cheyenne in hills above the valley where they would have to come. Smoke signals called other bands in those mountains to join us, run off the bluecoats.

But bluecoats could see the smoke, too, and know where we hid.

Soldiers attacked on foot, fired cannons, but cannon noise didn't scare us like before. Snow so deep we could not have much of a fight. Warriors used rifles and ammunition they took from bluecoats at the Greasy Grass fight. The froze-up soldiers that came for us wrapped themselves in buffalo robes, same as us. The fight flowed like two armies of frozen hairy worms. We retreated into the hills; the bluecoats gave up the chase. Crazy Bear wounded a bluecoat, earned himself a coup feather. He took much pride in that feather.

A Cheyenne camp had to abandon their belongings and tipis when they got overrun by soldiers, who set their tipis afire. We had to move camps faster and faster. Crazy Horse knew we could not survive without a time to rest. Not much food to feed many people in those mountains. Horses can eat only so much bark; women have to eat to have milk for babies. Maybe stealing cows wasn't a good idea—hurt Bearcoat's pride to have Indians steal his cows.

Was he my pa? Did he ever soldier in the Willamette Valley?

With no meat, roots, or berries, we began a horrible way to end life—starving.

CHAPTER TWENTY-FOUR
SURRENDER 1877

Indians who'd surrendered long ago to bluecoats showed up at our winter camp with an offer from the Great White Father— hunting land along the Powder River—great hunting lands.

No other way to keep us alive, Crazy Horse agreed.

"We go with you," Crazy Horse told the Indians who asked him to surrender. "Tell the soldiers we come. We come slow. Many old people, sick, many children." He stopped his talk, thought for a while, told them, "I want you to know, I have no Great White Father except the Great Spirit." First time I heard about a Great White Father, wondered what he looked like. Probably a great warrior like Crazy Horse who gave away most of what he had to poor people, like our chiefs did.

In the Moon of the Grass Appearing, bands headed out, strung out far as the eye could see. Many on foot, the sick on pony drags.

Medicine Feet Woman held her daughter's hand, walked beside me riding the army horse I kept. Some days I let her ride, and her daughter. We brought Gramma Eagle Nose Woman on a pony drag. The sky greeted us clear most days, but when rains came we sat under buffalo robes—with nothing to eat. The men were ready to fight if they sensed anything peculiar. We trusted no one, not even fort-hugging Indian who'd made peace with Long Knives.

We came to Fort Robinson, in a place they called Nebraska.

"You should have run with Two Horns," Medicine Feet said. "See the lines of Long Knives? Will they kill us when we ride through them?"

Her fear reached to me, a baby kicking in me, Two Horns's child.

Crazy Horse said not to trust wašíču. I don't think he ever planned to learn their ways, just get us food, hunt on the good land they promised us near the Elk River.

At the fort, we rode through two lines of soldiers, sitting quiet on horses, hands on holstered revolvers in case we attacked. Confused look on soldier faces when we walked and rode by—hard to figure they couldn't defeat in battle these skinny, sick, tattered-clothes people. But we held our heads high, did not surrender like dogs. Indians at the fort lined up and cheered us—we didn't surrender till we had no food. Made me proud—a feeling I never forgot.

We set up camp near Chief Red Cloud's people. Felt strange to be surrendered, camps looked the same. We cooked over fires, babies cried, kids chased hoops on prairie grass. The sun shined, grass grew, but inside we ached, hurt more than words could tell. No longer free. Best I could tell, wašíču wanted to turn us into cows, tamed, penned up.

I learned a general name of *Sheridan* planned us to live the cow life. He killed off our buffalo, wanted us to pound farm corn into flour, eat sugar till our teeth got rot. I told Crazy Bear, while I pounded corn from a husk, "If I come across this Sheridan, I'll shoot him, if I have a gun."

"Do not let soldiers hear those words," he said, looked around to see who might hear.

Sheridan wasn't at the fort, only a general we called Three Stars, who we sent running at the Rosebud fight. Three Stars would meet with Crazy Horse, work out our surrender. This meeting Three Stars planned got fouled up like many foul-ups after our surrender. Bad translating.

Medicine Feet Woman wore her doeskin dress around camp, fringed nice, cut off at the knee. Showed folks she slashed her legs how a wife should when our husband got killed. I'd tried one slash after the battle, all I could do to a leg. She was on the lookout for a husband. Medicine Feet Woman brought a stone to our tipi, handed her knife to me.

"I slashed my leg, sister," lifted my dress, showed her my cut.

"That cut you did for our husband," she said, not impressed. "You must grieve for your child."

"I grieve," I said, rubbed my womb, carrying Two Horns's baby.

"You must cut a fingertip, one of your little fingers. You have another. Here, put your finger on this rock, I will cut off the tip for you."

"Cut off the tip of a finger? You crazy? I need my fingers to care for this baby. Cut your own finger if you want to cut something."

"You shame our family if you do not cut a finger for your dead child. If you are one of us, you must live by our ways," she said.

"I'll cut off your fool head if you try to cut my finger." I grabbed a robe to shake clean outside.

Her beautiful eyes frowned, ran thoughts through her head, remembered our fight in the woods. She knew what I could do if I got riled, even if I was with child.

"All right. Keep your fingertip. You are not Lakóta."

I gave in. "Give me the knife. I will cut a finger or you will nag me about cutting a finger all summer." I put my left hand on the stone, looked at my little fingertip, took Medicine Feet's knife. Never knew how good fingertips looked till I had to cut one.

"No," Medicine Feet said, put away her knife. "I am sorry I

said those words. We might need your fingers to tear out Long Knife eyes. I am bored—go with me to the fort?"

I took my hand from the stone.

"Nothing at a fort except soldiers," I said, looked at the fingertip I almost cut off. "They drink *mni wakhaŋ*, stink up a place, try to get in the robes with us."

"I never met a soldier," Medicine Feet said. "A live one. I am curious."

"All right, but I'll ride our horse," I said. "You walk, I have a baby coming. And don't you even think about a soldier for a husband." We went a few miles under a hot sun to the fort, tied our horse outside, walked in like old friends of pony soldiers.

"Cage for people," I said, walking in front of the guardhouse. Medicine Feet Woman touched the metal bars on the window. I gave her and Crazy Bear some wašíču tongue when we headed for white man living. Medicine Feet now knew how to say, "What is that?"

"Jail."

In her tongue I said, "A cage for no-good folks."

"Why?"

"They break a wóope." In the wašíču tongue I said, "Break a law. *Lah.*"

"*Lahhh?*" she said, in the wašíču tongue.

"A wašíču wóope," I said in her tongue. "Like a buffalo drive wóope. Not supposed to ride ahead of Akhičíta leading a hunt. No one should hunt a herd alone."

Medicine Feet Woman touched two fingers to her pretty head. She'd seen hunters punished if they broke a buffalo hunt wóope.

A soldier stood guard at the jail, half asleep, noticed Medicine Feet Woman.

"Afternoon, ma'am," he said, tipped his hat, stood lodgepole straight. Medicine Feet, startled, grabbed my hand.

"Afternoon," I said. Surprised him to hear a Indian woman

speak his tongue.

"William's my name," he said, stared at the lovely eyes of Medicine Feet Woman though he talked to me. Medicine Feet stared back at him, flirted like a no-account witkowin. Red hair on William's head, bushy beard, freckled face—a man her age. I grabbed Medicine Feet's arm, we moved on. She looked back, sweet, at that soldier. Pretty women make no sense. We passed a barbershop, blacksmith's, a hospital where they cared for sick soldiers. We went in their feed store, soldiers coming and going, Indians walking around like they felt at home.

I gave Medicine Feet more learning of the tongue of our captors. She knew how to call corn, "wagméza," and beef, "taló." Coffee beans we called "pežuta sápa"—black medicine.

"Aǧúyapi," I said, pointed to bread. "Bread." Cornbread.

"Bread," Medicine Feet said, enjoyed her learning. "Aǧúyapi." Medicine Feet ate some. "Tastes like old buffalo lung."

"I never ate buffalo lung," I said. "Here, eggs, from pet hens. Not prairie hens. *Eggzzz*. Wítka."

"Eggzz," she said, tried to get her tongue around new sounds. "Sister, how do you say 'handsome man' in the wašíču tongue?"

I knew what she had on her mind. "Uhglee feller."

"That soldier we met, uhglee feller."

"Uhglee, yes."

Medicine Feet already knew sugar, too—čaŋháŋpi. She loved sugar but didn't like yamnúmnužapi—pepper. Made her sneeze. I peppered her nose, clear her head about a handsome wašíču.

Soldiers and Indians gathered in back of the store, laughing, chanting. We looked in. Soldiers had a black box with wires stuck in a bucket of water. A contest was going on between bluecoats, Cheyenne and Sioux medicine men. I saw Medicine Duck, who took care of Friend of Otter when he chopped off his finger. Medicine Duck had many snows and a wily mind to him, near short as me, two eagle feathers in his hair, wearing a breechclout tied around his waist, a medicine bundle around his neck. He rubbed the bundle.

"What's going on, grandfather?"

Medicine Duck motioned for me to be quiet. A medicine man friend of Medicine Duck's said he would take the challenge soldiers gave to any medicine man. Medicine Feet Woman and me joined in, laughed, praised him for taking the challenge. A bright silver dollar was at the bottom of the water bucket. The soldiers bet no medicine man could reach in, grab the dollar, pull it out while holding the wire from the heap big medicine box. Soldiers said their medicine and magic song had more power than medicine men. They'd throw in five more silver dollars if a medicine man could pull out a dollar while holding their medicine wire.

"Grab the wire, chief," a soldier yelled to the medicine man.

"Héehe'e," he said, took the challenge.

The medicine man got ready to enter his spirit world. He laid himself flat on the floor, chanted, sucked his magic stone, eyes closed, body shook when spirits came to help him. I slipped close to the soldiers' medicine box. I saw some at Fort Benton. Batteries. When you crank the handle, fire ran along the wire. Fort Benton folks called the fire—*juice,* said, "Give 'er more juice." Cranked faster. Not a spirit box just a white man machine—soldiers having sport with our medicine men.

The medicine man stood up, tranced, eyes stuck on the five more silver dollars on the table. He grabbed hold of the wire, nothing happened, soldiers not cranking the medicine box. The medicine man stuck his hand in the water. A soldier cranked the battery; other soldiers sang a magic song about a feller name of Pat Malloy. The medicine man felt the juice, shook so hard his teeth banged, eyes bugged, legs flapped the way a hen flaps with her neck cut.

"Eiiii!" Indians cried. Anyone try to grab the man, they shook, too.

"Heap big medicine, huh?" says the soldier who did the cranking.

The medicine man walked away. Indians wide-eyed the soldier medicine—no wonder they beat us in war. I whispered to Medicine Duck, "Take that challenge. Grandfather, when you flop round, holding that wire, kick the box. Say you want another go at the dollar."

He looked at me like I was crazy.

"Just a trick box—no spirit in the bucket. You get five more dollars, too," I told him.

Medicine Duck had his own bag of tricks, had learned wašíču card tricks to show off his medicine powers.

"This going to hurt?" he said, quiet, no one else heard.

"Not sure. But it won't kill you. Five dollars if you win."

Medicine Duck eyed me, gritted his teeth, stepped forward. Soldiers whooped, Indian women yelled to give him courage. The old man began his chant, eyed the medicine box. He grabbed the wire, stuck his hand in the bucket, his eyes nervous because he knew flopping was soon to come his way. Soldiers laughed, sang their Pat Malloy song, cranked juice to the Duck. The Duck bobbed like a horse not broke, arms jerked, legs bounced. I felt sorry I got him up to going for the dollar. After they stopped cranking, he took his hand out of the water. He looked my way, I nodded. He swung wild his arms and legs, kicked the box, knocked the wires loose. He gave a front tooth-missing grin to the soldiers, showed he wanted to have another go. Soldiers look feared, tried to get the wires hooked up. Medicine Duck chanted, stuck his hand in the bucket. Soldiers cranked, sang their medicine song without the wire stuck to the box. Medicine Duck grabbed the dollar, held it up for all to see.

We cheered, clapped, hooted. The old man thanked the

soldiers, grabbed the other shiny five silver dollars.

"Ith mo chac," I said to the soldier who cranked the machine.

"Ma'am?"

"Better medicine next time, soldier."

We left the feed store.

Medicine Duck gave me a dollar. "I owe you a favor, daughter," he said. "Anything you ask."

Medicine Feet Woman and me headed for our horse. The guardhouse soldier, William, ran to Medicine Feet, asked where we lived, what camp.

"Crazy Horse's camp," I said, though I didn't want to answer.

To Medicine Feet Woman he said, "Maybe I see you, ma'am, when we inspect for weapons. Could I say a howdy?"

I didn't want to but I translated. Medicine Feet smiled, flirted. I kicked her ankle. She gave me a glare, smiled at William before I yanked her away.

"See you later," William said. "Your name?"

"Her name is Medicine Feet Woman. You soldiers killed our husband, and my son. Leave us alone."

"Ma'am?"

We walked away. To Medicine Feet Woman I said, "Get some sense, sister."

She stopped, looked me in the eye. "You had a soldier father," she said.

Her words gave me pause in my judgments of her.

William showed at our tipi after searching for weapons at our camp. Medicine Feet snuck away with him while I looked after her daughter. She came back, wonder eyed.

"O, sister," she said, collapsed on buffalo robes, smiling.

"You haven't had a man in a year, woman," I said, angered, I wanted to slap her, get her some sense. "Do not think more of him than that."

She showed me the parasol he gave to keep the hot sun off her prettiness.

"I mourned our husband proper," she said. "You mourned for how long, *sister*?"

She knew I had not mourned the proper time. but I did not break the rule with a soldier.

"Do not let Crazy Horse know about this," I said.

"None of his concern," she said. "Your mother loved a blue-coat or you would not be here. Times change, *sister*, you think? I like his eyes, how he looks at me. Maybe I find a bluecoat husband. For my daughter, not just for me. Keep us safe. They would not harm my daughter if she had a bluecoat father."

"And maybe you get with another child? Like my mother did? And the skunk runs off?"

We stopped our fight, thinking on my words, held each other in our tipi. "Be careful, sister," I said. "I do not want you to get your heart hurt."

I took care of Medicine Feet Woman's daughter while her ma snuck out with that soldier.

Nighttime. I felt my baby kick harder in me, water flooded my legs. A boy? A girl, like me? I'd have to teach her how to be a woman—still learning about that myself. I feared having a daughter in those times, but that's who I hoped I'd birth.

Chapter Twenty-Five
A MOTHER AGAIN

"Get ready, sister," Medicine Feet said. She spread the robe, I grabbed the pole she stuck in the ground, stood on an old deer hide. She took off my tunic and skirt, put a rope around my belly, above the baby, pulled the rope tight. I got ready. Because I did it once, didn't mean I wasn't scared of what might happen to my body this time, and of the pain I knew would come. I feared we might not get my baby out alive. We had women in our band who died giving birth.

"You did this once. Easier this time," she said, pulled on the rope, moved my baby lower.

"You only birthed once, how do you know birthing comes easier?"

"Think about birthing. A woman gets loosed up giving birth, ready for another. That is what my mother told me."

"That is *all* I got to go on?"

The pain hit. I forgot how much hurt came from a baby. Medicine Feet Woman let loose of the rope around my belly, stood next to me, talking, rubbed my back, holding my free hand. The fire in my lower back, raged, calmed.

"Talk to your baby. 'Come, baby. Your mother wants you. Come, baby, come out to this world.' "

"Baby, come. Come out of me. Your mother wants you." I tried to stay calm, but I was sweated up, head to feet. Medicine Feet stuck a cloth in a bucket of water, wiped my forehead. I stood up. She took her skinning knife from under her dress, gave the knife for my teeth.

"Bite hard, sister."

I bit that knife hard as I could, pushed and pushed, pushed a baby out of me, caught the baby with my own hands. Oiled face and body, looked like the new birthed baby deer I saw born, only my baby had black hair, wetted down. My knees wobbled, I stood straight, took a deep breath, looked.

A girl. I loved her even before she hollered.

"Her name?" Medicine Feet Woman said, cut the cord, tied it off, cleaned up the mess, kept what I would bury in the ground and hide in trees. I'd thought about my baby's name, if she was a girl.

"Ȟewičiŋča." I named her Mountain Girl for where she began her life on this earth, on Wolf Mountain. We cleaned Mountain Girl, dried her hair and face, wrapped her in a blanket. She sucked my bosom like that was her purpose in life, looked in my eyes. A sight I'll never forget, when my baby looked at me, eye to eye. Probably wondered who she looked at. She had lovely Indian eyes, not round like mine.

Medicine Feet told her daughter to get me our bone backrest while she lit a fire in my tipi. They sat quiet, hugging each other, watched me nurse my baby. I wanted to show Mountain Girl to her father, Two Horns, see how happy our baby girl made him. I heard folks yell, outside our tipi. Women cried, old people gave a wail, children cried, too.

"Tašúŋke Witkó is dead!"

I tried to ignore what they said. Must be wrong, Crazy Horse had no sickness, no one could kill Crazy Horse, not in a fair fight. Bullets went right through him, no harm done him at the Greasy Grass fight. Crazy Bear slipped in to see my baby, tears flowing. A man that huge can cry a river once he gets going. I knew something bad happened. When he calmed down, I asked why the talk about Crazy Horse being dead.

"Crazy Horse thought he would meet Three Stars at the fort, get us good land. Fort soldiers tried to put him in a guardhouse, send him away then he would war no more. Crazy Horse fought Indian friends who brought him to the fort, who agreed he should be sent away. An Indian friend jumped him. The soldier with a knife on his rifle ran to stop their fight. The soldier's rifle-knife went in Crazy Horse, in his backside." Crazy Bear lay on my robes, buried his face.

"You sure?" I said.

"Died before the sun rose."

Crazy Bear let out a death chant.

"Stop that!" I said. "You sure he died?"

Crazy Horse's mother and father took his body, put him in a wood box behind a pony drag. I wanted to run, open the box, see for myself. I hoped Crazy Horse pretended death, hid out, would come back and take us with him. I never joined with the Sioux to surrender to nobody.

No one saw Crazy Horse again. His folks hid him, feared soldiers would steal his body.

Soldier William sent word to Medicine Feet Woman to meet him. She slipped away, came back, shaking, scared like I never saw her scared.

"What, sister?" I said, holding my baby, tired from nights of no sleep, nursing a crying child, grieving for our chief with all my heart.

"They sent him away."

"Who? Why?"

"Soldiers sent my William away. Our people can't kill him."

"Why would our people want to kill that bluecoat?"

"He held the rifle-knife that killed Crazy Horse, by accident."

I gave comfort to Medicine Feet, best I could. She'd become sweet on that soldier. She said there'd be no more bluecoats for her, shed more tears than I saw her cry since Lone Wolf died.

Crazy Horse's dying words to us, spoken to his dear friend, Touches the Clouds, follow his spirit to the Grandmother's Land.

Crazy Horse never gave up to wašíču, even as a spirit. I loved that man.

I wanted to find Two Horns in the Grandmother's Land. Me, Medicine Feet Woman, and Crazy Bear got us a plan, but we needed someone to guide us. Medicine Duck owed me a favor for the silver dollars he won. I always paid my debts and expected others to pay theirs. We gave him a invite for a talk about running north, across land he knew well.

Medicine Duck brought a nephew he could trust, Horses Loose, if we needed another warrior in a fight. Medicine Duck liked the idea, his nephew, too. Not much of a plan, but the best we could come up with. The old man was confident his medicine could get us there, safe.

We'd swipe supplies from the soldiers over the summer, get us dried meat, army beans, corn flour sacks, hardtack, pistol, carbine and cartridges. Hide what we could in the woods when we went for firewood, swipe army horses, get a pony drag ready for tipi hides and lodgepoles. Tell Eagle Nose Woman and let her agree we could go. Sneak off at night.

We'd make a run to the Grandmother's Land before snows fell, our last chance to live free.

Or die trying.

CHAPTER TWENTY-SIX
JOURNEY TO THE
GRANDMOTHER'S LAND
1877

We traveled nights, by moonlight. Days, we hid from miners and any soldiers who might notice we slipped camp. Moving quiet through the Pahá Sápa, Friend of Otter, still a man, scouted ahead on foot. Medicine Duck had a question for his nephew, Horses Loose, while we rode.

"Is Makhá round, not flat? What you think, nephew?"

"Uncle, if we go far enough north, maybe we will fall off Makhá, then you have the answer to your question," Horses Loose joked him. Plumes of air came from his nephew's mouth in the Black Hills air. When he breathed out, his chilled breath looked like feathers the male prairie chicken puts up when doing a mating dance for the hen.

Snows fell early that fall. We had buffalo robes wrapped around us, hair on the hides to keep out the chill. I had my baby girl wrapped to my chest, Medicine Feet Woman walked next to the pony drag where her daughter slept, Painted Calf Girl, trying not to fear her head would get cut off by miners. We heard about a Mexican in the town of Deadwood who used an Indian head for a target. Deadwood folks cheered his shooting. Someday I might have to fight white men to keep my baby alive, but no time now for fear.

"Crazy Horse said he thought this earth had a round shape, nephew. Use your eyes, learn from Makhá. Look in this night sky, and you see Haŋhépi wi, round and shining in the night. Aŋpétu wi shines hot in the day, round like a drum. Maybe the

Makhá we ride on is round, too, same as that night sun that shines on us. Maybe where we ride on Makhá, we would come back to the same place," Medicine Duck said. "Up there," he pointed far away to Bear Butte, bright in moonlight, "where I got my medicine. Saw a flock of paǧúŋta fly north. I had only fourteen snows; I took scalps later in my life, but remembered my spirit call from the mallard ducks, and ended the warrior life. Here I ride, now, near that same place, alone in this world—my wife and children dead from white man disease. A man needs a good wife, nephew, like your mother, my sister. No nagging in her."

The roundness of this earth, his want for a wife who didn't nag, was what Medicine Duck had on his mind while we made our way to the Grandmother's Land to find Sitting Bull.

Horses Loose told his uncle we had more problems to figure than whether Makhá looked the same as the moon or sun—how to not get our heads cut off by miners looking for yellow sand.

Medicine Duck had a curious mind, though, one that hung onto what had his interest—like a badger sets his jaws on a marmot. That's what made him a famous medicine man. He looked at everything close, let one part of this world teach him about other parts.

Although we rode quiet in the night on horses we swiped from the army, shod hooves striking rocks gave more noise than we liked. And the two lodgepole pony drags scratched loud, like carving on the side of a cliff with buffalo horn knives. One had Medicine Feet's daughter on top of tipi hides, the other with tipi poles and supplies for the trip. Being a mother again made me happy. Gave me a reason to live, and I hoped my ma would someday find me.

Horned owl hoots came from around the bend. Horses Loose signaled to stop. He slid off his horse, grabbed his war club, went to find out why Friend of Otter hooted.

They both came back on the run. I hushed my whimpering baby, tight against my chest.

"Wašíču on the ridge ahead," Horses Loose said.

Medicine Duck motioned for us to turn around, quiet, head back through the ravine we passed through. I got off my horse, let him be more sure-footed, while I walked next to our pony drag. Medicine Feet Woman's daughter woke. She saw fear in our eyes.

"Wašíču, my mother? Will they cut off my head?"

Medicine Feet motioned for her daughter to be quiet, ask no more questions. Gold miners. As much as Lone Wolf's people didn't understand the white man, the gophers who dug gold from the ground, killed each other over the useless stuff, seemed lunatics. Crazy men, to me, too. Medicine Duck told us about miners who got rubbed out when Lakóta caught them in our Pahá Sápa. When warriors found the miners' gold dust pouches, they poured out the yellow sand, kept the pouches for tobacco, hung around their necks. Another warring party on the Big Muddy got a mackinaw boat to tip, loaded with sacks of gold, *mázaskazi*—yellow metal. White men snuck back to get the sacks of gold, dodged arrows, for useless yellow sand.

"We will camp here," Medicine Duck whispered. "No campfires, čuŋkší," he said to me through his missing tooth. Called me his daughter. "Get us wasná to eat. We eat, then I take first watch. We bundle in robes after hobbling our horses. You take my knife, čuŋkší. Nephew, give your knife to Medicine Feet Woman. Everyone get some sleep. I look for waŋblí when the sun comes up; waŋblí will show us a safe path."

I didn't have confidence in a bird, waŋblí, a golden eagle, to give much help to reach the Little Muddy. If we found the Little Muddy, that river would guide us to the Big Muddy. We'd follow the Big Muddy to Fort Benton, head north from that town to find Sitting Bull. I whispered to my daughter before she fell asleep, wolves howling in the night, "You are going home, čuŋkší."

My baby sucked my bosoms, slow, most of the night. I flowed with milk like spruce sap in spring. While she sucked, I looked at my fingers, wondered if I should have cut a tip so I would not think about my dead son. Tearful thoughts came of him while I nursed my baby girl.

In the morning, Medicine Duck squinted his eye, spotted his waŋblí, circling high, hunting early, riding wind. He decided we would ride in the daylight. We broke camp, without breakfast we followed the eagle up a ravine.

"You tired, grandfather?" I said to Medicine Duck.

"Wakáŋtáŋka gives me energy, daughter." He believed strong in the Great Spirit, and his bird. "How is your child?" he asked, a concerned look on his old face, wrinkles around his eyes.

"I worry about her, grandfather. Looks bad colored in her face though I nurse her good."

"Keep her warm. We will get your baby to the Grandmother's Land. And she might need to know if we walk on a round earth, that she won't fall off, not fear to travel. Someday she might need to go back to some place in her life where she felt happy."

I said I'd give thought to his words. The elders said words you needed to think about before you understood all they meant.

Medicine Feet Woman rode next to me, wiped snow from her eyes, looked back at her daughter on a pony drag, said, "You will see my parents—your grandmother and grandfather. Does that make you happy, my daughter?"

"Yes, my mother," her daughter said, tried to be brave. "I think about them, I am not afraid. I miss my father. I try not to think about him, not say his name, but I think of him. He took good care of me."

"Think about happy times coming, my daughter. Not about what has gone. Your father would want that."

I would have to do that, too. I reached a hand to Medicine Feet. We rode hand in hand, said nothing. The early snowfall let up when we came to a high ridge of the ravine. Snow hung heavy on ponderosa branches, and the bull and lodgepole pines. What we didn't expect, the ravine curved back to join the ridge with the miner cabin. Friend of Otter saw no movement on the ridge; we rode slow to where the two ravines came together. Peaks climbed high around us and even in daylight the peaks looked like the head of a bull buffalo—dark, silent. Medicine Duck stopped, watched his waŋblí circling overhead. He took tobacco from his pouch, sprinkled tobacco in the wind, his offering to the eagle guiding us safe through the ravine.

"Let's go!" Friend of Otter said.

"Patience," Medicine Duck said. "Spirits guide us. We have to make prayer thanks to keep moving safe. These hills . . ."

A thunderclap echoed off the peaks; my heart leaped. Medicine Duck fell forward over his horse, like a cornsack thrown from a reservation agent's wagon.

"Shooting! Máza wakháŋ!" Horses Loose yelled.

Friend of Otter, riding behind Medicine Duck, turned his horse, hollered for us to get back to the trees. More thunder knocked limbs and snow off pine tree branches. My baby fussed, coughed, tight against my chest. We had to leave Medicine Duck in the snowed bush. We galloped to trees, slid off our horses, hid behind huge boulders that fell from peaks above.

Friend of Otter had our carbine and cartridges we stole from the army. He gave the carbine and cartridges to me.

"Where's the shooting come from?" Friend of Otter said to Horses Loose.

Horses Loose shook his head, not knowing. He fought the sadness in his heart at the killing of his uncle. The sound of the shooting echoed around the hills—we could not tell where the sound began.

Friend of Otter and Horses Loose grabbed war clubs that could smash a man's skull like a chokecherry. Their scalping knives were tucked in leather sheaths, around their waists. Horses Loose had his bow, and his arrows in a quiver. He set the sinew string around the bottom of his bow, gave it a twang— ready. Medicine Duck's nephew won shooting contests with that bow.

Horses Loose handed a knife to Medicine Feet Woman. She kept her daughter between her legs, tight against a boulder that towered over us. If miners killed our men, they expected us to defend ourselves. Hard to fight with a knife, your baby bundled to your body, holding a frightened daughter's hand. But we would make them pay, best we could, if they got up close, tried to have their way with us before they shot us, cut off our bosoms for souvenirs, and took their turns having Medicine Feet Woman's daughter.

Friend of Otter took medicine from the pouch around his neck, rubbed it on his war club and his growed-back hair after he threw down the beaver cap I made for him. They wore buckskin leggings under buffalo robes, elk hide boots, buckskin shirts. They dropped their buffalo robes to the snow, quietly chanted their death songs.

Having my baby to keep alive gave me courage I might not have had on my own, but my stomach turned upside down in me. I would be hunting men who hunted me.

We got ready for a fight to the death.

Them varmint miners or us.

CHAPTER TWENTY-SEVEN
DUCK POWER

Horses Loose put his beaver hat on a stick, stuck the hat around a boulder. Two shots hit the rock, knocked snow and rock chips in his face. He held up two fingers, bullets hit rock at the same time. Might be more, but he knew two miners shot at us. He pointed south, to the pine-covered ridge where Friend of Otter spotted a cabin.

I kissed my baby's cheek, handed her to Medicine Feet Woman, snuck with the carbine and pouch of shells through snowed bushes to hide behind a boulder, closer to the varmints on the ridge above.

I tried to stay calm, thought of my daughter, in need of her ma to shoot good this day. I looked at my hand holding the carbine—trembling. Horses Loose waved, ran low to the ground like a marmot, dove behind a rock. Thunderclaps filled the air, miner shells knocked snow and limbs off trees. Must be shooting Henrys, I thought, to knock a branch off a tree. A Henry shell would put a hole in me the size of a fist.

"Come on, you Red Devils," a miner yelled. "Get me another dead one for Custer. Eat lead, you sonsabitches."

Miners were having fun shooting at Indians for sport.

My hand stopped trembling, put the stock to my shoulder.

Friend of Otter signed—could I see them? I sighted movement on the ridge, took aim at a branch that moved. I knocked off that branch, gave miners something to think about—we had a rifle and knew how to shoot. Friend of Otter crouched, ran up

175

the ravine in the opposite direction of Horses Loose. Our army horses spooked, ran down the trail—Indian horses would have stayed put in a fight.

Someone higher up threw rocks down at the miners—we had a friend in the fight. The rocks showed us where they hid. Horses Loose and Friend of Otter began their owl hoots, one to the other.

The miners shot wild at the hooting and windblown snow falling from branches. A branch moved on the ridge, and I saw what looked like an arm aiming a rifle. I put lead in that arm, heard a scream.

The chilled air went quiet except for thumps war clubs make bashing in skulls.

Medicine Feet Woman's terrified tremolo filled the air.

I ran through snow fast as I could. My dress slowed my run, I held up the hem, charged like a mama bear through brush. A miner had snuck to get us from behind, stood between me and Medicine Feet, six-shooter in his hand. Seeing a baby in Medicine Feet's arms, a girl hid behind her ma's dress, gave pause to the miner. Medicine Feet Woman faced off with him, showed him her knife. His hand shook, tried aiming a gun at her. She lay my sleeping bundled baby on snow, moved her daughter away, handed the knife to her daughter to protect herself. Medicine Feet Woman opened her arms to the miner— shoot her if he wanted, do not harm our kids.

I cranked a shell to my carbine.

The sound of that shell came to his ear, he turned, fear in his eyes, scared of what gave the noise. He saw the end of his life—if he couldn't get me first.

Medicine Feet Woman ran at him from behind before I could shoot; she knocked him down, his six-shooter fell in the snow. She screamed like a crazed wolf, teeth bared, dug fingers in his eyes. He hit her hard as he could in her face, pounded her, but she wouldn't let loose of his eyeballs. She ripped his eyeballs from their sockets. Her daughter ran to her, gave her the knife. Medicine Feet Woman rammed the knife in the miner's face, jumped off him.

He rolled in the snow, screamed like a crazed badger caught in a trap, tried to pull the knife from his face, eyeballs hanging loose down his cheeks. I wondered if the eyes could see, hanging outside his head.

"Look the other way!" I yelled to Medicine Feet's daughter.

She looked away. I stuck the carbine next to the screaming man's head, put my foot on his head, pulled the trigger. The boom spattered the snow with his brains. Horses Loose and Friend of Otter ran to us.

"Any more?" Horses Loose said. He listened, heard nothing, picked up Medicine Feet's crying daughter to calm her. Friend of Otter put his arm around me, I shook all over.

"No more bad men," Horses Loose said to Medicine Feet's daughter. "You are safe."

Painted Calf Girl buried her face in the chest of Horses Loose. She cried and cried, too young to see what came to her eyes that day.

My baby fussed, wrapped in a blanket on the snow. Medicine Feet picked her up, rocked her in her arms, tried to quiet Mountain Girl. I dropped my carbine, took my baby, gave her my bosoms, tried to get calm myself. I never got used to bloodshed, even though the miners deserved what they got. I comforted Medicine Feet Woman—she never killed no one before. I felt proud of her. Lone Wolf would have been proud of his beautiful wife, how she fought, protected his daughter. I changed my mind about tipi women—they could fight good to protect kids.

We had to get out of there after we found Medicine Duck's

body, hide his body under rocks where other miners couldn't find him and cut him up—miners who might have heard the gunfight. Then we'd look for who friended us with rocks thrown at the miners.

Horses Loose rounded up our horses. Friend of Otter brought a pack mule and two miners' horses from their cabin, their weapons and scalps tied on the mule. We looked for Medicine Duck's body. Nowhere to be found—how'd an old man's body vanish to air?

A branch cracked.

"*Palani!*" shouted Horses Loose. Enemy!

The men grabbed their clubs.

Medicine Duck strolled in view from the hill above us. The old man faked he got shot, took off after the miners, threw rocks to show where they hid. My esteem for him rose high that day. I owed him a big favor.

"*Wówaš'ake paǧúŋta,*" he said. Mallard power, that's what gave him strong medicine. Nothing special he did, to his mind. We gathered for a talk—should we give up our plan to get to the Grandmother's Land? We almost got ourselves killed, our children orphaned or dead. We decided we'd keep heading north; being alive and not free, might as well be dead. I needed to find my husband.

In our hearts lived the spirit of the bravest man who ever walked this earth—Crazy Horse. If he told me to do something, I'd do it. He told us to follow his spirit north.

We covered the miner bodies with rocks in case their friends came looking. I made the men throw away their scalps—we might run into bluecoats.

We found a place to cross Belle Fourche River, reached the banks of the Little Muddy that flowed to near Fort Berthold on the Big Muddy. Easier traveling now, safer, too. Medicine Duck said he knew this land. Maybe we'd run into Slót'a, mixed blood Indian friends of Sitting Bull from his childhood days. We'd pay Slót'a with a miner horse to guide us to Sitting Bull's camp. By following the Big Muddy toward the setting sun, we'd come to Fort Benton. I knew that country. I thought about Medicine Duck's question about Makhá being round, me coming back to where I wifed Mr. McFadden. I feared what the old Scot would do if I ever ran into him.

Would I ever have peace, like when I lived in the Willamette, one day flowing gentle into another? Would my daughter grow up healthy and happy, maybe with a brother and sister coming from my body? Would I ever find a place to call my home on this earth?

That thought, those dreams, kept me going. I checked my skinning knife under my dress, ready for Mr. McFadden if he spotted me.

CHAPTER TWENTY-EIGHT
BACK ON THE BIG MUDDY

We made camp two moons later where the Little Muddy runs to the Big Muddy, far from gold miners, but near Fort Berthold, a Long Knife fort. We kept a lookout for fort soldiers and enemy Indians. Medicine Feet Woman and Friend of Otter set up our tipi; I nursed Mountain Girl. Medicine Duck kept watch. Horses Loose dug a firepit in the tipi; Medicine Feet's daughter gathered wood, got her ma's flint and dry leaves from our pony drag.

Horses Loose took his turn guarding on the knoll above us.

Medicine Duck relaxed by the fire in the tipi, shared stories. I liked his story about contests with a Húŋkpapa medicine man, Moon Rises Slow. In the old days, during the summer gathering of the seven council fires when Lakóta made the year's hunting plans, medicine men got together to see who had the best medicine. At a Kettle Dance, Medicine Duck challenged Moon to reach in the boiling kettle, pull out the head of a cut-up dog.

"Moon told me no one can do that anymore. 'I can,' I told my friend, 'and not get my hand hurt.' I reached in, pulled out the dog head, my hand not hurt at all. Moon asked how I did that. My best kolá, I showed him how to cook the *heyóka tapéžuta* root to protect his skin in boiling water. I want to see my good friend again."

Medicine Duck puffed his pipe, leaned against the backrest we brought for him, watched the fire die down. Skin over his eyes sagged from age. He fell asleep, snored how dogs do after chasing rabbits, pipe hanging from his mouth. He didn't look like a man who pretended he got shot, ran up a hill in snow, threw rocks at miners. All in a day's flow to him. Warriors didn't do much around a tipi except smoke the pipe and talk because of fear of attacks. They never knew when they would have to grab a club, protect children and women.

Friend of Otter had a long face in camp that night. When he got his feelings hurt, we let him be. We angered him because we wouldn't let him bring along his pet bird. He raised that crow bird ever since it fell from a nest at Fort Robinson. He named the crow, Parfleche. The bird could say "Hókahé," and liked learning new words. The bird might get us killed if he squawked when we ran into miners or bluecoats. Friend of Otter left Parfleche with a white trader by the name of Walton, at the reservation.

Next morning, after sunup, we came to wood piled alongside the Big Muddy where headed the last noisy fire-wagon of the fall. Medicine Duck had a plan. I'd use the wašíču tongue to ask the steamboat captain, when he docked for wood, if he might take us to Fort Benton, his final stop. We'd give him a mule and the miner horses for payment. I told the Duck I'd try. I thought about how I might charm the steamer captain with what I learned at Miss Brenda's. Medicine Feet Woman took my baby, wished me luck. I cleaned my face with snow, practiced a sweet smile while Friend of Otter combed my hair.

After the steamer docked, the captain put his eyes on me. Black hair stuck out the edge of his wool cap, pulled low above his sky color eyes. He spit tobacco, hand nervous on the revolver in his belt, eyed the peculiar Indians who wanted to talk.

"You have room on your steamer for our family, Cap'n? Take us to Fort Benton? Going back to the Grandmother's Land north of that town. We can pay for the ride with two horses and a mule."

The cap'n studied me, told his men to load the wood.

"You speak English—we met?" he said. "I ne'er forget a juicy colleen face, purty as yours."

Well, now, him thinking I looked purty gave me the upper hand. He spoke like the Ireland fellers who got blootered with Mr. McFadden. Steamboat captains played poker, downed whiskey with Mr. McFadden when they overnighted. I could not recall this feller at Miss Brenda's bordello or Mr. McFadden's trading post.

I smiled shy, how Miss Brenda said made a man want me more, looked down at his fanny-flap words.

"I do not think we met, kind sir. We want no trouble, not hostiles, as you can see. We are Slót'a Indians, from the Grandmother's Land. On a wander, trading along the way. We come from a visit to the miner yonder who married my sister, in the hills south. He gave us supplies and horses he had no need for, and a mule, to make our way home."

"Well, hallo, missy. Top of the mornin' to ya," he said, gave me a smile, chewed tobacco. "For aught I know, ya look familiar. Captain Féchin O'Shay here. What might be your name, Slót'a lady, if you please?"

"Pleased to meet you, Mr. O'Shay. Eagle Nose Woman here. This old man's my father. These others got blood with us, a Slót'a family headed home to the Grandmother's Land."

"Ya don't say? Eagle Nose Woman, huh? You think we run a bobtail steamer up this plash of a river for Indians? Just flag us down, hop aboard?"

He spit tobacco, wiped his mouth on his shirtsleeve, wanting me to sweet the offer. I knew what he wanted.

"I don't know what a bobtail steamer might be, sir."

"Well, Missy Eagle Nose, don't want to put the kibosh on

your family wander but I need more 'n a couple nags and a mule to ride this steamer. This ain't the Big Muddy streetcar for Indians. You sure we've not done a howdy somewhere on this slob of a river?"

I got nervous, tried to recall fellers I gave a night to at Miss Brenda's. Got me scared he might remember me, if he was a customer. Then the recall came—I spent time with Mr. O'Shay, bearded and plastered at the time with watered-down whiskey. Easy to call him to mind because he had his peculiarities in the robes. His religion would not let him get naked with a woman who was not his wife—he wore a wedding ring. He wore dirty pants and a wool shirt, had that same shirt on while we talked alongside the river.

Friend of Otter came while I thought on our predicament, signed for me to come with him.

" 'Scuse me, Mr. O'Shay, my cousin wants words." I smiled sweet, let him know I was considering what else I might offer him for a ride on his steamer. He spit tobacco, took his hand off his gun, folded his arms across his chest. He would get something real good, he figured—a squaw to warm him in his captain's bed on the Big Muddy steamer.

Friend of Otter took me to the miner's mule, showed me three pouches in the mule's bag. I had a look in the pouches.

I went back to Captain O'Shay.

"Maybe this will take care of the pay for a ride, Mr. O'Shay, a gift from my sister's husband to our father for letting him marry my lovely sister."

I handed him a pouch, let him look inside. He whistled. All thought of doing me in the captain's cabin on the steamer faded at the sight of gold. "Your sister must be a colleen perty as the Cliffs of Moher if a miner give such for her hand."

"She has that kind of beauty, Mr. O'Shay. And, since you seem kind, sir, our family has another gift, for you, and your men." I gave him another pouch.

He had a look in the pouch, ran yellow sand through his fingers. Smelled the gold.

"Eagle Nose, you make me a Tory with your fine gift. It'll git yours truly all the poteen and legal mash me and my boys can drink after we drop you and yours north side of this river. Good doing business with you and your family. Git your family on board, missy, and we be going to Fort Benton."

The steamer gave us a ramp up. I wouldn't have to shag this man to get my daughter and friends safe to the Grandmother's Land.

Mr. O'Shay blew the steamer whistle, fired the doctor engine, checked the ice shield on front, watched marks on the side to make sure we would not get stuck on a mud heap. We did a fire-wagon run to Fort Benton.

When we rounded the last bend in the river, a cannon fired from the levee of that old adobe fort. Once the steamboat unloaded whiskey barrels, drinks would drop to two bits, watered down at my Scot husband's robber house, four to one. I checked my skinning knife under my dress, thinking about what might happen if the old Scot saw me. Could I get him before he shot me?

Cannon fire meant the coming of more whiskey to Fort Benton folks, and all the crates crammed on the tween-deck. Medicine Duck climbed over the rail of the bottom deck when he heard the cannon. He would swim to get safe, urged us to join him.

"Just a wašíču way to say Hau," I said to Medicine Duck. "Don't jump, grandfather. River would freeze a body in no time."

Medicine Duck got off the rail, studied the sight. A crowd waited at the steamboat landing, traders lined up with their wagons, horses, and oxen for the barrels of whiskey to roll from the ship to the levee. I looked for Mr. McFadden, no sight of him in the crowd.

Medicine Duck slipped to my side. He had no idea wašíču had this much stuff as he saw roll down the plank from one fire-wagon. Ammunition, carbines, pistols, dolls, kerosene lamps, parasols, wool coats, blankets, tobacco, shovels, wood chairs, saws. Silk top hats that done in the beaver fur trade. Gloves, books, pots, knives, candles, medicines, wire, even candy, traded for furs, gold dust, or a night in the robes at a bordello.

"Do wašíču here make anything useful for themselves from this earth?" Medicine Duck said.

"Make their own troubles, grandfather."

He laughed, watched sights he never saw before. The sun shined bright that morning, coming up behind us, made the ice seem to dance on cottonwood branches. The streets were tore up, though fresh snow fell during the prior night. The wašíču world didn't look like what an Indian with any sense might want. I saw Keno Bill, who played cards with Mr. McFadden, smoking a cigar while barrels of *mní wakhaŋ* were loaded behind his mule team. No sight of my husband. Maybe if a wife cuts the tip off a man's privates, he doesn't show his face much around town.

Medicine Duck said, "They share this with kolá, daughter, have giveaway dances after they eat dog at a Kettle Dance?"

"No, grandfather. They sell this stuff for silver dollars. See the hide piles?"

More hides tied in bales than Medicine Duck imagined could come in this world. All shipped east. I saw over a hundred thousand buffalo hides and tongues shipped on one steamboat when I wifed Mr. McFadden. Mr. McFadden said over ten thousand beaver, fox, elk, bear, and deerskins were on that same steamer. A greenhorn hunter from Dodge City and his partner rode in without even a buffalo rifle. They got outfitted on what banks and mercantiles called credit. A wašíču could get six buffalo skinned a day, three dollars and fifty cents a hide to two fifty. Partners rode in not long after, paid off the credit, got enough money for a plow, mule, plow horse, seed, table and chairs. Become farmers.

Buffalo made farming possible like they made Indian life possible. But we used buffalo for food, knives, cooking paunches, needles, ribs made into snow sleds for kids. For clothes, robes to sleep under, tipis, beds, sinew for bows and leather for shields. Even boiled hooves for glue. The only thing Sioux didn't find a use for was the snort that comes out a buffalo nose. We used buffalo chips to light fires or tobacco in a pipe. Stuffed buffalo hair in a hide for an Indian ball game.

Now some Indians shot buffalo for the tongue, traded tongues for a whiskey jug.

I spotted the young wood-hawk customer of mine at Miss Brenda's—he waved his hat to the captain, pointed where he had his cut wood. Mr. O'Shay waved back, swigged on a whiskey jug. Living at Fort Benton, I saw two steamboat captains race on the river, crash their boats into each other, too drunk to turn.

After the wood-hawk sold his cottonwood to the captain, he'd drink the rewards of his labor, go to Miss Brenda's bordello, get shagged till he ran out of money.

We huddled like šuηka—dogs—on the mid-deck, between the main and the boiler decks where they stored hides. I thought on Medicine Duck's question about this earth. Here I came on my journey, back to the town where I wifed the ole Scot, but all had changed. The world didn't seem round to me. Lone Wolf, who met me along these shores, was with his ancestors. Our son was dead, too. I had a baby girl, no husband to protect me, and Custer couldn't write more books.

We walked off the steamboat later that day across the river, happy to be near the Holy Road, going to the Grandmother's Land. Mr. O'Shay waited for me at the end of the ramp, cap in hand.

"I won't forget you, missy. I ne'er forget a purty colleen face."

"Likewise, Mister O'Shay." I gave him a peck on his fuzzed cheek, for old time's sake. "And maybe get yourself a new wool shirt with our gift, Mr. O'Shay."

He laughed, waved to me as we rode north.

A Slót'a found us north of Milk River a day after we crossed the Marias River. "For one of your horses, I'll lead you to Tatáŋka Íyotake," the Slót'a said.

"Where's that?" Medicine Duck said.

"Cypress Hills, not far. Just cost you a horse."

We agreed on the terms of his kind offer. We rode with the Slót'a till sundown, set up camp. Next day we came to willows and water where we could rest, *Aŋpétu wi* overhead, shining bright.

Four soldiers in red coats rode from the willows, aimed rifles at our heads. The Slót'a laughed, waved, said, "Welcome to the Grandmother's Land, cousins."

The Slót'a rode off after redcoats paid him for the spying he did, never looked back.

Damn Injun took our miner horse, too.

We were prizners again.

CHAPTER TWENTY-NINE
THE GRANDMOTHER'S LAND

We stared at the redcoats, rifles aimed at our heads. A redcoat said *Hau,* motioned with his rifle to get off our horses. Not the welcome we expected from the Grandmother. Horses Loose and Friend of Otter looked to Medicine Duck. The Duck studied the redcoats, their rifles, motioned to get off our horses. I held my daughter, slid off my horse. Medicine Feet Woman ran to the pony drag to get her daughter.

The redcoats took our carbine, scalping knives, war clubs, Horses Loose's bow and quiver. We'd hid the pistols and rifles of the miners in tatáηka robes on the pony drag. They threw the robes to the ground, unwrapped them, found what we hid. The tall soldier had river otter hair under his nose; the other three stood shorter, clean shaved. They walked around stiff as lodge-pole pines, never smiled.

"Mini Wakan? Mini Wakan?" the big one yelled, the only Lakóta he knew besides *Hau.* We showed open hands. No firewater. Maybe these wašíču with red coats were going to line us up, shoot us in the back; we didn't know.

The redcoats didn't shoot us; they turned to the willows, out walked an Indian man. Redcoats needed help to figure what Indians came north with Sitting Bull, and which came with Nez Perce. Nez Perce, we heard, got near wiped out by Bearcoat's soldiers before Sitting Bull fought his way to the Grandmother's Land.

When the Indian saw Medicine Feet Woman, a big bent bow

smile crossed his face.

"Taŋkší!" he hollered.

Medicine Feet's worried eyes went happy. The Indian was Šiná Lúta—her older brother, Red Robe. She ran to him. "Tibló!" she said, tears flowed to see her "older brother." She took her daughter to hug the girl's uncle.

The soldiers held their rifles tight, taken aback by this Indian family stuff.

"That's her older brother, Red Robe," I said to a redcoat. He jumped, heard his tongue spoke by a woman who looked like she rolled in a buffalo wallow.

"Eh? Wha' you bloody sighin' ma'am?"

"What you say, soldier?"

"That wha' Ai astu. You speak our tongue, seem to my ear. You tahyken priznah by redskins?"

"I speak your tongue or you would not understand me, would you, but I do not understand what you say, soldier. You sick? Got a alder leaf stuck in your throat? I said that's her older brother, Red Robe."

One of the short ones, who spoke their tongue better, broke this up. "Where you folks headed? Looking for Bull's band, Little Knife's? Many Sioux bands here—Long Dog's, Crawler's, Four Horns's. Tell us and we'll see you get there safe."

"Tatáŋka Íyotake's tiyóšpaye," I said. We looked for Sitting Bull's band.

"Well, all right," the short one said, "Let's get a move on. We'll return your weapons at Fort Walsh. Chief Bull will be there, for a meeting with General Terry."

We got on our horses. The short one whispered to the big one with the otter hair under his nose; the big man nodded, studied me.

The short redcoat said, "Maybe you help translate at the

meeting, ma'am? Chief Bull does not trust the translator we use."

"That will be up to Chief Sitting Bull," I said. "He might not want a woman at a meeting of chiefs."

I rode to Red Robe, asked about the bluecoat general coming to meet chiefs. "One Star," Red Robe said, not happy about the meeting. "He sent bluecoats attacking us at Greasy Grass. Long Lance is chief of the redcoat fort where we head."

I thought we got away from bluecoats. Scared me to my freezing toes that a bluecoat general could reach across the Holy Road, and this General One Star would meet with our chiefs. If bluecoats got close enough to talk, that'd be close enough to kill.

That's what happened to Crazy Horse.

Medicine Duck said, through his missing tooth, "Čuŋkthi, these soldiers going to shoot us, take you women for themselves?"

"No, grandfather. A different kind of pony soldier—these Great Grandmother's soldiers."

I don't think he believed me. Medicine Duck rode on, hummed his death chant.

Medicine Duck said, "Great Grandmother? I know the four Great Grandfathers, do not know a wašíču Grandmother."

"Must be a powerful lady if pony soldiers do what she tells them," I said.

We traveled the rest of the day with our redcoat escort, over rolling, snowed hills, short grass, trees watered in ravines, and hills in the distance. Buffalo country. We came across deer at gully creeks. Šiná Lúta arrowed us a whitetail. I did the skinning with help from Medicine Feet. She cooked us a deer roast even redcoats wolfed down. For breakfast, redcoats served us beans and salted pork. I feared the pork would sour my milk for Mountain Girl.

With the sun straight up, we came over a ridge, caught sight of Fort Walsh on flat land below, a stockade fort. We whooped for joy—found our people, our kids still alive, and we kept our heads. I got off my horse, showed my daughter where she'd live, grow up, where we'd find her father. I couldn't wait to see him. I sat in the snow, cried like a baby. A whole new world opened up for us. Medicine Feet Woman hugged me, "Find him," she said, "find your husband."

Near the fort were log cabins and round canvas tents that came to a high point in the middle. Away from the tents given by the Grandmother's soldiers to our people, rose a buffalo hide tipi, Sitting Bull's lodge, the short redcoat said. Sioux families were coming to the fort in wheeled carts, like the carts Slót'a used, for the meeting with bluecoats.

What they called a Union Jack waved in wind on a pole inside the stockade. Women cooked outside tents to have food ready for friends coming from Cypress Hills. The men talked quiet around fires, wrapped in thick robes in the chilled air. Kids had buffalo rib sleds on a hill, slid down snow outside camp, filling the air with children's voices. My heart felt happy, seeing such sights, hearing sounds that meant we found a home.

Close to the fort I saw other Indians—Piegan Blackfoot, like those around Fort Benton. Also in the area, the soldier said—Assiniboine and Saulteaux, our old enemies.

"Come with me, please, ma'am?" the short redcoat said. "Sergeant will escort your friends to Red Robe's lodge. I want Major Walsh to meet you right away."

I said nothing, he had the carbine.

I left my friends, rode with the redcoat, nursed my baby. When I looked back, I saw Friend of Otter wave to a Húŋkpapa wíŋkte friend. Medicine Feet's folks ran from their lodge, and her cousins came, too, laughing, hugged her.

I kept an eye on everything. I'd hid a knife in my baby's

blanket when the redcoats searched for weapons. We rode through the stockade gate where the redcoat did a salute to soldiers. We stopped in front of a long wood building, curtains inside on glassed windows.

A soldier helped me from my horse, took him for watering.

"Thank you, soldier," I said.

He tipped his hat to me. Wašíču shake hands like sawing logs when you meet, tip hats like you want to see their hair when they leave. The raised palm of the Indian made more sense, showed no weapon in the hand. The hand shaking got our people a good laugh.

I entered Major Walsh's office.

Before me stood a big man with the most clear eyes I ever saw in a wašíču. I liked him before he said a word.

The short redcoat whispered to Walsh why he brought me. Walsh, called Long Lance by Red Robe, nodded, thanked the soldier, came around his desk to meet me. Black hair on his head, close cut above his ears, otter hair mustache above his lips. Fine-looking wašíču, in a clean, bright red coat.

"Madam, can I get anything for you, eh? Pot of tea? Something to eat?"

I spotted cattails in a tall vase under a window.

"Water, sir," I said. "And those cattails, if you can spare them, eh?" I talked his tongue like he did, best I could, like Mr. Tunbridge spoke.

He told the soldier to get me water.

"These?" Long Lance said, going to the cattails.

I nodded, unwrapped my baby from my chest, took a Seventh Cavalry scarf from my neck, spread the scarf on Long Lance's desk. He stared at the scarf like he saw a ghost. My baby fussed. Hard to hold a fussing baby and spread the scarf. Long Lance held out his arms, offered to take my child. He had large hands, eyes that hid no secrets, head cocked in a way men do when women live a world different than theirs.

"Pilámayaye," I said, thanked him, gave him my baby. "She needs a diaper."

"A nappy?"

"Whatever you call it, sir. She has need, as you can see."

My baby smelled worse than a buffalo wallow.

Major Long Lance put my baby over his shoulder, patted her back. Salted pork that redcoats cooked for breakfast soured my milk; Mountain Girl gave a heave of salted pork all over his pretty red uniform.

CHAPTER THIRTY
MEETING TATÁηKA ÍYOTAKE

I took my baby, laid her screaming self on the major's desk, broke the cattails open—their soft insides ready to do nappy work. Long Lance's uniform was covered with my daughter's throw up, his arms in the air like men do when a baby soils clothing plans for the day. He stared at the mess but held his tongue. A fine gentleman.

"You need translating, Major, eh?"

I put the knife in my belt that I'd hid in my baby's blanket.

"Oh. Yes, madam," he said, eyed my knife. "Uhh, General Terry comes with a commission from the Great White Father. Wants to talk with Chief Bull and other chiefs. We have a translator, but you could answer any questions General Terry has about the translation. Your English seems suitable. You speak Sioux?"

"Sweet Medicine Woman's my name. I speak our tongue, still learning. We speak Lakóta, *Lahkótah.*"

"Lakótah," he said, practicing.

"Means Joined Together Bands, sir."

He smiled like he understood, went around his desk to get a cloth from a drawer, wiped my child's breakfast from his uniform.

"Good, very good. La kótah, eh? Well, now. How aboot that? Bloody good, madam. You have a trader father? That how you learn the Queen's English?"

"Had me a white man stepfather from the Grandmother's Land taught me your tongue. I will translate at the meeting only if Tatáŋka Íyotake wants."

I took off my baby's wet clothes, washed her, used the water the soldier put on the desk. The soldier who stood in the corner hid a laugh at the sight. I gave him a smile. I liked these redcoats, different than the soldiers we'd fought.

"Čuŋkši," I whispered to my baby, "your mother's here."

My sweet daughter had an attack of *kajójoyeya*. The mess flew all over Major Long Lance's desk. Besides the smell came the noise, the horrid sound of a sick pony after chewing milkweed and drinking water. A flatulent Sioux pony could be heard by enemy Pawnee for a mile. My daughter alerted all the Pawnee between the Grandmother's Land and Omaha country with her performance. I left the messed cavalry neck scarf on Long Lance's desk, apologized, headed out the door with my squalling child.

"Will talk more later, sir. I have to take care of my child, as you can see, yourself. 'Scuse me, Major."

Friend of Otter waited for me outside the stockade, made sure I got safe out of the fort. He smelled my baby, laughed, took my daughter.

"*Kajójoyeya?*" he said, nuzzled by baby's neck.

"All over, kolā."

"I will make her more diapers. You hungry?"

"Pápa?"

"All the pápa you want."

Ahhh, real food.

I met Medicine Feet's folks again, first time was at Peži Slá Wakpá. They cheered when they saw my child. Sioux loved their children—that is why I liked to be with them. We ate and talked into the night, happy to be free. I asked Medicine Feet's father to introduce me to Chief Sitting Bull, had to know if he wanted me to translate. Bad translating at Fort Robinson got Crazy Horse killed. Medicine Feet's father feared taking me to meet

Chief Sitting Bull.

"I cannot do that," he said.

"Why not?"

"Sitting Bull mourns for his son," he said, "the son of his dead wife. That boy saw only nine winters. A white man sickness came in his chest. Our medicine men have no cure for white man sickness." He didn't say any names of the dead. "And he does not like One Star. Sitting Bull is in a very bad mood."

We heard scratches on the tent. Major Long Lance stood outside, soldier straight, a white dome hat under his arm. Beside him stood Tatáŋka Íyotake, my knees shaked. A chief never came to see anybody, folks went to see the chief.

"Chief Bull wants to meet the Oglála woman who speaks English," the major said. "I'm sorry. Can't recall her name."

My heart pounded. Mountain Girl was asleep; I laid her on a robe, got an encouraging hand from Medicine Feet Woman, went to meet Sitting Bull. Medicine Feet's mother stopped me, ran a wood comb through my squirrel's nest hair. I wore a clean doeskin dress. The major changed his uniform, too.

There Sitting Bull stood, over a head taller than me, in front of my short legs and pinhead, long arms, and wašíču nose. He seemed bigger than when I saw him hold a quick council with Húŋkpapa war chiefs at the Greasy Grass fight.

A silent time when Sitting Bull put his eyes on me, studied me, a not pretty girl going on seventeen snows. He stood taller than Crazy Horse, more 'n a few winters older. His chest, like the trunk of an old cottonwood. He could hold himself still, not breathe, study what had his interest. When his jaw clamped shut, his mouth looked like a beaver trap, his nose round as a wild onion. With a moon shape head, two braids hanging down his chest, dressed in dirty white man's clothes, old moccasins, held an old red blanket around his shoulders. One eagle feather

was braided in his hair. Medicine Feet's father got it right—
Tatáŋka Íyotake had himself a bad mood.

"Do not call me CHEEF," he said to Major Long Lance, in
the Lakóta tongue. That woke the redcoat. Sitting Bull spoke
Lakóta, expected me to translate. I looked at Long Lance,
translated firm and angry, like a wife giving words to a husband
who flirts with another woman.

"He does not want you to call him chief, sir."

Sitting Bull went on, loud, "I told you, I am no one's CHEEF
now. I have no land, nothing to give my people." He said to me,
gently, "Daughter, tell my words to this redcoat. Thank you."

I started to translate, realized what he said, could not stop
my words. "But you are our chief, of all the free Lakóta. We
have come here . . ."

"No, daughter. Have you no eyes? No awareness? Are you
not attentive? This,"—he backed up, opened his blanket to show
me his clothes—"is not a CHEEF, not in these rags."

His voice had anger, but I knew he had no anger at me; he
felt heated about the meeting with One Star. "We had to run
from bluecoats, grandfather," I said, "many moons, to be with
you, our chief. Where else can we run?"

Major Long Lance stood silent, not knowing what we talked
about with loud words. Probably figured I would not get to
translate for the chief I give a holler to, who hollered at me.

Friend of Otter snuck behind Sitting Bull, pacing back and
forth in his buckskin dress, giving me the eye stare of my life.
He feared my talking like that to the Húŋkpapa chief would get
us Oglála thrown out of the Húŋkpapa camp. I ignored him
because I believed in what I said. If Tatáŋka Íyotake wore nothing but a bull's tail around his neck, he'd be the chief of all us
free Sioux, in my view. Crazy Horse trusted him like a brother,
so I did.

I ran back in the tipi, grabbed my sleeping daughter, took her outside. I held out my daughter to Sitting Bull. He looked at her, confused. Did I want him to hold my baby?

"Tell my daughter you are not her chief. Go ahead, tell her. You will choke on your words, because they are not true. Where you go, we go. We do not care what clothes you wear, what warriors you have. All of us are warriors now. We die here, with you, if that has to be. Her, too."

Sitting Bull's mouth fell open, looked at Medicine Feet's father, behind me. "Where did you find this one?"

Medicine Feet's father looked down. Major Walsh looked down, too, fingered a button on his clean uniform. Sitting Bull stomped away. Friend of Otter motioned with his fingers for me to run after the chief, apologize for talking like that.

"Does he want you to translate?" Long Lance said.

Sitting Bull turned, held the blanket tight to his shoulders. "You bet!" he said in the wašíču tongue. The old fox knew some wašíču tongue. In Lakóta he said, "*That* voice can tell me what One Star lies about now."

Sitting Bull smiled to me, threw off the rag of a blanket from his huge shoulders, walked proud to his tipi. I found me a chief I'd follow anywhere, my daughter living free.

CHAPTER THIRTY-ONE
MEETING WITH GENERAL ONE STAR

Major Long Lance sent a redcoat to Red Robe's lodge to escort me to the meeting.

Medicine Feet's mother found a lovely doeskin dress for me, brushed my hair with the silver handle brush I gave Medicine Feet. I wore my old moccasins, a Hudson's Bay blanket around my shoulders that another woman shared, to keep out the chill. Medicine Feet Woman came with me to take care of my baby, but she would have to stay outside the meeting room. We didn't talk on the walk to the stockade fort. Friend of Otter stayed with friends the night before, joined us on our walk to the fort. He wore a buckskin dress.

Warmed my heart to see him, back to his spirit called self. We'd been through a lot together; it gave me courage, having them beside me. Scared me, too—going in a room of bluecoat who killed my son and husband.

Bluecoats waited for chiefs in the meeting room at the fort, and reporters for newspapers, too. I pretended I didn't understand a reporter who tried to talk with me after they learned I was a translator. Said he came from *Harper's Magazine*, a black and white paper I never heard about. Sitting Bull strode in, a Húŋkpapa woman with him. I wondered what the old fox had up his sleeve, bringing a woman to a talk of chiefs with Long Knives.

Chiefs shook hands with the redcoats, smiled like friends you invite to a party. General One Star and his officers stood to get in on the handshaking, Chiefs gave them the ignore, sat on the floor. Hate bounced off walls in that room.

Sitting Bull said, "We cannot see their faces over a table, tell them to sit on the floor like us."

The translator let the bluecoats know what Sitting Bull wanted. One Star didn't want to sit on the floor. He moved his chair in front of the table. Chiefs sat cross-legged on the floor, bluecoats on chairs. Long Lance sat me on the floor beside One Star. He told One Star he could ask me for translating that didn't make sense. One Star raised an eyebrow, gave me a look, nodded I could sit next to his chair. The idea of a talk between men who wanted to kill each other was a mystery to my mind.

One Star stood, gave his talk. Chiefs' bands would have a good life if they surrendered, came back peaceful, get good reservations, rations.

No chief looked at One Star while he spoke. The fancy pants General One Star seemed nearsighted as a buffalo, said, "You will receive cows, horses, and taught how to farm."

A chief could not help himself, he laughed at those words. One Star looked to me—maybe the translator had not got his words right?

"You promised farming to the chiefs," I said, *po*lite. "Farming does not hold much for wičaša, General. Digging holes in our mother, Makhá, is not respectful."

One Star got angered, grabbed his coat in front, his other hand behind his back. "If you return with your guns, you will be treated as enemy."

No one said a word after One Star sat down. After some time, chiefs spoke their mind, told One Star that the Great White Father broke every treaty made with Sioux—why make another one? One Star looked to me, see if the translator got the words right. I nodded that they did.

Tatáŋka Íyotake stood, everyone got quiet. This was the

savage the reporters thought killed Long Hair Custer in a one-on-one fight.

One Star sat on his chair with a leg over a knee, yellow stripes down his blue trousers. One of our chiefs wore a skinned-out buffalo head, feathers hanging from a buffalo horn. Sitting Bull's hair flowed over his chest, his right arm free of the blanket over his other shoulder. He wore a clean shirt, black leggings with red stripes—looked real good, not in rag clothes. Made me proud. Only one feather was in his hair, though from what I heard, he could wear more coup feathers than any chief—he counted over sixty coup. A elk teeth necklace hung around his neck. Sioux used only the front two teeth of elk for a necklace; more than twenty elk gave teeth for that necklace.

Bluecoats wore gold stars; Sitting Bull wore elk teeth and an eagle feather.

Sitting Bull began his talk.

"Wakáŋtáŋka gave us our land, not the white man. The white man came to look around, then you wanted to trade, wanted our tatáŋka hides, beaver skins, fox pelts, bear hides, elk and deerskins. We let trading posts come on our rivers. You brought firewater to trade with us. Our people got sick, in their minds, from your crazy water. We said we would trade with you, but our people would hunt our animals.

"Then you wanted to hunt on our land. We tried to get along. The white man broke every treaty ever made with us; name a treaty you ever kept with our people. Name one."

I looked to a window. Medicine Feet Woman lifted my baby to her chest, let me know my daughter was hungry. I touched two fingers to my head, would come soon as I could.

One Star looked at the floor, the talk not going good for our surrender. Newspaper reporters with the commission scribbled on paper like field mice digging mouse food hid in grass bundles.

Sitting Bull looked at One Star, yelled, "Get out of this land."

The room got quiet; Major Long Lance called a break to cool the room. I needed a rest, and milk leaked under my dress. I went outside, took Mountain Girl from Medicine Feet, put out of my mind the angry words and craziness in that room, hummed to my baby, nursed her.

"Well?" Medicine Feet said.

"Sister, I am too worn out from their angry words to talk."

"What do they say? We have to go back?" Her eyes intent, afraid.

"Chiefs tell them to sit on their flagpole, sister. We are not going back."

"Wašté," she said, calmed down.

One Star came to me, "Young woman, I have a message for Chief Bull. I am not getting the respect my rank entitles me."

"Yes, sir?" I said, *po*lite.

"Your people call me One Star, but you call General Crook, 'Three Star'—the one you fought at Rosebud Creek and sent running, tail between his legs. I have more stars than General Crook. Will you tell that to Chief Bull?"

I told him I would. He tipped his hat, showed me his hair. We went back to the meeting.

The Húŋkpapa woman, who came with Sitting Bull, gave her talk. She told about the harm white men gave her and her family. Pony soldiers attacked so often she didn't have time in the robes with her husband. Sitting Bull laughed from deep in his belly. I tried not to laugh, but couldn't stop, hid my face. One Star looked to me, "What did she say? What's funny? Time with her husband—what?"

"She said your soldiers didn't give her time in the robes with her husband, sir."

The reporters laughed, but not One Star.

"What does that mean?" he wanted to know. He motioned for me to come closer to him. I crawled close, whispered in what seemed his good ear.

"Your soldiers didn't give her time with her husband."

"Time for what?"

"Sir, there are others in this room. Lean closer, please." He put his good ear close to my lips. "No time to shag her husband, sir."

"No time to feed him, cook for him?" He leaned closer, my lips touched his good ear.

"No time, like you folks say, to F her husband, sir."

"Oh," One Star got red-faced.

The chiefs stood to leave.

"Your answer to the Great White Father is No?" One Star said.

Sitting Bull yelled, "This is our side of the Holy Road, go back to your side!"

Chiefs left the room, me too. Sitting Bull came to me. "Daughter, you give words to him how that woman spoke."

"Best I could."

He laughed, one of his huge Sitting Bull laughs. I told him One Star wanted him to know he had more stars than Three Stars. Sitting Bull roared, almost coughed, he laughed hard.

When he caught his breath, he said, "That man goes home with no stars, daughter."

Outside the fort, I said to him, "I need your help, grandfather."

Sitting Bull waited for me to speak.

"A Húŋkpapa man, who came north with you, asked me to be his wife, meet him here. I have his daughter to show him. Will you help me find him?"

"What man?"

"Two Horns," I said.

Sitting Bull took a breath, put a comforting hand on my shoulder.

"Come to our lodge, daughter, meet my mother, then we talk about your husband."

I got the shakes. Why could he not tell me where to find Two Horns? I took my baby from Medicine Feet Woman, followed Sitting Bull to his lodge.

He introduced me to Her Holy Door, his mother. How did such a big man as Sitting Bull come from such a little woman? Age and worry about her people were carved in her cheeks. They sat me beside a low fire, my baby in my arms. He whispered to his mother, sitting quiet on robes.

Sitting Bull rested against his bone backrest. "I knew your husband, daughter."

"*Knew* him? What do you mean?"

"On the way to the Grandmother's Land, a river flooded a camp. Your husband tried to save his uncle from drowning, the husband of Horse Tail Woman. Both men drowned. A very brave man. I am sorry."

His mother, Her Holy Door, came to me, put her arm around me. I could not get air, my mind left. Sobs came deep, I fell to her arms, fainted dead away. Never knew a kick to the head could make a mind shut to the world.

I put all my hope for happiness with Two Horns, to raise our daughter with him, have more babies. What Sitting Bull told me came out of nowhere, like the killing of my son and my dear Lone Wolf. No chance to get my mind ready. Always be *auda*cious my pa said, not give up. I think I gave up that day.

I woke in Sitting Bull's lodge. No one was in the lodge except Medicine Feet Woman and Friend of Otter, on robes near the fire, waiting for my mind to come back.

"We will cry with you, sister," Medicine Feet said. She came, lay down beside me on the robes, mothered me. Friend of Otter held my hand.

After they let my tears run, no more tears coming, my friends walked me to Red Robe's lodge. My feet didn't seem to touch ground. Friend of Otter held me, kept me walking. I asked to be alone.

When they saw I would not harm myself, they took my baby, left me to do my tears. They had in mind what a Cheyenne woman did after soldiers captured her in the freezing Wolf Mountains. She kept a revolver hid under her dress at the soldier camp. She could not stop her tears, thought her husband got killed in the fight, or ran off and left her. She didn't use the gun on bluecoats. When alone, she put the gun to her head, pulled the trigger.

I thought that night to put a gun to my head.

Medicine Feet took me to woods outside camp. I asked her to come. She lifted my dress, I took my knife, slashed my leg under the cut I did for Lone Wolf. Medicine Feet had her hand on my shoulder, spoke no words. The flow of blood felt good, felt right. I slashed my other leg, watched blood follow the blade across my skin, down my ankle, form a pool in my moccasin.

I moved the knife to slash my leg again. Medicine Feet grabbed my hand.

"Enough, sister," she said.

She took snow, rubbed snow on my cuts, the white of snow turning a cherry color. My mind was as numb as my leg. The blood flow stopped; Medicine Feet cleaned my knife with snow.

"We go home now," she said, handed me the knife.

I had a daughter to keep alive.

★ ★ ★ ★ ★

Part III
My Húŋkpapa Life

★ ★ ★ ★ ★

Chapter Thirty-Two
Becoming a Huŋka Daughter

I lived with the Húŋkpapa—Medicine Feet Woman's people—also my husband's and baby's people. Medicine Feet's family and Friend of Otter were all I had for family. I couldn't ask for more loving people in my life. We camped by a stream in Cypress Hills our first summer on the Grandmother's prairie and hills we called home. One day, Sitting Bull came to talk with me. With him came his mother, Her Holy Door. They got me scared—what did I do wrong now?

"My mother and I talked," Sitting Bull said. "I will do the Húŋkapi with you, if your heart agrees. My mother will teach you what you need to know. You should become a relative of Húŋkpapa, you have a Húŋkpapa child."

His mother smiled, her heart wanting me for her son's relative. I could not speak, choked up.

"Oooo," all I could say. "Oooo."

Sitting Bull touched my arm, gentle. "Is that how a peculiar woman agrees?"

I put two fingers to my forehead, lowered my eyes. They left.

The Húŋkapi was the making of relatives. I saw the Húŋkapi done at a Sun Dance before the Greasy Grass fight, didn't understand all the fuss. They said a holy man name of Matohošila learned the Húŋkapi from Wakáŋtáŋka, the Great Mystery, or maybe they meant the Great Mysteriousness of this whole world.

"Like the Wakáŋtáŋka and our people, that is how close love

must be between you and my son," the little lady said.

I cried. My own father didn't know he had a daughter. My ma traded me like a beaver skin. Now, near seventeen snows, there were few in my life who wanted to be close to me.

Her Holy Door wiped my tears. "Hush, čuŋkši. Much work to do, much you must learn. You speak our language, have a Húŋkpapa child. Now you become a relative of my son."

Her Holy Door said the next day, teaching me. "A holy day comes. You will learn to walk in a holy way. That is what Lakóta means, to walk in a holy way."

Holy way? I had no idea what the little lady talked about. I done killing, Quarter Hole work in a bordello, stole horses, killed men I didn't know.

The morning of the Húŋkapi, Friend of Otter scratched on our tipi, peeked in, all smiles.

"Hurry. No feast till after the Húŋkapi," he said. Friend of Otter opened his big arms to me; I ran to his chest. He wore a clean buckskin dress, beads around the neck of his dress, flowing over his shoulders. We both wore silver conch sashes around our middle, trailing to the ground. I felt like a doll, a pretty doll, a girl someone might want to hold close. I felt good.

"Aaiiii. You smear my dress," he said. My red cheek paint smeared on his buckskin.

"You look lovely," I said.

He looked down, shy at the words, but he liked what I said.

"Maybe I look better than when you had me cut my hair and we raided Crow horses," he joked.

"I still got my peculiarities," I said, joked him back.

He said if Tatáŋka Íyotake didn't mind my peculiarities, he wouldn't.

Medicine Duck waited in the big lodge, all dressed up, ready to do the first day's ceremony.

Sitting Bull stood quiet, waiting to become my húŋka Até,

my húŋka Father. He would be responsible for my proper upbringing. All those who'd gone through a Húŋka sat in the lodge. I sat next to Sitting Bull, a tiny seed next to a huge cottonwood.

Medicine Duck, his hands painted red, waved two sticks with horsehair over us. In front of us was a buffalo skull. On the skull, a stick stuck through an ear of corn they brought from Arikara friends, who grew corn. Her Holy Door taught me, "Čuŋkši, when you look at that corn, know corn comes from our Mother. We must treat Her with respect, and all Her animals she gives us for food. Like you feed your daughter from your body, our Mother feeds us. Understand?"

"Yes, grandmother."

I didn't understand, though, a heathen to any religion—but I wanted to.

Medicine Duck chanted, the people sang. Medicine Duck painted my face red and Sitting Bull's face got red paint with a blue circle and lines. I watched Medicine Duck's skinny legs in front of us while he did the face paint—his leg scars, old man veins, legs that ran up a hill to throw rocks at miners. Now, lonely legs with no woman to walk with him the last steps of his life. He tied eagle feathers in our hair, waved a stick over us while singers sang to the Sky, Earth, and the Four Directions of Makhá.

On the second day, Medicine Duck put a buffalo robe over Sitting Bull and me, crawled under the robe with us.

It was dark under the robe, I could hear those two men breathe, men who wanted to give me honor. I heard Major Walsh cough, an eagle screech above the lodge. Heat from Tatáŋka Íyotake's body warmed me—becoming my húŋka father. I had no idea how to feel like a man's daughter, closer than a blood relative, they said. Sweetgrass burned in the great lodge firepit, the smoke making everything smell holy. Even to me.

I thought back on what happened, and the prayer Medicine Duck sang on the first day. "O, Grandfather, Wakáŋtáŋka, we make peace and relatives. This smoke brings our prayer to You, Who are First, and our holy Mother Earth, and the Four Directions. May all people live in peace."

All this peace and love talk confused my mind, with the horse stealing, warring, scalping that went on right regular. Mr. McFadden got me baptized in Big Muddy water, got us a preacher to make us married, supposed to make doing me in the robes something proper. Somehow, doing things proper made them good. My father didn't think my ma was his wife till they married in his church. I decided to give Sitting Bull's idea a try with this Húŋka, learn how to live holy and proper.

Medicine Duck had a buffalo bladder on the ground in the great lodge the first day, offered tobacco to where the sun set, chanted in his old voice, "We make on earth the same relations between these two that the Wakáŋtáŋka has with us." The Wakáŋtáŋka—the Great Mystery. How could I ever hope to understand such things?

He put tobacco on the bladder. The bladder, Her Holy Door told me, was the world around us, a thought beyond my mind.

"Grandmother Earth," Medicine Duck sang, "two-leggeds, four-leggeds, creatures with wings and all that move on You, are Your children. We shall be relatives with all." Then he sang, "May we walk with love and mercy, O Mother, on a holy path."

The buffalo bladder with the offerings got passed around for everyone to kiss who went through a Húŋka ceremony. I never thought kissing a buffalo bladder might make me feel holy, but kissing the bladder gave me a holy feel—first time in my life. They passed the bladder outside the lodge to all waiting for the ceremony to end. Everyone kissed the bladder.

At the end of the second day, Sitting Bull and me sat under the robe; Medicine Duck lifted the robe and somehow he'd tied us together, our two closest arms and legs. Folks cheered. I wondered how the Duck did that; I never felt his hands tie nothing on me.

Then came gifts between my húŋka father and me. Friend of Otter led a horse from behind Sitting Bull's tipi. He gave the rope on the horse's neck to Tatáŋka Íyotake. Sitting Bull walked toward me, leading the most beautiful horse I ever saw, all white.

"To be Húŋkpapa is to own a horse. This horse is yours."

I walked to the beautiful horse, not believing my eyes.

"A horse? It is too, too . . ."

"No," Sitting Bull said. "Just right, what I give to you. Do not argue with your húŋka father." Then he whispered, "Not in front of our relatives. You must learn proper manners, daughter."

Not the time to argue with my chief, my húŋka father. I must gift him. With Medicine Feet's help, I beaded on leather around a pipe we traded for, with Blackfoot. The beads, not lined up straight, but I did the best my little fingers could do. I handed the beaded pipe to Sitting Bull with both my hands, hoped he liked what I gave him, the beading, too. His eyes wandered the beads on the pipe, looked at the crooked sewed beads, smiled. His smile warmed me, the kindness he showed this girl. I wanted to say, "Father, I can shoot the eye of a beaver at fifty paces, but I can't bead."

"When I smoke this pipe," Sitting Bull said, "I will think of my húŋka daughter, who learns to walk in a holy way with our people." He leaned to my ear, "You will act proper now? Not embarrass me?"

I touched two fingers to my forehead, understood his words. I thought that was all of the gifts.

He said, "Look there, čuŋkši. Your húŋka father is not a beggar, yet."

I looked in back of his tipi, walked over. Another tipi was there, with Sitting Bull's coup deeds painted on the sides. The setting sun glowed through the tipi. My knees got wobbly.

"Oooo," was all I could say.

My heart swam in my head. He lived so poor, he should not do this for me. Sitting Bull's two wives came from that glowing tipi, held open the flap to let us see all that a woman needed for a home, for me and my daughter. There were buffalo robes on the ground, dew liners up the sides, more metal pots than I knew what to do with, and a bone backrest.

I could not speak. My hands covered my mouth, I bit my lip, I would not embarrass him with words. I could not stop tears running down my not pretty face. I wanted to say, "I have nothing holy in me, how can I live holy?" But held my words. I wanted to give him another gift; I ran to Medicine Feet's tent.

When I returned, I said, "For you, father. All I have in this world, except my child and friends."

I handed him the most precious thing I owned, the coup feather Crazy Horse gave me, in memory, too, of Lone Wolf's fight at Greasy Grass.

Sitting Bull took the feather, curious.

"Tašúηke Witkó's coup feather that he gave to me," I said. "He gave the feather his blessing."

"Brother Crazy Horse gave you a coup feather?" He leaned to me, no one else could hear, "What did you do to earn this coup feather, daughter? This is a holy day. I cannot receive a gift that is not holy."

"Father, is horse stealing holy?" I said.

"That is how you earned this feather, you stole a horse?"

"Two."

"Depends on whose horses you stole." He studied me.

"Psáloka horses."

"Ahh, that is holy, daughter," he said, laughed till tears came.

Sitting Bull turned to Four Robes, one of his two lovely wives. She smiled to me, tied the coup feather in his hair. "I will wear brother Crazy Horse's feather," he said. Sitting Bull whispered to his mother. She pointed to the feather with her chin.

"Wašté," she said. Good.

I found my father for long as grass growed, rivers flowed, with me and him on this earth.

CHAPTER THIRTY-THREE
FAMILY QUARREL

Major Long Lance yelled in Sitting Bull's lodge next to my tipi. Scared me; I never heard Long Lance angered like that. "I told you, Chief Bull, your people should not raid south of the Holy Road! Should not raid for horses anywhere. Four of your men stole a hundred and fifty damn Slót'a ponies and if you don't punish them, I sure as hell will."

His translator told Sitting Bull what angered the major. Raiding horses was the most fun thing young Sioux could do. The winter had been peaceful in the Grandmother's Land, but with the coming of the Month When the Ponies Shed, bored boys snuck out on horse raids before their mothers woke up.

Sitting Bull slipped over to my tipi to give thought to what the major said. He sat slumped against the bone backrest.

"I understand a young man's heart, daughter," he said, made a fist in his lap, let it go. "They saw us earn coup feathers fighting Psáloka, Hohes, Šahíyela. They think life is not fair if they cannot earn feathers. But I have to punish these horse thieves."

"I thought stealing horses from enemy was holy," I said, gave him a buffalo horn of heated soup from the kettle hanging over buffalo chip coals in my firepit.

"Redcoats do not see raiding for horses like we do. Everything gets mixed up by the white man. They need to be more aware, daughter."

Sitting Bull used the word abléza meaning something like "be aware," to describe what wašiču needed. Without abléza, things

216

were only what they looked to the eye. A rock is a rock; horse stealing is bad, a crime. But with awareness, you could see the spirit of stone rise in the sweat lodge when water splashed on stone. And know a warrior's Guardian spirit was pleased when he stole horses from enemy.

Sitting Bull sipped soup from the horn, thought about his problems, talked to himself. "I sent tobacco to Chief Crow Foot last summer. I knew we had to get along with Blackfoot. Even named one of my twin sons Crow Foot. Yet his hunters came to our land. Daughter, if I have to watch our men, does not Crow Foot have to watch his?"

"Blackfoot know you fed their starving hunting party this spring?" I said, refilled his horn with venison soup.

"I loaded them down with bags of food," he said. "Hungry Blackfoot, I fed them. Just a bunch of horse thieves if you do not watch them. You helped my mother and wives and daughter cook for them. You saw what we gave, for three moons. This soup you made is real good, daughter."

My chest wanted to burst with pride at those words.

Sitting Bull fed Blackfoot to get their chief, Crow Foot, to join him in attacking Bearcoat across the Holy Road. Sitting Bull was not finished with his war. Crow Foot feared to attack, though. Bearcoat and Tatáŋka Íyotake had a grudge; neither would back down. The Nez Perce chief, White Bird, said he'd attack across the Holy Road with Sitting Bull. White Bird even put the idea into Sitting Bull's head to send tobacco to the Crow, see if they would join him in one final war against bluecoats. The Crow not only turned down the offer, they stole a hundred of our horses.

The problem with Sioux stealing Slót'a horses—Sitting Bull's own brother-in-law, Gray Eagle, led the raid on Slót'a horses. Sitting Bull gave his favorite horse so he could marry Gray Eagle's sister, the older sister of Sitting Bull's wife, Four Robes

Woman. Four Robes wanted her older sister, Seen by the Nation, as a co-wife. Not easy for Four Robes Woman to wife a chief by herself. To give a great horse, like Sitting Bull gave for another wife, showed how much Sitting Bull wanted to please Four Robes Woman.

Sitting Bull sighed, walked slow back to his lodge, heavy of heart.

I felt sorry for him, but there was nothing I could do.

The next day, Sitting Bull hollered at the four horse thieves, "No food or water for seven moons! You will be staked to the ground. Never again will you forget your people for your own selves."

I tried to mind my own business, shook robes outside my tipi. Mosquitoes swarmed around me like flies on buffalo chips, thick; you could suck in a mouthful after you yawned. Sitting Bull's wives followed him back into their lodge, pleaded for their brother. I could not hear what they said; I shook my robes closer to their lodge.

"He only did one wrong thing, his whole life," Four Robes Woman said. "My husband, do not punish our brother like that."

Seen by the Nation was on him, too. "He fought bravely at Greasy Grass. Do not punish Gray Eagle by staking him in the sun. Do not punish him like a dog. Or," she said, angered, "you will regret what you do."

The younger wife peeked outside their lodge, caught me trying to hear the fight. She motioned I should come in. When I walked past, she said, "Help us talk sense into our husband, he likes you."

Sitting Bull's mother took her leave, not wanting to get in the middle of a husband and wife fight. Sitting Bull sat across from the entrance to their lodge, leaned against his bone backrest. He had his stubborn jaw—an angered bull.

"He shamed our people," Sitting Bull said to the older sister.

"Yes. And now he is shamed enough," Seen by the Nation hollered back, eyes narrowed at her husband. "You make an enemy of Gray Eagle if you do this."

"Unnnnnnn," Sitting Bull muttered, his jaw tighter.

He married two sisters, he told me, because sisters got along. He hated nagging, sent away an earlier wife because of how she nagged. Now those sisters ganged up on him to save their brother.

Affection between a Sioux sister and her brother were stronger than with a husband. I left their lodge, not wanting in the middle of a family fight. That night, Four Robes Woman and Seen by the Nation brought their noisy kids to my tipi. The women said nary a word, didn't ask if they could move in. I'd become family, stuck in the middle of a family fight.

"Sleep by the fire, sisters," I said, scratched my head, wondered how this would go. I held the baby daughter of Four Robes Woman while she placed robes around my tipi. The two-year-old twin sons of Sitting Bull—Crow Foot and Run Away From—slipped quiet under a robe next to my dew liner. Even Sitting Bull's lovely teenage daughter, Many Horses, joined the fight to help her uncle, Gray Eagle. Sioux uncles and nieces and nephews hung together in family fights. Snuggling in the robes with Seen by the Nation were her two young boys from a dead husband. One of those boys was Little Soldier, the other was Blue Mountain—sometimes called Looking Horse. Sitting Bull adopted those boys.

The message of the wives to their husband was clear—Sitting Bull would sleep alone in his robes, get meals from his mother if he staked out their brother.

I felt sorry for my huŋka father. I took him soup that night, his mother welcomed me to their lodge.

"Father, may I speak?"

Sitting Bull, not happy, never looked up, motioned for me to sit across from him.

"You sure you want to stake out their brother?" I said.

"You, too?" he yelled, shook his head, not believing I sided with his wives. He sipped soup. "I hate nagging, daughter."

"I do not want to nag, father, but your family sleeps in my lodge. I do not mind. I worry about you, if you stake out their brother. They might leave you, take your children."

My concern calmed him. "You think that might happen?" he said, worry showed in his eyes. How could he be chief, set a good example, if his wives and kids moved out?

"I once had a Húŋkpapa woman angry at me," I said, "I would never want that again. You have two Húŋkpapa women angered now, father. Two of the best women in camp. It does not matter to them if you are chief. You told me—family should come first in my life. Seems to me that's what your wives want now. They are willing to give up a husband to protect a brother who looked after them, long before YOU came into their lives."

I went back to my lodge before he got more angered.

Next day, Gray Eagle got spared the staking out, but Sitting Bull made the horse thieves run across a field while other warriors fired rifles over their heads, scared them near to death. Three horse thieves got staked out on the grass for seven moons, no water or food. Their mosquito-sucked bodies looked like something a vulture would think twice on before ripping into.

Sitting Bull kept peace in his family. The sisters and their kids moved back to his lodge. I got my tipi back. Sitting Bull didn't speak to me for seven moons, never looked my way when I walked by.

I wanted to yell in his face, "You should thank me! I helped you stay warm at night, eat the best food in camp, and have love in your lodge—I did that for you, the girl *you* call peculiar."

I held my words. Maybe he'd never talk to me again, and I'd lose the only real father I ever had.

CHAPTER THIRTY-FOUR
LEARNING HOW TO ROAST ELK LEG

Sitting Bull showed up at my tipi, made me very happy, I almost hugged him.

"Too noisy in my lodge, daughter."

He talked like nothing bad happened between us.

"Sit, father, please," I said, my heart singing; we were on speaking terms again. I propped up his bone backrest near the fire. If a father and daughter argued, did they get over the fights, love each other no matter what happened? I didn't know.

I had a heháka leg outside, roasting over a fire. Me and Medicine Duck hunted the elk because Medicine Duck met the widow, Horse Tail. Two Horns tried to save her husband from drowning. The Duck wanted to impress the widow, looking as he was for another wife. I agreed to have a feast for her, her two married daughters, and Medicine Duck. I was determined to get the hang of Sioux cooking on my own, not be a peculiar woman.

Sitting Bull went outside to study the elk leg hung over the low flame fire, elk fat crackling. He had the pipe I gave him, filled the bowl with tobacco, took a light from the fire, came back in my tipi, smoked, sat peaceful against his bone backrest.

"That leg will not be ready until tomorrow, čunkši."

"I know, father. Tomorrow I feast a widow, her relatives, and Medicine Duck."

He puffed on his pipe, watched the flames outside my tipi flap. "I am glad you feast that widow. Good to share what you have, daughter."

I didn't say Medicine Duck had the idea for the feast, that he wanted the widow for a wife. I let our chief praise me. His moon face relaxed. Sometimes, looking at a new moon, I see his face, how he looked when he dropped in for a visit, sometimes with his mother, to get away from meetings with Long Lance, arguments with other chiefs about what to do about surrendering to bluecoats. The noise in his tipi could get fierce, with all their kids. The sisters wanted to share a large lodge, he agreed.

My daughter, Mountain Girl, fussed that night. Sitting Bull laid his pipe on a stone near my firepit, picked her up, placed her gentle over one of his huge shoulders, patted her back until she quieted, went to sleep. I quilled, kept watch on the elk leg roasting over the pit outside.

"Could I ask about your family?" I said.

"You want stories tonight, daughter?"

"Yes. Stories, about your family." I loved family stories.

"Stories about our tiyóšpaye. Well, you are not the first iyéska brought into our family, just the most peculiar," he said, laughing at what he thought about having a breed like me in his family.

He laid Mountain Girl in her cradle, pulled a robe over his legs, lit his pipe, leaned against the backrest.

I said, curious, "What breed was not peculiar as me?"

"He's not here, now. Went with that old woman, Chief Red Cloud, to a Gift House. He came from people who lived on an island in the Great Water." He pointed where the sun set.

"This a joke?"

"It is true."

He laughed, thinking about a crazy story.

"Now that I think about it, he was more peculiar than you. He became our enemy."

Sitting Bull told me about a man called Grabber, son of

Mormon missionary and woman who lived on an island where the sun set; he came to live in this land. Another missionary adopted the Grabber, but at fifteen snows he ran off, bored by how those people lived. He delivered mail by horse, became a bullwhacker for freight oxen, had fights with the law. Sioux captured him, but Sitting Bull saved his life, adopted him as a brother.

"My older sister, Good Feather, thought Grabber was a good man, taught him to speak our language. Later, he ran off to be with the Crazy Horse. Surely you saw him."

I told him I never saw Grabber but heard his name at Fort Robinson. He translated words of Crazy Horse, messed up the translation that got our chief killed. Oglála called him Standing Bear. Grabber was a nickname for the bear's way of grabbing.

"That crazy man came back to us, tried to talk me into surrendering, like Red Cloud. Said I should become a farmer. He ran away from that boring life. I made a mistake in adopting him. I will never farm. Never. Not a holy way to live. I tried to have him killed when he scouted for Three Star, before the Greasy Grass fight."

What he said got my attention—my father tried to kill a breed he adopted. He got perturbed, watching the elk roast.

"What? What?" I said, looked up from my quilling, poked my finger with a needle. I tried not to spill the turtle shell cups I used for dyeing quills.

"Too high, čunkši," he said. "The wíkaŋ tied to the leg should be lowered, or you must put more wood in the fire. You smoke the leg the way you do it. If a woman wants a husband, she has to know how to at least roast elk leg and make rabbit soup."

I glanced at my turtle shells, looked helpless at him. He grumbled like I asked him to move the Backbone of the Earth, but he lowered the elk leg. He felt better when he made the leg hang right.

"There. That's the way to do it, daughter. Who gave you this heháka? Or is it uηpáη?" Made a difference to a man who knew his food whether the elk I roasted was a male or a female. Different taste, they said.

I never could tell the difference.

"Heháka," I told him. A bull.

"That old man, Medicine Duck, can shoot a rifle? Must have good medicine. I didn't know old medicine men could hit snow on a mountain with a rock."

I figured praise was due where praise was earned. "Medicine Duck helped track the elk, that is all. I shot the elk, behind the ear."

Sitting Bull looked at me like I told a tale. "Unnnnn?" he said to that. Then he said, "Got a metal pot?"

I motioned with my chin to the supplies behind the dew liner. He found a pot we took from the gold miners, made a place for the pot in the fire outside, stuck the pot there. Elk fat dripped in the pot.

"Have mushrooms, daughter?" He got excited.

I shook my head—No. He got up slow, favored the leg below the hip where he got shot when younger, limped out. He returned with dried čhaηηákpa and spices his mother brought when Bearcoat chased Húηkpapa north. He dropped wild mushrooms and chokecherry leaves in the pot, added ground bear root, stirred the juice with a stick, didn't say a word. I learned a woman should bring her spices with her; even when rivers flood, bluecoats attack, babies get sick, and your son is the chief of all the confusion.

He smiled, bent over the pot, smelled the sauce for the roast. "Mmmmmm," he said. He returned to my tipi, sat down, leaned against his backrest. "Never get another husband if you do not learn how to cook, daughter. Húηkpapa women are the best cooks in the world."

225

"Not sure I want another husband," I said. "They get killed, or drown, and leave a woman with a child to care for by herself."

"That is foolish talk," he said. "A woman needs a man; a man needs a woman. Maybe you spend too much time with that wíŋkte. You should have more children. Let ancestors come to us in the bodies of babies. We only pass through this world in these bodies, like that heháka, passing through that smoke. The heháka spirit, though, it's goooooooone." He motioned with his arm towards the west. "Tó-kȟah'-aaaaaŋ."

He sat up straight, crossed his legs, alert. "You say you shot this elk? You?"

I told him I shot the elk. He squinted, studied me. "No need to lie, daughter."

"Wówičakhe šni? *Lie?* I never lie. Well, not to friends, never to you. I shot this elk with my own máza wakȟáŋ. That is the truth."

I threw down the dress and needle, crawled to the dew liner behind me, grabbed the carbine we stole at Fort Robinson. "This is mine," I said, angered, tossed the carbine to him, went back to quilling. He caught the carbine, looked down the gunsights.

"You would bite the knife and swear you shot that elk?" If I lied and bit the knife, I would die by a knife.

"I will bite anything to prove what I say is true."

He studied me. In his mind, a young woman, with no training he knew about, claimed she could track and shoot an elk. "How far away was that elk?" He narrowed his eyes, like he did when he suspected a lie.

"Opáwiŋǧe paces. Across a river."

"Opáwiŋǧe!" He knew a hundred-pace shot. He wasn't that good with a carbine, himself. He could not tolerate what he thought was lying. He reached into his sheath, pulled out his deer-handled steel blade, the middle part of that blade was wide as my hand.

"Bite the knife." He studied me, to see if I hesitated.

I took the knife, turned it flat, clamped down hard with my teeth. I looked fierce at him, he glared at me. I took the knife from my mouth, dropped it on the robe. He put the knife in his sheath, his stern look gone—a buffalo no longer interested in a fight.

"I believe you," he said.

I went on quilling. "Good," I said. "No need to ever doubt my word, father. I do not need to bite the knife to speak truth to you, ever. I can shoot the eye of a beaver at fifty paces, if the truth be told. My mother married a trapper from the Grandmother's Land. He taught me how to shoot good. I'm no good with a revolver, but I have no arm trembles with a carbine. One of the two gifts the Great Mystery gave to me."

I felt angered, I pricked my finger. "Sumbitch," I said.

He looked at my angry face. *"Sumbish?"*

"A wašiču word, father. Means I feel angry as a wolverine trapped in a hollow log."

He thought a while. "Sumbish," he said, chuckled at the wašiču tongue he learned.

Sitting Bull was tuckered, closed his eyes, went to sleep sitting up. We'd become father and daughter; warmed my heart. Father and daughter could have hot words, come back as friends.

I put buffalo chips on the fire, nursed my daughter till she fell asleep, me, too. When I woke, Sitting Bull was gone, but he stoked the fire before he left.

I know folks think of him as a warrior—what he was in his prime. That's not how I knew him. I knew him as a kind, stubborn man, taking care of two wives, many children, his mother, making plans for how to keep our people free.

Sitting Bull was a man who respected me and took care of me better than any man I ever knew.

We snuck off the next day with my carbine, just him and me. He wanted to shoot a hundred-pace shot, not miss. I showed him how to keep his right arm in tight, against his body, not out wide like shooting a bow and arrow. How to hold his breath before he pulled the trigger, to look his shell into what he aimed at. How to shoot sitting, standing, kneeling.

Many moons later, I tacked a can from Legaré's store to a tree a hundred paces away. He sat down, held his arms tight, fired. Dead center.

"Now I am good as you, daughter," he said, "thank you for teaching me."

I took the carbine, walked back another ten paces from where he sat for his shot, loaded up, knelt, put a shell in the same hole.

"You're right about that, father," I said.

We went back to camp.

CHAPTER THIRTY-FIVE
DUCK LOVE

I wanted to live a proper woman life, raise a child, cook, bead, sew, take care of my relatives, like Sitting Bull and his mother said I should. But there was more in doing the elk leg roast than showing I was a proper woman.

Medicine Duck met the Widow Horse Tail, wanted to court the lovely widow, but not obvious and she'd shun him before he even got the chance. Medicine Duck, nervous, came in my tipi after studying the elk leg roasting outside in the chilled air. He had a hand on his bony hip, other hand on his chin, finger rubbed his jaw missing a tooth in his mouth.

"Will the heháka be ready, čuŋkši? You know how to roast elk leg? Who taught you?" He danced on one foot, then the other, nervous.

"Tuŋkášila, Sitting Bull gave me mushrooms and chokecherry leaves for the drippings, in a metal pot we took from the miners. His mother helped, too. I know what to do for a roast."

That calmed the Duck, hearing I got help in how to roast elk leg.

"Wašté. I want this woman for my wife. Not too young for me, you think? Everyone says her husband lived a happy life, no nagging."

He beat my robes outside, get them fresh, no bugs or ash, the widow would sit on those robes. He cut pine boughs when we hunted the elk, hid them behind my dew liner out of sight, but giving off sweet smells. I added bedstraw—a love perfume I

229

learned from Medicine Feet Woman. The Duck checked the tipi-smoke flap poles to make sure smoke went straight up to the sky.

"We have to show our best manners around her, daughter."

"I will be taŋyáŋ," I told him. Proper.

"Čuŋkši," he said, "I do not want to offend you, but would you remember to sit with your legs under you, like a proper woman? Sometimes you do not sit proper and sit like a man. It offends the elders. I do not hurt your heart to say this?"

He squinted at me, feared his words hurt my feelings.

"No, grandfather. I'll sit proper, I give my word. That widow is fine looking, never gossips when we women get together. I like how she laughs. I do not think she's too young for you. You have . . ."

"Sixty-three snows. Fifty-three in her. Thank you, čuŋkthi, other men, good hunters, younger than me, look her way. Now, I shot the elk?"

"Yes, you shot the elk that we serve at our feast. I went with you to skin the elk."

"Just a little lie, daughter. Not a big lie."

"Mmmm," I said, agreed, thinking on my dear Lone Wolf. Without a little fib to get things going, how would man and woman get together?

But Widow Tail would not look at Medicine Duck during our feast for her. And he got all dressed up, too, in his best buckskin tunic and leggings, beaded by his wife before she died. Widow Tail sat properly between her two married daughters, with her unmarried son next to them, then Medicine Duck. She wore a fringed doeskin dress, quilled at the neck and beaded lovely down the arms. She talked on and on about what a great hunter she had had in her husband, never looking at Medicine Duck.

She said, "Most buffalo have gone south for the winter. Friends said they saw a lone pté head north. I have no husband to hunt for me now. I sure could use a buffalo hide, and meat for a party to honor my grandson who brought us his first deer."

Widow Horse Tail looked straight ahead. Her daughters laughed, hearing their mother flirt like that with Medicine Duck. I looked away, hid my smile.

Soon as Widow Horse Tail left, I knew what Medicine Duck had on his mind. "I want to hunt that buffalo. I need someone good with a máza wakháη if I do not have luck with my bow. You know anyone who has good medicine with a carbine, who maybe owes me a favor?"

He looked at the cold sky, rubbed a hand on his chin, gave thought to his question.

I owed the Duck a favor, for his help at our fight with the miners. I told him, "Grandfather, thank you for giving me the chance to pay back the favor I owe you. If you can find that buffalo, I will try my luck if your bow can't bring her down."

"Oh, daughter, I forgot you owe me a favor. You make my heart happy. I'll sit with your child if you watch dancing, or pick berries bearberry, sumac—pick whatever you want. I will make skin offerings to the Wakáηtáηka to have pity on me, show me where to find that buffalo. I will fast and pray. Love is not easy, daughter. I love that woman, my heart says I do."

He left, full of hope. Made me happy to see him hopping to his tipi, proud, head up—he'd be a man again, win a woman's heart. Medicine Feet Woman and Friend of Otter said they would take care of my daughter.

A new year, a froze winter, just after the Month of the Popping Trees.

Before the sun came up, we rode north toward higher ground, leading two packhorses that Medicine Duck got from his friend, Moon Rises Slow. The days came dark, wind blew cold to the bone, snowfall on hills left a cold white daisy blanket. Medicine

Duck and me bundled in buffalo robes, hair on the inside, warm fur leggings, buffalo hide boots. We wore wolverine hats I made for us, with tails hung down our backs. When I took a breath, let out air, a cloud flowed from my mouth, iced the edge of my hat pulled tight around my face.

The horse Sitting Bull gave me didn't want to be rid on such a cold day. I named him Até, My Father, in honor of Sitting Bull. Had my carbine in a leather case I sewed from the elk hide, hung it on the buffalo bone saddle Medicine Duck's nephew made for me. Felt good riding the horse, on rawhide stretched over a buffalo hip bone, tied tight around a blanket.

Medicine Duck rode bareback, on a blue horse blanket. Added a dyed eagle feather to his sorrel's tail to give him spirit help on our hunt. On his mare's neck he slung a bow and quiver, wanting to take the buffalo with an arrow. He worked at making that bow ever since he planned this hunt. He found a Slót'a who had the Osage orangewood he traded for from a Crow, who got the wood from a Cheyenne, who got the wood from a Pawnee, who maybe stole that wood from Osage all the way from around Fort Robinson. The Slót'a worked the wood, Crow, too. The wood came double bent when Medicine Duck got it, bent at both ends, like a eagle with spread wings. Double bends made the wood a buffalo bow. Medicine Duck had pride in that bow.

"See, daughter," he said when we went on a target shoot. "Straight grain wood, bends good but very strong."

He cut rawhide from the elk I shot, got the hide wet. Together we sewed hide around the orangewood. I put beadwork in the middle so his small hand fit between the beaded strips. Not perfect beadwork but the best I could do. He showed me how to twist sinew from a buffalo back for bowstring. The bowstring hung loose while we rode to not weaken that amazing wood. A warrior could drive an arrow shot from an orangewood bow through three enemy if they lined up right.

Medicine Duck brought a coup stick, tied to his quiver; enemy hair on the quiver, the hair he scalped before living a medicine man life.

"Are you cold, tuŋkášila?" I said. I needed a rest.

"Thoughts of that widow warm my heart," he said, turned on his horse, grinned, showed his missing tooth. "Not felt this way for—cannot remember how long. You should try what I do now. You should not live alone, daughter."

"Too many ghosts in me now, grandfather. Takes more than love to put the dog back together once you cut up dog for a Kettle Dance."

Least that gave Medicine Duck something to ponder besides marriage and if Makhá came with a round shape.

We trotted away from the snowed flat land, up hills that went higher and higher, covered in lodgepole pine. I saw peaks when sunlight touched the tops. Pink on top, where the climbing sun painted the snow. Snow hid all except fresh tracks and that was what we looked for. The best time to hunt—waníyetu—when the earth comes white—ská. Ská, far as the eye can see. Buffalo tracks, easy to follow.

Medicine Duck slid off his horse, looked at the first tracks we came across. Motioned for me to have a look.

"The tracks go south. Two horses and a man, walking. Maybe Blackfoot. Maybe a family. Maybe why the man walks. This horse walks heavy, this other horse does not walk heavy. A wife and child on the horses, maybe. We are safe."

"Safe from what?" I agreed to a buffalo hunt, not a fight.

"Blackfoot raiding party."

He squatted to study the footprints.

"Look. Leather strip behind one boot, wipes out the shape of the boot when the man walks. This man thinks he has two boots with scout leather trailing both. Must have lost one scout leather. The shape of the boot—not one I have seen. Must be Blackfoot. Crow tracks curve on the right, Pawnee curve on both sides near the toes. Arapaho have a hump to the right at the toes. Cheyenne, like ours, are straight on the inside, then curve around from the little toe to the big toe. This man was a scout, on raids. Not now."

We got back on our horses, rode slow towards mountains.

"How do you know he's not raiding now?"

"He'd be more careful. Probably taking a wife to visit her relatives."

We rode into a freezing wind. Like old times when I hunted with my stepfather, wind coming our way, what we hunted not catching our smell.

The Duck said we should rest our horses, eat pemmican for breakfast. With the sun up, the air felt passable warm. I took off my hat, scratched my head. Got our dried buffalo meat and water pouch. We squatted, ate wasná.

Medicine Duck, on his haunches, a happy squirrel holding wasná in his hands. After eating, we mounted, rode off, he called back, "You ask Sitting Bull if he thinks Makhá has a round shape?"

I said I forgot to ask the question.

"Ask him. A man of visions. Ask him if he ever had a round Makhá vision. Tell me what he says."

I told him I'd try to remember his question.

He stopped, jumped from his horse, went to grass stuck out of the snow, bundled over.

"Not good. No, daughter."

I prodded my horse to see what the Duck found that was not good.

"See?" he said.

"Tall grass, bundled over."

"Not 'bundled over.' Grass tied in a knot, pointing south.

Same direction of the horse and scout tracks. A trail marker. We have company."

He led his horse to a log, stood on the log, jumped belly first on his horse, got himself upright.

"Keep your eyes open for raiders. We ride where the sun goes down. But that buffalo might be where warm winds blow," he said, pointed south.

We rode down a ridge, through a gully where green pines hid us. He reined his horse, took off his mittens, signed for me not to move. He dropped the buffalo robe from his back, grabbed his bow, strung the sinew, grabbed an arrow, slid off his horse.

Got me scared we might have a fight on our hands. I reached for my carbine. I knew he could fight good after what he did to the miners on our trip north, but this fight would be against Blackfoot. I'd never been in a fight with Blackfoot, but heard they fought good.

He crouched behind a snowed bush, put fingers to his lips, took in air, made a sucking sound. A fat jackrabbit ran from a bush, looked for the female. Medicine Duck put an arrow in his double bent bow, pulled back the sinew string, took aimed, let fly the arrow. The arrow went right through the maštínčala like the rabbit was a cloud. He slid off his horse, grabbed the rabbit by the ears, found his arrow, and a log to stand on, let him mount up. We rode on. I'd probably have to cook the rabbit— never done that on my own.

No sign of the buffalo, no sign of Blackfoot, either. Medicine Duck said they'd likely not attack us because Sitting Bull made a peace with their chief. I hoped all Blackfoot knew about that peace, and that we were Sitting Bull's people. If not, Medicine Duck would give them an old man's scalp to decorate a lance, and I'd never see my daughter again.

CHAPTER THIRTY-SIX
WHEN THERE'S NOTHING
TO DO BUT PRAY

"Aŋpétuwi's almost down. Let's make camp, daughter, hunt that pté tomorrow," Medicine Duck said, reined in his horse.

Sounded good. I loose hobbled our horses, cleared off snow, laid down a deer hide for a place to do our meal. I got my flint, made us a fire with dry leaves from the Duck's skin bag, and firewood from our packhorses. I skinned the rabbit, cut out the liver and heart. Slit the legs down the middle like Lone Wolf's mother taught me, saved the bottom of the rabbit for a roast. Around the fire I propped up four tall sticks, with river stones. Got my dried buffalo paunch from a packhorse, put snow in the stomach while the Duck smoked his pipe. I dropped four river stones the size of my fist in the fire, waited while they heated up. Not long after, I got my forked stick to lay the fired-up stones in the paunch, to melt the snow, boil the water.

Roast rabbit and soup were Lone Wolf's favorite dinner. Took more 'n one lesson from his mother, but I never got it right. Here's my problem—I burnt the heart and liver. Now, I had to cook rabbit on my own. Medicine Duck puffed his pipe, sat on the deer hide near the fire.

"You know how to cook rabbit?" he said. "Want help?"

"Of course I know how to cook rabbit, grandfather. Any woman knows how. Enjoy your pipe." Hard to fool a duck who'd fooled many with his medicine tricks.

He eyed me, suspicious, closed his eyes, sucked calm on his pipe.

I cut the froze carcass in half, hacked through rib bones, had to pound my knife handle hard with a stone to cut through the bone. Medicine Duck opened his eyes to see what made the noise. The fire was low enough under the buffalo paunch for me to put the rib bones, with meat on them, in the boiling water. Made soup. I tossed in dry spice leaves from Sitting Bull's mother. Stuck two small sticks through liver and heart, set them above the fire coals to cook the best part of rabbit just right— liver and heart—pink on the inside. A lot to remember, hoped I'd not forget what came first, second.

"Don't burn the liver, daughter."

"I turned the sticks."

"Nothing worse than burnt liver."

How about burnt Duck arse?

Time for the roast. I rammed a stick in the bottom of the rabbit, propped it higher over the coals, added more wood, took the liver and heart sticks, offered them to Medicine Duck. He pulled the liver from the stick, smelled what I cooked, smiled big. I relaxed.

"You want some?" he said. I said no, liver—not to my liking. He plopped the liver in his mouth like I gave him candy, sucked it, smacked his lips. I sliced halfway through the heart, gave it to him, let him taste how tender I left the inside.

"You sure you don't want a husband?" he said, impressed by my skill after tasting the heart.

"Shush. You're too old for me. Ready for soup?"

He moved near the fire, buffalo robe around his shoulders, sat cross-legged on the deer hide. I got my buffalo horn ladle, let him scoop soup from the buffalo stomach.

He tasted my soup, looked to the sky, gave thanks. "Best rabbit soup I ever had, daughter," he said, wiped his lips with a froze sleeve.

"Thank you, tuŋkášila," I said, prouder than I let on.

"Roast rabbit will be ready after soup," I said. I was proud of what I did that day, on my own.

I cleaned up camp after supper, put the rest of the rabbit roast in snow to freeze for the next day. Medicine Duck took first watch. I bundled in a robe under pine trees, fell asleep in no time. When it came my turn to watch, he said to sleep, we were safe. He'd turn in, too.

I looked at stars in the sky. Never saw such a sight as campfires of the ancestors over our head. Black sky, countless stars. I could see what Her Holy Door taught me was the mind of Sky, and his Daughter, Falling Star. Stars fell that night— changing places in the sky, is what she called stars moving in the night. I watched stars change places for a long time, paid no mind to the chilled air. Thought of my ma, missed her, wondered if she ever thought of me. Wished I could live a buffalo life, roam free, no need for a tipi to keep me warm. I pulled up the buffalo robe to my chin, wiped a tear thinking about my ma, went to sleep.

Fog flowed around us when we woke, I couldn't even see trees. Medicine Duck found an iced stream or river, covered with snow. Couldn't tell how deep the water flowed. He dropped rocks on the ice edge, got fresh water in his water bag for us and our horses.

"We eat later," he said. "We'll follow this water. Flows from where the sun sets. The sun soon warms this fog and we can look for that buffalo. Ready, daughter?"

No, I wanted to say, I was stiff, cold, and hungry but said we could start.

Not long after, we spotted the buffalo.

We reined our horses, didn't move. The pté roamed on the other side of the snow-covered, iced-over, water. We still couldn't tell if the ice covered a stream or deep river—more fog slipped in from the woods. My heart ran fast and I got wide awake. I knew a hunt is never just about going for an animal—you never know what else might happen—you need to be aware.

The pté pawed for grass under snow on the other side of the froze water, a hundred paces from us, arse end our way. All I'd do, if I shot her from where we sat on our horses, is wound her, and she'd outrun us, hide in the woods.

Pine trees were heavy with snow far as I could see. Steam flowed from the buffalo's nose, fog moving in and out of our sight of the buffalo. Medicine Duck, on his horse, slid the buffalo hide from around his shoulders to the snow, without making a sound. He took off his gloves, hung them on his horse's neck, motioned for me to get my carbine. He took tobacco from a pouch around his neck, offered tobacco to the Grandfathers, scattered tobacco to the wind. Slowly, quietly, he got his bow and an arrow with a metal tip. I eased my horse next to his mare, held my carbine in my gloved hand. If I touched the carbine metal with my fingers they would get stuck.

"She looks beautiful, covered by snow," I whispered.

Medicine Duck nodded, didn't take his eyes from the hide his widow wanted.

The pté, under a blanket of snow, looked like the albino buffalo sacred to his people.

I thought about what Her Holy Door told me, in her Húŋka teaching, about a holy young woman, White Buffalo Calf Girl, who came to this earth as a lightning spark. She came to teach Sioux how to walk in a holy way. Sometimes she looked like a young albino buffalo, sometimes like a beautiful woman. Two Sioux men saw her when she came as a young woman, one going after her to have her without her agreeing. Lightning flashed, thunder rolled, turned that man to a heap of bones. The other man took the story to his people, teaching them that Sioux should treat women proper. When I heard that story, seemed I was a bit like her—came out of nowhere to this earth, like a spark of lightning.

The Duck whispered, "I need strong medicine for that pté. Might run if she gets our smell, hears our horses. We go slow, I ride beside her for my arrow. You follow. If I miss, I ride ahead of her, turn her, then you have one shot behind her head. One shot, all you will have. Understand? I think that pté will give herself to us, if that's what the Wakaŋtaŋka wants for me."

His eyes fixed on the buffalo, frost hanging from Medicine Duck's nose. We rode slow, his horse slipped on a rock, snorted. The pté looked our way, took off running.

"Hey, Hey," Medicine Duck yelled, kicked his sorrel, going full gallop after the buffalo.

I kicked my horse. Até took off like he loved nothing better than chasing a buffalo through fog, following an old man who wanted to win a widow's heart. Medicine Duck's legs kicked the flanks of his sorrel, gained fast on the short-legged buffalo, a hairy white snowball on the other side. I feared his horse would slip, break the old man's neck when Medicine Duck rode across the ice.

"*Hókahé!*" he yelled.

He galloped for the other side of the froze river or stream; his horse kicked up snow when she ran down the bank, eagle feather waving in her tail, tried to gallop on ice. I rode my horse along the bank, held the reins with one hand, carbine in the other, bent low—hoped Até had sure feet. Wind rushed past me, made tears come to my eyes. I saw the Duck's sorrel mare sliding on the ice.

A deep ice crack tore through the air, not a high sound like ice cracking on a shallow stream. Medicine Duck's horse broke through river ice, dove into a deep ice hole. They both crashed headfirst into the water. His horse tried to climb onto the edge of the ice, but she broke her front legs.

"Tuŋkášila!" I screamed.

He tumbled underwater, buffalo hide boots over his head, bow and arrow gone. I reined Até, walked him slow toward the hole in the ice, stopped. The ice might break more; Até stood bigger than Medicine Duck's sorrel. Medicine Duck's arms waved underwater, tried to swim. He came up, got air, grabbed his horse's head. His horse felt such pain; she flopped every which way, knocked off more ice, made the hole bigger, tossed Medicine Duck back under the freezing water.

When he came up for air, he yelled, "Crawwwwl, daughter!" He swung his arms, hung onto the edge of the ice.

I rammed my carbine in the case, jumped off Até, whacked his behind to get him off the ice. I got on my hands and knees, crawled fast as I could on the ice.

"I cannot hold on much longer, čuŋkkkkthi," he hollered, terrified, teeth clicking loud like a woodpecker on cottonwood. "Not a good day to die, daughter."

I crawled on my belly nearer the ice hole, hoped the ice would not crack more, swallow me, too. I stretched far as I could, reached my hand for him to grab, glad for the first time I had long arms like my pa. Medicine Duck had his gloves off to shoot his bow, his fingers were so froze he couldn't grab my hand.

Ice cracked, boomed, like a rifle shot in the cold air. I stopped. Should I get off the ice? I had a daughter to take care of.

The old man sang his death chant.

"Stop that!" I said, tears in my eyes at the thought of him dying. I didn't want to hear no death chant.

He breathed hard, fought the current to keep from going under ice. If he went under ice, it would be his death. Too froze up to speak, his arms slid off the ice. He looked my way, no fear in his eyes, ready to die. I crawled faster, ice cracking like spider legs all around me. I grabbed his arm before he went under, looked in his old eyes. "Tuŋkášila, I'll count to four. On four, you have to kick with all you got left. Help me pull you out. Kick on four, or you're dead."

He understood.

Waŋží.

Nuŋpa.

Yámni . . .

Tópaaaaa!

Kick, old man, *Gawdamnit!*

CHAPTER THIRTY-SEVEN
HOW DEEP IS DUCK LOVE?

He kicked harder, came onto the ice up to his armpits.

"Wašté, grandfather. One more, you got to kick one more time if you want that widow."

"I want that wwwwidow, daughter. Keep me warm nights, you know?"

"How much do you want her? How warm do you want to be? You have to kick again, grandfather, harder, if you want her. On four."

Waŋží.

Nuŋpa.

Yámni. Are you ready? Kick or die.

Tópaaa.

He kicked like a wild horse and I yanked him out.

The stormed picked up. I figured we had three moves of the sun between tipi poles before he froze to death. Wind howled around us louder than a pack of crazed wolves. On my hands and knees, I dragged him off the ice. My horse waited on the bank, the packhorses with our robes and change of furs were not to be seen. The buffalo was gone, too.

"Almost had her," he said, shivering. "Maybe the Wakáŋtáŋka does not want me to have that widow?"

"How do I get you warm? You can freeze here same as in that water."

Snow fell thick, could barely see his face. Wind blew hard, I couldn't hear his voice. He put his mouth to my ear, shouted.

"Daughter, get your horse, bring him here. Shoot your horse in the head. Cut open his belly, pull out his insides. Put *me* in the belly of your horse. Put your clothes around me, then you get in, without your clothes. Hurry, or we die."

I looked at my horse. Até waited to know what I wanted. I ran to him, led him next to Medicine Duck, got my carbine.

No time to say goodbye. The hardest part was not to tell Até why I had to put a shell in his lovable head that looked to me for sugar; tears on my cheeks, I put the carbine to his head, looked away, pulled the trigger. The boom knocked snow from pines. Até fell hard like his legs got roped. Blood flowed in the snow, down his sweet white head. His eye rolled, stared at me, how my baby, Flying Eagle, looked at me when the soldier's bullet hit his face at Greasy Grass.

I fell to my knees, fought tears, took my knife, cut Até's belly. Had to fight the want to throw up. I cleaned out animals before, but none I cared for. Steam flowed from his belly, stench, too. Opened him up good, pulled out his insides. I made a cave out of Até for the old man—a womb or a tomb for him.

"My clothes, get them off me, take your clothes off, too," he said, teeth banging together. "Put your clothes around me in the horse's belly. Hurry, daughter, before I freeze. I can't feel anything."

I tugged his soaked leather clothes, got everything off. He lay on the snow, curled up like a naked fish.

I dragged Medicine Duck to the steamy hot belly of Até, rolled him inside. Snow fell thick, wind blowing, I could barely breathe. From behind my saddle on Até, I unrolled a blanket, took off my clothes, my skin freezing when wind hit. I looked up over my dead horse—the pté was covered in white snow, walking out of the woods, looked our way. Fog came thick, and she vanished, like White Buffalo Calf Girl.

I grabbed my clothes and blanket, crawled in Até's belly,

tucked my clothes around Medicine Duck like he told me. I got the blanket hung outside, over Até's belly, to keep out the snow and wind. I curled my naked body around Medicine Duck's backside, gave him my body heat.

I had no belief in a Great Mystery, but in times like these, I prayed, "Do not take him, Grandfather. Let him live. If you hear me, damnit, save this old man."

"If I die, čuŋkši. Leave me. Got to save yourself," he said.

"Don't talk like that."

"Come back in the spring, get my body. I'll be dancing with the ancestors."

He curled up tighter, my arms and legs around him. Dark now, quiet in Até's belly except for the storm raging like a devil, outside. The thought came to me—I could die, too. I didn't know how long a dead horse had heat, or how to find our camp if the old man died. I wondered if our packhorses hung around.

My body was wrapped around his, a bare leg around his bony arse to get him warm. "Not had a woman in the robes for a long time," he said.

I moved away when he said that.

He laughed. "You need to work on your sense of humor, čuŋkthi."

"Makes me happy you get warm, joke me, but we are not out of this yet. I will laugh at your quacks when we get back to camp. Do not think of me as a woman, think of me as a blanket."

"That is how I think of you, daughter," he said. "Sorry you had to shoot your horse to save me. I will get you another horse, if I live. I give my word."

Até's belly stunk worse than boiled buffalo guts not cleaned good.

I thanked the Duck for his offer of another horse. He sucked in air, let it out slow, his body getting heat from my body. We lay quiet in the horse's belly, seemed the storm would never end.

When I could not hear wind, I pushed back the blanket. Snow fell in, but it was clearing outside.

"I'll look for our packhorses," I told Medicine Duck. "Wait here."

I booted my feet, kept the blanket around me, ran naked to look for the packhorses. They hid in woods, turning their arses to the wind. I jumped on the back of one, grabbed the reins of the other, rode to Até. I slid off, got two buffalo robes unwrapped from our packhorses. In one robe, I found my change of clothes, slipped into those furs. I got Medicine Duck's change of clothes, put a buffalo robe on the ground with the fur side up. He rolled from Até's belly onto the robe, got dressed fast as he could. We put on our spare hats, gloves, stuck a blanket over us, leaned back against Até's belly.

"You saved my life, daughter."

"Only did what you told me."

"What will we tell our people?"

"Whatever you say."

"Maybe, my horse broke through ice. We used the belly of your horse to get me warm. Leave out where our bodies touched, without clothes," he said.

"That will be the truth I tell. Only a little lie," I assured him.

"Wašté, daughter. Not a big lie. Let's eat, then look for that pté."

"What?"

"We almost had her, daughter—one more moon, we go back if we do not find her. Wašté?" His voice squeaked at the end—he knew what he asked was crazy.

I had to get firm. "Not wašté, grandfather," I said. "We must head back now. We almost died."

He took a breath, let out air, not happy at my words. I got

the remains of the froze rabbit I kept warm on the ride under my horse blanket. After we ate, I boosted him on a packhorse. We rode back the way we came.

Widow Horse Tail heard what Medicine Duck suffered to win her heart. She sent him beaded moccasins. He had me over to see the moccasins, all smiles on his face. Never saw such fine beading as on those moccasins, love beading is what she gave him. She beaded a duck's head on one moccasin, a horse tail on the other, her wily widow way to say, "You have a wife, my love, if you want her."

"Wakáŋtáŋka gave me a wife," Medicine Duck said. "Maybe this earth is round, daughter?" He did a little duck hop in his tipi. Warmed my heart to see him happy.

Moon Rises Slow gave me a pinto for saving his friend's life. I named that pinto Pağuŋta Wówaštelaka—Duck Love. The horse ran to me for sugar, when he heard, "Pağuŋta."

Medicine Duck moved into Widow Horse Tail's lodge the next full moon.

An even bigger surprise came when Medicine Feet Woman got a proposal from Widow Horse Tail's son, a handsome man who could hunt good. Medicine Feet Woman moved with her daughter to live at her husband's Minneconjou camp. I didn't talk much with Medicine Feet Woman after that in the Grandmother's Land.

It warmed my heart to know Medicine Duck got his widow. Their marriage brought my husband, Two Horns, closer to me—he gave his life trying to save Widow Horse Tail's husband. I gave her another one.

CHAPTER THIRTY-EIGHT
A MAGPIE BECOMES FAMOUS

The next summer, buffalo vanished from the Grandmother's Land. Nary a buffalo anywhere. Blackfoot said Sioux wiped out buffalo; the Sioux that came north, hunting buffalo that Blackfoot figured belonged to them.

Word came up from Piegan around Fort Benton that no one sighted buffalo, their parts, neither. Piegan further south in Crow country said they saw some, but that summer held the greatest mystery to ever hit Plains Indians, except the coming of the white man. Buffalo vanished to air.

I recalled a story told to me by Medicine Duck. When he was a young man, he and friends went on a horse raid to swipe Crow horses. They came upon a train stuck on tracks in the middle of nowhere. The train couldn't move because a buffalo herd strolled across the track, far as the eye could see—cows, calves, and bulls. Miles and miles and miles of buffalo, far as an eye could see. The horse raiders decided to use the time to trade with passengers on the train.

White folks relaxed—the Indians didn't want their scalps. Medicine Duck showed me a knife with an ivory handle that he got in trade from a lady on the train.

It took three moons for that buffalo herd to stroll across the tracks. Now, there were no buffalo anywhere.

Piegan medicine men said white men hid buffalo in caves. Sioux thought buffalo, like Sioux, came from this earth, from caves in the Black Hills. It made sense that, somehow, the white man hid buffalo where they'd come from, held buffalo captive while Indians starved, forced to live like pets, on handouts at army Gift Houses.

Sitting Bull said he wouldn't live off Gift House forts, would never farm, wouldn't dig holes in Mother Makhá. He went alone to pray and fast, cry for a vision on Wood Mountain. He figured if he lived back home near the Black Hills, spirits that friended him when younger would come, tell him where to find buffalo. Or what to do to get them back.

How could such mighty beasts vanish from Makhá, a mystery every medicine man, holy man, tried to figure. They sun danced, cut flesh from their arms, cried for visions, begged Wakáŋtáŋka to take pity, begged White Buffalo Calf Woman to let them know what we did wrong.

Nary a tatáŋka or pté came north of the Holy Road.

A hunting party sighted a herd south of the border. We couldn't cross it or bluecoats would come for us. Sitting Bull had a tough decision—obey the Grandmother's rules and starve, or hunt across the Holy Road.

Sitting Bull told his Akičita not to stop hunters from crossing the Holy Road to get buffalo. When I heard his decision, I said, "Our wičaša already hunt there, father. Surely you knew?"

"No, I didn't know. What kind of chief am I to not know this? Two moons, we hunt buffalo. One Bull will load your pony drag for you, daughter."

"Thank you, father," I said. "Sorry I had to shoot the horse you gave me."

"Family, friends, honor, are more important than a horse. You walked in a holy way, saved that old man's life," he said. Made me proud to hear those words.

We came across the herd at a creek that ran to Milk River. Wherever wašíču hid buffalo, some snuck out. Our hunters crawled under buffalo hides on the edge of the herd, how their fathers and uncles taught them.

Sitting Bull rode hard that day, shouted while he galloped next to a pté, sent many down with his lever Winchester carbine, a shot back of the head. The herd ran into the wind, made dust clouds. The men were happy to do what they knew better than any in this world, hunt buffalo.

Medicine Duck came to the hunt with his new bride, Widow Horse Tail. His nephew, Horses Loose, was also on the hunt. Medicine Duck's bride was ready with her skinning knife, Medicine Feet, Her Holy Door, Four Robes, all of us women were ready to skin hides.

When the hunt ended, we gave shouts of joy, and prayer thanks, for those buffalo. The meat would feed us, and the hides warm us, into winter. My daughter wouldn't starve.

Tatáŋka Íyotake, sweaty from the hunt, rode to our family, raised his carbine, his angered mood gone. "My wives, my mother, my children—Wakáŋtáŋka gives us buffalo."

We cheered, went to skin buffalo. I took my daughter, teach her about a hunt. On this hunt, men knelt beside women, skinning hides, passed fresh heart to chew. Still not to my liking. We sat back, looked at each other, laughed, happy.

Medicine Duck scattered tobacco to the Four Directions, chanted his prayerful thanks.

A scout rode in, dust flew under his horse's hooves. Meant trouble for a warrior to ride so hard on a hot day. Sitting Bull went to talk with the scout, One Bull, his nephew and adopted son.

Long Knives came for us.

Not again, here they come, to kill us, our men, women, and kids. Bearcoat coming, with his pony soldiers, Crow scouts in the lead. To kill Sitting Bull, if the truth be told.

One Bull said, "They know where we are, cousins."

Sitting Bull looked at the buffalo, flies on carcasses not yet skinned, looked at women and children, warriors, waiting for his decision. "Only warriors stay. We will fight. Women, children, elderlies—leave now," Sitting Bull said. He wanted one more battle with Bearcoat. I got fear for his life when I looked at Sitting Bull's angered eyes.

"Load the meat and hides!" One Bull shouted. "Hurry."

We quick loaded pony drags.

"How long till the Crow scouts come?" Sitting Bull said.

One Bull pointed to the dust cloud headed our way, raised one finger. One tipi pole move of the sun, about twenty minutes.

War chiefs set their warriors for a fight; others took meat and hides across the Holy Road. I stopped near the woods, gave my daughter to Medicine Duck. Medicine Duck gave me a Henry rifle and shells. I didn't want Sitting Bull to do anything foolish, figured I would watch from a distance, within rifle range.

Crow scouts for the Long Knives whooped over a ridge, eager for a fight; red bandannas were tied on their raised carbines. Our war chiefs thought they wanted to talk; our warriors went to talk. But the bandannas were to let soldiers know they were Crow, not Sioux, when the fighting began. Psáloka attacked, shot two of our warriors. Our men fired back, stopped their attack. Our warriors hid behind any rock or tree they could find, held them off while women and children escaped across the Holy Road. Sitting Bull, on his horse, made medicine prayers from a ridge out of rifle range, studied the battle.

A Crow rode out with a white flag. Our men went to learn what the Crow dog wanted. A warrior rode back with a message for Sitting Bull. Crow had a warrior named Magpie, with a challenge to Tatáŋka Íyotake—Magpie challenged him to a duel.

Sure enough, out rides a Crow at the other end of the field, sitting proud on his horse.

Sitting Bull thought on what he heard. He had over fifty snows, past his prime. He looked at his carbine, at his warriors.

We waited for what he would do. No, father, I prayed—don't fight him, you're too old—and you can't shoot good.

"For all my relations!" Sitting Bull yelled, hair flying, carbine in one hand, galloped at the Crow. A Crow had stabbed Sitting Bull's father in a fight long ago, killed him. Sitting Bull wanted more revenge for his father is all I could figure.

Magpie and Sitting Bull rode hard at each other.

I took a breath, raised my rifle, aimed at Magpie's chest, prayed to the Great Mystery with all my unbelieving heart. Sitting Bull was foolish, fighting a duel with a warrior in his prime.

Magpie wanted fame—kill the great Sioux chief in a duel. He reined his horse, aimed his rifle at Sitting Bull, riding hard. Sitting Bull reined his horse, dared the Crow to shoot him. My heart thumped, Crow men stood still, watched—our warriors, too. I had Magpie in my sights, my finger wanted to pull the trigger.

Magpie's rifle misfired. He sat on his horse, surprised at his bad medicine, slapped his carbine. He did his death chant, taunted Sitting Bull, a hundred paces away.

Sitting Bull took aim, his shooting arm tight to his side. Fired.

Top of Magpie's head blew off—he got his wish—became famous.

Our warriors cheered; Crow looked clubbed in the head. Sitting Bull rode slow to the man on the ground, took his knife, cut Magpie's scalp, held the scalp for all to see. He leaped on Magpie's horse, rode the dead man's horse slow back to our warriors, his head high, leading his own horse. Our men cheered. I felt proud of our chief.

The battle got going again.

Bearcoat and his bluecoats roared to the battle, their travel slowed by howitzers. Bearcoat didn't want to catch Tatáŋka Íyotake, plop him on a reserve; he wanted to blow Sitting Bull to pieces, high as the clouds.

Shells exploded, earth coughing her guts. Our carbines and bows were no match at that range. Our men scattered but stopped Bearcoat from attacking while we escaped.

We got far as Rock Creek, bluecoats on our tail. Bearcoat sent word he'd cross the Holy Road to get Sitting Bull. That brought Major Walsh, with our war chief, Long Dog, to hold council with Bearcoat. Long Lance asked me to translate.

Chief Long Dog sat with Bearcoat, told him jokes. I got to say, I never met a people more fond of joking than Sioux; they'd joke at the most peculiar times.

I kept a blanket over my face, didn't want Bearcoat to see me, recall our cow stealing raid. I laughed at jokes Long Dog told; Major Long Lance, too. Bearcoat looked serious—the man had no sense of humor. Long Dog told him what our warriors hollered when shells blew up around them at the fight.

"Big shoot! Goddamn!"

Long Dog laughed, hard, coughed. I got water for Long Dog from Major Walsh's canteen. Bearcoat sat on a rock, one leg hung over the other, not seeing the fun of what Long Dog said. Bearcoat studied me when I lowered the blanket to get water for Long Dog. His curious eyes looked at my wašiču nose.

My legs wobbled.

Did he recognize me? Was this officer my pa?

CHAPTER THIRTY-NINE
CURSING HEALS THE HEART

Our people agreed not to cross the Holy Road. Bluecoats agreed not to attack us if we stayed put in the Grandmother's Land. Bearcoat kept looking at me after the council ended.

"How'd you learn English, young lady?" Bearcoat said.

"Had a stepfather from the Grandmother's Land, sir," I told him, "and my ma taught me. I had a bluecoat officer Pa, like you, before I joined the Sioux—never met him."

I studied him like he did me. He seemed too tall to father a girl short as me. I liked his shoulders, broad, like they did work in his life, not just count army medals. Dark eyes, like mine. Ma would have found him handsome. Long arms, like mine.

Bearcoat asked me to his tent, for a talk. Major Long Lance thought he wanted help to understand what I translated, told me I should go with Bearcoat. Got me nervous—this day, my pa learns he has a Indian daughter? Would my pa put his own daughter in jail for stealing his army horses?

"No tricks?" I said to Bearcoat.

"I'm an officer and a gentleman of the U.S. Army, young lady. Why would I trick you?"

"They say you had Chief Lame Deer to your tent for a talk, shot him dead."

"Damn lie!" Bearcoat said, heated up. "Who said that?"

"No matter. Leave your gun. I'll come to your tent."

He gave a grunt, handed his revolver to Long Lance, waved me to follow him.

"Who are you?" Bearcoat said in his tent, before we sat down—a table, wood stool, trunk, and canvas cot in his tent. I wanted to ask the same question of him.

"When I was born, White folks called me Army Girl, sir. My mother is a Willamette Valley Indian. I married into the Sioux. My Sioux husband lost his life at the Greasy Grass fight. He named me Sweet Medicine Woman—take your pick, what to call me."

I watched his eyes, see if they showed familiarity with my Willamette story. Nothing showed in his eyes, he motioned for me to sit on the cot. He threw his hat to the ground, ran a hand through his hair. Maybe he was as good a liar as I'd become? Maybe his heart was running in his chest, like mine, thinking maybe I was his daughter?

"You look familiar, have we met?" he said. He sat on a wood stool across from me.

"I never forget a face, sir. Have not come across yours."

"Your mother?"

"An Indian, like I said. A beautiful woman from near the Great Water where the sun sets."

"Father?"

"Bluecoat soldier, like you, sir. Like I told you—an officer."

"A soldier for a father? Officer? WHO?" He got agitated—or was he nervous?

"I never met him. Folks called him Stump, a lieutenant at a Willamette Valley fort."

"Stump? Willamette Valley?" Bearcoat studied me, my round eyes, wašíču nose.

"You know him?"

"Maybe. Your face, I'll be damned," he said. He gritted his teeth—his truth coming to him?

"You see my father in my face?" My heart about flew out my chest—was this man going to fess up? If I was meeting my pa, I

255

hoped he liked what he saw—wished I'd fixed my hair.

He leaned to me, "You want to leave these savages? Meet your father, who I think he might be?"

"No, sir," I told him. If he wouldn't fess up, I'd not play his game. I looked closer at his hairy face—no sign he recognized me. Faking it?

"Don't want to meet your father?"

"Sitting Bull's a father to me now."

"Sitting Bull? *That sonofabitch?*"

His words angered me. I stood up, angered, didn't matter he might be my father.

"Please sit down, Army Girl, Sweet Medicine Woman . . . whoever you are."

"Apologize for your words, then I might."

"Apologize for what? What'd I say?"

"What you called Sitting Bull."

"He's worse than that, young lady! You have any idea the trouble he's caused?"

"Sitting Bull has more honor in one drop he takes in the woods than you Fat Eaters have in all your gawddamn medals." End of conversation. I flipped my head, ended talk with a silly man, left his tent.

Bearcoat didn't like getting the ignore from a woman. He yelled, "You have the foul mouth of your mother! Your father feared her mouth, one like your own!"

Major Long Lance gave Bearcoat's revolver back to him, tipped his hat, we rode away.

Long Lance and Long Dog heard Bearcoat yell, looked my way. I shrugged—Bearcoat had lots to yell about that day.

Bearcoat cursed louder, yelled, "I know you! *I know you!* Come back here, gawddamnit! *You stole my cows!*"

I shrugged to Major Walsh—I had no idea what Bearcoat yelled about.

Major Walsh muttered to me, "Maybe he lost some of his mind in the heat of today's battle? He didn't have any cows with him. If he tries to come across the border, bring his troops—that's war against Her Majesty, and will be dealt with."

On the ride back to camp, I realized I had a ma to be proud of, a mouth on her that gave fear to bluecoats. But Bearcoat brought to mind what I lied about to myself—I wanted my father to know he had a daughter. I wondered at the Greasy Grass fight if we shot my pa, if we cut him up, left his bones for hawks. Least I knew he might still live.

If Bearcoat had the right varmint in mind.

Dreams came to me that night, my bluecoat father held me in his arms. Handsome, loving eyes, a young man like when he lived in the Willamette Valley. He told me he loved me, proud he had a daughter, no matter I was Indian.

I woke in my tipi, hugged my daughter, cried myself to sleep. I put my father out of my mind best I could, after that. I had a daughter to keep alive, no time for tears, for dreams about a father, though Sioux taught dreams had more truth than what the eye could see.

CHAPTER FORTY
A ONE-ARM GROS VENTRES WÍŋKTÉ

Friend of Otter paid me a winter day visit in my tipi. "Meet my friend, White Owl," Friend Of Otter said, "from the Ĥewák-takta."

He introduced me to a one-armed Gros Ventres, from south of the Holy Road, who came with men from his village to trade with Blackfoot, and with Mr. Legaré at his trading post. White Owl stood a head shorter than Friend of Otter, his hair wrapped on the ends with trader cloth. He wore silver bracelets on his one wrist, a choker of seashells and silver bells around his neck, a tanned doeskin dress, fringed down the sleeve, leather leggings under the dress, fur boots. Softest face on a man I ever saw, a Gros Ventres wíŋkté, born without his left arm.

"Welcome," I signed to White Owl, didn't know his tongue.

White Owl smiled bashful, went to my tipi fire, smoothed his dress under him with the one arm he had, sat down, legs under him, out to the side. A proper woman.

I wondered what two wíŋkte had on their minds in the middle of a freezing, starving winter.

We had empty bellies, buffalo meat gone from the summer hunt. Mountain Girl said she could not see good, her eyes needed food. I feared she'd go blind. I gave my daughter all my food. Nary a buffalo roamed north of the Holy Road. What we ate came from Grandmother handouts.

Other chiefs said they would surrender to Bearcoat. Sitting Bull was not of a mind to give up; me, neither. I was not sure, though, how to feed me and my daughter through the winter.

"White Owl said I could live with his people this winter," Friend of Otter said. "A wašíču trader near his village has supplies. You and Mountain Girl could come with me."

I only got half the story, I figured. I knew when my friend tried to persuade me with less than truth.

"Thoughtful of you to think of me," I said. "But two more mouths to feed, and yours? That would be hard for his family."

"All right. White Owl's father is too old to hunt. White Owl's uncle is chief of his village. My friend has a younger sister. They have no one to hunt deer, elk, fox, bear, or beaver. You know how to trap and shoot like a wičaša, so," Friend of Otter said, "we need someone to hunt. You are no tipi woman, said so yourself. White Owl and me, we would care for your daughter, pray to the spirits to keep you safe. You could hunt, get us meat, trade furs for supplies."

"You called me oštéka when we stole cows," I told him. "I am trying to not act *strange*—what you called me—and to live a proper woman life."

"I said I was sorry I called you strange."

"NO, you didn't apologize, I still wait for your apology."

"You know how much love I have for you."

"What? Whose mouth says he has love for this woman?"

"My dearest kolá," he said. "In the whole world, who lives closer to Friend of Otter's heart than Sweet Medicine Woman? Did I not risk my life to help her husband steal horses? I could have lost my scalp. I dressed in warrior clothes, for you. You know the place you have in my heart."

"You felt sweet on my husband, that's why you did that," I teased him.

"Well, that, too. I didn't know Sweet Medicine Woman, then. Now I have love for her in my heart."

I figured I had a special place in his heart, but I only knew one wíŋkte, this one, as peculiar as he thought me.

"You heard my words of apology. Come with us?"

White Owl looked away, wondered what had gone on between us.

"I will think this night on what my friend said. We talk again tomorrow. Soon enough?"

Friend of Otter gave me a smile.

Next day, I bundled against the fierce wind and snow, walked bent over with my daughter to Sitting Bull's lodge. Our camp was scattered along the creek that ran past Legaré's trading post. Men and boys carried cottonwood bark for their best horses, staked outside tipis. The men and boys looked froze up, walking snowmen. Younger boys had a snowball fight across the creek.

I scratched on Sitting Bull's tipi, his ma said to enter.

Sitting Bull sat at the back of his tipi, leaned against a bone backrest, didn't look up when I came in—in a bad mood. I let my daughter and his twin boys run outside to ride a sled. My daughter was now old enough to play outside with other kids.

Sitting Bull had the buffalo skins from the summer hunt to put up another tipi, now only him, his mother, and his family with Four Robes Woman lived in this lodge. Four Robes was gathering firewood.

"How are you?" his mother said, looked up from cutting hide for moccasins. "Soup, daughter?"

"No, Uŋči. I ate."

I hadn't eaten that day, figured they only had enough food for their family. Her Holy Door gave me pemmican. I chewed pemmican while I sat, my knees under me, resting on my heels like a proper woman. I twiddled with the buckskin, waited for Sitting Bull to let me know I had permission to speak. He stared blank, looked older than when we came two snows earlier. Skin sagged around his eyes, jaw tight. He made a fist, let it go.

"I need to talk with you," I said.

Sitting Bull said nothing.

Her Holy Door motioned with her chin I should speak to her son.

I said, "Many mouths here, no food. Friend of Otter asked me to go south till the winter ends, live with Gros Ventres where his friend's uncle is chief."

He looked up. "Gros Ventres? Be careful, daughter. Our people had fights with Gros Ventres."

"I will, father. If I hunt for food and trap furs through the winter to help his friend's family, we can trade for supplies from the trader."

"No food here," he said. "Just a bunch of beggars. If you wish, go. Take care of your daughter. Come back when snows melt, I have become fond of your peculiarities."

"I will return. You are not a beggar."

"If the trader didn't help, there would not be much for us to eat. Even with his flour and cans of meat, I serve horse to my family," he said.

Her Holy Door pointed with her chin to the water that simmered in the kettle. Sioux ate dog at a Kettle Dance. But to eat horse hurt the Sioux heart. Horses, to them, were like gold to the white man.

"Crazy Horse had us eat horse," I said.

He looked up. "You say those words to make me feel better?"

"We ate horse in the froze mountains after Greasy Grass. Bluecoats attacked us in winter. We had to run, leave tipis for bluecoats to burn. No food in those froze mountains, our horses ate bark, we ate our horses."

He studied me for any lie. "Tašúŋke Witkó ate horse?"

"Down to skin on bone, old people, kids, mothers. Eating horse was better than starving."

"All right, we eat horse. I will not surrender to Bearcoat.

Daughter, go south. Come back when the snows melt. Wakáŋtáŋka will hear our prayers, buffalo will return."

He spoke softly. I looked at the arm of his hand holding mine. Scars on his arm, from the strips of his skin he cut, offered to Wakáŋtáŋka for the return of buffalo.

I stood to leave.

"I will return, father." But I didn't know if that would happen.

Two moons later, we readied to leave. Friend of Otter rode his big bay army horse from Fort Robinson, twirled a rope over his head. "Cow boy miš miye," he joked.

"You are a cow boy?"

My daughter, wrapped on robes on our pony drag, laughed at her uncle.

"A cow boy, my mother? What's a cow boy?"

"A wašíču who runs after spotted buffalo."

Friends came to wish us a safe trip, gave us food on a chilly but clear day when we rode by. Medicine Duck sprinkled medicine on Duck Love's nose, the horse his friend, Moon, gave me, then over my daughter's head and on my feet.

"May this horse take you safely," he said, worried about us living among enemy. If caught going across the Holy Road, soldiers could take us prisoner or shoot us for sport.

White Owl held the reins with his one arm, led the way wrapped in robes. I rode my pinto, my daughter under warm robes stretched across a pony drag. Friend of Otter rode last, wearing a beaver fur hat, warm leggings, and boots under a buckskin dress. He led a packhorse with my tipi and supplies on a pony drag. All we had in the world.

Near sunset, second day, we sighted a tatáŋka—a bull buffalo—north of the Milk River, on snow-covered plains. The wind came at us from the south; the bull had no idea we spotted him. We got the excite, meat for our bellies.

Friend of Otter said, "Get your máza wakháη, kolā."
I pulled the carbine from the case around my horse's neck,
hungry for something to eat, for me and my daughter.

CHAPTER FORTY-ONE
A STUBBORN WÍŋKTÉ

"I can only wound the bull from here," I told Friend of Otter, "he'll run. We have to get closer. Tie your packhorse to grass; you and White Owl ride around him, chase him my way. I'll untie our pony drag, leave Mountain Girl on the drag. I'll ride close for a shot before he knows we come for him."

Friend of Otter agreed to my plan, found grass under the snow, tied reins of his packhorse to a grass bundle. Him and White Owl rode right and left, circled the bull.

I left Mountain Girl with a doll on the drag, held the carbine stock in my gloved hand, hoped my horse wouldn't get flatulent. Buffalo can hear and smell better than any critter I knew except dog.

White Owl rode to the left, eased his horse down a ravine before he came to flat land where the buffalo pawed at snow, looked for grass. Friend of Otter was not in sight after he slipped to a grove of trees, edge of the flats.

I rode slow, quiet, got close enough for a shot.

The bull heard me, turned, lifted his legs like he got stung by bees, scattered snow. He let out a bellow. I had him in my sights, aimed the carbine behind his head, pulled the trigger.

Click—the only sound from my carbine. The carbine froze up or the shell had dirty casing. I rode hard, yelled to Friend of Otter that my carbine wouldn't shoot. The two wíŋkte came at him from the south, couldn't hear me. White Owl held reins in his teeth, wild waved a blanket in his one hand. The buffalo changed path, headed in front of Friend of Otter. A mighty coming together going to happen, my friend's horse and the buffalo's horns. The horns of the tatáŋka would stick in the horse's brave neck, send dear Friend of Otter to wíŋkté glory.

The buffalo turned, ran the other way. Friend of Otter gave chase with a whoop, pulled out his rope, got a loop in the rope, waved the loop over his head, kicked the horse in her flanks to hightail it faster through the snow.

First time I saw an Indian give chase like a cowboy with a rope. I laughed.

White Owl caught up to me, laughed himself.

"Get him, cowboy!" I hollered to Friend of Otter.

Friend of Otter chased that buffalo across the open field, snow flying underfoot. White Owl let out a scream, signed, "If he ropes that buffalo, he would get dragged to his death."

That stopped my laugh.

The buffalo did a circle, charged where I left my daughter.

I kicked Duck Love, rode fast as I could to my pony drag. "Daughter, get behind a tree!" I screamed—terror crawled through me.

My daughter could not hear me.

I feared the buffalo would run her over. Nothing I could do, the buffalo charging at her. My horse could not run fast through deep snow. I heard her cries when she saw the buffalo.

Friend of Otter galloped behind the buffalo, yelled, "Hey! Hey!" He let fly with a loop of his rope that circled the bull's horns, put the rope on the other side of his horse's neck, slowed down the bull. He got the buffalo turned from the path that would run over my daughter. Friend of Otter could not stop that bull, away they ran through deep snow, the rope around the bull's horns, but no longer could I see them when they ran over a knoll.

I got my terrified daughter, put her on my horse, calmed her down.

Over the knoll we came across a sight to behold—the buffalo got stuck in a ravine filled with snow. The buffalo was pinned like a big hairy rock, not able to touch ground. He snorted anger, shook his head, plumes of air flew from his nose. Friend of Otter's horse had longer legs and backed out of the ravine.

"Can you shoot the buffalo now?" Friend of Otter teased me.

"The carbine won't shoot. You want to hit that buffalo with your club?" I teased him right back.

I tried to shoot the buffalo, but the carbine only gave a click. We had ourselves a buffalo, but he wouldn't do us much good, stuck in snow.

White Owl and me went back for the packhorse and pony drag. We camped next to the ravine, made a fire with wood from the travois. Friend of Otter crawled on the ravine snow to grab his rope, but kept the loop on the buffalo's horns. He tied the rope around his horse's neck. Friend of Otter and White Owl took turns standing watch after supper. We bedded down in our tipi for the night, reckoned we were safe, and would figure next day what to do.

At sunrise, White Owl signed, "What do we do with the buffalo he roped?"

"I won't let him loose," Friend of Otter signed. A wíŋkte could be stubborn as a buffalo bull.

"What to do with him? Cut his throat? He melts snow with his body heat, soon ready to fight," I said.

"I am not . . ."

"But what do we do with that buffalo?"

The buffalo watched us. Mountain Girl said to Friend of Otter, "Feed him grass, my uncle."

"Feed a buffalo?"

"He's hungry, like us," she said.

Friend of Otter dug in the snow, cut grass, crawled on the ravine snowpack, offered grass to the buffalo.

"You will make a good farmer," I said, "feeding a four-legged."

"His eyes look in my eyes," Friend of Otter said, finding *dee*-light looked eye to eye by a buffalo. The buffalo chewed grass Friend of Otter gave him, paid no mind to us.

"Maybe if I keep the rope on him, he would follow behind my horse," Friend of Otter said.

"Why do that?" I said, put away the wasná. "You make a pet out of that buffalo, you would not let us eat him."

I sighed, knew we would not have buffalo stew.

We pulled the buffalo out from the ravine. The bull waited for Friend of Otter to lead him by a rope. Friend of Otter gave the name Tatáŋka Koyágya to his pet buffalo—The Buffalo to Rope.

Koyag, we called him.

We came to the Big Muddy at Cathedral Rock, rode tired across froze Eagle Creek. A few miles away, at the mouth of the Judith River, we reached White Owl's village. Mountain Girl peeked from her robe on the pony drag, needing kids to play with.

"We come to his village, my mother?"

"Yes, čuŋkši," I said, happy to call someplace home.

Folks in White Owl's village lined up to greet us, not believing their eyes when they saw Friend of Otter lead a buffalo by a rope.

Gros Ventres had a good place for a winter village, flat land along a river, pine trees above on the rim of the valley. Cotton-woods along the riverbanks gave them shelter from wind. They kept their horse herd on the grassy flats. Whatever Gros Ventres might be as a people, they kept busy winters, rounding up horses. We heard the pounding of drums beneath the laughter of children that came from their large village.

Would they welcome us when they learned we were Lakóta, their old enemy? Could a one-arm wíŋkte be trusted, now that we were away from our people? Would they steal my daughter? I ran to get her.

CHAPTER FORTY-TWO
CROW WOMAN CHIEF

White Owl's uncle, chief of the village, gave us a warm welcome, sign-talked with his huge paws. He gave us a invite for a hot meal. Gros Ventres spoke a strange tongue. They could talk other Indian tongues but no Indian I met, except Arapaho, could speak Gros Ventres. I used sign best I could. He didn't care we were Lakóta because we were friends of his one-arm nephew.

We sat on robes around a fire in the chief's lodge, the chief sitting on a couch he made. We'd stopped at trader log homes on the ride to their village. I learned that making a couch, like the white traders, became the Indian thing to do, using buffalo bones with stretched elk hide to sit on.

Bull's Head, the father of White Owl, entered the lodge; a rolled wad of hair on his head came to a peak two hands high. A sour feller, he told us Sun, a Great Spirit to his people, didn't take kindly to two-leggeds making a pet out of a wild four-legged buffalo. "Sun will hide animals if you lead a buffalo around by the neck, like a mule," Bull's Head signed, never smiled.

Later, me and his son, White Owl, gave thought to how I would live in their village.

"Will your father think me peculiar, a woman hunting and trapping like a man? Throw us out?" I said.

White Owl laughed, shared a story.

Not long ago, their great enemy, the Crow, captured a girl

from his people, her only going on ten snows. The Crow man who captured her raised her like his daughter, treated her good. Her Crow father saw the girl's interest in what men did, taught her all he knew about how to hunt with a bow, shoot a rifle.

"Her Crow father died," White Owl signed. "She took on caring for her Crow family. She could ride a horse, hunt, fight Blackfeet and us, better than any Crow warrior, wearing a buckskin dress. She smoked a pipe, got in fights with us—her own people—on horse raids."

"She fought against her own people?"

"Stole our horses, took scalps."

"Crow let her be a warrior, fight like a man?"

"Crow thought she had good medicine, made her a chief."

"You make up this crazy story?"

"All tribes feared Crow Woman Chief. She took four Crow women as wives, became the most rich and powerful chief of Crow." He stopped the story, I wanted to know more. I asked him to finish.

"My people wanted peace with Blackfeet, Crow, and Assiniboine, to stop the horse stealing and bloodshed. Crow chose Crow Woman Chief to come to the peace talk with my people."

"What happened?"

"My people remembered what she did in fights, the horses she stole, scalps she took."

"You make peace with Crow Woman Chief? Welcome her back to her people?"

"No."

He looked down, embarrassed, "My people shot her in the back, killed her." His story gave me pause. I would be careful how I lived around Gros Ventres.

White Owl's father said we could set up our tipi near his lodge after White Owl told him I'd hunt for furs and food, taught to hunt by a Grandmother trapper. We'd share what I got with White Owl's family. He even let us stake Koyag in back of our tipi. Friend of Otter, Mountain Girl, and kids in the camp gave Koyag grass for his belly.

White Owl's father, Bull's Head, liked the meat from my hunts that I shared with his family, invited us to a party to meet a white trader friend of his, C.W. Schultz. With Schultz came a young Piegan man, Wolverine. White Owl's father had no use for Wolverine.

A smelled-up whiskey trader from Fort Benton, Moose Jaw Calhoun, came to the party. Bull's Head wanted to give his daughter, Piksahki, to Moose Jaw to get all the whiskey Bull's Head might ever want. The Piegan, Wolverine, brought a tobacco peace offering for White Owl's father, to warn him and the village chief that Crow would raid Gros Ventres horses.

Bull's Head took the rope of tobacco, waved off Wolverine's story as not true. He hated Piegan, he said, because Piegan killed men in his family long ago. Piegan were liars, cheats, no-goods, even though Bull's Head married a Piegan woman—the one-arm wíŋkte's mother.

Moose Jaw had a burl in his jaw, like you see on a tree, and an eye that looked to the side no matter what way the other eye looked. Hard to tell whether Moose Jaw looked at me or a wall.

"How's business?" I said to Schultz, a fine-looking man from the east.

Schultz's head snapped my way when he heard his tongue.

"You speak English, ma'am?"

"Had a bluecoat father and a white trapper for a stepfather," I told him. "I married into Sioux. Went north from our reservation to the Grandmother's Land. No buffalo there, we came south for the winter, to live with White Owl's family. I'll hunt and trap through the winter. Trade at your post, if that is all right with you."

Schultz said that would be fine with him, motioned for me to step outside Bull's Head's lodge. Moose Jaw eyed me when I walked by him.

Outside, Schultz said, "You know White Owl's sister, Piksahki?"

"Met her," I said. "Lovely girl."

"My Piegan friend, Wolverine, wants to marry her."

I said White Owl told me about a Piegan man's yearning for his sister. Wolverine's offer of thirty horses for his sister only brought a laugh from the girl's father, who hated Piegan. None of my business, I told Schultz.

"Does Piksahki return his feelings?" Schultz said.

"From what White Owl told me, she does."

"Would you help my friend?" Schultz said. "No Crow will raid Gros Ventres horses. Wolverine wanted to get into the girl's village, find out if she loves him, if she wants to go with him. Could you ask her to meet him near the river tomorrow night when she goes for firewood? Much obliged if you could do that, ma'am."

"Mr. Schultz, I can't risk that. Gros Ventres might harm me and my daughter."

"No one would know. Will you think about it?"

I told him I'd tell the girl, give Piksahki the choice.

We went back to the lodge.

A hungry louse must have bit Moose Jaw Calhoun when we came in because he wriggled, scratched his crotch. When he wriggled, I heard a tinkle. A familiar sound I could not place right off. Moose Jaw spit tobacco juice in a can he held in his paw, each eye looking a different direction.

I recalled the tinkle at Miss Brenda's bordello—the customer at the Quarter Hole with silver bells sewed in his organ that Pancake worked on, the bear grease keeping the hound's tongue eager for the task.

Moose Jaw said, "I seen you someplace? Look familiar."

"Never forget a face," I said. "Would not forget yours, Mr. Calhoun, what with that big burr in your jaw."

Moose Jaw shut up after I noted his peculiar feature. I didn't want that sweet girl going to a man like Moose Jaw.

Chapter Forty-Three
A PIEGAN LOVE STORY

Next night, the young woman, Piksahki, went for the firewood. I gathered grass nearby for Koyag, acted as a guard for her. Piksahki looked around, scared her father might see her, kill the Piegan man. When Wolverine crept from the trees, Piksahki dropped her firewood, ran to him, threw her arms around Wolverine's neck with such beautiful longing I stumbled into a cottonwood tree, near knocked myself out.

Wolverine was happy when he left, I heard him singing. You have to root for a man who sings his love. The lovers planned on making a run for it the next night.

Horse raiders attacked near sundown.

I thought Wolverine lied about a Crow horse raid to get into the girl's village, but this was real.

Shots came from where the Gros Ventres kept their horses, which brought Chief Big Belly and his brother, Bull's Head, running with their Henry rifles. Chief Big Belly, huffing and puffing through the snow, yelled at Bull's Head that if the Crow stole his horses, he blamed Bull's Head for convincing him Wolverine lied about the horse raiding. He didn't put enough guards on the horses.

"That Piegan dog just wants my daughter," Bull's Head yelled, found a horse to mount.

"The Crow want your horses. Which will you guard, you old fool?" Big Belly shouted. Big Belly, so fat that a warrior had to

274

boost him on his horse.

"First the horses," Bull's Head shouted. "Then I shoot the thieving Piegan!"

Schultz and Wolverine rode by the girl's lodge, near trees where I hid. I pointed to the woods where Piksahki and her mother waited with the girl's bags packed.

Bull's Head burst out of the woods. I aimed my carbine at Bull's Head's horse if I had to stop him from killing Wolverine. Bull's Head raised his rifle, Wolverine rode at Bull's Head, jumped on the girl's father, knocked him off his horse. Bull's Head got up, reached for his knife. I didn't know what to shoot.

Piksahki galloped past Wolverine, shouted to him. He leaped behind her on the horse; away they rode, Schultz in the lead, dodging bullets and the cursing words of the girl's father. I snuck back to our tipi, crawled under robes like I was asleep.

The horse thieves were Indians from the Grandmother's Land, not Crow. Wolverine's lie saved Gros Ventres horses.

Chief Big Belly sent word that Wolverine was welcome to his lodge any time he might come to visit.

Me and Friend of Otter rode to Schultz's trading post next full moon with fox furs, elk hide, beaver, and a bearskin rug from the Grandmother's Land. We needed sewing needles, flour, beans, hardtack, sugar, canned meat, and shells for my carbine; candy and gingersnaps for my daughter.

Schultz had the most beautiful Piegan woman for a wife I ever saw, lived with her near her people. She had us over for tea when we visited her husband.

"Do not hunt bear, ma'am," Schultz told me, in a kind way. "Bear are sacred to my wife's people."

I wouldn't hunt bear come spring.

Me and C.W. became good friends, one of the finest white men I ever met, like Major Long Lance. I learned about the trading business from him when he had me and Friend of Otter look after his post when he and his breed partner had business upriver.

Friend of Otter had a happy heart, gave buffalo rides to Gros Ventres, a fun-loving bunch. Gros Ventres enjoyed his pet buffalo. I told him he had to charge them something for the rides, learn to do business like the white man. He charged a hunk of pemmican for a ride. We tied a rope around Koyag's belly for kids to hold onto. Even curious parents rode on the back of the tame buffalo. Friend of Otter led his buffalo with a rope, a brave child or parent on Koyag's back. Even White Owl's fat father had himself a ride.

In the spring, Koyag lay on his side, belly filled with air that comes to a dead buffalo. Friend of Otter knelt beside his friend, tears in his eyes, rubbed Koyag's horns. Broke my heart to see my kolā sad. But now we'd have meat, fresh pemmican, too, to last us through the summer, and feast our Gros Ventres friends, thank them for taking us in.

"Some sickness," I told him, gave a pat to his shoulder. "Maybe why he lost his wild. You kept him alive, long as you could."

I got my skinning knife.

"I'll not skin him," Friend of Otter said.

I put my knife away, knew better than to argue with my friend about one of his pets. I got my horse with the buffalo bone saddle, tied Friend of Otter's rope to the saddle horn, dragged Koyag over snow to the woods. Friend of Otter piled rocks on the buffalo to keep eagles and wolves from eating him. To tell the truth, I never understood my friend. You don't have to understand a friend to have a good one.

A couple lazy Gros Ventres thought they wanted me for a wife, seeing how good I could hunt. I had no interest in bearing another child, watch the child die or go blind from starving.

My heart stayed quiet those days, no man in my life. My daughter's eyes got better with the good food she got, though she never could see as good as before. I blamed that on the white man, killing off buffalo, making my daughter starve and never see well again.

Friend of Otter became friends with Gros Ventres who respected him, needed wíŋkte medicine. They gave Friend of Otter gifts, hides I cut and sewed for mittens. But a big part of his loving heart died with Koyag. We decided to stay another year with our Gros Ventres friends.

Word came down that Sitting Bull surrendered to keep family from starving to death. Broke my heart to think of him no longer free. I let down him and his family, not with them at the most sad time in their life. I went to the woods for three days, two nights, alone, to pray for him, to survive whatever came his way, though I didn't know how to pray. I cut strips of skin from my arm, like I saw Sitting Bull do, to get the attention of a Spirit to take care of him.

"You want a man?" Moose Jaw said to me in the lodge of White Owl's father, his good eye looking at me best I could tell.

"That a wifie proposal, Mr. Calhoun?"

"If that be what you hear," he said, spit tobacco in his tin can. PING. "Got me a cabin outside Fort Benton. Logs chinked good, warm for you winters. Better nights come for you than with the man who wears a dress." PING.

"You'd do me real good, Mr. Calhoun, in your robes? A hot little squaw?"

"That's the kind of talk I like from a purty young squaw," he said, gave me a grin. PING.

"Here's another kind of talk," I said, looked him in what seemed his good eye. "Figure a way to Quarter Hole yourself,

Mr. Calhoun. That be who you can do real good in your robes."
Moose Jaw stayed clear of me after that talk.

Friend of Otter and me figured we best surrender to bluecoats.
If Gros Ventres learned I helped a Piegan sneak off with Bull's
Head's daughter, who other Gros Ventres wanted for a wife,
they might shoot me in the back, take my daughter.

We said goodbye to C.W., his wife, and White Owl's family.
They gave us food for our journey. We rode out on our skinny
horses, my daughter on a pony drag, resting on tipi hides and
lodgepoles.

She played with a doll I made for her out of deer hide and
trader cloth.

We headed for the Dakotas, heavy of heart, to live a
penned-up cow life.

CHAPTER FORTY-FOUR
PAYING A DEBT

We rode east across prairie land, under a scorching summer sun. Prairie sun looks down at you like a great eye in the sky. I loved prairie land—prickly pear flowering, needlegrass rubbing our horses' bellies, sagebrush here and there with a meadowlark or two perched on a tired sage. A few upright junipers and antelope who gave us no mind. Prairie dogs chatted when we passed by. Nights, coyote songs kept us company, buffalo only memories here as if they never walked this earth.

"Eiiiiii!" came the cries. A horse raiding party galloped over a ridge. They looked Crow, but maybe our visitors were Blackfoot. They hollered the way warriors do who figure they look good with feathers in the hair, paint on the face, to count coup, swipe horses. They must have got bored, snuck off their reservation.

Young men on horseback, gathered around us, curious at the sight we offered.

Me and Friend of Otter held our hands high, palms open, let them see we had no weapons, no interest in a fight. We done all the fighting we had in us, a wíŋkte in a buckskin dress, leather leggings and boots; a young woman in a buckskin dress with leather leggings; and her daughter on a pony drag. Scrawny horses not even worth eating.

I slid off my horse, not sure what our painted-up visitors had a mind for, went to my daughter on the pony drag.

"If something bad happens to your ma, you must go on, daughter. That's what daughters do. They will not harm you," I told my daughter

My daughter cried, threw herself around my neck.

"Noooo. Please, Ma. I don't want to live without you. Let's fight these bastirts." She knew the wašíču tongue, Lakóta, too—it was up to her which to use. Her tearful, brave words— four snows in her—gave me pause.

If they took my daughter, no telling what would come her way. I thought on my life after Ma left me, all that came my way without her to take care of me. A hawk flew overhead, flapped wings and flew high, nothing yet to eat. He waited for bones that two-leggeds left on the prairie. I motioned with my chin to Friend of Otter to get his war club. He loved my daughter, and me, too. We faced death before, together, him and me.

The raiders watched us move in front of my daughter on the pony drag.

I lifted the hem of my dress, got my skinning knife, faced off with warriors on their horses, no bows drawed. My daughter got a skinning knife from the drag. She stood behind me, rattlesnake eyes, a knife in her hand, blade up at our attackers.

Friend of Otter took my lead, walked in front of me, war club in hand.

He lifted the buckskin dress over his head, dropped the dress to the grass. A mountain of a man stood in front of me. He raised his hand, pointed to the biggest raider, invited him to come, stand in front of him. Friend of Otter would take him on, man to man, if the warrior felt he had good medicine that day.

Then Friend of Otter dropped his club to the grass, held wide his arms. He signed to our curious visitors.

We fight, if you want. No weapons. I break your back, we move on, with our horses, the woman and her daughter.

You win, you do with me what you want. Best scalp you ever cut. Take my horse. The woman and her daughter ride away, unharmed.

The man who held the pipe on that raid rode from behind

the horse stealing circle, a man older than the others. He slid off his horse—not a big man, but he showed no fear of Friend of Otter. He looked at the sun, at us, stuck out his bottom jaw, gave the matter some thought. He looked at Friend of Otter's scrawny horse, see if the horse might be worth a fight. He motioned for Friend of Otter to come close.

Gonna be a helluva fight.

The Indians on horses gave a whoop—the best medicine they ever saw in Friend of Otter. The warrior who held the pipe on that raid bent over in mirth. I would know that laugh anywhere—Fox Tooth, the brother of Yellow Cloud.

These were Crow.

I got fear Fox Tooth would recognize me, eat my heart for stealing his horse, making a fool of his sister. Fox Tooth studied us, him in a breechclout and leather boots, painted face, bent eagle feather in his hair. He waved off his warriors, walked palms open to Friend of Otter, offered the crossed handshake of friendship.

Friend of Otter, a head taller than Fox Tooth, took the handshake. Everyone got calm, Fox Tooth signed for us to follow.

Friend of Otter got dressed, mounted up.

"Thank you, my uncle," Mountain Girl said. She put her knife on the robes, climbed on the pony drag, sang to herself the Mother Song I taught her, going always under my wings.

At their camp, Fox Tooth studied me, signed, "I know you?" He scratched his chin, looked at Friend of Otter in a dress, wondered what kind of a crazy family he came across.

"Maybe we met in another life," I said in his tongue, looking as sweet and charming as I could, under the peculiar circumstances. "Or we met in a dream. I spent time with Crow. I never forget a face, and I never saw yours. We are Lakóta, on our way to our reservation."

Hearing his own tongue, he stepped back, eyed me feet to hair. "Sure we have not met?" He put a hand over his eyes to shade the sun, looked me up and down. "You have a brother who speaks our tongue like you? A horse thief, ugly, not beautiful like you."

"Oh, that no-good skunk, Thunder Walks," I said. "My twin. That man shamed our family. His wife cut his throat, we do not speak of him."

"Did not know he had a sister," he said. "I will tell my sister the skunk went to his Father. Her heart will rise from the ground. He treated her bad, stole my best horse."

They took us to their village.

I again met Fox Tooth's lovely sister, Yellow Cloud, even more of a beauty since I last saw her. She had a fine Blackfoot husband. When Yellow Cloud learned Thunder Walks got his neck stabbed, and had a twin, she threw her arms around me, hugged me like a sister. Thunder Walks and her had been promised in marriage, she said, if only for a short while.

We sat in Yellow Cloud's lodge; she cooed to her new baby. "You visit Yellow Cloud anytime, with your daughter, now that we have no fights between our people."

Yellow Cloud stuck her baby in a crib, crawled to me, eyed Friend of Otter in his buckskin dress. She said, "Was your brother . . . peculiar?"

I said my brother was a little peculiar, though handsome and brave. Women had no complaints—called him *Big Thunder Walks*. That reputation with women got his fat wife to stab him in his neck.

"Good," Yellow Cloud said, took a pemmican stick, sucked pemmican, lost in thought about *Big* Thunder.

I told her she could visit us, too, when we got home.

Fox Tooth sent a cousin to her lodge—had an offer for me to consider. He'd give all the horses he stole from Gros Ventres to my family if I marry him.

I about fell over at that offer, considering everything, but honored. I brushed my hair, cleaned up, put on my best dress, went for a talk in front of Fox Tooth's lodge. He invited me in.

We sat on his robes, just him and me.

"I am Fox Tooth," he said, "son of Handsome Weasel and Plenty Horse Woman. My wife died, I raised two sons, with my mother's help. Our people have better land than where you go. I would take good care of your daughter."

"I am Sweet Medicine Woman, no mother or father now. Bluecoats killed my husband. I have my daughter and Lakóta relations to care for," I said. "I must return to our reservation to care for them. Do you understand?"

I sat on his robes with my legs under me, out to the side, like a proper woman.

"I never met a woman as fine, beautiful, and brave, as you," Fox Tooth said.

We sat on robes, not knowing what else to say. He slapped a hand on a knee, looked for words. "I could use relations with Lakóta, to hunt their land, not lose my scalp."

I looked down, held my smile at his words. Any man—Crow, Sioux, or white—who speaks honest words, not fanny-flap woman flatter, gets a woman to give thought to his words.

"Thank you for not harming my daughter, but I cannot be your wife."

He sweetened the offer. "My mother would cook for us. You bead, all you want. Bead dresses, pipes, moccasins. Bead my horse if you want. My horse is old and tired. You get fat from my mother's cooking. You have more babies, pretty like your daughter. Fox Tooth likes babies."

"Not more a woman could ask in being a wife," I said. "But I must care for the family I have."

"You are such a good and honest woman, makes my heart

want you more. Hard to find honest women these days."

"Thank you for your words, but I cannot leave my people," I said. I wanted him.

He looked down, accepted what I said. He could kill us, take my daughter for his own. I touched his cheek gentle.

"Fox Tooth never harmed a child or a woman. You are free to go," he said.

"I want to give you my thanks," I said.

I lay on his robes, opened my arms for him. His eyes got wide, he took a deep breath, nodded to himself that maybe this was his day of strong medicine. We lay together, in our clothes, arms around each other. Fox Tooth was even more handsome now, if the truth be told. I put his hand on my bosoms, let him know what I wanted to give him.

His robes felt soft after he lifted my dress. I lay back, waited for him. He ran his hands over my legs like he never saw a woman's legs before and admired what got offered to him. He paused, thought on my gift—should he take what I offered, one time only? Not many a man would pause, give thought to whether he should take what got offered him that day. But he did and I admired him for that.

He took off his clothes, lay beside me. His back felt strong, warm to my hands. I felt the woman in me come alive, flowing through my body—I wanted him. First time with a man in the robes since my night with Two Horns. I lay with our enemy, on a woman's wander, my heart leading the way. I could not be his wife, but could be his woman, one time. I stole his horse, made a fool of him. That raid got my dear Lone Wolf invited to join the Akičhita.

I owed Fox Tooth.

Fox Tooth took his time, slow, warmed my heart. I opened to him, broke more rules than this earth ever gave a woman. I moved on top of Fox Tooth; he moved his legs wide under me.

His eyes wandered my bosoms above his face, my hair loosed around my shoulders. He ran his lips on my bosoms, licked my berries, sent a quiver through me like the first time in the robes with Lone Wolf. I watched him taste what a man finds sweet in a woman's berries, that make a bird drunk. This Crow found berries that day that made his wings flutter, fly higher than he ever flew in a breeze that came his way.

"You can put yourself in me now, anyway you want," I whispered, looked him eye to eye, smiled. "All you want, I am ready for you."

"Can I buck? I feel like bucking. I do not want to offend you." He was even more a gentleman than I thought.

"I am not going anywhere. Buck all you want, sweetheart, I won't fall off, I know how to ride if you know how to buck." Wild horses roamed in hills around us. None more wild than Fox Tooth that day. Felt good to have a man in me, even if he was my enemy. Not my enemy now. We made a truce between our people that fit the times.

We took a rest from his bucking. I lay still, not knowing what to say. "I want you on top of me," I said. He groaned, more tired than me.

He rolled me over, nuzzled my neck, tender. A loving man in Fox Tooth, without firewater. I gave him a bucking few men know could come their way. I never bucked him off, but I popped his cork. I bucked off Lone Wolf and Two Horns, though they rode better next time, learned to hold me good when I bucked. Fox Tooth and me gave what we had, one to the other, till we had nothing left to give. I thanked him for sparing our lives, didn't mention I stole his horse.

I went back to my daughter, felt good that night, best time I had in the robes since Wolf Mountain with Two Horns. I'll say this about Crow—when they want to, they can make a woman's heart very happy.

At sunrise, Friend of Otter and me got ready to leave. Fox Tooth proved himself a gentleman, gave tanned doeskin hides for my daughter, to make her a dress.

I touched his cheek, rode off with Friend of Otter, my daughter on our pony drag.

Fox Tooth sat bareback on his pinto horse; war bonnet feathers flowed down his back. He looked handsome against the rising sun. Fox Tooth barked his sweet farewell, "I will dream of you till I dieeee. Till we meet in the next life, sweet womannnnn."

A better farewell than the first one he gave, to cut out my heart and eat it.

Friend of Otter's eyes perked, like I been peculiar. I said nothing, none of his business what I did with Fox Tooth.

I got two marriage proposals from that Crow family, one from the sister, the other from the brother.

I felt bad for all the things I said about Crow. Fine people.

Our life, best I could know what lay ahead—become cows herded by the Great White Father and his bluecoats, on a reservation.

But I had other plans—they might take a while.

★ ★ ★ ★ ★

PART IV
THIS EARTH ROUND?

★ ★ ★ ★ ★

CHAPTER FORTY-FIVE
CALLED BY A VISION

"Only one gunnysack, daughter?"

Mountain Girl, six snows in her, looked down. She only brought the one gunnysack, thinking she had two. The season was early spring, 1883, in the white man winter count, crocus blooming their purple flower. We'd settled to reservation life in the Dakotas. I walked alongside a prairie dog hill a mile from our reservation, on land dotted by red paint brush and small-ear cactus. Friend of Otter cut some of the cactus for making soup thick after we got home. A clear cool morning, no dust in the air, Friend of Otter held a shovel, I had a rake. We wore cotton shirts, overalls, and moccasins hunting rattlesnakes. My daughter chased meadowlarks and prairie dogs. I didn't want to bring more sadness to my daughter's heart; I told Friend of Otter to throw our snakes in the one sack. He stretched the sack over four forked sticks like the buffalo stomach for making soup. Near noon, we had a gunnysack half full of angered snakes.

"Rattler!" Friend of Otter yelled, pointed behind me beneath a tumbleweed. Before I turned, the snake struck my overalls, tried to get his poison in my ankle. I swooped the rattler with the rake, threw him over my shoulder to Friend of Otter. His pet crow, Parfleche, perched on his shoulder, kept for him by Trader Walton.

"Scares me when you throw rattlers at me," Friend of Otter said. "We don't need money this bad." He scooped a snake with the shovel after I flung one his way, dumped the rattler in the

289

sack with the corn flour picture. A dozen mad, just after snows, rattlers in a sack before I had enough for a day. At a dollar a snake for collectors back east, or skin for boot makers, we made good money. I wanted to be a business lady, like Miss Brenda. White folks called me Rattler Lady. Near twenty-two snows in me, a grown woman in my view, raising a daughter. Had to be practical in the white man's world. I planned on getting a trading post for me and Friend of Otter—like C.W. Schultz and Mr. McFadden. We needed money to build the post, to do what Miss Brenda taught me about not depending on a husband.

Parfleche flew off Friend of Otter's shoulder when a snake came his way, squawked, *"Hókahé!"* The bird came back to his roost on Friend of Otter's shoulder, waited for cornbread. The bird, like Friend of Otter, had no patience, followed his moods, had his own spirit calling. That bird was not of this world in any way the eye could see. The bird had spirits like those that roamed in Friend of Otter, who didn't want to only be a man. The bird didn't want to only be a bird—he wanted the respect two-leggeds gave to any who can talk.

"Ma, can we go home?" Mountain Girl said. She wanted to play with the daughter of Medicine Feet Woman.

Though Friend of Otter got only twelve dollars and fifty cents for his half of two gunnysacks of snakes, he bought calico dresses for my daughter, from traders. He spoiled her, gave my daughter an uncle in the family I put together for her. She called Lone Wolf's mother, "Uŋči," grandmother. Made my heart happy to know my daughter had a loving family. Her father's Húŋkpapa people would visit us when they could. I walked behind my daughter and Friend of Otter after the rattler tried to bite me. I felt dizzy, looked up. There he sat, on a rock near the gully that led past our camp, in white buckskin, a red-striped hawk on his head, lightning bolt painted on his cheek.

"Tašúŋke Witkó?" I said.

My knees gave way, I sat down, dizzy, dropped the sack of squirming snakes. Did I work too hard, the sun get to my head? Or did snake poison get to my ankle? Seemed a vision, but I wanted no part of any spirit world.

"Am I dreaming? Is that you, my chief? You dead? Or you fake dying, hid out in these hills?"

"Dead as I will ever be," Crazy Horse said, jumped off the rock, came toward me, a teasing look on his face, how he looked when he told stories to kids around a campfire.

Friend of Otter yelled for me to hurry. I told him to get our lunch, I'd come along shortly. Friend of Otter grumbled, went on ahead.

"What you want, my chief?" I said.

Can a body have a waking dream, or was I wrong about the spirit world? To me, when you died, that was the end of you. You lived in folks' memory. Any spirit to me was just wind rubbing tall grass together on a quiet day.

Crazy Horse motioned for me to come closer.

I looked through fog at faces above me. Friend of Otter held my hand, the doc wrapped my ankle. Mountain Girl was doing her tears, holding the doll I made for her—tanned deerskin and cattail cotton from the gully where that snake got his poison in my ankle.

"Will she always talk crazy?" Friend of Otter said to the doc.

"A *dee*lirium," Doc said, closed his satchel, patted my hand while I lay on my robes. "I got most of the poison out of her."

"Where am I?" I said, looking around. I was in my cabin. Seemed I'd been talking to Crazy Horse, enjoyed seeing him, even if in the spirit world.

"Ma!" my daughter said, threw her arms around my neck.

"You got a snake bite, you crazy Rattler Lady," Friend of Otter said. "I told you we had no need for more snake." Then he spoke soft, tried to, asked how I felt. Men don't know how to comfort none, but Friend of Otter gave a try; wearing a dress don't give a woman's heart to a man.

"I have felt better in my life," I said, tried to comfort my daughter, but another vision came. Fog flowed through my head. Crazy Horse sat in my shack, legs crossed, his back straight.

"Why have you come?" I said. "What do you want from me, my chief?"

"The man who planned the blood spilled by our people, who killed off our buffalo—a good day for him to die."

"*Sher i dan?*"

"Mmmmmm," Crazy Horse said. "You heard from the black and white paper of the trader that Sheridan comes to Yellowstone Park, to show off the park to their Great White Father."

"Yes. Trader Walton read us that crazy story."

"Go there, rub him out."

The vision vanished, or I had me a *dee*lirium. Was my heart speaking, wanted revenge for the dog treatment we got from the white man, or did Crazy Horse find a way back to this world?

I felt I had a mission for my people, for my son and husbands, for the starving life Sheridan gave us, the army lying about our reservation on the Powder River, lying about the Pahá Sápa being ours for as long as the grass growed and water flowed. And for the mood that came to me—I reckon a snake bite can do that to a body.

When I got over the fever, me and Friend of Otter readied for a ride through the Black Hills.

"Our duty to our people," I told him—he was not happy about my new belief in spirit visions.

"All the money we saved for a trading post will go for a stagecoach ride to rub out a Long Knife chief, and maybe we get hung?" He didn't want to go, but he was my friend.

Trader Walton had put on specs in his cabin to read us about a trip West by General Sheridan with a Great White Father, to get more pay for his soldiers, and keep poachers out of the park.

I never heard about a white man park.

"How long will we be gone?" Friend of Otter said.

"We come back when cherries get ripe. It depends if we have to hide after we do him in, or we look like Friendlies on a wander."

"And Mountain Girl?" he said, loading coffee, beans, pemmican, molasses, flour, Saratoga potatoes, and pans for cooking, on the packhorse. "She's never been away from you."

"Two new moons without me won't harm my daughter."

I felt guilty—how he wanted me to feel.

Time to go. We got two lard cans hid beneath the floor of my shack—seventy-two dollars and forty-five cents in the cans, a fortune to my way of thinking. I put the cans in my skin bag, petted my horse, ran some of Friend of Otter's medicine up my horse's nose, and on his tail. I figured I'd use Sioux medicine for a Sioux vision. Friend of Otter offered the stem of his pipe to the Four Directions, the earth and sky before we took off for Deadwood. There, we'd catch a stage to Milestown, a town of varmints near where we stole Bearcoat's cows on that cold winter.

"Ma, don't leave me," my daughter cried, watched us strap our last pack on the horse.

"Your Aunt Medicine Feet Woman and Gramma will take good care of you."

I hid the fear clouding my heart, hugged her close, kissed her, rode off to Deadwood. My daughter's voice followed me in the breeze, singing the Mother Song I taught her, wanting to be safe under her mother's wings. It broke my heart to leave her.

Friend of Otter had one condition for coming along—we had to bring his pet crow, Parfleche.

CHAPTER FORTY-SIX
JOURNEY TO DEADWOOD

"Two Jacks?" Friend of Otter asked his question on our ride north. I'd taught him a little English, just enough to probably get us in trouble.

"The black and white paper said Two Jacks hunted buffalo for those who built the iron horse, a kolā with General Sheridan, says Trader Walton. A fancy pants," I said. "No more buffalo to shoot. To make a living, Two Jacks plans Indian shows for the railroad man bringing guests from across the Great Water. They'll see the park and his hotel the same time the Great White Father comes with the army."

"Two Jacks will want *us* for a show?" Friend of Otter joked about my plan to settle scores with the general. "I don't think so."

"Do your spirit man prayers, let me do the planning. Do something you're good at."

"Prayers give no help to those who don't believe."

"Preach to me later."

Friend of Otter, dressed like a man, rode ahead of me, his legs hung over the sides of his sorrel while he bobbed along. He sang to his horse how he'd grown used to her pace, her ups, downs, and horse ways. His pet crow, Parfleche, perched on his shoulder; the bird's cage tied on a packhorse behind me. After me, that bird gave him his best friend. We came to White River; ahead through the Black Hills lay our destination—Deadwood, the most Indian hating town in the West. I would use what I learned in Fort Benton about how to get along with murdering monsters.

It would take three moons to reach where we'd buy tickets for the stagecoach to Milestown. Between Deadwood and Milestown was nothing except prairie, sagebrush, prickly pear, and robbers.

"You have Parfleche, and I can shoot and ride like a wild Indian," I said. "A bird who says 'A good day to die' in the wašíču tongue might hold interest for Two Jacks's Indian show. I can cook, too, Indian style."

"You can't cook good, you crazy iyéska."

He called me a breed, *iyéska*, knew that word riled me, reminded me of my bluecoat Pa. I trotted to his horse, whacked the horse's *be*hind, sent him bucking till Friend of Otter fell off. We coaxed the sorrel back with a sack of oats. Parfleche got upset at what I did, flew at my head, calmed down when I tossed him a biscuit.

Friend of Otter apologized for what he called me, and the hurt eased between us. Parfleche flied to the arse of Friend of Otter's horse, watched me, not trusting me no more.

The black and white paper that Trader Walton read to us said the Great White Father and soldier escorts would take a train from Washington City to the Mississippi River, go by train till they rode horses up the Snake River to the park with a soldier escort, led by Sheridan. With a senator potentate from Missouri. Trader Walton read us about an Indian show at that same time, planned by a railroad man to impress *too*rists, show off his hotel in the park. The supplies for the show would be shipped up the Elk River, what wašíču called the Yellowstone. The supplies came from Bismarck to Milestown, a wild town that sprouted near the fort built by Bearcoat the winter after we wiped out Custer. White men named the town in honor of Bearcoat, whose family name was Miles. Soldier names for prairie land sprouted like weeds after a fire, where before were only Indian names for rivers and mountains.

I took a look in the pouches Friend of Otter got from an Omaha friend. An Omaha chief done in seven of his enemy at a dinner, slipped poison mushrooms, with pepper— *yamnúmnužapi*—in their dinner. That's how I'd do in this general who planned the wipeout of buffalo, killed my baby son and husband—I'd poison him.

"Don't spook my horse again," Friend of Otter said when I checked the *žapi*.

I gave him my apology. "And in this other pouch?"

"Vision mushrooms from my friend," he said.

"Only vision that might come to the general will be ancestors lifting his scalp in the spirit world."

The thought gave Friend of Otter a laugh.

We looked where we might pitch camp our second night in the Pahá Sápa.

I saw why Crazy Horse didn't fear dying to keep those awesome hills. Streams flowed, with wildflower meadows, pine trees prettier than any painted picture. From afar, forests made the hills look like a tatáŋka head. Prairie dog towns here and there, and buffalo grass grew so high you could not see over the grass standing up, if you're short as me. Deer, elk, and bear roamed in valleys. So quiet, filled with mystery, you could see spirits float around the rocky peaks. Fish jumped in lakes and streams, searched for flies and mosquitoes while we rode by. Crazy Horse had visions in these hills when younger, up on Bear Butte. When clouds came, it seemed a buffalo robe fell over us, made dark the grass and hills. I felt close to the mystery of this earth in those hills. Spirit caves ran deep in them. And we rode by old gold holes dug by prospectors.

"Someone follows," Friend of Otter said when we stopped to water our horses.

"Why do you say that?"

"Maybe I saw a shadow, on horseback. Behind us."

Sundown.

We hobbled our horses in a meadow, made camp. Friend of Otter cooked us supper. I laid our robes in a dry creek bed, grabbed a river stone for a headrest, put my wolfskin pillow on the mudded stone. I took the revolver I stole from a soldier who tried to sweet-talk me, loaded up, got my skinning knife.

We left a fire burn to give pause to any varmint who might follow.

Bright stars that night—would take more 'n a hundred lifetimes to count the stars, ancestors' campfires. Ants and rattler holes in the grass made you look twice where you stepped. Parfleche squawked about something—the only sound in the night. Cornbread shut up his empty belly.

"Hi, sweetheart," the bird said, enjoyed his supper.

"Like when we stole Psáloka ponies?" I said to Friend of Otter, watched the black night come over us.

All I heard were snores.

I hoped Lone Wolf approved my plan. I said goodnight to Lone Wolf, told him revenge was on the way for his death at Greasy Grass. I gave a goodnight to Two Horns, brave father of my daughter.

I crawled under my robes, my turn to watch for shadows.

I fell asleep on my watch.

CHAPTER FORTY-SEVEN
NEVER TRUST A SINGING CHEYENNE

Parfleche squawked, woke me up.

"Hi, sweetheart! Hókahé! Whohhhk. Aaaaarrrk."

The Indian ran at me, waving a knife and war club, let out a whoop. I looked to Friend of Otter's robe—empty. My heart about flew out my chest, cocked my gun, aimed at the Indian.

Friend of Otter leaped from behind a boulder, whacked him with a club. The varmint fell like a cannonball hit him.

Friend of Otter studied him. "Šahíyela," he said. Cheyenne.

I had me a look. I saw this Cheyenne at the sweetheart dance at Peži Slá Wakpá, the night before Custer attacked.

"Why would a Cheyenne want to do us in?" I said. Cheyenne were friends of Sioux.

We needed explaining from our prisoner before we sent him to his *re*ward.

Friend of Otter tied our knocked-out prisoner's hands behind his back, around a pine trunk, stuck his legs apart with rawhide tied to pony stakes. I went to a rattler hole, got a snake mad enough to come out, rammed a pronged stick on the snake's head, grabbed the snake behind his head, not let him get his fangs in me. Friend of Otter tied the rattler's tail to rawhide rope. We staked the rattler near the Cheyenne; the snake's striking barely missed the varmint's foot.

A scared Cheyenne woke when the sun came up.

"Eeeeeahhhh!"

"Good morning," I signed, a little rattler brother of his—not knowing his tongue. I got coffee going on a flat stone near the fire. The snake hissed, gave what rattle a snake can with his tail staked. We had us an old snake, going by the number of beads on the tail. His tongue darted out, sniffed air due to poor eyesight, searched for a target in his angered mood. I once cut a rattler's head only to have the head run along the ground, snap fangs at me till I gave the head a whack. Never knew a critter so wanting to make enemy pay for disrespecting a snake warning, or for getting food in his belly.

"Why you attack Lakóta?" Friend of Otter signed, picked up a stone, sharpened his knife while the Cheyenne watched, eyes on that blade.

"Didn't know you were Lakóta," the Šahíyela said, in Lakóta He whimpered like a baby, a bump on the side of his head. The snake coiled, rattled. I threw a stick, the smell of ash on the stick. The snake bit the stick hard.

"Uhhhh," the Cheyenne groaned, saw his fate.

He lied that he didn't know he attacked Lakóta. I took molasses from our pony drag, ran some on the Cheyenne's bare foot, up his leg, across his skinny belly, up his neck, over his mouth and nose, around his eye, into his ear.

"Ant feeding time," I said.

I got me a cup of hot coffee and a biscuit.

"You ride far from your reservation, cousin," I told him.

Ants crawled up the Cheyenne's leg in no time, over his bare belly.

"They bite hard," Friend of Otter said, chewed a biscuit. "Sound like a wagon cannon blowing up in your ear. Then they dig in your head, cousin."

"I am just a poor Cheyenne," he said, looked for pity, embarrassed his relatives. "Shoot me and have me done with." His relatives would have been proud of those brave words.

We ignored him.

"I have a wife, Lakóta like you, three kids. I need the rifle and supplies the white chief offered for the woman's head. We starve at our reservation."

"What white chief offered that for her head?" Friend of Otter said, angered, threw down his biscuit, went to the Cheyenne who looked so scared I feared he might wet himself.

"*Mr. McFadden?*" I said.

I'd forgot about my no-account husband. I heard of angry *dee*vorces, but this one between my husband and me took all prizes. I cut his privates; he wanted my head cut off.

"WHO?" Friend of Otter said.

"Hi, sweetheart," Parfleche said.

"Shut your mouth," Friend of Otter told his bird. Parfleche cocked his head like he never heard Friend of Otter talk to him like that before.

"My no-good husband before I joined the Lakóta," I told him.

"She made him almost Not A Man," the Cheyenne said. He laughed, ants crawled up his neck, over the molasses on his lips, to his ear. The rattler coiled, popped at his foot, and this Real Human laughed. Impressed me. He laughed at the thought, he said, of an Indian woman cutting the tip of a white man's organ, who probably had the cut coming.

"They call you Barber Lady," the Cheyenne said, getting words out between his laughs. "But not your husband. Noooo. Hee. Hee. Hah. Strong medicine woman, you."

I could not help myself, I laughed. I liked this Cheyenne. Friend of Otter didn't join our fun. "Should I slit the Šahíyela's throat or let him die laughing?" he said.

That got our prisoner laughing till tears flowed.

"A good day to die," the Cheyenne joked, made fun of our passing warrior days. "Count coup on me, cousin."

"A good day to die," Parfleche squawked. I threw a stick at

the cage to shut him up, but the bird had more of a sense of humor than Friend of Otter.

The Cheyenne said, "If I had money for a gun, her head would be in my bag. My poverty did me in."

"No, cousin," Friend of Otter said, "you don't know how to track without being spotted. Do not blame your lack of skill on your poverty."

We got our robes rolled, packed everything to continue our trip. We'd let the Cheyenne get bit by ants or the rattler, after the snake broke off his tail. I tripped on a log, fell on my turnip head. When I came to, Crazy Horse sat by our dying fire.

"What? What now?" I said, perturbed.

"Who are you talking to?" Friend of Otter said.

Crazy Horse said to me, "You really want to do in this Šahíyela?"

"Why not? He tried to cut off my head."

"Maybe he would make a useful kolá on your mission. Think on that."

"I will. Now, go away."

"All right. But take that muddy stone you used for a pillow, as good medicine. Put the stone in your skin bag. Call this place, *The Ravine With One Bad Šahíyela and One Good Crow.* The bird saved your scalp, be more careful."

"Hokahé!" Friend of Otter hollered, impatient to get going.

"Hokahé," Parfleche said.

No patience in that man or his bird.

I packed the stone, asked the Cheyenne if he wanted to see his wife and kids again. He surely would. Would he help us on a mission, then see his wife and kids again? He surely would. Against Friend of Otter's wishes, I cut free the man's hands and feet, threw the snake in weeds, gave our Cheyenne a cold biscuit. I told Friend of Otter we had a change of plan. He grumbled.

"I owe you my life," the Cheyenne said, happy, rubbed off

ants, chewed his biscuit.

"Don't forget what you owe," I told him.

He rounded up his horse, rode off with us. The Cheyenne had the name Old Hand.

Friend of Otter asked who I talked to before the Cheyenne. To myself, I told him, and to wind rubbing grass together.

We rode through a meadow filled with cattails and dancing butterflies. The Cheyenne asked why we needed his help.

"To rub out a no-account army chief," I told him.

"Oh," he said. "Good."

After some thought, he said, "Coup counting days are over, cousin."

"We are not counting coup. We are gonna settle a score, kill."

"Unnn," he said to that. "Good." Hearing him say that, Friend of Otter took a liking to our new friend.

Old Hand sang while he rode; we had a singing Cheyenne, singing in his own tongue. A sweet voice on him, crooning to the skies and pine woods about whatever gave Cheyenne a happy heart.

I would learn, never trust a singing Cheyenne with a secret.

CHAPTER FORTY-EIGHT
DEADWOOD

The town looked hungover from a winter drunk, drunks staggering on the mud streets.

A muddy road sloshed through Deadwood for the local inhabitants, the prospectors, horse thieves, gamblers, pay-money women, and drunks who called the wood shacks their homes. More preachers than saloons, making a living saving worthless souls.

We stopped at a stage office with my skin bag, the lard cans with our snake money in the bag, and the good medicine stone Crazy Horse told me to keep. I emptied the bag on the counter, let the agent see he had paying customers, not drunk Indians.

The agent said I didn't have enough money for three tickets. I told him the Cheyenne would ride his horse, we only needed two tickets.

"If you came here few years back, you'da got your heads cut, clean off, and we'd have shooting contests at Injun heads," he said. "Now get outa here." He waved his arm at us.

A little weasel meandered up from the end of the counter, eyed the stone. "Lord, save us. Know what you got, little lady?" the short feller said.

"A stone and lard cans with money."

"No, ma'am. No, sirree. Rub mud off that rock; feast your gaze on Beelzebub's Eye. A stone of pure gold, missy," he said. "Biggest hunk of Devil's metal I ever saw."

"Where'd you find the rock, sweetheart?" the agent said,

rubbed off the dried mud like a crazy man. "You could buy the whole stage line, horses, too, if you want."

The short feller smiled with his missing teeth mouth, "Where'd you find the rock, honey?"

He talked to me like I was a dumb Indian. I knew gold, just not mudded gold. "I wondered when you fellers would notice," I said, gave a smile.

The little man put his nose to the rock like he could smell yellow metal. I drew maps for the intruder and the agent that would lead them to hellholes in the Badlands.

"Missy," the little intruder said, "the upstanding citizens here had a two-hundred-dollar reward for heads like yours. You seem to have a Indian head on your shoulders. Might I be of service to protect your person and your lovely scalp?" He bowed low, give a toothy grin. One of the best liars I ever met, almost good as me.

"And who might you be, sir?"

"I spent time in the company of the Indian. Adopted son of a chief among the Cheyenne. At your service, missy."

"Well, sir, I have Cheyenne protection," I said, nodded outside the window to Old Hand.

The agent grabbed a map from the counter, pointed me to the assay office. The little man grabbed a map for himself, tipped his hat, took off for the Badlands.

And I became a rich widow.

We gave our horses to the Cheyenne, sent him back to his wife. No need for a singing Cheyenne who couldn't track a wíŋkte and woman without being spotted. We loaded him with presents for his kids, a rifle for himself. He kept his bow and arrows, proudly hung that rifle and case on his new saddle. He gave us the crossed handshake of friendship, apologized for trying to take my head. He said if we ever visited his reservation, a pot of stew would be ready. He rode off with his head high, bow and quiver across his back, singing a song. He had the heart of my Lone Wolf, a man too kind to kill for money. A minstrel, with the heart of a boy.

Friend of Otter and me bought fancy clothes for our mission. White folks called me *Señora*. I must have looked to them like a cross between a Mex and a white. I drew fake maps to where I found the gold, gave maps to folks all bent over to help us now that we were rich Indians.

We put our Indian clothes in a trunk, with the žapi and paper money, got hot baths at the fancy but stinking No. 11 in that hellhole. I bought more pretty dresses than I knew came in this world—calico, silk, cotton, some with humps on the *behind*. I discovered I liked to shop for fancy clothes as much as I loved bear grease on roast elk, becoming more like my ma. Friend of Otter got himself a lovely suit, silk shirts with fancy buttons, and a black derby. He cut a hole in the derby hat, let his akičhita feather stick through it. He had his first taste of firewater and a hangover. At least he stopped nagging about our mission.

I bought dresses for my daughter, put the dresses with mine, folded nice in the trunk. I bought the prettiest lever Winchester I ever laid eyes on, gold inlay in the wood stock. I loaded the rifle, took practice shots in the hills. One sweet rifle. I fixed the sights for a long shot in case our poison couldn't do in a blue-coat general.

We readied for the journey to Milestown.

"Some rules before we git on, folks."

We gave our attention to the stage driver, a rusted skin feller name of Deek Malone.

"Listen up, only give 'em one time," Mr. Deek said. "No drinking, less you share your bottle. No *ceegar* smoke, got the gentler sex on board. If you chew, spit out the window, with the wind, not in the wind. You got that?"

Only passenger in the coach with Friend of Otter and me was a feller the stage driver knew name of Cal. Cal wore an old leather hat, plaid flannel shirt buttoned at the neck, suspenders to hold his mudded pants that flowed over boots. A pistol at his waist stuck in a rope that belted his trousers. More ugly and smelly than a wolverine that came with a den full of pups.

Cal waved his hand, understood the rules. Me and Friend of Otter nodded; we got his words.

"Couple more," Mr. Deek said, lifted his broad brim to wipe the sweatband. "No snoring if you catch some winks. We travel nights to keep the horses cooled. You can keep firearms on your person, but no practice shoots out a window; it scares the horses. They git scared, run wild for any reason, no jumping off the stage. That's important, ya got that? Don't follow rules, off ya go. Final word, no talk about robbers. No gold on this run, should be an easy ride. Say howdy to each other and we'll be on our way."

He spit tobacco to the ground, slammed the coach door like we were a nuisance.

"Wanna drink?" Cal kindly offered his bottle when we pulled out of Deadwood. He had a peculiar voice—I learned killers came in all shapes and peculiarities. I didn't like the pistol at his waist, if he got an anger on, whiskeyed up, suspect I had money in my trunk.

"I don't drink," I told Cal.

Friend of Otter wanted a swallow, but I stared him out of it.

"Pity," Cal said, swigged his bottle, gave a belch from his belly like a toad full of water. " 'Scuse me," he said, stuck the bottle in his pocket, let loose another cannon shot our way.

We had ourselves a long trip, some two hundred miles as the crow flies, the agent said. They stuck my trunk with my dresses and paper money, and Friend of Otter's bag, under a canvas cover in the rear boot. The bigger metal cage I got for Parfleche in Deadwood was roped on top, give the bird good air, enjoy the sights. Parfleche earned his keep, with his squawks about the Cheyenne trying to lift my head. Two men rode up front; the older, bushy faced feller had a shotgun and lever Winchester. Him and Mr. Deek carried Colt six-shooters, two apiece to keep us safe from robbers.

I wore my new yellow bonnet with a fake daisy on the top, brown cotton skirt to my ankles, white silk blouse frilled nice at the neck—looking the lady. Friend of Otter had the derby hat he cut a hole in for his coup feather, long hair combed down his back, under the derby. Green suspenders held up his buckskin trousers that fell over the moccasins I'd cut and beaded for him, a green silk shirt, open at the neck. I could not talk him out of this unusual regalia. Wiŋkte could have peculiarities to go with their spirit calling, least this one could. But Friend of Otter looked good, seemed to me, given how big and tall the man stood. He wore the derby on Deadwood boardwalks, strutted proud as a prairie chicken showing feathers. No one in Deadwood messed with him.

His coup feather bent on the coach roof; he took off his derby, untied the feather, slipped the derby and feather under his seat next to me. Six horses pulled us along, harnessed good. The sway bar under the coach carried us in more comfort than I thought possible in that contraption. Curtains rolled up on the windows gave us fresh prairie air, except for the smell that came from Cal.

When we stopped to do our privates in bushes, I learned Cal came into this world a woman.

CHAPTER FORTY-NINE

NEVER SHAG A LADY IN
A PRICKLY PEAR RAVINE

She called herself California Pearl, came with her folks from California, her folks looking to strike it rich. When her folks got the fever, died, she seen them buried and she stayed put. Said she lost her money gambling in Deadwood. Our Indian names bothered her so Miss Pearl gave me the name of Alice. Friend of Otter got called Bob. Bob and Alice—no mind to me what we got called. She had a cabin outside Milestown. "What be the nature of your travels, Alice?" Miss Pearl said.

"Bob, my cousin, and me, are on our way to Milestown to buy property," I said, made up my story while we bumped along. "Gonna try our hand at farming, run some cows. Got us money for finding more yellow than the moon."

"You're a good liar, Alice," Miss Pearl said, "done a bit of that myself." She drank from her bottle while we swapped yarns. Right fine lady, Miss Pearl. "Your cousin is the biggest damn Injun I ever laid eyes on," she said, not knowing Friend of Otter knew some wašíču tongue.

"*Hau,* miss," Friend of Otter said. She shook her head at his knowing her tongue, laughed at the peculiar Indians who shared her coach.

Couple days later, the stage still had some miles to the town named after Bearcoat. More than a thousand hooligans lived in Milestown, Miss Pearl said. "Milestown's wild, makes Deadwood a gathering of Sunday preachers, but they don't shoot Indians, not like in Deadwood. Not in town, anyways."

Around a bend, from behind the only trees along the trail for miles, two men rode out before our sleeping guard woke to his task. Red kerchiefs on the face—I saw them out my window, was going to wave, meet new companions but one hollered to the guard, "Don't give it a thought! Put your hands above your heads and no one gits shot up." They pointed six-shooters, long barrels; Mr. Deek reined the horses. I opened the stage door to see what our new friends wanted.

"No gold on board, gents," Deek said, calm, spit tobacco juice that fell on our window. "Sorry to waste your time."

"O, tarnation," Miss Pearl said, sobered up. "Robbers." I got fear. Paper money was hid in the bottom of my trunk and I needed the money for my trading post after we wiped out Sheridan.

"Hi, sweetheart," Parfleche said to the robbers. A robber, not knowing crow humor, shot lead in the bars on the cage. We near tumbled out of the stage, raised our hands. Parfleche squawked, "Kiss my arse. Kiss my . . ."

"Shut that bird up," a robber said, angered, "or I'll shut him up."

Friend of Otter scrambled to the top of the stage, threw a coat over the cage.

"Put your valuables in my brother's hat. No tricks, and no one takes lead. Rings, watches, guns, all the money on your person. Any gold dust, too. Throw down the bags from the back and front stage boots. Sorry, ma'am, all the bother this fine day," what seemed the older robber said to me, tipped his dusty cowboy hat, showed me his hair.

I signed to Friend of Otter to do what they said while I figured a plan. Friend of Otter threw down his bag and my trunk from the rear boot. Deek grabbed Miss Pearl's bag from the front boot, dropped it to the ground. We put our valuables, what they were, in the younger feller's hat. Deek said to a robber, "Zeke, come on, I know you boys and your ma. She'd not want you robbing stages."

The one he talked to lifted his kerchief, spit. "She sent us, so shut up, Deek, and forgit who you think robs you. Ma needs some silver for cows, after Pa passed on. Throw down their bags from the boots, we know you got no gold."

I asked if I could scratch my knee because I had a itch there, itched like the devil in the hot sun.

"Course, ma'am," the older robber said, the one who wasn't Zeke. Real *po*lite, he was. "First, throw down all guns and knives."

Miss Pearl unhitched the pistol from her belt, threw her gun to the grass. Me and Friend of Otter showed open hands, no guns or knives. Guard and driver tossed down the shotgun, Winchester, and six-shooters. Friend of Otter pulled a knife from his boot, dropped it—an honest Indian. I eyed him—no need to throw in a knife they *don't know about.*

The younger one, Zeke, saw Friend of Otter and me, said, "What are Indins doing on this stage, Deek?" I saw my way to save my trunk full of money. "I'm only part Indin," I said. "Rest of me is like you boys, white. Not white like a lily, if you know what I mean." I gave a smile, looked sweet as I could, their six-shooters shifting to aim at my head. "Thank you for letting me scratch the itch," I said, hefted my skirt slow to above my knees, showed some leg to our robbers. Though I came not pretty to this world, had me legs that came in handy. I saw them look, pulled the hem higher, moved my legs apart more while I scratched the itch. A little higher on the hem, they'd see the derringer I bought in Deadwood, stuck in my garter. A one shot—not sure right then how I might do in two varmints.

"I always dreamed about being with outlaws," I said, made my eyes wide to the robbers how I saw Medicine Feet Woman do to her Ireland William at Fort Robinson. "I could show you boys a good time, if you take me, leave these boring folks ride on."

They said nothing, but one gave a look to the other—they warmed to the offer.

"Well, little lady, maybe you can have your dream. What say you, Zechiel?" said the older robber.

"Ain't had none I didn't have to pay for in a long time, Will," Zechiel said. He winked at me over his kerchief. "Not have to worry none about getting diseased up, neither. Some half 'n half sounds good, if the rest is like her legs."

"Gentlemen," I said, "could we proceed to the bushes, get these bags after you do me? I've not been done good in a long time."

"Well, of course, ma'am," Will said, lifted his kerchief, spit tobacco.

"Git," he said to Deek. "You pick her up, after."

Friend of Otter and Miss Pearl got back in the coach. "Hókahé," Friend of Otter hollered out the window to Mr. Deek. Deek looked my way, see if I would be all right. I waved. Mr. Deek slapped the reins and the horses took a lope. I headed for the ravine with bushes and prickly pear cactus; robbers rode slow behind me. I swayed how Miss Brenda taught worked a man's mind, swayed fine as horse's arse if the woman swayed right. Held my hand to the back of my head, patted the bun like my hair might fall out of the ribbons holding my hair, like a pony's tail ready for war.

"Oooo," I said. "Men would pay a gold piece for what you boys gonna git. Best half 'n half to ever come your way." They jumped off their horses, tied reins to brush. "Me first, Zeke," said Will.

"No. Me first, brother. Don't like seconds."

"My idee, hold up this stage," Will said.

"No, it was Ma's idee."

But Will won the battle.

"I git shy, boys, when a man does me. You do me, one at a time, private?" I said.

"Sure, ma'am," Will said. "What you say, brother?"

Zeke gave a nod.

The older brother, Will, followed me down the ravine where grew fewer prickly pears, for shagging. Will had a mustache above his mouth, bushy and dark, reminded me of skunk tail.

"Hang your gun on a bush, cowboy? Limits my charms to have guns on a man when he does me."

Skunk Will peeled off his gun belt, hung the belt on a bush. I took my hat with the daisy flower, dropped the hat to grass, unbuttoned my blouse at the back. I blew him a kiss, licked my lips, gave him a smile. To his eyes, he had a mare in considerable heat waiting for him.

"Boots, Honey Will?"

Will near jumped out of his boots, dropped them to the grass.

"Trousers, too? Rough on a girl's skin."

He pulled off his boots, dropped his trousers—old long johns underneath.

"Oooo, what a man you are," I said, let him see me run my tongue over my lips, Miss Brenda's learning coming in handy. His brother shouted, "Hurry up, ain't got all day. It's hot up here."

"Almost there," Will yelled. "Plenty here to go around."

I loosed my skirt at the waist, pulled up the hem, slow, teased him, got his mind cloudy, showed him more leg. A wet cedar color to my leg, curved down nice to my ankle. He grinned, liked what he saw, spit tobacco.

"Can't wait no more, woman," Will said, coming to me. "Not had none since at Annie Turner's. A good whore, but you look sweeter." He wore his hat, and I thought that was fair—let him wear his hat on the way to his *re*ward—cowboys loved their hats.

I pulled my skirt higher, kept a leg away from his eyes, took hold of the derringer, waited till he breathed on me, whipped out that derringer, stuck the little gun in his face. His eyes got big as apples. "You rob the wrong lady, cowboy. Got me a daughter to care for, and she needs my money more than your ma." I pulled the trigger. Lead hit him between his eyes; he went down like his legs got roped. I ran for his six-shooter, had me more business to take care of.

His brother hollered, ran through bush, busting twigs, "You shoot her? Didn't get my turn."

I ran too late for the gun. Zechiel stood on top of the ravine, six-shooter in hand. His hat fell off during his run; he squinted, sun shining on his face, an old scar under one eye. He saw his brother with the blooded hole in his head, cocked his six-shooter, aimed at my head, screamed, "You shot my brother, you bitch breed!"

I've been called worse by men with more standing in a community than Zeke. I thought of my daughter in the moment before he pulled the trigger, closed my eyes to what was coming my way, my daughter growing up without me, her ma dead because I needed the money to give her a good life. Zeke groaned, I looked up. He plopped like a pine cone, straight to the ground, face leading the way, an arrow in his back. The singing Cheyenne walked into view, waved, hung his bow over his back, skipping like a boy down the ravine. He busted off feathers on the arrow—no one'd know what tribe done in the robber. Zeke still had life, moaned, cried for mercy. Old Hand gave me a grin, scalped Zeke, who still had life. I turned my head, not able to watch. The robber screamed when the knife cut into his scalp. Old Hand told him to shut up.

"More coup this way," Old Hand said to me. "Repay you for

my life, Good Medicine Woman." He scalped the dead robber. Was ready to go.

"You can't leave him like that," I said, pointed with my chin to Zeke, still sucking air in his lungs, eyes wide at this world that had become strange. Old Hand took a robber six-shooter, BAM, sent Zechiel to his *re*ward. I let Old Hand keep their scalps and guns; we split their horses. I used their lariats to tie our bags and my trunk, dragged them while I rode the robber horse to the stage Friend of Otter stopped around the bend. I got the shakes at what happened that day.

Mr. Deek and the guard never asked what happened, but looked around when they saw Old Hand, worried more Indians might be hiding. The Cheyenne helped Friend of Otter load my trunk and Friend of Otter's bag in the rear boot, put Miss Pearl's in the front boot. Old Hand mounted his horse, waved, rode off with a robber horse, his honor returned. He rode off singing another song.

"What took you so long?" Friend of Otter said, lifted the coat off Parfleche's cage.

"I only had a one shot; Old Hand gave the other an arrow. Took time to get the scalps."

Mr. Deek asked Miss Pearl for a swig from her bottle to calm his nerves, shared the bottle with his partner. My esteem in Miss Pearl's eyes knew no limits. The stage drivers picked up their guns; Miss Pearl asked for her bottle back. We continued our trip to Milestown, a robber horse tied to the rear. Miss Pearl said she owed me a supper at her cabin.

Mr. Deek kindly got the stage company to return my ticket money. Our adventure spread through that town of varmints and I became a heroine to Milestown folks who held vigilantes like me in high regard. We saw a hanging tree outside town on the stage ride in. Two fellers hung from ropes around their necks, not moving on a quiet noon.

No, sir. Robbers, cheats, and liars didn't find pay in Miles-town.

Well, liars might.

CHAPTER FIFTY
MILESTOWN

We got us fancy rooms at the MacQueen House. For supper, they served roast mutton, Saratoga potatoes, coffee, strawberry tarts, and Yorkshire pudding. No more good eating days with this boring wašíču food. A smiley preacher name of Brother Van invited me and Friend of Otter to be saved at his church. "Been saved, brother," I said, "baptized in waters of the Big Muddy up north. Praise the Lord."

Town folks thought me a Mexican. I let them think what they wanted. I told them, "This man with me is my cousin, from my marrying into the Sioux. We came to buy land and cows for a ranch. Settle down." Then the story got going I had a rich miner husband I killed and scalped before taking his gold.

I let that story run, too.

Dirt streets in Milestown came decorated with horse shite, stray dogs, lost cows, and drunks. A hog or two. Only the third town I been to, after Fort Benton and Deadwood. Brick and wood buildings lined up on streets for no reason that came to my eye, stores, saloons, bordellos, churches with steeples pointed to the sky, blacksmith yards, a newspaper office. Those who could, read about local mysteries and goings-on that sell newspapers.

Towns, best I could tell, were where men rocked on porches, read newspapers, never slept in the same bed twice—least not with the same woman, if they could help it. The Sioux way made more sense—tipis in circles show everyone comes equal to this world, and the great Hoop of Life. You enter a village from where the sun comes up, East. Towns weren't built with anything more in mind than where you find water, flat land, and trees to cut.

Miss Pearl said Bearcoat Miles threw coffee cooler folks out of nearby Fort Keogh where he built barracks the winter we stole his cows. The loafers set up tents across the river. Two saloons doing business, and a gambling hall, before the sun even went down. Bordellos and churches came to keep the boys civilized. The trail that went from that tent city to Bismarck and Deadwood in the Dakotas became the main street of Miles-town, where our stage wheeled in. From Milestown, you could ride a stage to Bozeman, or to Fort Buford, further west. Could ride a steamer from Milestown, on what they called Yellowstone River—Elk River to Sioux—all the way to the Little Bighorn. When the iron horse came, Miss Pearl said steamer travel would end.

Folks were coming and going day and night like they had some almighty important things needed done. Freight wagons with supplies for buffalo hunters gave a mercantile start to many towns. Everything bought on what they called credit. Buffalo hides and tongues had paid off the credit. The drunks in Milestown shot six-shooters to the air; women wore pretty dresses to make everything look civilized. We strolled by a jail for those the vigilantes didn't hang, and a brick courthouse, newspaper office, two-seated jerkies, and two-wheel contraptions with a seat in the middle running the streets. They had something they talked into, to folks not even in the room—a white man contraption Friend of Otter thought had spirits.

Weasels lined up at MacQueen House to meet me, walk me to the Tongue River, court me and my money. Had to talk to my suitors at the river, didn't want to stink our boots in what horse,

317

cow, and hog drop on a street. Doors of saloons hung open day and night, noise and craziness flying from faro tables to the boardwalks. Annie Turner's bordello kept the boys calm, run by a black wašíču madam. A lady no one showed a heel to.

More saloons than churches.

What I had in mind—meet John J. Perkins, who would bring supplies to Yellowstone Park for his Indian show. They called him Two Jacks, a peculiar name to my ear. I wondered what he'd be like, how I'd get the invite to join his Indian show. Maybe use my woman charms, limited though they were.

Miss Pearl, over roasted grouse hen at her cabin, said Two Jacks seemed a gentleman to her, educated to a point, and he never got drunked up. He saw only one woman when in town, a high-priced lady at Annie Turner's he called Princess.

"Waits on him like his mother. Sees no other when he's in town. I don't like her," she said. "Snooty bitch, 'scuse my English. Men from here to Dodge spend a week's wages for a night with her. I'd give them better for a bottle of tangle leg. Has herself a fancy room at Annie Turner's where she meets Two Jacks."

I figured I best forget my woman charms on Two Jacks. Had himself a pay-woman, probably prettier than me and better in the robes.

"What does Two Jacks like to do?"

"Shooting contests, Alice," Pearl said. "Two Jacks beat every sharpshooter between here and the Rio Grande with his buffalo rifle. A hundred dollars to the man who can beat him at a hundred paces. Alice, I tried and I can shoot, believe you me. He's good. Braces his Henry, squeezes the trigger sweet." She showed how gentle he fingered a trigger. I could tell, she was in love.

"Could I meet your friend, Two Jacks? Just curious, you know."

"Of course, Alice. Any friend of mine is a friend of Two Jacks."

Friend of Otter got fed up with the noise and craziness of that town, said he'd come back after a while. He took his crow bird and cage, his war club, rode out on the robber's horse.

"Remember why we came here," I said. "I might need you to rescue my scalp."

The singing Cheyenne waited for him outside town; they rode north to hunt antelope.

"Psáloka country here!" I yelled, Crow country. "Be careful!"

"Two Jacks, meet my friend, Alice," Miss Pearl said to the man in buckskin sitting in the Cottage Saloon, puffing a cigar, telling Indian fighting stories to wašíču drunks.

"Howdy, Miss Alice," Two Jacks said, stood, took off his hat. He grabbed a chair for me next to him, asked if I wanted a drink. His *po*lite manners impressed me.

"Heard about you, ma'am. Boys," he said to his friends, "come back later. Pearl and me have a lovely guest, a veritable Helen of Troy, for whom any Paris would launch many a ship."

His words made no sense about a Helen of Troy, but his voice sounded nice, deep meadowlark song. Always struck a pose, showing off a mustache that curled up at the tips. Biggest bear in the berry patch to his mind and dressed in fine buckskin under a broad brim rawhide hat.

"Thank you, sir, for your kind words," I said, looked down, shy of his flatter. "Maybe a cool sass'parilla on this hot day."

I heard ladies order a sass'parilla at Keno Bill's in Fort Benton. I had no idea about the taste. We sat around the table; Miss Pearl ordered a double whiskey, put her boots on a chair. When her drink came, she threw down her whiskey in one swallow, held up the glass for another. I sat proper next to Two Jacks, straight-backed, like a lady—how Miss Brenda taught us at the bordello. I wore a dress I bought in Deadwood, frilled at the neck, sashed around the middle, tied in a bow at the back, and my yellow hat with the fake flower. Below the dress I wore fancy boots, brown of color, wiped clean and spit polished.

Miss Pearl entertained her friend with the story about me and the robbers.

"The fairer sex has more courage than most men know," Two Jacks said, eyed me with a curiosity and respect for a kind like his own. Him and me were respectable killers.

"To tell the truth, sir, I'd be honored if you give me a chance to win that hundred you offer for a shooting contest. I can shoot pretty good."

Two Jacks smiled, shook his head.

"Good madam," he said, "I don't take money from women, except from Pearl."

"Good sir," I said, sipped my horrible tasting sass'parilla, "I can shoot the eye of a beaver at some distance, not harm the hide."

A cowboy heard my challenge. "Feared of a half-breed Mex?" he said to Two Jacks. "She can afford to lose. Take her money, Two Jacks, or the stories will fly."

The cowboy's words didn't sit right with Two Jacks. He opened his coat, loosed his pistols in their holsters, told the man, "Why don't you bite your worm before I give you another hole in your belly?"

The cowboy tipped his hat, took his leave. Two Jacks nodded to me—we had us a shoot.

Before we left, Two Jacks's pay-woman sashayed down the stairs, a red fake feather scarf around her neck. She stood between me and Two Jacks.

"Honey," she said to Two Jacks, "don't be late." She would not look my way, except for a moment, see if my charms might turn her man's head. She ran her eyes over me like I was a bug she could squash with a heel. I understood why Pearl didn't like her.

"Of course not, Princess," he said. "I have to settle this, then I'll see you, a hundred richer. Get you presents."

We left the saloon. I stopped at the MacQueen House, got my Winchester with the gold inlay. I slid the rifle out from the case, loaded it, ready for a shoot, placed it back in the case. I looked at myself in the mirror, fear showing—could this buffalo hunter shoot better 'n me?

They put two cottonwood stumps alongside the river after they paced off a hundred steps, put an empty whiskey bottle on each stump. We got ready; Two Jacks pulled out his Henry, patted his rifle like it was a pet, removed his broad brim and buckskin jacket, winked at me. I removed my hat with the fake flower, loosed my sleeves, slid my Winchester from the leather case.

Two Jacks's eyes froze when he saw that rifle.

First shots I took standing. The bottle looked smaller than a deer's ear but I sighted it in, let out my breath, pulled the trigger. The bottle flew to pieces. The crowd let out a cheer, clapped, respectful of my aim.

"Very nice, ma'am," Two Jacks said, sweat on his face. He set his brace, knee-high, knelt on a knee, squeezed his trigger, broke the bottle clean. Maybe this buffalo killer could shoot better than me—he squeezed the trigger real gentle.

The crowd clapped, waved hats. "You can take her, Two Jacks," folks yelled.

We took turns, broke eight bottles each. A mosquito buzzed him when he pulled the trigger, missed, his shot roamed through trees.

I wiped sweat from my forehead, said, "Since things look good for me, I want to raise our wager from a hundred, if you are open to that; five hundred."

Two Jacks was not a happy buffalo killer right then, but he had a gracious way and he had pride. "If, ma'am, you agree to move the target back another ten."

Like a fool I agreed.

I missed at a hundred and ten.

He didn't.

CHAPTER FIFTY-ONE
SURPRISE AT ANNIE TURNER'S

Two Jacks and me now tied on our shoot, I had to try something else. I said, "For the last shot, how about ten more paces?" He had to accept, odds were in his favor because he won at a hundred and ten. I sat down for my shot, how Chub showed me, my arms steady as a rock. Broke the bottle clean.

Sweat run on Two Jacks's face. He laid flat, lowered his rifle brace, aimed, pulled his Henry trigger. The noise of that shot echoed through cottonwoods. The whiskey bottle rested quiet on the stump—the crowd did a groan. Local hero got whupped.

Later, when we walked alongside the river, Two Jacks said he'd need a while to get that much cash. He had to take a caravan to Yellowstone Park, put on an Indian show, get money from railroad folks who hired him, pay me his considerable debt. He asked me to say nothing about that debt.

"Of course not, my friend. But I would like to see that wondrous park," I said. "Consider the debt paid if you invite me and my cousin on your trip. I could cook Injun style for the dignitaries, too, do an Indian dance."

He smiled at saving his five hundred, we shook hands.

"Got to see my Princess, ma'am," he said, tipped his hat, walked away knowing his reputation had suffered.

I rested on my bed at MacQueen House, planned out my poison killing in the park, thinking on my daughter. Then it came to me—I sat up, jumped off the bed, ran for the door. Crazed thoughts while I ran through the streets. No, not possible, my heart thumping in my chest—maybe this earth came in a round shape, like Medicine Duck said? You could return to where your journey began.

At the door of Two Jacks's lady, second floor of Annie Turner's bordello, I turned the knob. Two Jacks wore his boots and a six-shooter belted around his middle, nothing else, standing on a table, waving his hat. His woman lay on her bed, her naked *be*hind raised in his direction.

Two Jacks shouting, "Yahoo!"

She saying, "Come on, sweetheart!"

Molly, near eight snows older, still using her charms to perfection.

"Why'd you ABANDON me, *MOTHERRRR?*"

Tears came to me, my heart broke, tore to pieces like a cattail pulled apart, its insides blowing nowhere, the pain to see I meant nothing to this woman whose body bore me.

"Leave, honey, please," Molly said to Two Jacks. He put on his pants, ran out of the room.

"Sit down, daughter, please," Molly said. She got a robe, we sat on the edge of her bed, tears slid down my cheeks.

"You became a grown woman," Ma said, wiped my tears. "Good to see you, daughter. I missed you. Truly. Sorry you found me like this, but . . . *you could have knocked.*"

I wiped more tears. "Where the hell you been, Ma?"

"You have anger at me, daughter, so, listen," Molly said. "Did I ask to have my world tore up when I was a girl? Whites coming from all over, disease, women's virtue taken because we were *squaws*. Our land taken. Me, a chief's niece, raised to marry some chief's son, live out my life in the world I saw in my mother's life. They gave me to a soldier—for my people I did that. And, yes, I got nice dresses . . ."

Dresses. I wanted to slap her pretty face.

"And when Chub started his looks at you, I got you a

husband, a rich one. When Chub took a younger woman, he threw me out. Two Jacks became a good friend after I started work here . . . where I came *looking for you.*"

"Oh, Ma," I said. I wanted to believe my ears, but I knew my ma. "You came here, looking for me?"

Molly cried, stopped her tears for a glance my way, see if I took her story.

"Oh, Ma. I never knew you came looking for me. Truly, you came looking for me?" I hugged her, hoped she didn't make up that story. "I am sorry about your life, Ma, but, why'd you come looking for me only after Mr. Tunbridge took another woman?"

Ma stopped her tears, gave thought to my words. "Might seem like that. Well, here's the truth, daughter. I swear, this is the truth, your mother's truth. My trouble with Chub got going only after I told him I wanted to find you, missed you. That got him looking on another woman."

Ma looked me eye to eye, time to let our sad times go away, I figured. I found my mother. Tears came to both of us.

"I'm sorry you found me in this kind of work," Ma said, looked down.

"Don't mean nothing. I been in this line of work myself. Ma, we have a daughter."

Ma's beautiful eyes got wide at the news.

"A lovely girl, only six snows in her. Has an Indian father, dead now," I said.

She held my hand, looked me in the eye. "I'm sorry, my daughter. Tell me your life."

I told her my life, and that I came on a mission to rub out the army general who gave the plan that killed my son and husbands, and for all their lies. Ma dried her pretty eyes, stared blank at me like she birthed a crazy daughter.

"Two Jacks gave me the invite, Ma, to entertain railroad folks and the Great White Father, in what they call a park." The thought came to me, if this woman loved me, she might come along, take care of me and I didn't get hung. "Come with me, Ma?"

Molly stood, looked out the window. We heard a gunfight below.

"Daughter, let me think on this. You could get hung; me, too, like those Cascades got hung for scalping settlers and an agent, not for killing a *general.*"

I walked to the door.

"What I figured. Well, Ma, nice to see you." I turned the knob. "Just talk, how you missed me."

"No, my daughter. Wait, please. I never killed nobody. Let me think on this. You ever kill anybody?"

I let loose of the knob. "I rubbed out no-good fellers who had the rubout coming," I said. Would be up to Molly if she wanted a daughter in her life.

"How will you do in this general, daughter?"

I let loose of the knob.

"My friend has poison mushrooms. An Indian chief, friend of his, done in his guests at a dinner with those mushrooms. Should be able to do in an old bluecoat. I'll poison the supper I cook for him."

"You learn how to cook, daughter?" She studied me, wondered who she'd raised.

"I can make rabbit soup, roast elk leg, no thanks to you. Well, you going with me?"

Ma stared out the window, let her thoughts run, then I saw that look come to her eye, how she looked when she told me she'd blow up the Willard. "We must not get caught, daughter. They would hang us by a rope around our necks. But first— they got to catch us."

I had me my ma back. We hugged, talked, and laughed

through the night. Not how I thought we might come together, but this would have to do.

Two weeks later, Two Jacks had his wagons loaded with crates from the last steamboat to ever run that river. We got ready to entertain a railroad potentate and the Great White Father. Miss Pearl gave me sourdough bread she baked and wishes for a safe journey. Friend of Otter rode in with a present from him and the singing Cheyenne who went to be with his wife and kids.

Their gift—the scalp of Mr. McFadden.

"That man will not bother you anymore," Friend of Otter said. "We sent him to his Father."

I touched my heart at his words, thanking him, but I also felt sorry my marriage to Mr. McFadden had to end this way. I wiped tears.

My daughter had more need of my head than the old Scot. I threw Mr. McFadden's scalp in the Yellowstone River—our *dee*vorce final, my honor avenged right proper.

Now, to kill a no-account general and not get hung.

CHAPTER FIFTY-TWO
JOURNEY TO RUB OUT A GENERAL

We rode on the rutted stage trail next to the Yellowstone River, heading west to Fort Ellis. Two Jacks said the army built the trail that ran east, behind us, to forts in the Dakotas. The last spike, Two Jacks said, got knocked in the track just before we began our journey. Train tracks reflected sunlight alongside the trail.

At Fort Ellis we picked up Bannock and Shoshone Indians, and supplies waiting for Two Jacks—some Shoshone lances with scalps the soldiers took from their reservation. Soldiers at Fort Ellis told us about a crazy rumor going around the fort—Texas outlaws were coming with Shoshone and Bannock to kidnap the Great White Father, hold him for ransom. They showed Two Jacks an Idaho newspaper story. Army folks said they'd escort us to the park just in case. A soldier climbed in the back of Two Jacks's covered wagons to make sure no Texas outlaws hid in the wagon. In the last wagon, Friend of Otter was feeding cornbread to his bird.

"Kiss my arse," Parfleche squawked to the soldier.

The soldier fell out of the wagon. I wondered how soldiers could protect the Great White Father if a bird scared them.

The army got part of the story right, but no Texas outlaws were coming for the Great White Father. A Spirit Man, crow bird, me, and my ma were coming—not to kidnap a Great White Father nobody ever heard of. We were coming to kill a no-account general who planned the wipeout of buffalo and us living like penned-up cows.

Our singing Cheyenne, Old Hand, must have fanny-flapped tales to soldiers at his reservation about what we were up to in the park, and his story got turned to Texas outlaws and Indians going after the Great White Father, a story picked up by a newspaper.

I never again trusted a secret to a singing Cheyenne.

Ma came down sick, Two Jacks had her rest at Fort Ellis. She'd join us later in the park, with a soldier escort. We rode back to the main street of the railroad depot town, Cinnabar, that we'd passed through. A hotel, couple saloons, wood shacks, and churches sprouting like weeds in the middle of nowhere after a fire. Cinnabar was the last train stop, then *too*rists had to ride a stage to get to the park, or rent a horse and buggy.

I rode alongside Two Jacks, getting saddle sore, but I enjoyed his yarns. He got curious about our ways. "What's the meaning of the word you use for us—*washeechoo?*"

"Maybe means 'fat eaters.' "

"Eat fat?" He could not get the point.

"Folks who take the good part of everything that comes from this earth," I said. "And don't share." Can anything on this sweet earth survive such folks? I wanted to ask him.

"Oh. Am I a fat eater?"

"What do you think?"

"Let's talk on other matters."

Two Jacks asked about Friend of Otter, resting most of the trip in the back of a covered wagon on sacks of sugar, coffee, salt and pepper, beans, tea, Saratoga potatoes, and salted pork. He fed cornbread to Parfleche when his bird squawked.

"When he smiles my way, and he does that a lot," Two Jacks said, "makes me uncomfortable." I laughed, Friend of Otter had a huge liking for the fancy pants Two Jacks.

"My cousin, Bob, is a wíŋkte."

329

"Winktay? Bob—some kind of Spirit Man?"

"His spirit calling, live a wíŋkte life, came to him in a dream. Has his peculiarities. If he gets an anger on, he becomes Crazy Bear. He don't like to kill, though, hurts his heart."

Two Jacks nodded that he understood. Of course, he had no understanding of a man like my dear friend. Two Jacks called a rest for lunch. Shoshone whooped, rode off to the side of the trail, used their hunting knives to dig roots, came back happy, loaded with roots.

"Camas, camas," they said. "Cowse. Many. Good."

Shoshone got excited, Two Jacks let them dig a round pit, a foot deep, put camas roots in the pit. The roots looked like a wild onion. They used army shovels to dig up grass, put the sod grass-side down on the roots. They heated flat rocks in another pit, put heated rocks on the sod, cooked camas underneath. I ate Indian food again, like camas Ma cooked, brought tears to my eyes. Tasted sweet, too. They pounded roots, made flour to eat down the road.

I asked Friend of Otter to help me dig camas—I'd never dug them before. We dug a bunch, to the curious eye of our Shoshone companions. They laughed. Shoshone said we dug the poison camas, not the sweet camas. Camas all looked the same to my eye.

If poison mushrooms didn't do what we needed done, I snuck poison camas to Friend of Otter's pouch.

We camped that night at Mammoth Springs in the park. Two Jacks and me put our bedrolls near. I had a question: "Why do you call where we camp a park?"

Two Jacks studied stars in the night sky, thought on my question. "Maybe the idea came from back east, Alice. Set land aside, with rules for using this Wonderland, open to all citizens. Really, though, what got the park idea going, seems to me, rich folk back east who like to hunt and fish. They wanted reserves set up, be places for them to hunt deer, elk, and catch fish forever."

He lit a cigar, I lit tobacco in the short stem pipe I got in Milestown.

"Why does General Sheridan come?" I said, blew smoke to the night air. "Why does a general and Great White Father come to a park? To hunt and fish?"

Two Jacks moved his broad brim to see me.

"Phil wants to protect what's left of the wildness of this land. Poachers already took forty thousand elk from this park. You have no idea how this country works, Alice. Know who pressures our council of chiefs, our Congress, to get control of this park? Railroad men. Same bunch that hired me for this Indian show."

"Railroad men like to fish and hunt?"

Two Jacks cleared his throat, "No, for the money. They want to run rail to the hotel they built in the park, and more to come. You saw train tracks alongside the trail on our way. The west, to railroad folks, means freight and tourists. Folks for seeing the sights."

"You favor that?" I said. *Too*rists. Fat eaters.

"No, not in regards to this beautiful park," he said. "But, I have to make a living, Alice, I do this show for a railroad man, Mr. Rufus Hatch. We have a senator coming up the Snake River south of us who thinks like Phil and me. We want to keep railroad folks out of these mountain cathedrals, allow no rail in the park. And Phil—General Sheridan—wants soldiers to enforce no hunting rules in this park. It's a big fight, about money."

I tapped out my pipe, slipped lower in my bedroll. Made no sense. Two Jacks worked for a railroad man who wanted to put rails in a park that Two Jacks wanted to protect from train tracks.

I had a hard time sleeping, thinking about what lay ahead,

wondered if I should give up my mission.
Could I poison a man who never, himself, attacked me?

Chapter Fifty-Three
*Too*rists

We left at sunup.

Noon, we took a break. I looked up a grassed hill, sighted fellers ride down the hill on two-wheeled contraptions like I saw on streets in Milestown.

"O, gawd," Two Jacks said, took off his hat like he had himself a vision. "Wheelmen. The West's going to hell, Alice."

We gawked at six men on machines with a big front wheel, small back wheel, and a bar to hold while they sat on a seat in the middle. They came flying down the hill, legs up.

"Riding their ordinaries in the park," Two Jacks said, *dis*gust in his voice. "What the hell?"

The men, legs in the air, rolled fast down the hill, yelled, "Yahooooo."

"Is that why they set up this park, Two Jacks? Let ordinary folks, on their ordinaries, enjoy a park?" I teased him.

"I want to remember this land as a little wild. That too much to ask?"

"You folks might not know wild, Two Jacks, if wild bit your arse."

He eyed me, looked at the ordinaries, gave thought to what I said. Two Jacks got an anger on, hollered, "Wagons, Ho!" Waved his hat, reared his one-eye horse he called Cyclops.

Friend of Otter hollered to me from a supply wagon, "Wagons, Ho?"

The wagons rolled faster.

"Maybe a white man hókahé," I yelled to Friend of Otter. "I don't know."

I looked back at the men riding down the trail on their ordinaries, derby hats on their heads, a sight to make you sick—*too*rists I rode to the end of our wagons, signed to Shoshone that Two Jacks wanted them to get painted up, scare the derby hats. Shoshone laughed, gave me an invite to have some fun. We got painted up, gave war cries, took off after the wheelmen.

The derby hats saw us, pedaled faster on the flat trail at the bottom of the hill, chased by Shoshone and me yelling death chants. I laughed till tears came. We caught up, surrounded those scared fellers. The Shoshone had lances, scalps tied to the tips, pointed at the derby hats.

"You there, what you call yourself?" I talked in a mean voice to their leader, my face painted red with black around my wolf eyes—like my dear husband's for a fight, looking like the devil himself.

"Peter, ma'am, Mr. Peter McKiddie. I have a wife and two kids. We belong to the Ordinary Club, Wyoming Territory—an honorable group of men, I assure you. Don't kill us, I beg you." He took off his derby, held the hat in front of his shaking body, knelt on one knee.

"Mr. Kiddie, you don't honor our ancestors, riding ordinaries on our sacred ground. Do *we* ride on *your* sacred ground?"

"No, ma'am, but we didn't know we rode on sacred ground—right, boys?" He spoke to his companions, them shaking so much I feared they'd fall over dead. A Shoshone missing an ear, Buffalo Hump, got off his horse, walked slow to the men. Two scars crossed Buffalo Hump's face from both sides of his forehead to his jaws, his face painted white like a ghost. He grabbed Mr. Kiddie's curly hair, held the hair for us to see.

"My friend wants your scalp, Peter Kid," I said. "I'm not a savage like Buffalo Hump, who'd scalp his own mother. I don't want him to have your hair . . . if we might work something out." Mr. Kiddie begged, "We have money—how much to not lift my scalp?" His hand reached inside his coat, pulled out a silver money clip, holding green paper.

I signed to Hump what Mr. Kiddie said. Hump shook his head, fingered the man's curly hair, said something to his companions. They hooted, yelled—the wheelmen dropped to their knees, begged for mercy, hands folded. Hump signed to me. I put two fingers to my head—understood, rocked back and forth in my saddle, pondered the fate of wheelmen scalps.

"Tell you what, Pete," I said. "Okay, if I call you Pete?" He nodded I could call him Pete.

"Put your clip away, Pete. The Great Mystery don't appreciate paper. We have ways from the Great Mystery to make amends for dishonoring ancestors—*The Holy Kiss To Make Amends.*"

"Anything, ma'am. We'll do the Holy Kiss. You want us to kiss you?"

"No, Pete. Kiss Buffalo Hump's horse on the mouth. All of you, right on the mouth. Show us you mean no harm to our sacred ground. The Shoshone way to make amends, heal the insult, wash the stain. Forgive the wicked sin."

I signed to Shoshone what we agreed. They hooted, got quiet, glared at the wheelmen. Mr. Kiddie told his friends to kiss Buffalo Hump's horse on the mouth. Shoshone laughed to see white men put their lips on a horse's mouth. The horse looked at Hump, wondered what Hump wanted from him, but the horse never backed away from the affection.

"Your scalp got saved," I said. "Go in peace, Pete. Don't let us catch you riding on our sacred hills no more. Tell your family that savages let you live because you did the honorable thing, the Holy Kiss To Make Amends."

They jumped on their ordinaries, rode fast as a white man's

legs could move such a contraption.

When we got back to the wagons, I told Two Jacks what me and the Shoshone did to the derby hats. Two Jacks took off his broad brim, kissed my cheek.

"Much obliged, Alice. You got spark, like your mother."

But the Shoshone, me, and Friend of Otter would put on a show for soldiers and their chief—entertain them who stole our land, killed our families. Seemed crazy to me, to turn our ways into a show for those who done us in.

Our show would bring *dee*light to a Great White Father, President Chester Arthur. I wondered who he was. While we rode I asked Two Jacks, "Did Mr. Chester count coup in battles to become Great White Father?"

Two Jacks laughed at my question. "Count coup? My dear Alice, he only knows how to count votes."

"How'd he become Great White Father, what great deeds he do?"

Two Jacks lifted his hat, scratched his head. "He outlived the real Great White Father—Chester Arthur came second in command before the real Great White Father got shot and killed. I don't know much about him. They say he ran a Custom House in New York City before serving our country, a crooked Custom House. Kickbacks."

"Will wašíču sing and dance in Chester's honor when he dies?"

"Hell, Alice, in twenty years, no one will remember the damn fool's name."

I wore a short brim Stetson to keep the sun off, a flannel shirt, sheepskin chaps Two Jacks gave so my legs would not get rubbed raw. My *be*hind gave me a prayer the ride would soon end.

Two Jacks admired the park around us while we rode, green-leafed aspen and lodgepole pine that ran far as the eye could see. He gave me more learning about a park. "A hunter discovered this land, Alice. No one believed his stories about steam and water flying higher than Douglas fir. The army took a look; the hunter's report told the truth. Phil Sheridan and me, we fought to keep this land wild ever since." Two Jacks stuck out his chest for a medal.

"Why do you say this park got discovered by a white man? Indians used this land for more Winter Counts than wašíču ever came around here. Damnation, man, you know that."

"Well, discovered the park for our people, maybe what I should have said."

"And thought that. Not just the words, Two Jacks."

"I see you got opinions, Alice. Like your mother when she gets going."

"Damnit, man," I said, angered. "Alice is not my name. Pearl gave me that name for white folks to call me. *Pežúta Skúyawin* is my name—you folks don't even know how to say my name. You give names to everything—rivers, hills, like nothing had a name before you came. My ma named me Army Girl."

"Army Girl? Why'd your mother give you such a peculiar name?"

"Two Jacks is not a peculiar name?"

"I was named for my folks' fathers. Both had the same name—John."

"John? Your name is *John John*? Why don't folks call you Two Johns?"

"Can we talk about something else?"

I told him I had a bluecoat father, and that's how I got the name Army Girl. He leaned back in his saddle, let out a whistle. "An Army officer father? I never knew that, about your mother, having a child with a soldier."

"I never met him," I said, wondered what else Ma never told this man.

A Shoshone rode in fast from scouting ahead. What Two Jacks called Old Faithful was coming up, dignitaries waiting, guarded by bluecoat soldiers to stop Texas outlaws and Indians from kidnapping the Great White Father.

I hadn't planned on soldiers standing guard when I poisoned their general.

CHAPTER FIFTY-FOUR
SHOW TIME

Two Jacks called a halt.

"Get your clean uniforms, boys," he ordered our soldier escort. They'd agreed to give a hand for his show, fake an Indian fight for the Great White Father. "Raise your cavalry flags, flank the wagons with horses carrying the colors. And get the American flag. Where's the flag? What? You forgot the *flag*?

"Rub salt off your horses. Well, get water from the river—you can see the river, right? Geezus. Eagle Feather, get your warriors in war paint. Dig out the shields I brought in the wagons, lances with feathers. I don't give a damn if they are Crow lances. This is a show, we're not going to scalp the Great White Father.

"You, Bob, take off that derby. And take off that silk vest. Yes, the bear tooth necklace would look good. Look like Indians. Geezus. What you want, Eagle Claw? No, Eagle Claw, no firewater for Shoshone. How'd you know we had firewater? Who's been sipping the claret? All right, later, you each get a sip. No, just one. One, gawddamnit! All right. Two.

"Soldier, bring me my trunk. Get my white buckskin. Indians, wear breechclouts. Braid your hair. Yes, like in battle. You don't braid your hair in battle? Well, braid your damn hair for a pretend battle. *Pretend*. Not a real battle. No damn scalp taking. *Geezus*."

I put on my clean doeskin dress to look the Indian woman for the show. They gave us mirrors to put on war paint. Shoshone and Bannock liked to look at themselves in a mirror, peeked behind the mirror to see what was there.

We got ready.

Two Jacks rode in the lead on his washed down, smart-stepping one-eye Cyclops; a bugler rode behind Two Jacks. Next came wagons flanked by soldiers. The plan—soldiers ride in, salute the Great White Father and dignitaries from across the Great Water brought by the railroad potentate, Mr. Rufus Hatch. Half of us Indians circle through woods, wait to attack. The rest attack from behind. The wagons circle, we ride like crazed redskins, shoot rifles and arrows in the air, scream like devils. Do fake fights with soldiers, all Indians fall over dead except me. I'd wait till after the attack, run in looking for my husband. A soldier would take me prisoner; I'd cry out the tremolo of grief.

And that would be the show.

We'd get up, bow, meet the Great White Father.

Eat lunch.

Dignitaries watched our show. Soldiers rode in, proud, to the noise of a bugler blowing his horn, Old Faithful shooting water and steam higher than pines. Indians attacked the soldiers, got carried away in the spirit of the battle, whacked soldier boys in the head with clubs. That angered the soldiers—scuffles broke out, a soldier got an arrow in his foot. Friend of Otter, in a breechclout and leather leggings, biggest feller there, got his horse shot in the neck. The horse fell over, Friend of Otter landed on his feet, so angered I feared what he'd do. We came to poison a general, not fight soldiers. Two bluecoats rode past him on either side. Friend of Otter jumped high, got his arms around their necks, threw the soldiers to the ground. He picked up a bluecoat, threw that soldier to the air like a feather. The other soldier ran away fast as he could.

They hid President Arthur in a tent to protect his scalp. Two Jacks got whacked in the head, knocked cold. I never got to do my tremolo, but it was great fun. Tempers cooled. They made Indians camp away from bluecoats, except for me and Friend of Otter. We had our tents next to Two Jacks. President Arthur said he never saw such a wonderful sight as our show, shook everyone's hand. When Two Jacks woke, the president shook his hand. Two Jacks had a lump over his blue and black eye.

Two Jacks wanted to introduce me to General Sheridan. I wondered what he'd look like. My legs shook under my dress—got ready to meet the man I'd poison. Sheridan was short, only a couple inches taller than me, with puffy cheeks, a mustache above his lips that hid his mouth, and hair on his head turning a gray wolf's color. His mudded black boots climbed to his knees, a bluecoat jacket hid a fat eater belly. Hard for me to figure this little feller planned the rubout of buffalo, and the penned-up life of Indians. A wedding ring on his finger. Would be hard to poison a woman's man, but that was the way this would have to go for what he did to our women, kids, families.

Two Jacks, smiling big, said, "Phil, I want you to meet my friend, Alice. Speaks English. One of the Texas outlaws that came with me and the Shoshone to kidnap the president." He joked about the rumor that got Sheridan to bring extra soldiers on the trip.

Sheridan took off his hat, real *po*lite, spoke in a voice showing his life of whiskey and cigars, "Pleased to make your acquaintance, Miss Alice. From Texas? I worked there on my first command."

I gave him a Miss Brenda curtsy in my doeskin dress. "Not from Texas, General."

"Shoshone?" His eyes wandered my clothing.

"Sioux." I looked him eye to eye.

Sheridan blinked. "Which band? Red Cloud's?"

"No, sir. Tašúŋke Witkó's."

"Don't think I heard of him," Sheridan said.

"Crazy Horse, General."

"Oh. Great warrior, Crazy Horse. Tragedy how he died."

"We learn white man ways now—run cows and grow corn."

I wanted him to trust me.

"Very good. We must learn to live in peace, under the, uh, Great Spirit," Sheridan said.

Two Jacks broke in, "Alice offered to do Indian cooking. And, Phil, this young lady whupped me in a shooting contest. A real dead eye." Two Jacks twirled his mustache tips, eyes afire at knowing such a celebrity as me. "And her mother's coming from Fort Ellis, after she gets over what ails her. A lady friend of mine from Milestown."

Sheridan looked curious at Two Jacks—Milestown had women, but no ladies to his mind.

President Arthur waddled up, "Good show, Two Jacks. Good show, man." They shook hands. Two Jacks introduced me to the Great White Father—a fat old man in buckskin. I curtsied, gave him a bordello girl smile. President Arthur kissed the back of my hand.

A funny looking man in a cowboy hat ran up to get in on the greet—Mr. Rufus himself, the railroad potentate who wanted to run rail to the park. Two Jacks walked me to meet the big bug folks that hatched from across the Great Water who Mr. Rufus brought to show off his hotel at Mammoth Hot Springs. He wanted to stir up *too*rist business from across the Great Water. They didn't even speak the English tongue. Some wore tight pants that I never saw before on a man. Two looked at me through round glasses held in the eye, what they called a monocle. They had unusual names, even for white men—*Duke, Earl, Lord*. I met a man they called *Count*, and an old man and a woman shaped like potatoes they called *Baron and Baroness*. Their names made Alice seem a good white man name.

General Sheridan said, "Get your men and Indians bivouacked, Two Jacks. And I hope to see you, Miss Alice, at the show."

It's not easy to kill a man you just met. Hard to steel your heart when enemy laugh like boys, smoke cigars, like they are chief of the mountain. Hard to remember you are Indian when they treat you white.

In my tent, taking a nap, I dreamed of Crazy Horse. "What are you learning, Sweet Medicine Woman?" Crazy Horse said.

"Being Indian is becoming only a memory, my chief."

"Not easy?"

"No."

"Who said our way comes easy?"

Pehíŋ Háŋska—Longhair Custer—came in a dream, his buckskin cleaned up from the battle.

"Don't kill him," Custer said, a begging to his voice. "Don't kill my friend, Phil. He only did his duty."

"No excuse for what he did!" I yelled, woke myself up.

Friend of Otter ran from his tent. I told him I had me a Pehíŋ Háŋska dream and Crazy Horse dream, too. "Leave dreaming to me," he said, went back to his tent.

I took a walk.

The wind blew from the north. When Old Faithful water came from under the earth, the spray drifted to the Grandfather of the South. A kettle boiled in the belly of this land, a Kettle Dance going on under this earth. I would throw the general dog in the kettle. The Great Mystery that flowed under us seemed angered, heating waters under this earth with a fire about what we knew nothing. Before water shot to air, there was hissing, a roar, a bubbling that made me feel I didn't walk alone on this earth. Over the rim of the crater came hot water. Mist and spray flew in the air. Earth shook like a woman giving birth, or a man drunk on firewater trying to heave his guts. Steam clouds filled the air. Our horses and the army mules stomped nervous in the distance when Old Faithful blew to the sky. Indian tents stood quiet, guarded by soldiers with rifles. That thought got me angered. I crawled to my bedroll. Later that day, I'd cook the poison *žapi*, count coup for my son, husbands, and every buffalo shot for a tongue and a wild drunk.

CHAPTER FIFTY-FIVE
COUNTING FINAL COUP

More men rode in before we started our show, waved hats like they knew Mr. Rufus and Sheridan. Sheridan waved, told the newcomers to sit on the ground, watch an Indian show.

Shoshone danced for the spruced-up dignitaries, drums beat loud. Shoshone danced with bonnet feathers down their backs— the Indian for *too*rists Show upon us. The audience didn't know Indians held dance sacred. I watched Sheridan, tapping a boot to the drumming, a silver goblet of claret in his hand, hat tipped back on greased-down hair. He liked the show. Shoshone stomped and twirled, bodies painted yellow, black, red; jumping through hoops, acting out counting coup on soldiers.

I felt the drum in my bones.

My silver earrings shook, dangling from my ears; braids swayed down my back that Friend of Otter wove in my hair. I leaned over, whispered to Two Jacks—I wanted to dance. Don't know why I wanted to do what Mr. McFadden said came with the parts of a woman. Maybe it was the drum. Maybe I had more Indian in me than only my mother's blood.

"Give 'em hell, Alice," Two Jacks said, had his interpreter tell the Shoshone drummers I would dance.

I thought about the dancing Lone Wolf taught me the night before Long Hair killed my family at Greasy Grass.

I took off my moccasins, let me feel the earth beneath my feet, stood straight like a proper woman for a dance, eyes looked ahead, shuffled my feet slow to the beat of that beautiful drum.

I looked at Sheridan, stomped slow his way. Drummers chanted, my braids swayed with blue ribbons tied at the ends, doeskin dress bounced above my ankles. Dust rose from under my feet. With my dead child, Flying Eagle, in my heart, I did a coup dance around Sheridan, acted out how I wanted to eat a heart— Sheridan's. I didn't like raw heart, but I would have chewed his.

Spirits must have got to me because my shyness lifted like mist in bright sun. Cries came from my throat, I howled like my sweet Lone Wolf. If I had my skinning knife in hand, hid under my dress, I could slit Sheridan's throat. His eyes got wide, hands grabbed the arm of his chair, dropped his goblet when I did what our dancing was supposed to do.

Tell truth.

Crazed up, maybe with spirits, I grabbed Sheridan's saber before he knew what I had going. I held the steel to his neck while I stomped around him. The Shoshone yelled, wanted me to cut his throat, have us a real party.

Two Jacks jumped to his feet, not knowing if this was part of the dance or I had other intentions. Sheridan didn't move a whisker with the blade to his neck. The drumming got louder. I sang in Lakóta that Sheridan came from Dog, that his Bitch Ma mated with Coyote who had such a big organ, she never could please Coyote.

I stabbed the saber in the ground between his shaking legs, a Lakóta song came from my throat about the death of relatives. Spirits left me. I bowed to the applause of dignitaries, slipped to my tent. Cried myself to another afternoon sleep.

More dreams came.

The water; land; mist; blood, and where was I and needing my ma . . . smell of an old Scot on my body . . . and where am I and why am I . . . buffalo . . . guns . . . my legs around men I love . . . wind and the saber I had at his throat . . . wanting him dead . . . my daughter's life ahead without me if they caught me . . . my son

Flying Eagle's eyes . . . Lone Wolf's flute hands on me . . . Two
Horns loving me . . . all the laughter we shared . . . soldiers catching
me and Ma . . . hanging us . . . the moments of my horrible dying.

After I woke, I went for a walk, cleared my head.

Friend of Otter and me got asked to cook an Indian meal for
the dignitaries. The luminaries included their Secretary of War,
Governor of Montana Territory, Senator Vest, and the man we
knew as White Hat. Also came General Sheridan's squirrelly
soldier brother, and a few others. The newcomer *too*rists to the
party were desk soldiers from Washington City who came by
train to Cinnabar. Sheridan introduced me to his good friend,
General Callahan, gray hair starting on his head, bushy hair
under his nose—a short feller like Sheridan. I gave General
Callahan a curtsy, him fat in the belly, dressed in buckskin, not
an army uniform. General Callahan looked like any fool *too*rist
who fancied himself a mountain man.

"Pleased to meet you," I said.

"Likewise, young lady," Callahan said. He gave me a smile,
went for whiskey and cigar with Sheridan.

In the cook tent, I pounded poison mushrooms I got from
Friend of Otter's pouch. I steeled my heart hard, like the sabers
they stuck in our bodies.

"How much poison to do him in?" Friend of Otter said.

"Not sure, I'll put in a lot."

"Will he yell?"

"Heart give-outs kill old men," I said. "Folks will think he
got a heart give-out. Look sad, feel sorry at his dying."

I cooked the mushrooms in grouse drippings, chopped them
up good. I'd serve Sheridan's plate myself.

"Mmm," I said, tasted the heháka I started to roast the day
prior with Friend of Otter's help, remembering what Sitting
Bull showed me about roasting elk leg. Friend of Otter added
chopped roots he dug and gooseberry leaves on the elk. In a

metal pan over a fire, he poached trout the president caught that day. He added sweet camas root for flavor. White man salt, Friend of Otter said, killed the taste, not pepper. Cooked fish smelled bad to him, like wet dog hide.

We served the tables of dignitaries in what they called the Officer's Mess. Quite a sight—Friend of Otter wore his breech-clout, a white cloth on his arm like the MacQueen House restaurant waiter we saw in Milestown, who served us. He poured claret in silver goblets for the Great White Father and old fat men, eating more fat.

I put the plate of elk leg with poison mushroom gravy in front of Sheridan.

"Smells *dee*licious, Miss Alice," he said.

"Thank you, General," I said, curtsied. "Hope you enjoy Indian cooking."

I got another plate for his friend, General Callahan, went to scrub my pots. Later, Sheridan, the life of the party, drank whiskey, swapped war stories with his friends. President Arthur acted strange.

"Hoo. Hooooo," the president sang. Two Jacks asked the Great White Father what he hooed about.

"The owl, man!" The president was having a vision. I got worried.

"Friend of Otter," I said to my friend, "did you . . . ?"

Friend of Otter gave a sloppy grin.

"No!" I said. "You didn't!"

If you want help in the spirit world, a spirit man is the way to go. If you want to poison a general and not get hung, not good.

The Great White Father flew high on the vision mushrooms Friend of Otter slipped in the gravy on his elk roast. I wanted to strangle my friend; he might get us hung if Sheridan croaked and the Great White Father saw owls after they ate our cooking.

I hoped they'd think the president got blootered from whiskey and claret.

"Great claret," President Arthur said, asked for more.

Sheridan said he felt under the weather, maybe had too much whiskey. He excused himself, stumbled to his tent. My knees got weak.

General Callahan 'scused himself, too, went to the tent soldiers gave him.

Mr. Rufus didn't have enough rooms at his hotel at Mammoth for all his guests. Some of his guests came with servants. I was glad newspaper reporters on his big bug tour stayed back at his hotel to write their stories, didn't get to see our show, or write about us.

I took heated water to Sheridan's tent—no one would think a woman who cared for his sickness done him in. Sheridan staggered around in his tent like a wounded buffalo. He crawled to his cot, white in the face. There were shadows on his canvas walls of Shoshone entertaining soldiers with a coup dance; their dance showed the killing of bluecoats in battles they fought.

"Can you hear me?" I said to Sheridan, his eyes closed, resting on his cot.

"Mmm, Miss Alice. I don't feel good. Think I'll be all right. Fine dancing. Check on General Callahan; I hear him throwing up in the tent next door, a desk soldier, not used to camp life anymore. That's an order, young lady."

Though I could see Sheridan had a kind heart, wanting me to look after his sick friend, I wanted to watch him die. I had to do what he ordered, took heated water and cloths to Callahan's tent.

The general wiped puke from his mouth, leaning over his cot when I came in his tent. He tried to smile.

"Wonderful meal, ma'am. Sorry I got sick. Too much whiskey and your wild food. Turkey's about as wild as I eat these days.

You looked lovely tonight, Miss Alice."

"Thank you, sir. I'm sorry you came down sick."

My mind did a run—maybe I poisoned two generals? No matter—I wanted questions answered before he went to his reward.

"All these wars, General. Can I ask you a question about all this warring?"

"My head hurts, Miss Alice. You worked hard on our supper, wonderful dancing. Your question?"

"You have feelings about all the Indians your army killed?"

"Oooo, Miss Alice, they protected their lands. What else were they to do? We wiped out their buffalo, they fought us to the death. Brave people, what else were they to do? My head spins. Stomach hurts. More water, please." My hand shaking, I poured water in a cup from the pitcher on the table beside his cot. I saw a picture of his wife, a younger white woman in a fancy dress, half the snows he had, and two young daughters. He opened his eyes, looked at me. "I have come to regret all we did." He fell asleep, going to his reward. I would watch him go there, then do dishes in the cook tent. Two Jacks rushed in, Ma with him. "Can you help him, Princess?" Two Jacks said to Ma. Ma took the hot water, threw it out the tent, poured in cool water, soaked a cloth, went to General Callahan. Ma mopped his brow, looked at him.

"Oh, my," Ma said. General Callahan opened his puffy eyes, small like the slice of a dying moon. "Mmmolly? That you, Molly, honey?"

"Stump?" she said. "Is that you?"

Two Jacks said, "You know each other?"

Molly said, angered, "This is Stump, who left me after he took me to live with him in the Willamette Valley."

My knees knocked together; blood left my body. I felt weak as a child's tooth ready to fall out.

350

The wašíču general I poisoned was my pa—the beginning of my troubles on this earth.

CHAPTER FIFTY-SIX
KILLING A GENERAL

General Callahan puked his guts, Molly held the pan.

"Like old times," Ma said, angered. I ran out of the tent, got a pan of cool water and towels. My heart raced fast; I knew I should tell Ma what I done to pa. There were enough soldiers nearby to hang me, Ma, and Friend of Otter, like they hung the Cascades. White man justice came quick to hanging Indians.

My heart ached, too, flopping in me, killing my own pa. I wanted him dead at Greasy Grass, for what his soldiers did to my baby and husband, but not now. Our warring days with soldiers had come to the end. I only wanted Sheridan dead.

I found Friend of Otter sweet-talking a drunk bluecoat.

"Don't ask any of your dumb questions. One of those generals we poisoned is my pa, my bluecoat pa. What are we gonna do?" I said.

"You dreaming, again?" He was calm, studied my eyes for any craziness. He heard me talk with Custer in my dream, I couldn't blame my dear friend for thinking I'd become a lunatic.

"Listen to me," I told him. "I'm not dreaming. General Callahan is the army man how I got my name, Army Girl. He's my father, in his tent, puking his guts, dying. We poisoned him; help me."

Friend of Otter got serious, thought about what I said, pulled a pouch from his breechclout, waved it in front of my face.

"I think you gave generals the wrong pouch, kolā."

I watched the pouch swing left, right.

"What's that?"

"Mushrooms—they let you see the Other Side."

"I used the wrong pouch?"

"Maybe. Maybe the generals only have visions, throw up like squirrels," he said. "Or, they die. It's in the hands of the Great Spirit—and it's not such a bad road—the happy forgetting of home."

I ran back to Pa's tent, heard them shout—my ma and pa. Felt good to hear *my* pa and *my* ma talk, even if she was angered and he was dying from my poison.

Two Jacks ran out of that tent. "Too crazy for me, Alice," he said, went to tell war stories with soldiers, grabbed meat from the cook tent for his hurt eye.

I went in Pa's tent where Molly had words for him.

"You left me with child in Washington City. This girl's your daughter—a finer woman than the two girls I see pictures of on your trunk. You *never* wrote to me after the war, wandered free of me. You married a white woman—I see her picture by your cot—not a lice hair squaw, like *me*. I loved you, still do, and I hate you, too. Now you're a big shot general and my life's been buffalo chips."

Pa put up his hands, waved them at her, "Molly, honey, please calm down," Pa said. "Me and Phil feel bad what we did to you and your cousin. You say Alice is my *daughter*, honey?"

Ma quieted when he called her honey.

Made my heart happy to hear my pa call Ma, honey. I could tell, he had feelings for Molly, her still more beautiful than the woman in his picture. Molly said, "Get to know your flesh and blood, Stump. I'll have me a whiskey with Two Jacks, first time. Then I'll tell Lieutenant Weasel, who you call General Sheridan, what our people think of him, for what he did to my cousin in the Willamette Valley. Sheridan looked familiar, puking in his tent, when I walked by."

Ma walked out of Pa's tent. When she passed by me, she gave me a hug, looked me in the eye.

"Get to know your father, child, limited though he is. Don't make the mistake I made, loving a worthless man. I still love him, was faithful to him in my heart. Least I got you in all that."

Ma joined Two Jacks, flying high with whiskey, challenging all to a shoot.

I looked around, got my bearings before meeting my pa for the first time as his daughter. The United States Secretary of War was dancing drunked up in a war bonnet with Shoshone. President Arthur, best I could tell, talked with Parfleche in the woods. Parfleche perched on the Great White Father's shoulder, squawked, "Hi, sweetheart. Good day to die, hókahé."

The president roared his laugh, yelled, "Hókahé." I liked this Great White Father who learned from a bird what life is about— you got to keep going.

Would my father accept me if he knew I poisoned him?

I entered his tent; he wiped vomit from his lips, eyes grogged. I felt sorry for him, tried to put myself in his boots, learning he had an Indian daughter. We said nothing while I cleaned him up, helped him out of his spoiled clothes, got him clothes like I did for little Flying Eagle.

"Let's talk by the river," Pa said.

I helped him stand.

We walked past the mayhem around us beneath what Two Jacks called Nature's Cathedrals, headed toward the Firehole River where flowed heated water from Old Faithful. Firehole seemed a good name for the river and how my life flowed—a good place for a talk with the father I never met before. We climbed down a rocky bank, sat beside the deep flowing river.

"Let me look at you," Pa said, held my face in his hands. His eyes searched mine for something, maybe a story from his lonesome days as a young man when a beautiful young Indian woman warmed him in his journeys far from home, loved him with all her heart, and he loved her.

"You look like me," he said. "Sorry I wasn't more handsome."

"Oh, Pa," I said, laughed. Felt good to call him Pa—know he had a sense of humor.

My pa.

"You cook some wild food, daughter."

He called me his daughter. Tears flowed when he called me *daughter.* Such joy I never knew, to have a man claim me as his flesh and blood, not a lightning spark that flew to this earth for no reason, smoldered stubborn. I cried, sitting there, Pa holding my face in his hands like he saw a flower he never knew before, the prettiest flower that ever grew on this earth, a lovely bloom like Molly.

Tears I held all my life ran down my face, tears like geysers bring water from this earth, crying the sadness life holds.

"Oooo, Pa," I said, wrapped my arms around him, hugged him for the first time in my life. "Pa, I needed you, I've been hurt so much in my life." I sobbed, could not stop my tears, covered his cheeks with wet from my own. He hugged me, cried, too.

"I never knew," he said. "I'm sorry, so, sorry."

"Your soldiers killed my baby, Pa, your own flesh and blood, at the Custer fight. A bullet through his eye. And my husband, the man I loved—your soldiers shot off his face. Your soldiers chased us like dogs through freezing mountains. We had nothing to eat, ate horse. I needed a father to protect me, show folks I was SOMEBODY on this earth. I loved—and hated you—all my life. Now, Pa, I only love you. I don't want to hate you no more."

He stood. "Daughter, help me," he said, stared straight ahead, eyes wide.

"What, Pa?"

"Blood. Buffalo blood, Custer's blood, your baby's blood, soldier blood. *O, gawd.*"

I held him, the same pinhead as me, short legs, bull-snake arms. A varmint, but my pa.

"Twojur Lahdass," I whispered in his ear.

"What'd you say, daughter?"

"Twojur Lahdass. Always be *au*dacious. Ma taught me, said you taught her. What you learned at soldier school."

He perked, "Were you, daughter, audacious, like Napoleon said? Like I wished for my life. I only sat at a desk later, wasted my life."

"Best I could, Pa. I'm not big, not pretty. My life's been hard, traveled far, looking for a home. I killed men I didn't know, been a pay-woman. I still have a whole life to live. Oooo, Pa, I have to tell you—I came here to rub out Sheridan for all he done to us. I came to poison him, in his dinner. Pa, I think that poison made you sick, too."

That got him sober. "Poison? You say you POISONED the dinner you cooked for me? But we just met!" He studied my face, thought on his fate. "I'm going to die? That's what you say, daughter?"

"Poison or vision mushrooms, Pa, I don't know what I cooked in your gravy. You might die. I am so sorry."

"Sorry? Sorry you POISONED me?" His voice squeaked at the end of those words. We spotted Two Jacks and Molly running over a ridge, naked as sparrows, drunk as birds that eat summer berries when berry sweetness turns to firewater. They jumped in the Firehole River upstream from pa and me, floated our way, feet up, laughing.

That pa might be dying gave him pause. He searched through

his mind for everything that might have been important in his life, now that his daughter was killing him.

"Oooo, *gawd*," he said, took a breath. "This how my journey ends, daughter? My just deserts?"

"Guess so, Pa," I said. "But, maybe I got pouches mixed up. Maybe you'll only have visions, or you're dying—I don't how to cook good."

He calmed down, hearing those words, "Oh, thank gawd. Neither did your mother." He looked at me, tried to understand the craziness we got caught up in, if my lack of learning woman's work from Ma might save his life. "Well, no matter," he said. "Through you, I had me a helluva life. And you're beautiful to me, daughter." I felt beautiful as my mother for the first time in my life, and never worried about my looks after that.

Pa caught sight of Molly and Two Jacks floating down the river, laughing, coming our way.

"Molly, honey!" he hollered, fire in his eyes. Pa ripped off his clothes, nodded to me. I tore off my doeskin dress. We ran to the river naked as babes, looked at each other, held hands, jumped in the Firehole River. Molly floated by. I put an arm around her neck, hung my other arm around Pa's neck—my family, Indian and white, together, what I wanted all my life. I looked ahead to me and Ma digging Pa's grave, putting him in the ground, dead from my poison. The water flowed around me, not caring if I was a girl or a fish, telling me—*Enjoy these moments with your family while you can—all is wandering, change, fire, and smoke on this earth, Girl.*

We whooshed around an outcropping boulder that narrowed the river, became fish dumped on the shore. Two Jacks gave me a nod that he understood what this day meant to me, having my folks together—he took his leave. I appreciated his understanding.

Ma and Pa smiled to me, touched my shoulders, held hands

like sweethearts, walked together to the woods, him telling her he never felt so alive as when he lived with her, each day maybe bringing his death. He said he'd give Ma some of his army pension.

Molly said she didn't want no Army money. (I'd have taken the money.)

I walked over the knoll, put on my dress, picked up Pa's buckskin, sat on a rock. I tried to be attentive, aware, like Sitting Bull taught me about life, death, what the time in between might mean. What the journey of my life had been about—killing my pa.

I heard my parents in the woods, crying, Pa on the way to his grave.

The crying stopped. I put my face in my hands, not able to think about what I'd done to him.

I got my heart ready to fall apart, to know more sadness than I ever knew—then heard them two varmints again.

"You are a flower of the mountain, Molly, honey. . . ." Pa saying.

"Yes! O, Yes, yes, yes, sweetheart," Molly, in a late bloom of love, saying, "however you want me."

"I missed your sweet breasts, honey," Pa saying.

I put hands over my ears to not hear them doing for the last time what those two varmints did to make the spark that became me.

I must say, I didn't come a quiet spark to this earth, and understood for the first time why they got along so well in the Willamette Valley.

But . . . *THIS IS DAMN HARD TO LISTEN TO, MY PARENTS.*

CHAPTER FIFTY-SEVEN
THIS EARTH ROUND?

Next day Ma, Friend of Otter, and me rode horses slow back to Cinnabar.

I wouldn't see my father again, though he and Sheridan lived the night. I realized Sitting Bull was the only real father I ever had. Stump was just my idea of a father. Ma and me were glad we didn't have to live as killers of the man she loved, my father. And rubbing out Sheridan wouldn't bring back buffalo.

Crazy Horse understood, no more visions came.

Pa said to keep to ourselves what we did, wouldn't get hung for trying to kill a general.

We never told no one.

No reporter came with the Great White Father, what happened that day didn't get writ up in a newspaper. A man with a camera did come with the Expedition, took pictures of Sheridan and President Arthur's companions posing at Old Faithful, but missed our show when he was away looking at what had his interest in the park. He never took a picture of my pa, either, hung over in his tent. Our family story—no need to put it in wašiču history books.

"Ma," I said, while we rode, swaying slow in the saddle, "thank you for teaching me what I need to know to live these times—and not teaching me to cook. Saved Pa's life."

"You're welcome, daughter," Ma said, thinking on her life, calm now that she made peace with my pa, knew he had love for her in his heart.

My horse swayed beneath my legs while we rode; his sweat under the blanket came to me like perfume from this earth. I rubbed the Appaloosa's neck, felt his heat under my hand, thought about my dead son and husbands. I thought about all those I loved, who loved me—Medicine Duck, Medicine Feet Woman, Sitting Bull, and his dear ma.

"Hókahé," Parfleche squawked, staring at me, perched on Friend of Otter's shoulder.

Time to move on, like the bird said.

Two Jacks sold his wagons, horses, and supplies to folks in Cinnabar to sell the stuff to *too*rists that came to see the park. He said this was the last time he'd work for the railroad.

Two Jacks got us a ride on the train back to Milestown. My first ride on a train—like riding a cloud. There were ladies all dressed up, fancy hats, drinking tea at tables while we rumbled along the tracks. They gave us looks—peculiar Indians on a train.

Two Jacks showed us the pile of money Mr. Rufus gave him for doing the show. He bought us dinner on the train, bread for Parfleche. Parfleche kept his thoughts to himself, in his cage. He got looks at sights he never saw before. Out the window flowed the Yellowstone River, the blue of sky reflected on water, fenced-in cows chewing grass. The bored cows didn't even look up when the train gave a whistle.

We sat on stuffed green chairs, wood panels on walls around us with pictures and maps, and a stuffed fish that looked alive. Parfleche could not take his eyes off the fish.

I should hate the iron horse because of what trains did to end our way of living but, I got to admit, I fell in love with whatever came with a train. I especially loved the yahoo train squeals and whistles when we came to towns, the want to keep the smolder going from the lightning spark from Ma and Pa that became me, till no more life ran through me.

We holed up in Milestown. Later, I went to get Mountain Girl, and on the way back, picked up more gold rocks in the Pahá Sápa from the Ravine With One Good Crow.

With the nuggets, I built this trading post east of the Black Hills that I came to love. I built it on Beaver Creek near railroad tracks that ran past Buffalo Gap, alongside a horse and buggy road. At night, train whistles blew, and rumbles on tracks hummed under my four-poster. Coyote songs came—a *doo*-ette to my ear—train and coyote music put me to sleep.

Molly married Two Jacks. They stayed friends with Miss Pearl, farmed with her outside a railroad town, Terry—named for ole One Star, near Milestown.

Friend of Otter, still my best kolá in the world, gave a hand to run my post. We hung Parfleche's cage from the ceiling behind the counter at our post. Nights, we let that bird fly around however he wanted.

I gave the white man name, Helen, to my daughter, so white folks would not think her peculiar, named after the Helen of Troy Two Jacks talked about. We had our misunderstandings after she grew up, due to how beautiful she became, and where all that beauty took her in the even crazier times Indian women had to live. She never could see good, after near starving in the Grandmother's Land.

A few years after we built this trading post, up rides a man. He tied his horse to the rail in front of where I sat in my rocker on the porch, in my white doeskin dress, smoking my pipe late in the day. An Indian man, long hair headed to gray, a ponytail hung under his Stetson, wearing dusty boots and a pressed checkered shirt. Handsome, to my eye.

"See any buffalo?" he said, speaking the wašíču tongue. "I hear there might be a pretty one wandered these parts."

What he said got me a laugh.

He walked a bit bent from his ride, his age, but he took his steps, I could see, with pride.

"Just this buffalo, sir, on her rocker. Want some coffee, frybread? Rabbit soup? Rest a spell from your travels—or stay long as you want, sweetheart."

Fox Tooth had come calling from across the border. He had himself the white man name, Adam. I told him folks now called me Miss Alice. We had our talks, Adam Fox Tooth and me, watching stars change places, nights, in the sky.

We lived with Friend of Otter above our trading post.

One night, a few weeks after Adam came, I put on my new blue nightgown, bought especially for this night, brushed my hair, looked in a mirror. The woman looking at me was older 'n how I felt. Wrinkles around my eyes showed the trails of my life. I saw in my eyes the same want when I was young to keep the smolder going from the lightning spark that became me, till no more life ran through me.

I gave the invite to Adam Fox Tooth, come to my bedroom, if he wanted.

"Welcome to the next life," I said after he came in, closed the door. Fox Tooth stood in his shirt, trousers, bone necklace, polished cowboy boots. He looked at me, my bedroom, the white lace curtains on windows. He walked to a chair, sat down like he got hit in the head.

"You got yourself a wife, if you still want her," I said, smiled shy because that's how I felt. I glanced in my vanity mirror, saw a woman's face powdered by what we endured in the west, washed pure by snow and pain, tears wetting my cheeks. I'll never forget Fox Tooth's words.

"I never wanted nothing this much in my whole life."

I don't know how I lived without a loving man. I'd tried to live proper, honor my dead husbands like Lone Wolf's mother did. But it was time, I reckoned, to let go of being proper, time to live what came my way, live wild and true like all I loved on the land that roamed around me, train whistle blowing across grassland. Like Fox Tooth was, truth be told, wild.

Fox Tooth gave me a love night I never forgot—though our bucking days were over. And all the nights after—I had me a loving husband, hoped this would be my last one.

Fox Tooth helped run the trading post. He knew how to strike a fair deal with customers, then the *too*-rists that came. I cooked for him, though not as good as his mother. He set our dinner table with knives, spoons, tin plates, and cloth napkins. He cleaned up after dinner, gave up firewater. At night, he brought me a blanket for my shoulders, a gift from his sister. I got him a rocker to sit beside me and Friend of Otter, enjoy sunsets, the smell of rabbitbrush and longleaf sage. We planted green ash and California Laurel pine trees along Beaver Creek for tea, buckbrush to keep the wind down. Him and Friend of Otter laid in chokecherry trees—I'd not have to go far for cherries, surrounding my trading post, seeming to hold it up when it sagged over the years. We dug hare's-foot clover from hills, chickweed, bedstraw and bitterroot, too, that gave a lovely pink flower around our place.

When Parfleche passed on, Friend of Otter got his bird stuffed in Rapid City, like the stuffed fish he saw on Mr. Rufus's train. That bird had more 'n twenty snows in him. We hung Parfleche in his cage on the porch. To us, only his bird body died, not his spirit. We let Parfleche have sight of prairie grass, trees, sky—what he liked. I'd come to love that bird, taught him new words, like *auto-mo-bile*. He got cranky if he had no new words. I miss making cornbread to feed his belly.

We got us a Model T when they came out, to see the sights— Fox Tooth, Friend of Otter, Parfleche in his cage, and me. We took in powwows all the way from Idaho to Wyoming, brought chains for mud roads. Brought a car jack, too, slipped inner tubes in tires that gave out, camped along the way.

Hard to believe, we became *too*-rists in our own land.

I had big giveaways at our place, summers, for white friends and Fox Tooth's people, mine, and Friend of Otter's. We shared stories, ate fry bread, wild plums, prairie turnip—whatever we could hunt or pick. I hunted us duck, rabbit, deer; picked hackberry and chokecherry. We celebrated my daughter's life while she grew up to be a beautiful woman, like my mother, by sharing in her honor what we had with our friends, at our giveaways. I lived holy by sharing, like Her Holy Door and Sitting Bull taught me I should live.

Before my husband passed on, I fessed up about stealing his horse. Fox Tooth near died laughing, said not to tell his sister.

When Fox Tooth passed away, his family and the South Dakota gover'ment let me bury him out my back window.

Later, I buried Friend of Otter next to my husband, back there, outside my window. I kept Parfleche in his cage on the porch. There he is, over there, in his cage, enjoying the sights.

Is this earth round, like Medicine Duck said? You can return to your home after a long journey away?

Maybe, if you look at this earth from afar, but if you walk around this earth, I don't think you ever come back to the same place where you began.

Three Sioux men took off to see if this earth came in a round shape like the sun and moon. One did a high wire act; two on the ground beat the drum, wore feathers in their hair. Those boys got to the Grandmother's country across the Great Water, on to Europe, on to what they call Persia and China. Relatives ran into them in a city by a bay where the sun sets, begging on streets, out of silver dollars. Took those boys three winter counts to learn this earth had a round shape, nary an edge. No way to fall off. Same lesson I hear that white folks had to learn, longer ago, when one of their ships got lost, landed somewhere near here.

Relatives brought them home.

But everything changed on the land they came back to. All is change, fire, and smoke in this world, grandson. But who you are, what flows in you, does not have to change. You have to find who you are, grandson, even if you are half 'n half like me. I hope these stories give you direction. Maybe we're all half 'n half of something. And it's time we all got along.

Sitting Bull got back to where he lived as a child. Indian tribal police, his own people, shot him dead when the Ghost Dance scared the U.S. Army.

A loving part of me died when Sitting Bull died.

More of my heart died when Custer's Seventh soldiers slaughtered my friends at Wounded Knee. Soldiers shot Medicine Feet Woman in her back, killed her daughter and her Minneconjou husband. They shot Medicine Duck and his lovely Widow Horse Tail, too, who had no weapons in their hands. Those soldiers were getting payback in a coward's way for losing the Little Bighorn fight, though they would not admit what they did.

Not easy to walk in a holy way, like Sitting Bull's mother taught I should walk, my heart sad.

Angered, too. Hard to feel sad, angry, and live holy, at the same time.

One day, two women younger than me, Brigid and Caitlin, came looking for me at my trading post. I never met two white women like that, short as me. We hugged, laughed, cried, drank hot chokecherry tea, walked around my place, looked at the graves of my dear husband and Friend of Otter. They took me to Rapid City to buy clothes like they wore, to get ready for the last journey of my life. We bought sun-color lampshade tunics to wear over long black underskirts, with waistlines high under our bosoms. I looked good. In New York City we got skirts wide at the hips, so narrow at the ankle I walked like a hobbled horse. They got me stockings—cotton socks for the day and silk stockings for dinners on the ship. I had the lady make me a pair of silk stockings hand-embroidered with a crow bird, to keep my legs ready for whatever mysteries that lay ahead.

I was a fancy lady on that trip, like my dear sisters—us Callahan girls.

My dear father told his daughters to look for me after he passed on. Together we voyaged across the Great Water to visit our relatives on my father's side. I came to love them, my sisters, and the journey we took together. Here's a picture of me and my sisters, overlooking the lovely Cliffs of Moher in Ireland, grandson, like Cap'n O'Shay said. Nary a tree in sight on that magical isle. I found peace—how I fit in this world, on this earth.

I'm an Irish-Indian. So are you, grandson.

Get my cane, please, behind the kitchen table. I made rabbit soup for us, snared the rabbit myself. And give your gram a hug. I need that from you, I surely do. *Ahhh,* feels good. Pilámayaye. Such a good boy.

Last story, then we eat.

A *too*rist saw a picture at my post of my lovely daughter—your mother, grandson. He looked at me in my rocker. How'd I get such a beautiful daughter, he unkindly asked. Adam Fox Tooth heard the question.

"Cousin, she don't make babies with her face," my dear Adam said, grabbed a shotgun off the wall, gave me a white man wink. The wide-eyed *too*-rist ran from my post.

My dear Adam ran out the door, yelled, "She made babies with her heart, and you can *Ith mo chac, you sonofabitch!*"

He fired the shotgun in the air, a warning shot, then put

buckshot in the Ford's paint, the *too*rist stirring up dust on the
road in his getaway.

I laughed till tears came.

Well, that's my life.

Heċetu ye. It is as I have said, for all my relations.

Let's eat soup, grandson. We got chores to do.

Alice Callahan died October 10, 1966, at 103 years of age.
Alice's Trading Post burned to the ground February 16, 1995.
Homer "Half Big" Phipps died in the fire at 95 years of age.
Sweet Medicine Woman/Alice Callahan asked that her stories be
dedicated to girls who come half 'n half to this world, whose courage
is monumental.
We honor her wishes.

Report Issued April 12, 2018

Respectfully,

Marjorie Callahan Phipps, Secretary

Buffalo Gap Historical Society, Ltd.

ABOUT THE AUTHOR

Kerry Dean Feldman was born in Terry, Montana, near One Star Terry's "Landing" along the Yellowstone River, 1940. He spent weekends visiting relatives thirty miles away in Miles City (orig., Milestown) near the cantonment Bearcoat Miles built after the Little Bighorn battle, where the Tongue and Yellowstone Rivers meet. His earliest photograph has him sitting on a blanket at the Little Bighorn battlefield, on a picnic with his parents and dear uncle who admired Custer. He played basketball and football against Crow athletes, including the legendary Larry Pretty Weasel, often winning in football, not as often in basketball, admiring their athleticism, team spirit, talent, and humility. He holds a PhD in anthropology from the University of Colorado, Boulder (1973) and is currently Professor Emeritus at the University of Alaska Anchorage. Cirque Press published a collection of his short stories, *Drunk on Love: Twelve Stories to Savor Responsibly* (2019). His research has resulted in tribal status recognition by two Alaska Native groups: New Salmon Tribe and *Qutekcat* Tribe of Seward, Alaska.

The employees of Five Star Publishing hope you have enjoyed this book.

Our Five Star novels explore little-known chapters from America's history, stories told from unique perspectives that will entertain a broad range of readers.

Other Five Star books are available at your local library, bookstore, all major book distributors, and directly from Five Star/Gale.

Connect with Five Star Publishing

Visit us on Facebook:
https://www.facebook.com/FiveStarCengage

Email:
FiveStar@cengage.com

For information about titles and placing orders:
(800) 223-1244
gale.orders@cengage.com

To share your comments, write to us:
Five Star Publishing
Attn: Publisher
10 Water St., Suite 310
Waterville, ME 04901